All Mine

Pippa Nixon lives in Guildford with her husband and four teenage boys where she has a reputation for watching horror films from behind cushions and never failing to burn garlic bread. Always a fan of words and with a career in PR and Marketing, she is an alumnus of the Faber Academy.

Pippa Nixon

QUERCUS

First published in Great Britain in 2025 by Quercus
Part of John Murray Group

1

A CIP catalogue record for this book is available
from the British Library

PB ISBN 978 1 52944 604 3
EBOOK ISBN 978 1 52944 606 7

Typeset in Swift by CC Book Production

Printed and bound in Great Britain by Clays Ltd, Elcograf S.p.A.

MIX
Paper | Supporting
responsible forestry
FSC® C104740

Papers used by Quercus are from well-managed forests and other responsible sources.

Quercus
Carmelite House
50 Victoria Embankment
London EC4Y 0DZ

John Murray Group
Part of Hodder & Stoughton Limited
An Hachette UK company

The authorised representative in the EEA is Hachette Ireland,
8 Castlecourt Centre, Dublin 15, D15 XTP3, Ireland (email: info@hbgi.ie)

For all the amazing women in my life

Chapter One

Isabella

'Your keys, Mrs Tucci.' The estate agent passed her a bundle of keys of varying shapes and sizes on a large steel keyring. Isabella had not met this man before, but her usual agent was sick. This last-minute substitute was maybe fortysomething in a badly fitting suit.

'Ms,' she corrected absently, taking a step back to survey the building in front of her. Not that there was currently much to admire. Boarded windows. Flaking paint. But she could see past that. She could see its future, and her own. She took a deep breath, and a smile brightened her face.

'Unusual name, Tucci,' he said, unperturbed – and nosy. 'Italian?'

'My family is Italian,' she said. 'You can call me Isabella.'

'This is a huge project.' The estate agent rocked back on his heels and blew out his cheeks. 'Should keep you busy for a while.'

He might think that, but she didn't have the luxury of time.

She had barely three months to turn the building around and meet her goal of a new life within a year. Nine long months to find the right property, to win the bid at auction and for all the never-ending paperwork to go through. And now, finally, she gripped the keys in her hand with ninety days left to open.

'Could be a real money pit too . . .' he said, deciding to give her advice she hadn't asked for. 'You know, when you have to—' She stopped his mansplaining with a raised hand.

'The survey was clean. Nothing structurally wrong with the building. Just a lot of cosmetic work and maybe some rewiring.'

Even as she said the words, her stomach lurched. She'd gone through the figures a million times because it was everything she had in the world, everything from her old life to fund the new. Proceeds from the divorce settlement, the sale of their house, the life she had thought she would live for the rest of her days. She'd checked and double-checked fees and duties, because there was nobody else to back her up now. No one to share the costs or the charges. She felt sick at the thought.

She looked again at the building in the pleasant warmth of the late August sun. A smallish, whiteish building facing the pedestrianised town square. Nothing distinctive to write home about – yet. But she could already imagine the frontage painted cleanly and flowers blooming in the window boxes. She could hear the music coming from the open windows. She glanced at the space above the door where the old sign had been, and the thought of putting her own sign up there turned the anxiety back into excitement. This was all hers and she was going to make it a success.

'Shall I help you in?' the estate agent asked, reaching to take the keys back.

'I'm fine, Mr Reynolds. The removals people will be here shortly. But thanks for everything.' This was something she wanted to do herself.

'Is your husband coming soon? To help?' he asked, looking around. She forced a smile, even though the comment irritated her. Why did everyone think you had to have a man to do anything in life?

'No, it's only me.'

Better that way by far, she reminded herself as she tossed her hair back over her shoulder, even as a flash of hurt made her press her lips together. The images were still too fresh. The good ones were deeply embedded – the first flush of love, the anticipation, the planning of dates, holidays, the engagement ring, her white dress, their first house together – and they all rushed into her mind at once, like watching a home movie. Laughing at the kitchen table. Spooning on the sofa to watch a film. But as always now, these were followed by the more recent bad ones – the ones she never wanted to think about again. Who would have thought she'd be married and divorced by thirty-three?

'So, what's the plan for this place then?' he asked, tucking his hands into his trouser pockets and jiggling keys around rather suspiciously near his balls. 'Beauty parlour? Nail salon?'

She swallowed her frustration. Another common misconception. They looked at her and saw long, wavy brown hair that tumbled down her back. They saw olive skin, high cheekbones and even, white teeth. They saw that she was slim and fit and toned, with curves in all the right places. So, they didn't bother to look for a brain. They merely associated her with her looks.

Not that there was anything wrong with nail and beauty salons, they were essential services. But she had different plans for this place.

'A restaurant,' she said firmly.

His eyes shot up towards his prematurely receding hairline.

'Wow, hard work.' She shrugged; she wasn't afraid of that. But he wasn't finished. 'Long hours. Hard to get staff sometimes too.'

He was like a walking Wikipedia of doom, this guy. She ignored him, her attention caught by the glint of copper on the pavement at her feet. A penny. A good omen. She bent to pick it up, taking a second to press it hard into her palm for luck before tucking it into her pocket.

'Not married then?' he asked from his position behind her, which made her roll her eyes as she straightened up. Turning to reply, she caught his look of appreciation as he swept his eyes up and down her body and got stuck on her chest. She cleared her throat and he bolted his eyes back up to head level.

'No,' she said pointedly. 'I'm very happily single.'

He puffed up his chest and she spoke quickly to ward off any more questions.

'I'm not looking for distractions. Not until this place is a success.'

Three months left, she reminded herself. Not even that, actually, until the start of her new life and until her year-long, self-imposed man ban was over. She'd sworn after the split with Daniel she would be single and sex-free for a year. Who needed a man, the hassles, the lies? Or the heartache, the anxiety, the loss of confidence, come to think of it? She would dedicate time to healing and focusing on herself, before she let another man into her life in any kind of serious way. Or even any kind of one-night way.

It was easier than she'd thought to start with. Despite having had a regular and healthy sex life since university, she'd not missed it at the beginning. Word got around she was single again, even though she certainly didn't go bragging about it. In fact, it was probably the shock of the divorce that kept her numb, and she didn't hesitate in turning down any invitations or dates. She kept her head down at the gym and avoided the muscle corner. She focused on her work at the marketing agency until she handed her notice in and managed to avoid any drunken hook-ups at her leaving party. She was protecting herself at all costs. After the trauma of the year before, she figured a year to herself was exactly what she needed. Enough to feel stronger again – and to prove everyone else, especially *Daniel*, wrong. But lately, there'd been the odd, familiar tug in the pit of her stomach. She'd felt her senses coming back to life, her needs emerging from the cocoon of shock. She'd bought a stack of spicy romances and had to replace the batteries in her vibrator twice in the last month. She was most definitely going to have an itch to scratch when the year was up. Three months left. And counting.

'Have you checked out your local competition?' The estate agent nodded at the opposite side of the square and she followed his gaze.

The Bistro had leaded windows and a brick frontage. Its roof was low, and already she could imagine the ambience inside, all cosy nooks and candlelit corners and beamed ceilings. She had looked up its menu online – minute steaks, frites, coq au vin.

It might be another restaurant, but it wasn't direct competition to what she had planned.

Hers would be a traditional Italian restaurant, cooking the food passed down her family for generations. The recipe written by her grandmother's hand and the ones typed and printed painstakingly by her mother. The food of her childhood, her family, her past was going to be the path to the future.

As she looked, a man appeared and leaned in the doorway of The Bistro, observing them. Even from here she could see that his jeans were just the right sort of tight across his thighs and his light blue shirt fit in all the best places. A tea towel was hooked into his belt and hung from his hip. A waiter? The manager? She found herself straightening her spine slightly, lifting her chin. Conscious of his eyes on her, she wondered if he liked what he saw too.

'Ahem.' The estate agent cleared his throat loudly beside her, but Isabella ignored him.

The man opposite nodded at a blonde woman as she passed, called out something that made the woman laugh. Then he leaned on the door jamb and watched them again. It was an obvious surveillance. A moment later, somebody inside called out and he straightened himself to his full height. Before he went, he lifted his hand in a wave, and she felt a smile nudging her mouth upwards as she lifted hers in return. Okay, okay. So, she's not allowed to touch but it's always good to have something nice to look at.

'Right, I'll leave you to it, if you're sure I can't help you inside?'

Gotta love a trier, and this guy was persistent. But he wasn't to her taste. She flicked her eyes to the empty doorway across the square again. He would be much more her type of snack. She shook herself. What was she thinking? She finally had the keys to her future in her hand; this was no time to be lusting after a good-looking stranger.

'I'm fine, Mr Reynolds, thank you.' She crossed to the door. The biggest key slid easily into the lock and turned with a pleasing clunk. As she opened the door, he called out once more.

'What's it going to be called then, Isabella? This restaurant?' She smiled a real smile this time, dazzling him.

'Tutto Mio,' she said.

He frowned in confusion. 'Tutti . . . ?'

'Tutto Mio,' she repeated. 'It means all mine, Mr Reynolds. All mine.'

She stepped inside.

The darkness inside the restaurant was a shock after the brightness of the late summer sun on the square. The boarded-up windows barely allowed any light through, and Isabella was impatient to see all the potential that had made her certain this site was the one. She swept her hand along the wall until she found a light switch and then flicked it on, chest banging with excitement.

There it was. Illuminated by a few spotlights and a hanging fluorescent whose days were numbered. In all its dirty, broken glory: her restaurant.

The main dining room was spacious enough to seat sixty easily. Maybe more if she changed the seating configuration for certain celebrations, but she'd built her business plan on sixty to be sure. A pile of mismatched plastic tables and chairs were stacked against the far wall; they would all have to go. Formica tabletops and school chairs were definitely not going to fit the design she had in mind.

Bold floral wallpaper had peeled in an arc from one wall, revealing some rather flaky-looking plaster. The carpet made a tacky sound as she turned in a slow circle in the middle of the room, imagining how it might look in a few months' time.

She wanted an eclectic aesthetic. Something that reminded you of home cooking and was familiar and relaxed. She wanted to encourage diners to linger around the table, feeling no pressure to leave, watch them order another bottle of wine or chat over coffees. She envisaged wooden tables that you might find in your mother's kitchen. No stuffy tablecloths or placemats. She imagined chairs with cushions, brightly coloured salt and pepper pots. Tiny vases on every table filled with the spoils of local hedgerows or seasonal bunches of daffodils or snowdrops. She saw a bookshelf for lone diners, with today's paper and a range of books to browse over a solo meal. She saw a games cupboard for those with young families to play snakes and ladders or Connect 4 between courses. She pressed her eyes shut for a moment and could almost hear the low-level laughter and conversation of people to come. She opened her eyes again to the harsh reality of it, but the smile stayed on her face.

She made her way through to the kitchen. The building had most recently been a café, although it had been closed now for the best part of two years. The facilities were probably perfectly functional, but Isabella knew she had to upgrade for Tutto Mio. A catering standard oven was already on order and should be arriving in about a month's time, to fit into a new sleek and hygienic area for food preparation, as well as a large area for refrigeration and freezers.

Everything had been budgeted for and itemised, many times, but the scale of the investment still flipped her stomach. Infuriatingly, it also brought to mind Daniel's face, his eyebrows bunched together in doubt, forehead furrowed under his floppy blond hair. She shook the thought away, but she could just imagine what he'd be saying now, in the oh-so-slightly patronising tone of someone who thought she couldn't or shouldn't do this. The lines about how 'restaurants are tricky businesses' and 'it might be safer to invest' and 'we need to focus on one business at a time and obviously it makes sense to prioritise mine', as well as the unsaid line 'as you might not be able to run yours in a few years, when the babies come along . . .' Well, screw him. And he never believed in this dream anyway. It was always hers.

She'd wanted this for as long as she could remember. When she met Daniel at university, it was one of the early 'big' conversations they had, when they first dared to tell each other about their ambitions for the future over late-night vodka and Cokes. She was studying business, purely to ensure she ran her future restaurant right. She had already completed summer school cookery courses and had the requisite certificates. She knew already the food she wanted to serve: the same as she'd enjoyed as a child, a teenager, a young woman, at her mother's table. She told Daniel all of this and his eyes widened as he told her it would be amazing. Because she was amazing, he said.

Somewhere along the line, though, that dream had been

overtaken by Daniel's own. His university placement evolved into a full-time offer, and they moved to London after graduation for him to be near his swanky office, all glass windows and views of the Thames. Isabella took a marketing job, which used her business degree, but didn't get her anywhere nearer to where she wanted to be. But Daniel's long hours brought in the big bucks which funded the deposit on their first house and paid for a honeymoon in St Lucia. Whenever she mentioned the idea of the restaurant, he changed the subject. Besides, he said he always loved coming home at the end of the day and knowing she'd be there. She couldn't begrudge him that; she loved it too. He'd throw his coat on the banister and call her name as he came in the door. He'd kiss the back of her neck as she chopped vegetables or marinaded meat for their dinner. He'd smell of the city, the tube, the night air, and he always said that she smelled like home. She sighed. It still stung.

She brushed the counter clean of debris and jumped up to sit cross-legged on top. Now was as good a time as any to tell the world what she was up to. She'd been quiet socially for months, not updating on Instagram or keeping up with her old crowd. Divorce always split friends down the middle anyway, and the only people that mattered were her university friend Jesse and her cousin Gabriella. She knew they'd stick by her no matter what.

She'd kept her head down, too hurt and embarrassed after what happened. She felt as though she was under a spotlight, that people were talking about her, which of course they were. That's what happens when you catch your husband having an affair. One that he'd been having for several years. Half of their married life, in fact. How could she have been so blind?

She could still remember picking up his phone to book a restaurant for that night and seeing the message pop up. The explicit message that called him Danny, when Isabella was the only person she knew that ever called him that. The message that made it clear that she shouldn't bother with date night, as Daniel was obviously already having his cake AND eating it too. Deep disappointment and humiliation shot through her, knowing that her marriage was going to end in such a such a clichéd way. A wife finding proof on her husband's phone. Because of course, she scrolled back. She found others, some equally sexual and some – even worse – loving.

When they first separated, Isabella was so heartbroken that it had been all she could do to get out of bed. Gabi turned up on the doorstep and moved into the spare room without being asked. She gave Isabella space when she needed it and hugged her when she didn't. She forced Isabella to see her parents on Sundays so that they didn't worry. She accompanied her on the tube to get her to her desk three days a week. On her work-from-home days, Isabella still rarely got out of her pyjamas, but Gabi made random food concoctions she saw on TikTok and they ate together in front of the TV. Isabella avoided all other contact apart from Jesse, who rang her every night and told her men were no-good shits. And he should know. She left phone messages from other friends unanswered. She cried in bed and in the bath and the front room with the hollowness of the house and her heart. Gabi replaced the tissues.

After a while, her feelings started to change. She was embarrassed Dan had cheated on her and angry she was the one to lose the entire life she'd built up. They had been the poster couple from their university group, the ones that fell in love in the first year and married straight after graduation. Jesse had got drunk on champagne and told her he wanted 'one just like Daniel'. They were the ones that bought a house and worked hard and saved money. They were the couple that were planning a family, a future. How dare he take all of that away from her? She still wanted it – and him – for many months afterwards. Even if he was an arsehole. She couldn't help it. He'd been her arsehole.

She'd come a long way in the nine months since signing the divorce papers, and now, here, in her restaurant, she finally felt strong enough to start spreading the word. She was back. She pulled out her phone and activated Instagram. New account.

A few moments later, she shared her first post from Tutto Mio, albeit with a 'new Italian restaurant coming soon' type of holding caption. But she would add to her profile over the coming months and had major plans for the launch already. She wanted to use her social media expertise to create buzz and attract locals and those willing to travel for a good meal.

Holding the phone in her palm, she stared at the screen for a moment, feeling a tug of sentimentality. The lure of her old life. Unable to resist, she clicked on her former profile picture, a happy circle of her beaming face, blue sky behind, sun reflecting on her sunglasses. She scrolled through some of her posts. Photographs of beach holidays and rainbows and reflections in puddles on muddy walks. Two pairs of wellies at the back door. A Christmas tree lit up in front of a window. Drinks next to each other on a pub garden table – one pint, one Pinot Grigio. Everything screamed happy. Pain stabbed through her. To think she'd believed that Daniel was going to be her 'happy ever after'. She supposed she should be grateful now to know there was no such thing.

The beep of a horn outside announced the arrival of the removals truck and brought her back to the present. She jumped off the counter and put her phone face down.

Men. No wonder she wanted nothing to do with them.

Chapter Two

Etienne

Etienne leaned against the door frame of The Bistro, watching the square, as he did every morning. He'd been for his usual morning run, a quick five kilometres around the town. He always hated it at the beginning but loved it by the time he'd been through the park and hit the river path. Especially at this time of year now the oppressive summer heat had passed. He'd showered and dressed, although he could still feel his heart rate was heightened under his blue shirt, and his hair was slightly damp. It was a good moment to take a breath, before the workday started. It was also a good vantage point to see the comings and goings of the town. He spotted Millie, blonde and tiny and who ran the local PR firm, on her way to the office, and gave her a quick hello. She blushed slightly as she waved back and he recalled the same flush of pleasure had spread across her cheeks when she'd unbuttoned her blouse in front of him a few weeks before. That had been fun. Now, watching the swing of her hips in her suit as she walked away, he considered a repeat performance. Fleetingly. But then pushed it aside. Nope. None of that. Better to keep things light, casual. A one-night-only performance. Always better that way.

A clutch of market stalls were setting up along the south side of the square. The greengrocer, a fish stall, a family selling local gins, another with cheese and olives by the bucket load.

A couple stood with their backs to him on the opposite side of the square. They were facing the old Keeper's Café, which had been shut for the past couple of years. He had heard a rumour that someone was taking it on. Maybe this was them, the new owners.

But something told him they weren't a couple. They seemed mismatched. She had long hair tumbling down her back and black jeans that curved nicely around her hips. He had on a rumpled suit jacket and his scalp showed beneath his thin hair. He looked squat. She looked lithe. He watched them talking and then noticed the man's clipboard, and the pass of the keys. Aha. Estate agent.

So, it was her that was taking over the Keeper's. His eyes flicked around the square, trying to spot if she had a partner, business or otherwise. But the only other people he saw were locals. He knew most of them by name, and some of the women by touch as well. So, she was alone.

At that moment, the woman turned to face him. Etienne hummed in appreciation. Even from this distance he could see she was stunning. Her gaze was direct as she took him in. She tilted her head slightly, and her hair fell over her shoulder.

He was considering going over to introduce himself when he heard his name called from inside the restaurant. He let his eyes linger for another moment and then raised a hand, saluting her. *Welcome to the neighbourhood, babe.* She lifted her hand to return his wave and his interest pricked.

Time to get on with the day. And a frisson of anticipation was sometimes a good thing. Although, let's face it, he didn't normally have to wait that long before he got what he wanted.

He opened his phone and scrolled to the top group chat, Brothers from Another Mother. Etienne was so close with Fox, the silver-haired games designer, and Walker, the local firefighter, they were quite often known as the 'three amigos' in town.

Etienne: New girl in town, boys. Taking on the old Keeper's Café.

The ticks turned blue within a second.

Walker: You introduced yourself yet and offered her one night of heaven?

Etienne: Nope – just saw her getting the keys.

Walker: Maybe I'll swing by to check out her fire escape?

Etienne: Could be a good idea. She's hot stuff.

Etienne cringed at his own bad joke.

Fox: This information might be of interest if I had the time or the energy. But I have a deadline on the new game . . .

Fox took a moment and Etienne could see he was still typing.

Fox: Reggie has a school project to hand in on Monday where we have to make a bloody dinosaur . . .

A pause. Typing again.

Fox: And George has been projectile sick twice this morning already.

Etienne grimaced. Fox's boys were the best. Wild, funny, freckled dynamos that didn't seem to stop moving until they were asleep. But they were a lot for Fox to manage on his own since his wife died.

Etienne: Need anything, Fox?

He knew Walker would be watching for the reply too. Because despite the banter, they'd do anything for each other. Had done before. Would do again.

Fox: I'm good, man. Unless you fancy helping Reggie make a T-Rex this weekend?

Etienne considered his waiting staff rota for a split second.

Etienne: Saturday afternoon? About 3?
Fox: Lifesaver.
Walker: Shift finishes at 4. I'll join you then.
Fox: Boys, you're the best.

Etienne clicked off the group chat and googled 'how to make a dinosaur' as he walked through to the kitchen.

Chapter Three

Isabella

A few days later, Tutto Mio was so busy with tradespeople that Isabella was lucky to get ten minutes on her own from the moment they turned up in the morning until they all left for the day. She had to fight to even have enough time to go to the toilet without being needed to answer a question. And usually, like now, it was on the loo that she'd find a minute to reply to her mamma's messages begging for updates.

Mia Famiglia WhatsApp group

Mamma: How's it going?

Isabella: It's going! Ten people on site today.

Papà: Show them who's boss, Isabella!

Isabella: They already know, Papà!

Mamma: Send me a picture?

Isabella: I'll send progress pics tonight.

Mamma: Have you eaten?

Isabella: Of course, Mamma. Don't worry!

She grimaced at the white lie, pocketed the phone again and grabbed a ciabatta roll on her way back downstairs.

She'd spent the first few days, music speaker blaring, cleaning the flat above the restaurant from top to bottom. It was her new home. She washed walls, painted a few even, and steam cleaned the carpets. She had now moved her furniture in and although she didn't have a lot, it was all her taste, her choice. She'd not wanted to bring the old sofa where she and Daniel used to snuggle, or their marriage bed where they slept and dreamed and made love. Once she'd calmed down enough not to want to set it on fire, she'd sold that on a local website, along with everything else Daniel left behind. She found that she didn't have much emotional attachment to things when the heart had gone out of her marriage. The atmospheric pictures they'd bought together at a market on the Thames now looked bleak. The cabinet they bought in a junk yard and upcycled to look shabby chic now looked just shabby. Everything went apart from her clothes, her photo albums, her kitchen utensils, her TV and her portable speaker. The proceeds had been enough to start over and the flat upstairs was already homely, if a bit sparse. She'd added lamps and throws and cushions and rugs; the front room and the bedroom were comfortable, cosy. She sent photos to Jesse, who replied immediately with a thumbs up or a love heart. Not that she'd had any time to invite anyone around yet. But at least it was welcoming at the end of a long day when her back ached and she only had enough energy, ironically, to heat up a ready meal before falling into bed.

The team's focus today was on clearing the cabinets and sorting the new electric sockets in the kitchen. Isabella would start stripping wallpaper, a steamy, sticky job. She pushed her hair into a messy bun on the top of her head and secured it with a bright blue scarf. She wore an old cropped white T-shirt and faded jeans that were already paint speckled, perfect for the job. She snapped a selfie for Gabi, flexing her muscle as she held the wallpaper steamer in the air.

> **Gabi**: Girl power!
> **Isabella**: You know it.

She couldn't wait to see the back of the floral paper. And she needed it done now so that the plasterer could come next week to skim the walls. Walls first, then reclaimed wooden flooring, then décor. The list was endless. She fired up her steamer, turned on the radio, picked up her stripping knife and got to work.

An hour in, she'd found a rhythm. It was a strangely satisfying job. When the music stopped between tracks, she heard someone shout from the kitchen. Then another voice joined in, then swearing and more shouting. She slammed the off button and ran towards the noise.

The door opened to chaos. Water sprayed from a pipe on the wall at waist height. One builder was already soaked and trying to remove electrical tools from the area, while another guy in overalls was trying to block the hole with his thumb, which just made the water jet in different directions. It was him that was swearing like a trooper. He stopped when he saw her and said, with a shake of his head, 'Hit a pipe taking out the cabinets.'

The third tradesman had his head in the cupboard under the sink, the crack of his buttocks showing where his jeans hung low.

'It's not here . . .' he shouted before pulling his head out and spotting Isabella. 'Ah! Where's your stopcock, love?'

Isabella frowned for a second, trying to think where she'd seen it. Then splashed across the wet floor tiles and yanked open the door to the utility area, where the washing machine used to be for the café. She opened the cupboard in the corner and pointed triumphantly. 'There.'

Phil slip-slid his way towards her, belly hanging out the bottom of his T-shirt, and once more stuck his head in a cupboard with a spanner. She heard him grunting with effort and then, 'FUCK!'

The stopcock had split in half. Water sprayed out directly at Isabella, a jet that soaked her T-shirt and her face. Great.

'What now?' she asked his upturned bottom. He withdrew his head and the water sprayed straight at her again, full on. He tried to block it with a cloth, but it was no good. Water was everywhere. Even dripping off her chin.

'Call a plumber, I guess, love. An emergency one at that. Unless you know where your mains stopcock is.'

Isabella stared at him for a split second in disbelief then stalked back into the restaurant.

She picked up her phone and googled 'where to find your mains stopcock'. She scanned the top few listings and they all concurred: *mainly outside, sometimes shared with a neighbour. Can be on the pavement outside the home rather than inside the premises.* It was worth a try.

Isabella ran out onto the square. The chill of the September morning hit her skin and she realised how flushed her face was from steaming the walls. She checked immediately in front of the restaurant, but wasn't even sure what she was looking for. A tap? No. A cover on the ground with a tap beneath it? Probably.

There was nothing to the right of the door under the windows, and she ran to the other side. The weeds had taken hold there and she had to pull up a few handfuls of straggly grass to get a proper look. Yes. That could be it. A square metal cover, like a mini manhole. She prised her fingers in the side but there was no way of lifting the lid. She needed a tool. Dammit.

Knowing that every minute this took to resolve, the more damage was being done to her restaurant spurred her into action. She shouted back in through the front door.

'Anyone got a crowbar? Or a lever?'

Muttering, and more muttering, and she could hear someone looking in a toolbox, but the shout came back as a no. She turned around again in frustration, looking for help. A movement caught her eye.

The guy in the restaurant opposite was in his doorway again, watching. Isabella decided that now was the time to meet her neighbour, but it wasn't a cup of sugar she needed. She sprinted across the square towards him and saw his eyes flash wider as she approached.

'Hi. Don't suppose you've got a crowbar, or a lever of some kind?' He blinked and then shook himself as though trying to concentrate. 'I need to turn off my water at the mains before I flood the whole place!'

She flashed a smile, trying to show she was friendly but in desperate need and he jumped into action.

'Hold on,' he said and turned inside, returning a moment later with an assortment of tools that might do the job. He held them in his hands for inspection and she threw him another smile.

'Thanks.'

'Come on,' he said, pulling a hoodie on over his head. 'I'll help.'

She was surprised by the offer but didn't have time to decline as he set off in front of her across the square. Men! Always needing to be in charge.

They knelt on the ground side by side, but she budged him slightly, putting her hand out for a tool. This was her job to do. The cover came up easily and, sure enough, the stopcock was beneath. The restaurant guy pushed a wrench towards her and she managed to clasp the tap in her hand and turn it closed. When she was sure it was firm, she ran to the front door and called through.

'Has it stopped?' There was a split second of silence inside followed by cheers, and her shoulders dropped as she breathed a sigh of relief. She turned, beaming to the restaurant guy.

'Done!' she said triumphantly, walking back towards him. 'Thanks so much for your help.'

'I didn't do anything,' he said. 'You did it all yourself.'

He stood, brushing his jeans at the knee. As he faced her, his eyes widened again, the same look he'd given as she ran across the square towards him. A flash of appreciation. It made her feel curiously naked. In a good way.

'But without your tools, I'd be flooded by now.' She extended her hand. 'I'm Isabella.'

A slow smile spread across his face, making his eyes crinkle at the corners. Shit. He was extraordinarily attractive. Green eyes and dark brown hair were a striking combination. Not that much older than her. Nearer forty and all man.

'Etienne,' he said. 'I own The Bistro.' His hand dwarfed hers as they shook, holding it momentarily before they both let go. Steady there, girl, Isabella thought, tucking her hand back into her pocket.

'Have you been here long?' she asked.

'About four years,' he said. 'It's a good spot. Near the theatre and bang in the middle of town. I saw the planning permission for this place. So – a new restaurant.'

'You worried by the competition?' Isabella challenged.

'Nope.' Etienne chuckled and it made her smile in return. 'I think it could be a good thing for the square. Bring more people in for the evenings. So, is it your family taking this on?'

'Nope, just me.' This time she was not frustrated by the question, because some part of her wanted him to know that she was single. That there was nobody else in the picture. He raised an eyebrow again and she felt a flush on her neck.

'Well, there's a good social scene in Honeybridge if you fancy it. Depends on what you're into?'

Isabella considered for a second. A single social scene. A whole new ball game. Oh God, it wasn't the best to be thinking about balls with this gorgeous man in front of her. He carried on.

'The Bolthole is the best bar in town and does theme nights which are fun if you want a night out. The Lit Lounge bookshop has a book club if you like reading. The gym is always organising events if you're into fitness. The rowing club has a monthly party . . .'

It was exactly what she'd hoped for. A vibrant, fun place to live. But not yet.

'Sounds perfect – for when I've got a bit more time on my hands.'

'How's it going then?' he said, indicating the front door. 'The renovation?'

She laughed.

'It *was* going well until now! But the workmen accidentally hit a water pipe and then the stopcock broke. Honestly, it's like Niagara Falls in there.' She ran her hand over her cheeks, still feeling the moisture on them. For the first time she wondered what she must look like, half her hair still up in a messy bun, no make-up, flushed from the steaming, wet from the flood. Especially when he looked so good, like fresh laundry and just out of the shower good. She bet he smelled good up close. God, he was distracting. 'The kitchen's soaked, the utility is soaked, I'm soaked . . .'

He lowered his eyes and nodded slowly.

'Yes, I can see that . . .' he said with another smile, raising an eyebrow. That look again. The one that made her feel undressed. Like he was looking right through her clothes.

Curious, she followed his gaze and looked down at herself. She was drenched. Not just her face, but her clothes. Top, jeans, the lot. She hadn't felt it in the urgency of the situation. And she had completely forgotten that she was wearing a thin, white T-shirt, which was now completely transparent. Her nipples stood proud and dark through the wet material in the early autumn air, and they were the focus of Etienne's slow smile. She gasped, clapping her hands to her front, cupping her own breasts. She could feel her nipples pebbled against her palms.

A commotion sounded at the restaurant door behind her as the builders piled out and leaned on the front of the building, starting to roll cigarettes and sip tea from mugs. Obviously, it was time for tea break.

'Oh God,' Isabella said to herself, knowing now that she looked half naked and so keeping her back to them. Which kept her front to Etienne. He grinned and allowed himself a quiet laugh as he looked from her to the builders and back again. Then he shook his head, regretfully, as he seemed to make a decision.

'Here,' he said, pulling his hoodie off over his head, flashing her a tiny glimpse of taut stomach with a trail of dark hair heading downwards as his T-shirt lifted. He passed it to her and she grabbed it and clutched it to her front. 'I have to say I'm enjoying the view, but I think maybe it's not for public consumption.'

She knew she was blushing as she pulled the hoodie over her head and covered her badly behaved nipples that seemed to be quite enjoying the attention. The rub of his sweatshirt against them almost hurt.

'Thanks,' she managed, and then laughed self-consciously, pulling the hoodie around her. It smelled of his cologne, deep and woody.

'Wouldn't have missed it for the world,' he replied and then walked back across the square, whistling. 'See you soon.'

She realised she was still holding his wrench in her hand as she watched him go, thinking about today's date. Months stretching out in front of her.

The next evening, about six, when all the workmen had left for a pint and a packet of crisps, there was a ring on the doorbell. Isabella's first thought was that it might be him, Etienne. She wasn't interested or anything, but she stopped to check her teeth in the mirror and toss her curls over her shoulder as she headed to the door. When she glanced at the Ring camera and spied two women on the doorstep, she wanted to laugh at herself.

'Hi!' The shorter blonde woman smiled, eyes twinkling through oversized tortoiseshell glasses as Isabella swung open the door.

'Hello,' the taller, more willowy redhead said simultaneously.

They both held out a bag towards Isabella.

'Welcome to Honeybridge,' the blonde said.

Isabella stared blankly, unsure as to whether they were a welcome party or a sales delegation. Did they want her to buy something? Sign a petition?

The redhead saw her confusion.

'Sorry, I'm Wren.'

'And I'm Rosie.' The blonde nodded.

'We own The Lit Lounge.'

'The bookshop.'

'And we wanted to welcome you to the neighbourhood.'

'So we bought you this.' Rosie, the blonde, pulled out a tourist information guide to Honeybridge from her bag.

'And this,' the redhead, Wren, said, pulling a bottle of white wine from her bag, followed by a bottle of rosé.

'We didn't know what you drink!' They both laughed.

'Both!' Isabella opened the door wide and welcomed them in.

Within ten minutes, one of the bottles was open, Isabella

had found a family bag of crisps to share, and Wren and Rosie were sitting on the sofa, feet tucked up under them, like they had been there a thousand times before.

'So, what's your story?' Rosie asked.

'Sorry?' Isabella said.

'Don't worry about her,' Wren said. 'To her, everything is a story. She's the biggest book nerd I've ever met. That's why we run a bookshop.'

'I can't help it,' Rosie said. 'I find it fascinating – the stories of people's lives.' Both women focused their full attention on her.

'Well . . .' Isabella wasn't sure where to start. Primary school? Going to uni? How far back did they want her to go? She cleared her throat but nothing came out.

'What brought you here?' Rosie asked. Her eyes were wide and interested behind her huge glasses, which she pushed up her nose with amazing frequency.

'I got divorced,' Isabella said, which made Wren sit forward and Rosie look like she was going to start taking notes.

'Sorry to hear that,' Wren said.

'That's a shame,' said Rosie.

Isabella took a second, shrugged, then sighed.

'Turns out he'd been having an affair for a couple of years.'

'Bastard!' muttered Rosie and Wren together.

'So I kind of feel like I'm the mug.'

'Never.' Both women rolled their eyes.

'I didn't see it coming,' she went on.

'He hid it well then?' Rosie rested her elbows on her knees like she was watching a gripping film.

'I thought we were happy,' Isabella said. 'We'd just booked a holiday when I found out.'

'Unbelievable!' Wren chipped in.

'And once I saw the text message, he still tried to deny it.'

'Arsehole,' they said together and collapsed back on the sofa.

Isabella laughed. They were right. And in the time it had taken to drink half a glass of wine together she felt like she'd found new friends.

'So why are you here, though?'

Isabella took a deep breath, topped up their glasses and started to talk. Telling Wren and Rosie the abbreviated version of her marriage, her divorce, her hopes and dreams. As she talked, Rosie tucked herself casually against Wren, who laid an arm behind her on the sofa, and Isabella realised their double act was more, much more, than a working relationship. The way that they touched, finished each other's sentences and frequently shared smiles reminded her of how she and Daniel were a million years ago. The memory stabbed at her with a second of loss. But that thought led to wondering how many times he'd sat next to her on the sofa with his phone in his pocket, waiting to feel the thrilling vibration of his lover's text message. Or how many times he'd arrived home with flowers 'just because' when he meant they were 'just because I've been shagging my work colleague over the photocopier all evening'.

'Anyway, so now Honeybridge is my home and this restaurant is my future.' She finished her glass of wine in one gulp and went to refill but the white was empty. She crossed to the fridge and pulled out the rosé, holding it up towards them in question.

'Why not?'

'Definitely.'

She already loved their enthusiasm for stories and now it seemed they shared a passion for wine too. Things couldn't be better.

'We don't normally drink in the week,' Wren said as she held out her glass for a top-up.

'But it's our night off,' Rosie finished, waiting her turn with the pour.

'Riley goes to her daddy on a Wednesday night.'

'Riley is our daughter.' Rosie flashed her phone screen towards Isabella, and there was a grinning three-year-old with the same shade of red hair as Wren, wearing a baseball cap on backwards and a smudge of dirt up her cheek.

'She looks like a handful,' Isabella said, laughing.

'You're not wrong,' Rosie said, looking at the image herself before putting the phone away.

'She's a character all right.'

'So, you used a donor?' Isabella asked Wren. 'To get pregnant?' She settled back in her chair, intrigued to now hear their own story.

'Oh, I didn't get pregnant!' Wren said. 'Everyone assumes that. Because of Riley's hair. And they're not wrong – she is my child. But I didn't carry her.'

Isabella frowned, slightly confused and not wanting to say the wrong thing.

'I did,' Rosie said proudly and Wren pulled her in close for a squeeze before explaining.

'My egg – fertilised by our friend Toby – was implanted into Rosie. She carried the pregnancy and gave birth to Riley.'

It made perfect sense. The couple that finished each other's sentences, why wouldn't they also finish each other's pregnancies?

'So, you're her biological mother' – she nodded to Wren – 'and you're her birth mother' – and she tipped her chin to Rosie.

They both grinned.

'Bingo.'

'And the dad?'

'Our old friend Toby, who has been the most wonderful man through all of this, although I think he's a bit disappointed Riley's not interested in letting him play hairdresser.'

'Yes, she hasn't got time to sit still for that sort of thing.' Rosie's smile was soft.

'But he has her every Wednesday night without fail and every other weekend too.'

'Which means we get wine and grown-up time, if you know what I mean.' Wren was grinning at Isabella, but the look that she flashed at Rosie was something else entirely. A glint in her eye told Isabella everything she needed to know about what the girls would be up to later. And it didn't include Scrabble.

'I know what you mean,' she agreed with a sigh and a glug of wine. 'But I'm definitely not getting any of that.' She stretched her arms above her head and let them fall to her sides.

Rosie and Wren straightened up again, flirting on the back burner till later.

'Why on earth not?'

'You're stunning. I'm sure the men are falling over each other for a chance with you.'

'It's not so much them as me.' Isabella took a gulp of her wine and told them about her self-imposed sex ban. Rosie's eyes grew wider and rounder behind her glasses, until she looked like a beautiful blonde owl.

'A whole year?' Wren exploded. 'I mean, I get your reasoning, I do, your last partner was a lying no-good cheat, but a whole year without sex?'

'I've done over nine months already . . .' Isabella said. 'Only two months and twenty-three days to go.'

'Not that you're counting!'

'I guess it's like a palate cleanser between courses?' Rosie suggested. 'Give yourself a bit of time to get over the bad taste left by the last one?'

Isabella laughed and shrugged.

'It's that and it's the fact I want to prove to him that I can do this on my own. I can be single and successful. I don't need anyone else.'

'But I guess you own a good vibrator.' Wren wasn't asking a question. It was a statement of fact.

'Several,' Isabella agreed and all three women nodded.

'So, have you not seen anything to tempt you since you got here?' Wren asked, still in disbelief.

Isabella thought of the way she'd felt as Etienne's eyes burned into her yesterday.

'No.' She shook her head. 'But I've hardly had time to venture past the supermarket and the DIY store.'

'Well, you never know, you might find some of the men in Honeybridge are irresistible.'

'No, thank you. Not until after my year is up and this restaurant is open.'

'We'll see,' Wren said, lifting herself off the sofa and helping Rosie up afterwards. 'We'd better be off.'

'Now that we've drunk all your wine! Sorry about that!' Rosie said, not looking sorry in the slightest. In fact, looking happy and mildly drunk.

Wren handed her phone over. 'Pop your number in for me. I'll set up a WhatsApp group.'

Rosie hiccupped. 'And you'll love our friend Amber. She only moved here a year or so ago too. We normally go to The Bolthole every few weeks if you fancy it?'

Isabella did.

After the front door had closed, Isabella picked up her phone.

Mia Famiglia WhatsApp group

Isabella: I made some new friends!

Papà: Great! Who?

Isabella: Rosie and Wren. They run the local bookshop.

Papà: Other local businesswomen! A great start.

Isabella: They wrought bine with them.

Mamma: Do you mean brought wine?

Isabella: Yes. They're lovely!

Mamma: Drink some water, Isabella. Have you eaten?

Isabella: Don't worry, Mamma.

She licked the empty packet of crisps as she went to bed.

Chapter Four

Etienne

Etienne's phone buzzed as he jogged back from the gym. A text from Mile End Mickey, the chef, asking for fresh dill. Etienne pocketed the phone and detoured to the farm shop on the high street.

As he browsed the shelves and selected a bunch of the freshest herbs, his phone vibrated again, this time with a notification from one of his dating apps, telling him he'd matched with several women. Now, that could be important. He scrolled quickly through their profiles, making a mental note to look at them in more detail when he got home. But something more interesting caught his eye as he recognised the new restaurateur, Isabella, browsing the olive oil shelf beside him. She was lost in thought, holding two different bottles in her hands, comparing the labels on the back of each.

'Hi?' he said and she started. Shock flickered lightly across her face and then the hint of a blush as she recognised him.

'Hi,' she replied.

'How's it going? Any more floods?'

She laughed.

'Not so far, thanks to you. I must pop your wrench back over to you – and your top!'

That messy bun, those eyes. The image of her with her T-shirt as see-through as if she were wrapped in cling film flashed through his mind. He grinned. He'd relish the thought of unwrapping that dish.

'Shopping for supplies?' he asked, and she nodded.

'I can't seem to find my normal brand of Italian olive oil.' She weighed the two bottles in her hands. 'So I'm trying to figure out which of these is best.'

'There are testers round the corner on the counter,' he said, thumbing over his shoulder. 'I'll show you.' He took her by the elbow to lead the way. She smelled softly of lemons, fresh and light.

The sample table was laden with a dozen small bowls of oil arranged around a basket of bread. Colours ranged from almost clear to golden syrup, and some had additional infusions such as chilli or garlic.

'Great range in this shop,' Isabella said.

'Here are the Italian ones,' Etienne said, indicating two bowls on the back row.

Isabella peered at them both, then lifted the edge of the bowls to see the way the oil moved. He watched her face, intense with concentration, and noticed a small beauty spot beside her mouth as she pursed her lips in consideration.

'Here,' he said, offering her the bread basket. 'Try them.'

She lifted a finger of bread and held it in the first bowl for a few seconds, letting the oil soak in before taking a bite. She chewed and nodded at him, before doing the same with the second one.

'What do you think?' he said.

'Both good,' she admitted.

'So, which one do you prefer?' he asked.

'In Italy, the consistency is just as important as the taste,' she said. 'We do the skin test to see how fast it absorbs.'

He cocked his head, intrigued.

'Never heard of that!'

'The only problem is, I have hand cream on, so it won't work.' She held her two palms up to him as if in defeat, but then grinned as if with a flash of inspiration. 'But I could use yours?'

'My hands?' Etienne said, surprised.

'Just for a moment,' she said and took his hands in hers, holding them flat at waist height, palms down. 'If you don't mind?'

'You know me, happy to help.' Etienne wasn't sure what he was helping her with, but was happy to go along with it, her small, smooth hands supporting his.

'Good, you're not too hot or too cold . . .' she said, almost to herself, surveying the backs of his hands.

'And you don't have any cream on?' She looked up at him under black eyelashes. He shook his head, and she nodded in return. 'Perfect. Now, keep them flat.'

She carefully held the first bowl above his left hand and tilted it just enough to let a drop escape and fall on his skin. She repeated the procedure with the second bowl onto his right hand. The two drops glistened against his tanned skin, perfect beads of oil. She took his hands in hers again, letting his palms rest on her palms, leaving her thumbs free to smooth the oil into his skin. Her movements were rhythmic and gentle. He liked the intensity on her face as she watched how the oil sank into his skin. He didn't mind this type of experiment at all.

'Look' – she lifted her eyes – 'this one is better.' She raised his left hand. 'See how the oil has immediately been absorbed?'

He touched the point she had been stroking and found it soft and moisturised. He raised his gaze again to her and was caught by the truest blue of her eyes as she smiled at him. Their hands remained entwined and his skin felt warm from her touch.

His phone buzzed.

'I'll leave you to that,' she said, releasing him and stepping away. 'See you around.' She selected the biggest sized bottle of olive oil available and headed off up the aisle.

He watched her turn the corner before sliding his phone out again, expecting it to be Mile End Mickey with another request. He froze when he saw the name on his screen. One he'd been waiting for four years to see again.

Alex. His twin brother.

Chapter Five

Isabella

A few days later, Isabella decided she should return Etienne's wrench. He might need it, she justified to herself, and it would be best to be on good terms with the competition. He also didn't wear a wedding ring; she'd noticed when she rubbed oil into his hands in the shop. Not that it mattered of course, but it was a point of fact.

He had his back to her as Isabella stepped into his restaurant kitchen. It was glisteningly clean, modern stainless steel, gleaming pans. He stood on the far side, dressed in jeans and a T-shirt, apron knotted at his waist, staring intently at his phone, before putting it to one side and gathering ingredients. The muscles across his shoulders moved lightly under his T-shirt, the fabric stretching across them as he reached for a bowl from a shelf above. He was lost in his task. Isabella leaned against the door frame, admiring the view for a moment as he cracked an egg one-handed into the bowl and began to whisk. There was an intensity about him that made her run her tongue over her bottom lip, an energy in his movement as though he was making magic. She might not be allowed to have sex for another two and a half months, but she could surely allow herself the simple pleasure of looking at a beautiful man?

He dipped his little finger into the bowl and lifted it to his mouth. Her own mouth watered in response. He made a sound, of thought, or consideration, and added a few drops from a tiny glass bottle on the counter, whisked, tasted again. This time the noise he made was of pure pleasure. The sound tugged inside her. She gasped as he suddenly turned from the counter, bowl in hand, and saw her there. His eyes flashed wide, but a one-sided smile followed immediately afterwards.

'Hi,' he said, as though women turned up in his kitchen all the time. Which, Isabella thought, if that was the case, she couldn't blame them.

'Sorry,' she stammered. 'I didn't mean to disturb you. Your waitress let me through.'

He rested the bowl on the stainless-steel island in the middle of the kitchen and wiped his hands down the front of his apron, pressing them clean against his thighs.

'Not at all. Nice to see you.' His grin was sincere. 'How's the renovation coming?'

Isabella held up the wrench to show she was returning it.

'Slowly,' she said. 'But I promised you I'd drop this back.'

He leaned against the counter on one hip, and Isabella was aware of the height of him. His legs came almost up to her waist.

'Don't worry, I have another one. You can keep it if you need it.'

'Thanks. But I should probably kit myself out better.' She

stretched the tool out towards him, and he put his hand on the other end. It linked them for a second before Isabella let it go.

'Well, you always know where I am if you need it,' he said. 'Or anything else.' His eyes met hers and this time they held. Was this kitchen hot all of a sudden? She swallowed and shook herself mentally. A year of no sex. A year of *no sex*. The mantra flicked through her mind.

'And I'm putting your hoodie through the wash, but I'll bring that back too.'

Again, the tiny lift of his eyebrow and she felt a flush hit her neck at the memory of what she must have looked like before he gave it to her to wear. Cold day, overheated woman, soaked white T-shirt and two brown nipples standing to attention.

'What are you making?' She nodded at the bowl to distract his attention.

'Don't you know what day it is?' he asked.

She frowned. All she knew was she'd been supervising plumbing work or carpenters for eternity.

'Tuesday?' she suggested.

He nodded and smiled.

'Right.' The batter was smooth and creamy-looking as he tilted the bowl towards her. 'So, it's pancake day.'

'But I thought Shrove Tuesday was around Easter?' Isabella was more than confused.

'Believe me, my pancakes are far too good to only have once a year.' He looked extremely confident about the fact. Her stomach rumbled loudly, and she pressed a hand against herself.

'Hungry?' he asked. 'Stay for brunch?'

The temptation was there. And not for pancakes. The idea of

it flashed through her head, staying, talking, topping pancakes with banana and Nutella, or lemon and sugar. Sitting together. Maybe brushing hands, holding eyes. She shook herself mentally. However nice he was to look at, she didn't need this type of distraction. In fact, she didn't need any distractions at all if she was to get the restaurant open in time. She tapped her watch and smiled ruefully.

'Got an electrician coming in ten. Better get back. But thanks,' she added.

'Another time,' he said and it wasn't a question. He was certainly confident. And surely getting brunch with him wouldn't hurt? It wasn't like she couldn't control herself around him, was it?

'Thanks again for the wrench – or whatever you call it,' she said, standing up to leave.

'Taste the mixture for me, Isabella?' he asked. 'Before you go?' It was the first time he'd used her name and it sounded strange.

He held out a spoon. Her stomach rumbled again, and he laughed.

'Seriously, it sounds like you need it.'

His eyes were such a clear green and they held a challenge in them. One which she couldn't resist. She stepped forward, close enough to smell the soap on his skin.

He dipped the tip of the spoon and stirred, the sleeve of his T-shirt catching on his bicep. Scooping the batter, he held the spoon out to her, as if to feed her, one eyebrow lifted. But that was a step too far. Isabella laughed.

'I'll do it,' she said and took the spoon from him. She tasted the mix, not afraid of the raw eggs in it, having tasted cake mixtures and recipes in her mother's kitchen ever since she could remember. The batter was sublime. Silky, with added vanilla. It would make the fluffiest, lightest, most delicious pancakes. She shut her eyes in appreciation and then laughed.

'Not bad.' She shrugged cheekily and he grinned back, knowing all too well how good it was.

As Isabella reached to pass the spoon back, Etienne stretched for it and their knuckles knocked awkwardly. The cutlery went flying out of her hands, through the air and back into the bowl, sending pancake mix in all directions. The batter was everywhere: over the table, spattering the immaculate worktop. There was a moment of silence as they surveyed the mess. Isabella held her breath, not sure whether to laugh or not. He broke the silence.

'You don't have to sabotage my recipe, you know. Your restaurant's not even open yet!' Etienne was smiling as he turned towards her, obviously joking, making her wonder if that was how he operated. Whether it was all just charm, just banter. But then his smile slipped and he nodded at her arm, more seriously. A large streak of pale cream batter rested on the inside of her wrist. She held it out in front of her so as not to let it drip further. He stepped closer and took hold of her hand, gentle pressure from his fingers holding her in place. Her mouth went dry. The second time they'd touched in a few days, only this time it felt very much like he was in control.

'What a mess,' Etienne said quietly, watching the batter glisten on her olive skin. She was surprised by his warmth, the way his palm took the weight of her hand in his, so that it felt weightless, tiny. He eyed her wrist solemnly and then lifted his eyes in question. 'Can I clean that up for you?'

He was so close. She could see the glint of different greens in his eyes, framed by the darkness of his lashes, his brows. Isabella swallowed and nodded as though hypnotised, conscious of his skin on her skin. Every cell in her body felt alert, the hair on her arms stood up like antennae. She stood transfixed and heard the breath catch in her own throat as, instead of reaching for a cloth or a paper towel to clean her skin, he brought her wrist up to his parted lips without taking his eyes from her own for a single second. The heat of his open mouth on the tenderest part of her arm, the sudden slick of his tongue as he licked the batter from her skin, sent a jolt of excitement straight through her.

He lifted his lips and showed her the clean, glossy skin of her own arm.

'All gone,' he said, with that damned smile.

Isabella opened her mouth to say something, but shut it again. Wait. What was happening here? She was a career woman. She had qualifications. She was independent and she was fierce. So why couldn't she string a single sentence together? He was watching her intently, pressing his lips together as though to savour the taste.

'The plumber,' she muttered.

'I thought it was an electrician.' Etienne grinned.

She tugged her arm free, and he let it go instantly. She wasn't sure if she was happy or disappointed about that. The press of his mouth still scorched her skin and she felt an intense desire to hold her wrist with her fingers, to touch the site of his kiss.

'I'd better go. Thanks again.' God, this sex ban was making her into a stammering fool.

'You liked the pancake mix, though?' Etienne asked as she

reached the door. She paused and glanced over her shoulder, conscious of the flush in her cheeks. 'Because, personally, I thought it was *delicious*.' He brought his fingers to his mouth in a chef's kiss of appreciation. Isabella fled.

Suddenly the next two months and seventeen days felt like they might be a challenge.

Girl Gang WhatsApp group

Wren: Want to come over for afternoon tea?

Isabella: Thanks, but I'm waiting on a plasterer.

Rosie: Shame to miss out on cake, though!

Isabella: Don't worry, I actually had a little taste of something naughty earlier . . .

Chapter Six

Etienne

Etienne grinned every time he thought of it over the next few days. The way her mouth had fallen slightly open as his lips had touched her wrist. The way he'd heard her quick intake of breath – a real-life gasp – as he had opened his mouth and pressed his tongue against that gorgeous olive skin. How those blue eyes of hers had widened and the pupils had darkened even as he watched.

'What's put a smile on your face then, mate?' Mickey asked. He was in early, apron over his chef's whites, preparing for the new seasonal menu, chopping vegetables at a million miles an hour. Autumn was on its way and it was time to move away from the chicken braised in mustard and on to the beef bourguignon. Every season, Etienne made a slight variation to a starter, main and dessert, to ensure all the regular customers had something new to try when they came in. Over the past four years he had built up a solid customer base. However, with no catering experience himself, he relied on Mile End Mickey to bring the dishes to life. And he'd never failed him yet. The chef came from the East End of London, but he nailed French cuisine as if he'd been born in Paris.

'Get lucky last night, did you?' Mickey nudged him in the ribs with a meaty elbow and Etienne grunted, shaking his head. Funny. He'd not responded to anyone on his dating apps. Not since he got the message from Alex. Or since Isabella turned up on the square. Although the two things were unconnected, he felt that they were both giving him issues. He was slightly off his game.

'I don't see it myself, mate,' Mickey continued with a wink. 'All these women that throw themselves at your feet. Or into your bed. I mean . . .' – he paused and looked him up and down – 'it's not like you're a six-foot-three sex god, is it!'

Etienne rolled his eyes and passed him a serving plate. Mickey spooned out the beef and handed him a fork. They both took a mouthful and stared at each other for a reaction as they ate. Etienne caved in first, making a long, low moan of appreciation. Mickey then smacked his lips together and broke into a smile of victory.

'Right, out of my way then. I've got a batch to make for tonight.' Mickey pointed at the door. Etienne swiped another forkful of meat before he left.

The restaurant was empty. The places were set. Etienne wandered aimlessly between tables for a moment, looking for something to do. Not wanting to think about the text he'd had, the one he'd been waiting to see for four years, but unable to focus on anything else.

Alex: I want to come home.

After all this time. More than 1,500 days of calling or checking for messages. Over fifty months of hoping to hear something. Anything.

Etienne had replied, almost immediately. His fingers trembled as he typed the message.

Come back.

It was only as he pressed send and exhaled that he realised he'd been holding his breath. But since then, nothing. He pulled out his phone and looked at the stream of messages he had sent since.

Hello?
Are you okay?
Hello?
Did you get this?
Talk to me.

And then, again, in desperation last night.

Just come back. We can sort it out.

Nothing.
He flicked to the WhatsApp that was always busy instead.

Brothers from Another Mother WhatsApp group

Walker: Seen the new restaurant owner again, Etienne?
Etienne: Saw her yesterday. Long story but licked her arm.
Walker: I wouldn't expect anything else.

Fox: Has she fallen into your bed yet?

Etienne: No. Although happy to keep trying.

Fox: By the way, Reggie won the dinosaur project. Got the class certificate for best talons.

Walker: Told you those acrylic nails would do the job.

Fox: Next project is to make a rocket. Anyone up for that? This games deadline is still kicking my arse.

Walker: Count me in.

Etienne: And me. And if he wins again, you owe us a beer.

Fox: Boys, I owe you much, much more than a beer.

Etienne pocketed his phone with a sigh. If only everything was as easily resolved.

Chapter Seven

Isabella

The morning briefing was almost finished. Isabella stood in the middle of the tradesmen on the restaurant floor – or what would be the restaurant floor in a matter of weeks. Carpenters stood alongside plumbers and decorators. Everyone held a mug of tea or coffee to warm their hands; autumn was getting chillier by the day.

The briefing had been Isabella's idea after an altercation broke out in the early days of the renovation between a group of plumbers and decorators wanting to work the same wall at the same time. She'd managed to step in before any punches were thrown, but it showed her she needed to project manage better. Planning was vital; communication was key.

So, she called a site meeting with the main guys from each trade. Found out what they needed access to and when. Worked out how long each stage would take. Then came up with a project plan which everyone could work around.

The morning briefing had become a part of her day. She

knew most of the traders' names now. If not their real names, then the names they were called on site. And they all, without exception, called her Boss.

'So, are we all clear for today then?' she asked the group, making sure everyone was listening and was reassured with a responding number of grunts and nods.

Isabella exhaled, feeling a sense of calm. Since she'd been holding the morning briefing, there'd been no major problems. A few spats maybe, but there were a lot of people in a confined space and arguments were bound to happen. But at this point in the day, with a cuppa and a plate of biscuits she'd made for them, they were all in it together. And it felt great.

'Right, let's get on with it then.' Her phone rang as everyone heaved themselves to their feet and left in different directions, carrying toolboxes and power cables.

'Hi, Mamma.' Isabella moved to the window, no longer boarded, to look out at the square while they spoke.

'*Ciao*, darling,' her mum, Natalia, said down the phone. 'How's it going?'

They spoke most days, even with the constant chat on the WhatsApp group. It was reassuring to know that her parents were there for her, even if they weren't physically present. In fact, at this moment in time, they were currently backpacking in Thailand, with a vague plan of moving on to Cambodia 'sometime soon'. Both in their mid fifties, they'd quit their day jobs, downsized the house and used everything they had to fund a gap year, which had now reached almost eighteen months and showed no signs of ending anytime soon. It was one thing they all agreed on, when Isabella told them of her plan to invest her life savings and divorce settlement in a restaurant. Do what makes you happy.

'Any gossip?' her mother asked now. Isabella grinned and rolled her eyes. She knew her mum was waiting for her to say she'd met someone new. Well, she'd have to wait at least another two months and – she glanced at the date on her watch – twelve days. Not that she was going to tell her that.

'No gossip, Mamma,' she said, but she couldn't help her eyes flicking across the square.

'Any news of Daniel?' her mother asked then and the nice feeling in her tummy disappeared.

'No,' she said. 'Why?'

'Just checking.' Isabella could practically hear her mother straighten her back the other end. 'I don't want him to come sniffing back when he realises what he lost.'

'He won't, Mamma. I'm sure of that.'

'Be careful. You know how hurt you were.'

That was the understatement of the year. Or the decade maybe. She'd been heartbroken. Her long-term love had betrayed her. She'd never felt pain like it.

'So, all on track for opening day?' Mamma asked.

That certainly brought her back to the present. That date was imprinted in her brain. The same day as the end of her sex ban. When she would feel independent enough and successful enough in her own right to open herself up to a new relationship.

'All on plan. Do you think you and Papà will make it?' Isabella asked.

'We'll try our best, darling, but it's tricky. Our route means we'll be very rural at that time.'

They chatted shop for a while, and Isabella mentioned the need to start sourcing suppliers.

'Is there not someone that could help you with that, darling?'

'It's okay, Mamma. I can do it.'

'I know you *can* do it,' her mum said. 'But everyone needs a bit of help sometimes, you know.'

Isabella hummed in agreement to appease her mum without any intention of complying. She didn't need any help. She wanted to do it all herself. Then Tutto Mio really would feel like it was 'all hers'. After a moment, Isabella blew kisses and promised to speak the next day.

As she pocketed her phone, she watched as the front door of The Bistro opened. A woman came out, a blonde with a pixie cut. Trendy vibes. The stranger lingered in the doorway, adjusting her bag on her shoulder. Etienne came out after her. Bit early for a business meeting, she would have thought. He leaned casually against the door frame while they spoke. They laughed, then the woman leaned forward to kiss Etienne on the cheek and walked away. Isabella could tell by the way the woman was walking she was desperate to turn back and look over her shoulder but wouldn't let herself.

Isabella studied Etienne, still leaning against the door jamb. Only when the woman turned onto the high street did Etienne head back inside. Isabella had the feeling the woman might have rubbed more than his hand. And for some reason that pissed her off.

Girl Gang WhatsApp group

Wren: Amber needs a night out.

Isabella: Who's Amber?

Rosie: She rocks. You'll love her.

Wren: The Bolthole on Thursday? We've swapped baby daddy nights with Toby.

Isabella: I'm in. Dress code?

Wren: Isabella, you could wear a sack and still look gorgeous.

Chapter Eight

Etienne

When Samantha turned onto the high street, Etienne let out a long sigh. He'd never had a night like it. Shaking his head at himself, he turned to head back inside.

Mile End Mickey was prepping in the kitchen, the radio blasting, so Etienne started to sort the bar for the day. There were several trays full of glasses to be polished and hung. He picked up a cloth and got to work, letting his mind run back over the night before.

It all started innocently enough. Samantha and he had matched on an app. Determined to end his dry spell, he'd messaged her. Their chat had been great, flirty and surprisingly funny, and he knew he was off to a good start.

They'd arranged to meet for a drink in town. The bar was noisy and had a younger crowd, one of his normal venues for a date or a hook-up. Samantha was lovely. Perched on her stool, she made sure to put her hand on his forearm when talking or nudge his thigh with her knee when she leaned in close to listen. She licked her lips after sipping her drink, her pink tongue glistening. Everything was going in the right direction.

A bottle of wine later, she was coming back to his, for one reason and one reason only. She'd expressly said so in the bar. And he didn't need asking twice.

It was when they got back to his flat above the restaurant that things started to get weird.

'You all right, mate?' Mickey asked, jolting him back to the present. He held a tiny espresso cup in his hand and was peering at him over the bar. 'Looking a bit peaky.'

Etienne ran his hands through his hair.

'Late night, that's all.'

Mickey sipped, then winked.

'Saw you showing the lady out this morning.'

Etienne grimaced but tried to turn it into a grin.

'Another in the long line of one-night stands?' Mickey said. 'I don't know how you do it, mate.'

'Well, actually . . .' Etienne said, before he could stop himself. 'I didn't.'

Mickey paused, coffee cup halfway to his lips, mouth half open.

'You what?' he asked.

'Nothing happened,' Etienne admitted.

Mickey held his eyes for a long second before snorting.

'Pull the other one, Et. It's got bells on!'

'I'm serious,' Etienne replied.

'Why?' Mickey plonked himself on a bar stool, confused and intrigued. Almost as much as Etienne himself.

It was a good question. They'd got home, he'd poured more

drinks, put on some music. They'd sat on the couch, slowly getting closer until they were pressed tightly together. When she answered his question, she let her face remain close, tilted towards him, her lips slightly parted. She smelled as good as she looked. Normally he'd move in at that exact moment. Kiss her. Wrap his arms around her, move things along. But last night, that hadn't happened.

Instead, he'd found himself moving away, forcing space between them. He gave an excuse of needing some water, before returning from the kitchen to sit on the single chair, Samantha's eyes widening in confusion.

'Are you feeling okay?' she'd asked, hesitantly. And that's when Etienne said it. The thing he'd never said before.

'No, sorry. I have a headache.'

He certainly didn't have a headache. But he also certainly didn't have any desire to sleep with Samantha. If it hadn't been so serious, it would have been funny.

She was polite, caring, offered him some painkillers from her handbag, but he kept up the pretence and ordered her an Uber. It wasn't the service she was expecting from him, but it felt like the least he could do. Soon he was escorting her back down the stairs again and out into the square. His first ever one-night nothing.

'So, did she just sleep over?' Mickey prompted.

'No, she left last night and came back this morning because she'd left her handbag here.'

He'd been surprised – and a bit embarrassed to be honest – when she turned up again. It was true, her handbag was lying forgotten against the side of the sofa, but it was also quite obvious that she was trying to get another date in the diary.

Etienne, whilst being pleased with the way he managed to avoid committing himself, was also questioning why he wasn't jumping at the chance. He'd never turned down sex since he discovered it aged fifteen.

He wondered briefly if he was ill. He hadn't felt a spark of interest for anyone since meeting Isabella. Or, if he thought about it, he hadn't felt anything much since the message. *I want to come home.*

'Well, well.' Mickey chuckled to himself. 'Maybe you're losing your touch.'

Etienne rolled his eyes and flicked Mickey with his tea towel. He might have other things on his mind right now, but he'd never lose his touch.

Brothers from Another Mother WhatsApp group

Etienne: You guys ever not fancied having sex?

Fox: I have two young kids. I don't even have time to fancy having sex.

Walker: Depends on what shift I've just come off.

Etienne: Both answers make me feel slightly better. I didn't fancy it last night.

Fox: Ha! You've finally broken your cock.

Walker: It just needs a break. Listen to its needs.

Etienne: Fuck off.

Fox: I have good news. I met my deadline.

Walker: Welcome back to life, mate.

Fox: And I have a babysitter for Throwback Thursday.

Etienne: Bolthole?

Fox: Bolthole!

Walker: Bolthole!

Chapter Nine

Isabella

The Bolthole was all low lighting, wooden floors, live music and loud. It was everything Isabella needed to remind her she was young(ish) and wanted to have fun just as much, or almost as much, as she wanted to have Tutto Mio up and running. It had been all work and no play for her first few weeks in Honeybridge and she would be the first to admit she wanted to let her hair down. Literally. It flowed over her shoulders in tumbling waves tonight, and she could feel it against her bare back as she shook her head. Her shoestring-strap camisole almost met the top of her jeans but not quite, allowing a glimpse of olive skin just at her waist. She felt good.

Wren waved a hand from a booth and Isabella scooted in, landing beside a beautiful woman – presumably the Amber who needed a night out.

'Damn, woman,' Wren said, 'the men will be tripping over their tongues.'

'Looking good yourself,' said Isabella, admiring Wren's sleek and sexy topknot, which was perfect with the plunging white shirt she wore tucked into skintight leather trousers. 'And you, Rosie. Love the hair.'

Rosie's blonde braids were wrapped around her head like a crown tonight and her tortoiseshell glasses sat at the end of her snub nose.

'Hey, what about me?' Amber who needed a night out said, and Isabella turned to get a good look at her, ready to say something complimentary. But no words came out as she took in the caramel tones of Amber's skin, the halo of curly hair held back in a top pony, and eyes the colour of the sea. And that was before she could take in the full bosom almost spilling out of a black top. She let out a low whistle instead.

'Good answer.' Amber laughed and then, to Rosie and Wren, she said, 'You're right, I like her already.'

'Welcome to Throwback Thursday,' said Rosie, raising her glass. 'The most fun you can have with your clothes on.'

An hour later, drinks were flowing and the bar was always three-deep. The women had decided it was better to buy two bottles at a time to prevent wasted time queuing. Amber was drinking Blue Lagoon cocktails instead and transferring the umbrellas from her drink to behind her ear. The crowd was just Isabella's type: up for it, young, but not too young. Old, but not old enough to know better.

A steady stream of locals popped over to say hello. Between them, Amber, Rosie and Wren appeared to know everyone in town. Rosie and Wren were like a double act, while Amber had a way of tilting her head to one side as she listened, and touching people's arms as she replied. Before long, Isabella felt like she'd been introduced to everyone she'd ever need. Lizelle, the striking South African hairdresser who gave the best blow-dry; Ben, the rowing coach, whose chest hair merged with his full beard; Ellie, with jewelled nails that glowed in the dark, who offered Isabella a discount on her first manicure; and Jamie from the greengrocer's, who promised her a free squeeze of his produce with a wink. She committed their names to memory and told them she'd love to see them at the grand opening of Tutto Mio. The booze was loosening her up, untying the knots in her shoulders from sanding and painting. Gabi would love it in here. She couldn't wait for her to visit.

'So how do you guys know each other?' she asked the women at the table as they poured another round.

'We met a couple of years ago when Amber and Jayden moved here and joined River Rats.' Rosie pointed between the three women. 'Bonded over a secret flask of brandy on the bankside on a bitterly cold winter's day while the kids did rafting.'

'River Rats?' Isabella asked.

'It's a club that does stuff on the water every weekend,' said Amber. 'My son, Jayden, goes. He's ten.'

'So does our daughter, Riley. She's three. And she has a massive crush on Jayden.'

'Sounds perfect,' Isabella said.

'Almost as perfect as when the men's team capsized and came out of the water looking like four Mr Darcys. Dripping fringes, broody eyes, the lot.' Amber closed her eyes with pleasure.

'Ah, yes. A famous Etienne incident.' Rosie sipped her wine. Isabella's ears pricked up at the name.

'I think I've met him actually,' Isabella made herself casually announce.

Wren put a hand out expectantly across the table. 'I win,' she said triumphantly.

Rosie groaned loudly, opened her purse and put a ten-pound note in her partner's palm with a rueful smile.

'I *knew* he'd make a beeline for you the moment he saw you!' Wren proclaimed.

'Do you all know him then?' Isabella asked.

'Think every straight woman in Honeybridge knows him,' Wren said. 'Or would like to.'

'Makes me almost wish I was straight when I see him at the rowing club, top off, leaning into the stroke.' Rosie fanned herself with her hand, and Isabella thought her glasses steamed slightly.

'Yes, you could say Etienne is something of a local celebrity,' Amber added. 'In the bedroom department.'

'Never seen him with the same woman more than once.'

So, it was as Isabella suspected. He was a player. A gorgeous one, to be fair. But bad news altogether.

'Where did you meet him? Did he come over and introduce himself?'

Isabella told them the whole embarrassing story. Firstly, the wet T-shirt and then the licking of the batter.

The girls roared.

'Well, if you're looking for a relationship, he's probably not the one.'

'But from what we hear, he'd probably be a good palate cleanser,' Rosie added and they all dissolved into giggles again.

'Nope,' Isabella said. 'Nothing happening. I told you, I'm not interested. I'm not having sex for another two months – give or take a day or two.' She explained her man ban to a confused-looking Amber.

'So, he's licked your arm and seen your nipples,' Wren said.

'Yes. But not in that order,' Isabella clarified.

'But you're still not tempted? Not even a tiny bit?' Wren held her finger and thumb an inch apart while looking highly suspicious.

Isabella fervently shook her head and buried her face in the massive glass of wine to avoid further questioning.

'Have you ever been Etienne'd?' Wren asked Amber across the booth. She forced a large swallow of her drink down as though it were stuck in her throat and then put her hands out definitively in a stop sign.

'No way! I mean, you can't help but notice him and his friends, Fox and Walker.'

Isabella noted the other unusual names. Wren nodded; Rosie smiled.

'I've known Walker since we were kids at secondary school, after he moved down from Scotland,' Rosie said.

'He was the only boyfriend she ever had,' Wren said.

'Luckily I realised I was gay before we got to any of the hetero sex stuff.' Rosie squirmed and laughed. 'Been friends ever since, though. He helped me through a lot when I came out.'

'Well, it should be illegal for them to all walk round together, they're all gorgeous,' Amber said. 'But when it comes to Etienne Martin, the answer is no. I'm raising a little man and I want any big man I bring home to be daddy material. Until then I'm doing a great job on my own.' She raised her glass again to her mouth but came away disappointed when it was already empty.

'I've been burned twice already. Jayden's real dad took off when we found out about Jayden's hearing loss and he's never been back. I know it's a lot to take on, but I expected more of him.' She shrugged and peered into her glass again. 'Then the only other relationship I've had ended with one broken heart – mine – and one very confused boy. And while I can forgive most things, I can't forgive someone letting Jayden down.'

Isabella banged her glass against Amber's empty one, partly in recognition of her efforts to be a good parent, and partly in relief that she hadn't shagged Etienne. Although, of course, she reminded herself, it made no difference to her.

Chapter Ten

Etienne

Etienne and Fox gathered round their usual high table in the far corner of The Bolthole. Fox had swapped his soft flannel checked shirt of the day for a different flannel checked shirt and wore it open over a white T and jeans. His silver hair stood up in a messy side quiff, his grey and black speckled stubble completing the picture. He lifted a bottle of beer to his mouth and as he lowered it, smiled unselfconsciously at a passing blonde, who fell off her heel as a result and nearly died of embarrassment. The Fox Effect. Women loved him. Especially when they realised the silver god of a man was the softest and most sentimental guy. They'd fall at his feet and offer to have his babies if he didn't already have two of his own. They'd offer to step in as stepmum if he so much as looked in their direction. But Fox would just smile and make polite chat, never going further than that. He wasn't interested in the slightest. He just wanted a night out with the big boys, before he went home again to his little ones.

Etienne had on a long-sleeved T-shirt that he liked the fit of, almost as much as the female population of Honeybridge did. He knew his jeans fit his butt with precision and he was aware of the complimentary glances coming his way, but his mood was still lower than normal. Walker was trying his best to solve this by buying another round of beers.

'Bar's busy,' he said, appearing through the crowd and placing a tray containing six bottles of beer on the table. 'So I bought doubles.'

Everyone lifted a bottle and sank a cold mouthful.

'So, deadline over then, Fox?' Walker shifted onto the stool beside him. His voice was a soft Scottish burr. 'What you gonna do now?'

'Hopefully have a couple of weeks off with the boys. This game's been going on for months.'

'How do you explain to them that playing computer games is your job?' Etienne said.

'I do have to design them first before I can play them, you know. And playing them is only to check that everything works. No glitches.'

'So how many times have you played this one?'

Fox blew out his breath.

'I've lost count. But I didn't sleep at all Tuesday night so that I could get to the final level.'

'Such dedication.' Walker laughed. 'I didn't sleep either on Tuesday night, but it was more to do with saving people trapped in a rolled bus than playing on my computer.'

'Yeah, yeah. We know you're amazing . . .'

'Firefighters are everyday heroes, you know,' Walker announced proudly, as if this was news.

'It's only because everyone wants to see your hose,' Fox said.

'Or climb your pole,' Etienne added.

'Fuck off. At least *my* pole's working,' Walker said good-naturedly.

Etienne thought about retaliating but realised he hadn't thought about his cock once all night, even when he was surrounded by gorgeous women. Maybe he really was broken.

'Seriously, though,' Fox said. 'I've got a good feeling about this game. I think it could be popular.' He lifted his beer and they all cheersed.

'When will you hear?'

'The investors' meeting is next month. Gives them time to personally play it and get feedback from user groups.'

'Then what?'

'They'll either produce it or they won't, or they might ask for some changes or extensions. Have to wait and see. And spend some time with the hooligans until then.'

'You could dedicate some time to getting laid too, you know,' Walker suggested.

'The only laying I'm going to be doing is down – for long naps when the kids are at school and lie-ins on Sundays to watch cartoons with them in bed.'

'Seriously, one day someone will catch your eye again.'

'And I'll have to hope my body can keep up.' Fox seemed completely happy with his lot. He'd come a long way from the first time Etienne met him, sitting at the corner table of The Bistro with a toddler in a high chair and a baby in a sling on his chest. He was trying to feed chopped-up Poulet Breton to the oldest as he banged a spoon repeatedly on the table, and balance a bottle under his chin to keep in direct contact with the baby's crying mouth, all the while Fox's own plate of boeuf bourguignon went cold and congealed.

'Shall I feed you while you feed them?' Etienne had joked, but the look of absolute despair on Fox's face made him pull out a chair and take over the feeding of a very vocal two-year-old.

'Thanks. You're a lifesaver,' Fox had said.

Fox's wife had died the week before. Reggie was old enough to notice, George just clung to his daddy instead.

Now, four years later, Fox had hit his stride with the boys. His career was on the up, with his 'FoxFun' gaming designs gaining attention. He was a hot single daddy who had everything except time to focus on himself.

'What about your sex drive then?' Walker nudged Etienne. 'Has it resurfaced?'

'Not as yet,' Etienne acknowledged. 'Last brief appearance was when I licked Isabella's arm.'

'Whose?' Walker said.

'Isabella. The new restaurant owner.'

'So, it worked for her then. All is not lost.'

Etienne swigged from his bottle and allowed himself to think of her. That gorgeous olive skin. The small freckle beside her mouth when she opened it in surprise.

'Maybe you're stressed. That can do it,' Walker said. Etienne's train of thought was interrupted by the vibration of his phone against his leg. He tugged it free of his pocket but the message was from his service provider, an update on his plan. He tossed it on the table in frustration and looked up to see both men watching him closely.

'What's that phone ever done to you?' Walker frowned.

'Nothing.' Etienne sighed and rubbed a hand over his face. 'I'm waiting to hear from someone.'

'Who?'

'Why?' Four elbows hit the table as the two men leaned in.

Etienne looked between them both for a long second before shaking his head.

'My brother.'

Fox sat up straighter on his stool, and Walker cocked his head.

'In fact, my twin.'

Fox and Walker glanced at each other, checking whether the other knew. By the confusion on each other's faces, it was clear that it was new news to them both.

'Why have we never heard about him before?' Walker said, who Etienne knew had an older sister living in the Highlands.

'Where have you been hiding him all these years?' Fox said, who Etienne knew had a younger sister living in Barcelona.

'It's not so much that I've been hiding him,' he said with a sigh. 'It's more that we're not close any more. My fault entirely.'

'So why's it bothering you now?' Walker said.

'It's complicated.' Etienne swigged his beer.

The other two men both waited.

'I fucked up in the past. Long ago. Before I moved here.' He shut his eyes briefly against the flash of memory, Kira in his arms, nothing else mattering.

'Can you put it right now?'

Etienne shook his head angrily. 'No. Like I said, I fucked up. He left. In fact, he ran away. It was dangerous for him to stay. All because of me.'

Walker nodded. 'Like you said, sounds complicated.'

'But he got back in touch last week. A single message. And now he's not answering again.' He banged the table.

Fox, the patron saint of patience due to living with two demanding bosses under his roof day and night, nodded sagely. 'If he's contacted you once, he'll do it again. And then you can fix it.'

Etienne searched Fox's kind eyes and hoped to God he was right.

Walker nodded along. 'Sounds like this could also be the problem with your penis.'

Etienne looked into his laughing eyes and gave him a swift dead arm.

The band ran onto the stage and put an end to their banter.

Chapter Eleven

Isabella

Wren's topknot was still in impeccable shape, even if she was slightly worse for wear. Rosie was delightfully squiffy and in the middle of a long story about the latest book she was reading.

'Honestly, the sex! So well depicted!' She rolled her eyes in pleasure.

'There's me thinking she'd be all highbrow when we met,' interjected Wren, 'but she's as happy with *Bridgerton* as she is with Jane Austen. The more sex, the better.' They grinned at each other, infuriatingly in love. The music in the bar turned up a notch.

'Yes!' Wren exclaimed. 'Let's dance!' She threw back the last mouthful in her glass and strode out of the booth.

'How *did* you two meet?' Isabella asked.

'Wren used to be a dancer,' Rosie said, looking lovingly at her partner who was now purposefully moving onto the dance floor.

'I can totally see that,' Isabella said. 'Was it ballet?'

'Not quite,' Rosie said with a giggle as Wren stepped up to the silver pole in the middle of the dance floor. Placing one hand on it, high above her head, she turned a tight pirouette underneath her own arm until she stood with her back to the pole. Lifting her knee, she placed her heel back against the steel and flicked a heavy-lidded look in their direction.

'She used to work with Cirque du Soleil a long time ago, but I met her doing what she does best, on a pole, in a club.'

Wren stepped round the bar in two long strides; people made room, someone whistled. Then she lifted herself as though weightless, circling the pole perfectly with one arm, one knee leading the way, the other straight out behind her, flying without effort. A moment later, she was upside down, still circumnavigating the pole.

'She's incredible,' Amber whispered, stirring her new blue cocktail with a steel straw.

'She's amazing!' Isabella gasped.

'She's *hot*,' Rosie said with a proud smile.

The song ended and Wren landed elegantly on her heels to a roar of approval from the crowd. Next moment, the band bounded on stage.

'Let's get up there,' said Rosie, scooting along the booth. Amber downed her drink and then she and Isabella followed. 'It's Throwback Thursday time!'

The guitarist started a well-known riff and then Isabella was dancing, hands in the air, happy.

Chapter Twelve

Etienne

Etienne saw Wren doing her thing on the pole. That woman had moves. He'd seen it before, but she never failed to amaze him. You'd think that people that ran a bookshop were quiet types, but Rosie and Wren were a riot. Walker had introduced them when Etienne first arrived in town, fondly describing Rosie as the only girl in Honeybridge who had ever turned him down, before pulling her in for a side hug.

The band, The Runaway Train, ran onto the stage next. They were always entertaining. Throwback Thursdays were a chance for them to play anything and everything from the past few decades – the cheesier, the better. The fact that most of the people in the bar hadn't been alive more than forty years didn't stop them dancing to music from before they were born.

He then saw Rosie coming across the floor to join Wren and, behind her, Amber from River Rats and Isabella, who was *almost* wearing a strappy camisole, jeans and heels. Etienne took a swig of his beer. She looked good.

He watched her smiling as she started to dance, arms above her head. That satin camisole lifting higher, showing more of her olive midriff, the muscles in her lower back, the soft curve of her stomach as she turned in the lights. Correct that, she looked *damned* good.

'That's Isabella, the new neighbour,' he said to the guys and indicated the dance floor with his head. 'Strappy top, long brown hair.'

Walker turned to see and Fox squinted onto the dance floor until they found her.

They all turned back to the high table at the same time.

'I think I could use her to model my next sexy avatar,' said Fox appreciatively.

'I think she has a fire in her pants I could put out,' Walker said. Etienne gave him his second dead arm of the night. There was no way he was letting Walker anywhere near her. Not with his hero status and his massive shoulders from saving people from burning buildings and the like. He let his eyes rest on her a while longer; her own were shut now, as she moved to the music.

'We're out of beer,' Fox said. 'Whose round?'

'Mine,' Etienne said, checking his wallet in his back pocket. 'Time for whisky.'

The Bolthole was now rammed. The dance floor spilled out into the aisles, customers dancing in their booths, some on their tables.

'Might cut across the dance floor,' he said and both his friends shook their heads.

'Thought you might.'

He edged closer to the middle of the dance floor, around couples and friends in circles, until he was surrounded by a hot, heaving party. It only took him a moment and then he was beside her. She was laughing and holding on to Amber and totally unaware of his proximity. Her strap had slipped from her shoulder and he could imagine pushing it further down her arm, freeing those wonderful breasts he'd glimpsed that day on the square. He couldn't help smiling, even though he hadn't had the chance to talk to her. He moved on to the bar as the song changed to 'Livin' on a Prayer'.

Chapter Thirteen

Isabella

'I need water!' Isabella said, wafting her face with both hands, feeling a bead of sweat run down her cleavage. The tribute section to Bon Jovi was finished and the band were starting on Tina Turner, fifty people all around her running on the spot to the beginning of 'Proud Mary'. Amber gave her a thumbs up and Isabella weaved her way through the crowd in the general direction of the bar.

She'd chosen a good time as the dance floor was pulling people in and she slid in between a girl group who were organising their order and a man leaning over a beer. A barman with long hair was busy at one end pulling pints and another was filling a tray with shots at the other. Isabella rested her elbows on the bar, feeling the breeze on her hot skin from the fan on the back wall.

'Well, hello.' The voice was so close to her ear that she jumped. She looked at the sweaty face of the thirtysomething man next to her. He looked like he should have gone home an hour ago.

'Hi,' she said politely and returned her gaze to the bar.

'Haven't seen you here before?' he slurred.

'No,' she said, not wanting to be rude but not wanting to encourage him either. Suddenly wishing she was joining in with the whooping along to Tina Turner.

'I'd remember a face like yours for certain . . .' he continued, using all his best chat-up lines at once.

She smiled politely, checked both ends of the bar, but both bar staff were still busy. One shaking a cocktail, one shovelling ice into a bucket.

'Wanna drink?' He lifted his beer towards her. 'I'll buy you a drink . . .'

'No thanks,' Isabella said firmly. 'I'm buying a round.' She took her phone out of her jeans pocket and studied it pointedly to avoid further conversation.

'So, what's your name then?' the man said suddenly, banging his chin on her shoulder.

Isabella's stomach lurched. He wasn't getting the message.

'Isabella,' she said. The girls next to her gave up the wait and succumbed to the dance floor frenzy in full swing. She watched them go. Someone else moved round the bar to take their place beside her.

'Fancy a dance, Issy?' he said, placing a clammy hand on her arm.

'No thanks.' Her voice was firm, but she smiled politely.

'Ah, come on, be friendly,' he said, moving his arm to put it around her shoulders. That was enough.

'Just to be clear, I'm not interested in you sexually, at all,' she said with a straight face as she physically lifted his arm away from her. His eyes widened and then flicked around himself as if checking she was addressing him. She continued: 'But it was nice to meet you and if you ever want to take your mum out somewhere nice for dinner, then I'd love to see you at my new restaurant. Tutto Mio. It's on the square. Opening soon.' She flashed him a smile then which increased his confusion.

'Eh?' he said. 'How did you know I live with my mum?'

'I didn't. But the clues were there,' she said. 'Now, sorry, I don't know your name?'

'Andy,' he stammered.

'Well, Andy, if you ever want to improve how you approach women, I can recommend a guy called Tongue Tied on TikTok. He gives great advice on conversation starters that might come in handy.'

The man was out of his depth now, mouth opening and closing.

She smiled and nodded to show him she had finished when the person standing on her other side leaned in.

'Everything okay here?' Etienne said and just like that she was looking into those green eyes and black eyelashes. He was so close.

'Everything's fine, thanks,' replied Isabella. 'Isn't it, Andy?'

Andy nodded, muttered something unintelligible and slid off his bar stool. He shuffled towards the exit, leaving his pint half-finished on the bar. Isabella turned back to Etienne.

'I didn't need rescuing,' she said and it came out sharper than she meant.

'I know that. I heard you.' Etienne raised a dark eyebrow in appreciation and then laughed. 'I bet Andy's never been given dating advice before.'

'Maybe someone should have done it earlier,' Isabella said. At this close range, she could see the designer-length stubble. She could smell the woody scent of his cologne. She could feel the heat from his body.

'Got a night off then?' she asked.

'Celebrating with my friend. He's finished a deadline.' He chatted for a bit about the game and Isabella recognised the names Fox and Walker the girls had mentioned earlier.

'Good to see you out, though,' he said. 'I see you've met some of the locals.' He nodded at the dance floor where Wren was now on a podium in the middle of the floor. Rosie and Amber were holding each other's hands above their heads and dancing back to back. Someone had started a conga which snaked around the back of the stage. The place was chaos.

The long-haired barman finally appeared in front of them and Etienne indicated that Isabella should order first. The bartender departed again to fetch another Blue Lagoon for Amber, three shots of toffee vodka and a pint of water, no ice.

'It's great here,' Isabella laughed, turning her attention back to Etienne. 'Honestly, I haven't been out like this in so long.' She took a second, trying to remember, but then realised it would have been in the Daniel Days. She blinked the image away. Better to forget that. Daniel had probably been texting his lover every time he was at the bar, while Isabella was on the dance floor.

'How come?' Etienne asked, leaning on the bar next to her, his thigh casually pressed against the curve of her hip. She felt the warmth of him, his proximity the closest contact she'd had in months. Something in her longed to press back.

'I haven't felt like dancing for a while,' she said and again those eyes found hers. Probing, searching, as if to see her story. Read her like a book. Uncover her secrets. Jesus, she sounded like one of Rosie's steamy romances. NO SEX FOR A YEAR. She shook herself. 'It's been one of those years.'

'I've had one of those before,' Etienne surprised her by saying and she thought she saw something like regret cross his face, just for an instant.

'But it's a good break from decorating!' She rolled her shoulders and saw his attention flash to the strap of her top as it slipped off her shoulder. She lifted it back into place. 'I never realised how exhausting it is. My body aches all over . . .'

He flexed his hands together.

'I give a good massage, so I've been told.' He grinned wolfishly.

'Don't worry!' she said as his eyes met hers again. 'Nothing a long, hot soak won't solve . . .'

'I've got a big tub. Room for two?' he asked, one eyebrow lifted. 'You know where I am . . .'

He caught his lower lip under a pointed, white incisor.

Good God. The thought of those white teeth on her own skin. Stop! She laughed and shook her hair away from her neck, which was suddenly burning hot. The action drew his eyes before they dropped to her chest, where she knew her breasts were on show again through the silky satin of her top.

'I do,' she said, grinning back. 'But I think maybe tonight . . .'

He was leaning in now, his face mere inches from hers, and she didn't pull away. His eyes sparked as the knuckles of his hand brushed against hers, a soft touch which set off some kind of chain reaction right the way to her pants. One finger lazily stroked a single line on her forearm from wrist to inner elbow, where the skin was smoother and more sensitive, without taking his eyes from hers. Get a grip, woman. The man is hypnotising you into having sex with him.

'What you need is a long, cold shower,' she said. He laughed, head back. She couldn't help but smile. He glanced at her phone.

'Do you have NameDrop on that?' he asked. She nodded and he tapped his phone to it, transferring his details automatically.

'My number,' he said. 'For whenever.' The one-sided smile made her want to lean forward and kiss him. To see what it would feel like to press into his body. To twine her arms around his neck and pull his face to hers.

'Eighteen quid, please,' the long-haired bartender said and Isabella threw him the money and grabbed the tray, taking it and her throbbing nipples back onto the dance floor.

Chapter Fourteen

Etienne

Etienne placed the whiskies on the table and the three each lifted a glass. The Runaway Train were now playing Michael Jackson and the dance floor was crammed with people moonwalking and grabbing their own crotches with abandon.

'You took your time,' Walker said.

'Got a bit distracted.' Etienne grinned.

'We saw,' Fox said, clinking their glasses together.

'So, when are you getting together?'

Etienne took a long swallow of beer.

'Don't know yet,' he said, finally. 'The fun is in the chase at the moment.'

'That makes a change for you.' Fox laughed.

'Maybe she's holding out for me,' Walker suggested, earning himself his third and final dead arm of the night.

'One thing I do know, though . . .' Etienne took another drink. 'My cock's working fine.'

Chapter Fifteen

Isabella

Girl Gang WhatsApp group

Wren: My head hurts.

Rosie: My eyeballs hurt.

Isabella: I woke up on the sofa fully clothed ten minutes ago.

Amber: My lips are stained blue.

Isabella: OMIGOD, they are drilling downstairs.

Amber: I found five paper umbrellas on my pillow.

Wren: Come to The Lit Lounge in an hour.

Rosie: We'll put the coffee on.

The door jangled, making Wren cringe and put her hands to her head, as Isabella stepped inside The Lit Lounge. Rosie had replaced her usual oversized tortoiseshell glasses with oversized prescription sunglasses and her plaits were spiralled around her head like a bandage. Amber, still with bright blue lips, slumped in one of the stuffed armchairs with a large cup of coffee in front of her, her eyes shut.

Every wall was lined floor to ceiling with bookshelves, and Isabella spied a ladder on one side. Hand-illustrated signs showed customers to the 'kids' corner'; another to 'killer thrillers'; a third happily announced 'cliterary fiction'. The bare floorboards were covered in colourful rugs, coffee tables were made from painted pallets and old travel trunks, and every armchair had a brightly crocheted cushion on it.

'How do you take your coffee?' Rosie asked, which would have made Isabella smile if she weren't so hungover that it hurt to move unnecessarily. Funny that they all knew each other's favourite cocktails, throwback anthems and dance moves, but not how they took their coffee.

'Espresso,' said Isabella.

She let herself collapse back into the armchair next to Amber as Rosie shouted, 'Watch out for Barney!' and Wren said, 'Wait!' But it was too late and she landed on an old ginger cat, who shot out from under her with a yowl.

Barney strolled away nonchalantly and jumped into one of the other armchairs. Isabella then noticed the tiny tabby cat in Amber's lap. Scanning the room, she spotted at least another four, in all colours and sizes, in various poses of sleep. There was even one in the window, curled up in the smallest puddle of sun.

'Sorry, should have warned you,' Rosie said. 'We have a lot of cats.'

'You're not allergic, are you?' Wren added.

'The only thing I'm allergic to is obviously alcohol,' Isabella said. 'I feel like death.'

Amber nodded without opening her eyes. Rosie and Wren

brought the coffees over and pulled their own armchairs into a circle.

'Welcome to Honeybridge. You're a local now you've survived a Throwback Thursday.'

Isabella managed a weak smile. 'I can't wait to take Gabi when she visits.'

'You okay in there, Amber?' Rosie said.

Amber nodded her head, then shook it.

'Never again.'

'That's what you said last time,' Wren deadpanned.

'I found Etienne's number in my phone this morning when I woke up,' Isabella confessed, showing the women her contacts list. Amber managed to crank open one eyelid to look at the evidence.

'He's definitely keen,' Rosie said.

'Are you going to message him?' Wren asked.

Isabella blew out her breath. 'Nope,' she said. 'Two words, remember? Sex ban.'

'Sex bomb more like,' Amber's blue lips said.

Three coffees later, all eyes were open, and hangovers were under control enough for Rosie to start talking about food.

'I never did find out why you needed a night out?' Isabella asked Amber.

Amber exhaled slowly.

'I'm losing my job. As of the end of this month I'll be unemployed.'

Rosie and Wren shook their heads, obviously already in the know.

'What do you do?' She couldn't believe they hadn't covered

this the night before, although thinking back to the rate that Amber was downing Blue Lagoons, maybe she just didn't want to talk about it.

'I do a bit of everything at the rowing club. It suits me so well – and I'm going to be hard pushed to find something that means I can be there when Jayden gets home from after-school club.'

'They're making a massive mistake,' Rosie said.

'They don't realise the half of what she does ...' Wren said to Isabella.

'So, what happened?'

'The club's been bought by a fancy leisure company. They're bringing in their own hospitality manager and so I'm not needed any more.'

'But she doesn't just do the hospitality side of things,' Rosie said, sitting up straight for the first time that morning. She raised her hand and started checking things off on her fingers.

'She runs the rowing meet schedule ...' Rosie.

'She set up River Rats to expand the membership ...' Wren.

'She manages stock for the outdoor café ...' Rosie.

'She also does the staff rotas for the café!' Wren added.

'And she manages the membership fees too.' Rosie snapped her thumb down at the last point. Both looked outraged. Amber blew them a kiss and smiled weakly.

'Maybe I'll let you help me write my CV. You make me sound fabulous.'

Isabella thought about Tutto Mio. How all these skills would be essential in the coming months. How things were starting to become overwhelming and she felt anxious when she went to bed at night. How she hadn't even started to think about staffing the restaurant yet.

She remembered admiring Amber's way with people the night before. The genuine way she listened. The way people reciprocated her smile.

'I would have started looking around town today for vacancies, but probably not the best look!' She pouted blue lips at them and laughed. 'I'll start tomorrow.' She nodded to them all. 'I'll find something great.'

Isabella felt Amber's determination as if it were her own. She admired her positive attitude. She remembered Amber saying last night about how, until she found someone good enough to be daddy material, she was more than enough on her own. It resonated.

'Have you ever waitressed?' she asked, as casually as she could.

'Girl, my parents own a beach restaurant in Jamaica. I grew up waiting tables.'

'And you know lots of people locally?' Isabella said.

Amber focused those ocean-coloured eyes on Isabella curiously.

'I know pretty much everyone,' she said. 'And those I don't know, I just haven't met yet.'

'So, you could staff a restaurant so that you didn't have to be there in the evenings?' Isabella asked.

'Yes, I could,' said Amber, cautiously optimistic now. Wren and Rosie were leaning forward in their seats. From the corner of her eye, Isabella saw Rosie take Wren's hand and squeeze it.

Isabella made her decision. It wasn't a hard one.

'Then I'd like to offer you a job.'

Amber straightened her back and her blue smile lit her face.

'And I'd like to accept.'

They shook hands solemnly while Rosie and Wren clapped.

'Sorry to interrupt.' A teenage girl wearing Doc Martens approached hesitantly and all eyes turned to her. She shuffled, kicking the heels of her boots against each other. Her eyeliner was heavy, her eyebrow had a lightning bolt through it and she wore her hair in space buns on the side of her head.

'Do you need help finding something?' Rosie said, already moving to stand.

'Yes please,' the girl said and turned to Amber, pointing at her big, blue grin. 'Where did you get your lipstick from? It's wicked.'

Mia Famiglia WhatsApp group

Isabella: I found my right-hand woman today!

Mamma: Hope you hired her?

Isabella: On the spot!

Papà: What experience does she bring?

Isabella: Great at organising kids' river rafting and drinking blue cocktails.

Mamma: Hmmmm.

Isabella: She's perfect, Mamma. Trust me.

Chapter Sixteen

Etienne

Etienne worked his own hangover off with a five-mile run at 7 a.m., followed by a three-mile row down the river and back, topped off with a bacon sandwich dripping with ketchup that Mile End Mickey presented to him on his return.

He lounged against the prepping table while he ate, licking his fingers and smacking his lips as he finished.

'Good night then?' Mickey asked, his knife a blur as he chopped vegetables for the day.

Etienne had to agree. He felt better this morning, reassured on two counts. Firstly, Fox and Walker had been certain he'd have the chance to put things right with Alex. And secondly, that his cock was in perfect working order. Or it was for Isabella Tucci, that was for certain.

He'd seen her at the bar and the well-concealed roll of her eyes as Andy started to talk to her. He'd strolled over there fully expecting to go in as the hero, the protector. But she hadn't needed anyone to save her. She'd been direct but not rude, plain speaking but helpful, and he hadn't needed to say a word. He only chipped in at the end because he wanted her to see him there.

He wondered when she might text. She didn't seem like one of those game players who left it a certain number of days before messaging, to show they're in control or not that bothered. From last night's performance, she seemed like the kind of woman that could handle herself and would message when she wanted to.

A flicker of doubt went through him, which was unusual when it came to women. What if she didn't text? She'd already turned away from his mouth on her skin. What if she simply wasn't interested?

'You all right, mate?' Mile End Mickey said. 'You've gone a bit pale.'

Etienne shook his head, clearing it. Of course she'd be interested.

'Fine,' he insisted. 'Absolutely fine.'

At that exact moment, his phone buzzed with a text.

'Even better now, in fact.' He grinned, picking it up and waving cockily over his shoulder as he went through to the empty restaurant.

He flicked to messages. But it wasn't Isabella.

Alex: I want to come home. But it might be dangerous.

Etienne sank down at a nearby empty table. His fingers trembled and he was glad of autocorrect as he quickly typed a reply, desperate to keep the conversation going.

Etienne: I can help. Tell me what you need me to do.

He would do anything to put this right. It was his fault that he hadn't been able to see his brother for all this time. It was down to him that his twin had had to run because Etienne had let him down when he needed him most.

Alex: I don't want to bring trouble back to you.

The reply felt like a kick in the gut to Etienne. He'd take all the trouble. He'd face it for Alex, like he should have done all those years ago.

Etienne: I'm in. What kind of trouble are we looking at?
Alex: The Dougalls still need paying back.

Etienne inhaled sharply. So, the rumours were right.

When their parents died five years before, Alex and Etienne were in very different places in their lives. Etienne was set on a path of owning a restaurant and immediately decided to use his inheritance to buy The Bistro. Alex was following his own path of playing the online slots, picking a horse or two at the weekend and finally moving on to local poker games. Not the ones for fun and sharing a bottle of whisky with the boys. The ones in back rooms of the local pubs, where the doors were locked and the stakes were high. Too high. When Alex got his share of the inheritance – a small fortune, enough to set him up in the business of his choice for the rest of his life – he instead decided to bet it on a full house which he thought was a sure thing, only to have Mason Dougall turn over a straight flush. Which would have been fine if he'd stopped then. But Alex was a gambler.

Etienne: How much do you owe them?

The wait was excruciating, longer than between the last messages. How much over the inheritance had Alex gone? He knew it must be a significant amount to have to run. The rumours said it was worth a chopped-off hand or a kneecapping unless it got paid back. Etienne had also heard that the Dougalls made you choose which hand you wanted them to cut off, and then always took the one you wanted to keep. Etienne felt his eyeballs drying out as he stared at his phone. Finally, another message.

Alex: 50k.

His stomach dropped. He didn't have enough to cover that. He was sure of it. He shook his head. He'd have to find a way.

Etienne: Leave it with me.

Alex: It might have to be cash. Or a transfer. They haven't said yet.

Suddenly Etienne felt like he was in some kind of gangster movie. This was way outside his normal life of cook, serve, sex, sleep. But he'd do anything for Alex and the chance to bring him home. It was his fault he'd had to leave in the first place.

Etienne: Are you still gambling, Al?

Etienne stared intently at the screen. He had to ask.

Alex: Haven't even played bingo since I left.

Etienne breathed out slowly, but the next message jolted him to standing.

Alex: How's Kiera?

Etienne: Long gone.

He shook his head at the complete and utter waste of the last four years. If only he'd picked up the phone when Alex called. He could have paid the money there and then. The papers weren't yet signed on The Bistro. He could have given him the money and put him into some kind of gambling rehab. Alex wouldn't have had to run and live on his own with no friends or family. They could have been together.

But it wasn't as simple as that. After living through Alex's addiction over the years, he'd learned the hard way that addiction trumps family – every time. He'd lent Alex money in the early days for him to pay off someone he'd lost a bet to, only to find out Alex used the money to try double or quits. The debt always doubled. Another time, he'd given him his entire month's wages, to try to help Alex out without their parents knowing, only for Alex to take it to the local casino and put it on black.

So, when Alex rang that night all those years ago, and Etienne saw his name flashing on the screen, he ignored it because he'd finally got his latest crush, Kiera, to go out with him after a few weeks of thinking she'd be the love of his life. As it was, they only actually dated for a month. But that night, as they kissed, he missed frantic message after frantic message from his brother, asking for help, begging for money, and finally explaining he had to disappear. And Etienne had blamed himself ever since.

So this time, he'd take the risk. He'd give him the money. He had to.

Alex: I'll contact the Dougalls. And I'll arrange how to get them the money.

Etienne could imagine how terrifying typing those words must be.

The Dougall family name was feared across south London where they used to live. They were notoriously violent, and people would cross the road rather than risk getting in the Dougalls' way. He'd first heard of them when his parents' car got stolen and the police confirmed a car theft operation run by the Dougall family. Later, when he was at university, the Dougalls seemed to run a loan shark operation preying on skint students needing a quick cash flow. They didn't know what they were getting themselves into and ended up owing more than they ever borrowed. It seemed that the Dougalls had fingers in lots of illegal pies, because it was also them who organised the illicit poker nights across the city, acting as a bank until someone like Alex owed them too much and they wanted it back – with interest.

Keep in touch. Etienne didn't want the conversation to end but knew he had to leave Alex to do this part alone.

Love you, bro, Alex said and Etienne's eyes squeezed shut. Visions of Alex sprung into his mind. The two of them with their arms around each other's shoulders, spinning in circles in the back garden. Fiercely objecting to being dressed the same. Wrestling in the pool on holiday. Kicking each other's legs under the table during tea. Standing side by side at their parents' funeral as the coffins were lowered in the joint plot. A million memories. Always together. The Twins.

Love you too, he typed, never meaning anything more in his life.

Etienne's chest was hurting as he let his phone fall to his side.

This was love. This was what he'd risked by trying to have a relationship with a woman. And that's why one-night stands were all that he'd allowed himself ever since.

Chapter Seventeen

Isabella

Isabella viewed herself in the full-length mirror and pulled the belt on her wrap dress tight. It cinched her in at the waist, before the skirt skimmed her hips and landed above her knee. Strappy heeled sandals gave her an extra few inches of height and made her legs long and lean. She looked good. She shook her hair out in the mirror, watching her curls tumble around her shoulders. No messy bun today. And no wet T-shirts. Although a fair bit of cleavage, she thought with a mischievous grin, pulling her dress down just that inch lower at the front.

She'd been doing competition visits all week. Starting with the local cafés for brunch and then a few of the other restaurants for dinner. Checking out their menus, their service standards, their staff. She'd eaten everything from eggs and avocado on sourdough to Murgh Makhani. She'd sipped cocktails and smoothies and caffè lattes. But she'd never made so much effort with what she wore until tonight, when she was booked into The Bistro. Funny that.

She'd not only tasted the competition, she'd learned about them too. She'd listened to what other customers were saying and heard all sorts of insights. Not just about the food either. Especially at one café where she'd been sitting next to a table of young women, similar in age to her. One of them had obviously moved away from the town and was back visiting her friends. They'd been exchanging stories and catching up on life, and Isabella inconspicuously listened in when she heard the name of her neighbour, Etienne.

'Any new encounters with the gorgeous Etienne?'

'Not me. I got Etienne'd last year,' one of them said with a giggle.

'I was the year before that,' another said, rolling her eyes. 'Been thinking about it ever since.'

'Saw him out on his run last week. How does he look sexy at seven in the morning?'

'He'd look sexy any time of day.' They all laughed and conversation moved on. Etienne certainly seemed to be in demand.

Isabella spritzed some perfume, firstly on her throat and then on her wrist where Etienne's mouth had been, and felt the tug of it again, deep in her groin. God, that man was sexy. She checked her watch. Time to go. She tied her coat at the waist, cinching her figure, and headed over the square.

He was leaning over his bookings diary when she pulled open the door to step inside, and she took the opportunity to survey the restaurant. The ambience was good. Tables all pretty much full. Lighting soft enough to make everyone more attractive. Music was low enough to talk over. She nodded to herself in approval. He ran a good place.

Etienne lifted his head to see who'd come in, a professionally welcoming smile on his face which turned into a wider smile when he saw it was her. She felt her stomach flip. Oh, for God's sake. Just because he's handsome.

'Hi,' she said. 'Table booked for eight p.m.'

He ran his finger down the bookings and then across the line.

'Ms Tucci, I presume? How nice to see you. Table for one?'

She nodded. She had become accustomed to dining alone over the last ten months. Since Daniel left, she'd forced herself to get back into the habit of doing all manner of things on her own. From going to the cinema to watching a play; joining a new book club to booking a weekend away. She'd even gone to a comedy club, knowing she might be comedy fodder for the comedians, sitting on her own in the corner. But she'd survived and, more than that, she'd enjoyed it. With every outing or challenge, she'd grown in confidence, feeling more like her old self, the one before she'd been half of a couple. When she was just Isabella and not Mrs Simmonds. Now, a table for one didn't faze her in the slightest.

Etienne helped her slide out of her coat, his hands resting momentarily on her shoulders, and hung it for her on a hook before leading her to the corner. A round table, with a single placemat. Which was a nice touch, she thought. Often when she booked a table for one, she'd find it set for two, which made it for ever look like she must have been stood up. This looked perfectly set for someone enjoying a meal out on their own – by choice. He pulled the chair out for her, and she slid into her seat.

'Checking out the competition?' he asked with a grin as he handed her the menu.

'Got to know what I'm up against,' she responded good-naturedly, 'so that I can beat it.'

He laughed outright.

'Let me get you a drink,' he said. 'As a welcome to the neighbourhood.'

Isabella asked him to suggest a dry white wine and asked for a side glass of ice. As Etienne navigated confidently through the tables, Isabella forced herself to look away and studied the menu.

After choosing moules marinière and placing her order with an elfin waitress with a French bob, who she noticed was younger than her and rather gorgeous, Isabella sat back to take mental notes.

The staff wore a uniform of black shirts and black jeans, with black waist aprons tied at the back. The menu was not extensive, but had a fair amount of choice, with new 'dishes of the season' highlighted on a board on the wall. There were all the usual considerations, options for gluten free or vegetarian. It was all very different from how she planned to run Tutto Mio, but she would keep that to herself.

Her wine arrived, delivered by the waitress with a welcoming smile. 'Etienne said to tell you that he could recommend the pancake dessert,' she said, which made Isabella clench her thighs together under the table.

Her food arrived. The mussels were plump and soft, the sauce creamy. She mopped up the remaining broth with chunks of homemade bread and wiped her bowl clean.

'I love to see a woman with a good appetite,' Etienne said, appearing beside her. How was it that he seemed to make everything sound sexual? She leaned back in her chair and crossed her legs under the table. His eyes flicked over her body, the slightest, quickest glance.

'It was delicious. Can you tell your chef for me?' she said, and then, grinning mischievously, 'In fact, who is your chef?'

'Uh-uh, hands off,' Etienne said, catching on immediately. 'You're not having him!'

Isabella feigned disappointment and they both laughed. But to be fair, her food would have to be good to keep up with the standards here. It was by far the best food in town.

'So, how are you?' he asked. She opened her mouth to answer but was interrupted by a crash from the kitchen. Etienne excused himself and was gone. Isabella sipped her wine slowly, wanting to make it last as long as possible. A few moments later, Etienne exited the kitchen with his arm around the beautiful young waitress. A strange stab of jealousy shot through Isabella until she realised he was supporting her, not cuddling her. She leaned heavily on his other arm and was limping badly, face pale and strained with pain. He got her to the coat rack and wrapped her coat around her shoulders before helping her out the front door to a taxi parked up on the kerb. Through the window, Isabella watched how carefully he shut the door behind the young girl. He ran both hands through his hair before turning back to the restaurant. A moment later, he was back in front of Isabella.

'Sorry about that,' he said, exhaling. 'Katie's sprained her ankle and my other waitress, Annie, called in sick so I'm now without assistance for the night.'

Isabella grimaced at him in sympathy. His gaze swept across the restaurant, taking in the busy tables, the diners still only on their starters who had another two courses to come. The ones already looking about them to get another drink. It was too much for one person to handle, that much was clear.

She removed her napkin from her lap and put it on her placemat. This was a good chance for her to get a look in that kitchen. To see who the chef was and find out what she could about how he ran things. She told herself all those things, whilst also admitting it would give her the opportunity to hang around longer. Appreciate the view.

'I can help,' she said.

He swung his face towards her in surprise.

'No—' he started, but she pushed her chair back and stood up.

'Of course I can,' she said. 'I'm good.'

He hesitated for a split second.

'I don't doubt it for a second,' he said, slowly. Their eyes crashed together in flirty little fireworks that fluttered all the way to her stomach.

'Well then. Hand me an apron.' She paused for a beat before saying, 'Boss.'

A smile crept over his face.

'I like the sound of that,' he said.

The next two hours flashed by. Etienne showed her the table number plan and took her through to the kitchen, where Mile End Mickey wasted no time in ringing his bell and pointing at two plates waiting on the hotplate. Isabella tied her apron over her dress, washed her hands in the sink and then got to work.

Over the course of the evening, she served every dish on the menu. She saw the presentation of the starters, the size of the portions, the accompaniments to each meal. She watched as Mickey seasoned and accessorised each plate. His attention to detail was fabulous, even if his language was foul.

She spoke to the diners, and they all told her what they'd especially enjoyed – and she promised to pass it on to the chef, whilst simultaneously filing it for her own use. She paused to talk to customers as they paid their bills, she smiled and laughed and chatted as she printed their receipts. She paused by one old man in the restaurant, the only other lone diner, who ate so slowly that she felt like she knew his entire charming life story by the time he left. A retired French teacher at the local school, he told her he ate there every week, but the last three years alone since his wife died. How he'd recently moved into the Heart of Honeybridge home for the elderly and was happily beating everyone at dominoes. Before he left, he smiled the most wonderful toothy smile. His pale blue eyes twinkled so brightly as he thanked her for her company that she gave him a hug on impulse, and he chuckled into his white moustache.

It was all such valuable customer research, but more than that, it was fun. She was enjoying herself. She felt alive, in an environment she loved. Doing something she was good at. She felt eyes on her at one point and turned to see Etienne staring from across the room. He pulled a questioning face, as if to check if all was okay, and she smiled at him, giving the slightest nod. Then made sure to swing her hips as she walked away from him to the kitchen. Might as well give him something to look at.

Mickey eventually turned off the oven after serving the last hot dessert and put the ice cream back in the freezer after adding a scoop of vanilla to the dish. Service was finished and his kitchen porters were cleaning up for the night. Mickey saluted Etienne, thanked Isabella and was out the back door. The kitchen assistants were gone a few minutes later. It was a case now of clearing tables as the stragglers left the restaurant and closing up.

Isabella's feet were screaming by the time Etienne closed the front door and locked it. She peeled off her apron and slumped into a chair, moaning dramatically.

'Oh my God! I'd forgotten how brutal waitressing is!'

'You were right, though,' Etienne said, turning the open sign to closed. 'You *are* good.'

She laughed.

'Drink?' he asked, moving to the bar. 'By way of a thank you?'

She couldn't think of anything better.

'Surprise me,' she said and a few moments later he placed a whisky on ice in front of her, and another on his side of the table. It all felt collegiate and friendly and nice.

'Honestly, I couldn't have coped without you tonight.' He raised his glass to her in a toast. 'Thank you.'

Their glasses clinked together, and she sipped. It scorched her throat on the way down.

'It was nothing,' she said. 'But next time, remind me to change my shoes.' She unbuckled her strappy sandal and let it drop to the floor, flexing her foot backwards and forwards to relieve the strain. He watched as he sipped his drink thoughtfully.

'So, where did you get all your front-of-house experience?' he asked.

'I waitressed my way through uni,' she said. 'The grant was never enough. And I always got good tips.'

'What a surprise,' he said, dryly.

She laughed and told him about her experiences in different restaurants. Serving curries so hot they made grown men dribble. Dropping a whole goulash in someone's lap. Sharing out tips from the jar at the end of the night and going home with pockets so heavy they tore the seams of her coat.

'What about you?' She surveyed the dark restaurant. 'You said you'd been here four years. Where were you before then?'

He glanced away before saying, vaguely, 'London.'

'So, why here?' she pressed, wondering where his easy smile had gone. He shrugged and his face closed down.

'Change of scene, I guess.'

'A new start?' Isabella said, feeling the connection of something in common. Suddenly she wanted to share how excited she was for her new beginning, but also how terrified. But he simply nodded and didn't elaborate. She pursed her lips, thinking. There was something about him that she liked, and not only the fact that he was hot as hell. She couldn't think about that for the next couple of months anyway, however delicious he might be. But he was as closed as a clam before baking. How to open him up?

'So, what can you tell a newbie like me about the area?'

His eyes crinkled then.

'Not sure I should divulge any secrets. You are the competition after all.' So, the banter was back. It seemed light conversation and flirting was fine. Maybe he was just a private person.

'You're joking, right? After I gave myself blisters for you?'

She pointed her toe at him across the divide between them. He laughed and caught her foot in his hand. She flinched at the thought of it, hot and tired in his palm, and tugged it back but he held on, insistent, before resting her ankle gently on his thigh. They faced each other in their chairs, her foot in his lap, and she wondered for a split second how she'd got there. She'd only come in for dinner.

'I guess I do owe you,' he said, lightly.

'So, what should a fellow restaurateur know?'

He tilted his head, considering, his fingers burning a ring around her ankle, holding it still before speaking.

'First, get your fish from McKenzie's. You might be tempted by the lower prices at Harry's, but the quality is not as good and the deliveries are not as reliable.' His fingers started to move lightly, stroking the top of her foot as he spoke. She watched his hand move against her skin, and her breath turned shallow. Nobody had ever touched her foot so gently. In fact, she couldn't remember anyone ever touching her feet at all. Daniel had an aversion to feet generally. He always used to grimace and make noises of disgust if she put her bare toes anywhere near him on the sofa, or if she tucked them under him in bed. It had been a standing joke. But now, in this instant, she realised how sensitive her feet were to touch. How sensual it felt to have someone massage them. What she'd been missing out on all these years. Etienne's fingers traced so lightly that it should tickle, but it didn't. It seemed to burn a trail instead.

'Second, the farm shop *will* give you an account. They say they won't, but they will if you pay upfront for a month and then ask again. Helps with your cash flow.'

'I know about cash flow,' she couldn't help but say. 'I did a business degree.'

His eyebrow acknowledged this information with a tiny arch and he nodded, but he was not to be distracted from his work. His thumb found the sole of her foot and she blinked at the sensation as he pressed a line, heel to ball, following a row of tiny pressure points. The energy his thumb gave to each spot as it pushed it to its core and released. The way it started to bring her aching feet back to life. The blood being recharged. The skin tingling. Her foot moved of its own volition in his lap, flexing to his touch. Pressing back against his thumb pad. Like it craved his attention. Traitor, she thought. Traitor.

'And finally, watch out if you get a booking from the Balham family. Every time they come in they find a hair in their meal and get it for free. I swear to God they must walk round with a bundle of hair in a plastic bag in their pockets, ready to drop in a breakfast, lunch or dinner.'

She laughed but it came out slightly breathless. He glanced up from his viewpoint and found her eyes.

'I'll watch out for them,' she managed to say, wondering why she sounded so serious.

'Good,' he said, taking hold of her big toe between finger and thumb and pulling it gently away from the foot, stretching the joint then letting it go. She heard herself gasp and he smiled to himself at the response before repeating the move on all her toes. She pressed her lips together to suppress a moan.

'Better?' he asked, eyeing her from the other end of her leg. She didn't trust herself to speak, but nodded, once.

'Shall I do the other one?' he asked, holding his hand out towards her other leg, indicating she should put it on his lap. Almost in a trance, Isabella started to lift her knee, to do his bidding. It wasn't just her foot that wanted his touch. Her whole body was betraying her, moving towards him, wanting skin on skin on skin. Her nipples felt as they had that day in the square, hard and begging for his attention. Just from him rubbing her foot. The tiniest smile started at his lips. His eyes were darker than before, the green glinting in the lamps of the restaurant.

Reality hit her like a punch in the gut. What exactly was she doing here? Letting this stranger rub her feet and then progress to her legs and then what? Have wild and wonderful sex with him on his workplace floor? Because that's what she sure as hell felt like doing. But that *wasn't the plan*. She'd only come over for dinner. And then taken the opportunity in front of her, to waitress and see the kitchen, the backstage operations. It was all good market research.

God, she could see why he had the reputation he had. He was *good*. If this was a seduction routine, he was damn fine at it. No wonder half of the women in Honeybridge seemed to have had sex with him. Or fantasised about it at least. She scrambled upwards in her chair, realising she had almost slid horizontal with the attention on her soles, like some swooning Victorian damsel. Where was the strong independent woman now? She shook herself mentally and physically as she took her foot from his lap.

'No,' she said, reaching for her shoe, missing it three times before she managed to get her foot into it, fingers fumbling the buckle. 'Better go.' When she looked up, he'd repositioned himself too, shifting in his chair until his elbows were on his knees, his face close and intent on hers.

'You haven't even finished your drink.' He nodded at the whisky on the table, ice all melted.

Isabella glanced at the drink. She had to get out of there before she broke her promise to herself. NO SEX FOR A YEAR. The mantra was circling in her head, practically screaming at her. She picked up the whisky and threw the whole lot back in one. It burned its way to her gut.

'Have now,' she coughed. 'I should go. Loads to do in the morning.'

He stood and put his hand out to help her up, but she pushed herself up and headed to the door.

'It was fun, though,' she said, fighting to pull on her coat, getting her arm stuck in the inside-out sleeve.

'Thanks for being my waitress.' He leaned on the supporting beam of the restaurant, between her and the door.

'Thanks for the foot rub,' she said, adding – she couldn't resist, one last time – 'Boss.'

His hand was already on the door handle but he paused at the word.

'Sure you don't fancy another nightcap?'

She grinned, back in control, and shook her head.

'Another time then,' he said and again she knew it wasn't a question.

The cool of the night air hit her face. She knew she was flushed. Somewhere inside her the fuse of her body had been reignited. A spark that had been damped down since Daniel broke her heart. Even if Etienne was a player, she was already thinking she might play with him a bit when her ban was up. She had the feeling their game would be a good one.

She turned to say goodbye, hoping to catch sight of him again before he shut the door. He was still there, leaning in the doorway, but his attention was not on her any more. It had already moved on, in those few seconds. She saw his face searching, his fingers scrolling. All his attention on his phone. Disappointment hit her like a sledgehammer and she wrapped her arms around herself in the September night chill.

She turned back to the deserted square and her heels echoed on the paving as she clipped across to Tutto Mio. Men. What did she expect?

Girl Gang WhatsApp group

Isabella: Etienne gave me a foot rub.

Wren: What? When?

Isabella: After work last night.

Rosie: This is more like it.

Wren: Did he have good technique?

Isabella: If he can make me feel that good when we're both fully clothed,

then just think if we were naked . . .

Chapter Eighteen

Etienne

No matter how many times he checked his phone, there were no other messages from Alex.

Isabella had been a good distraction the night before, keeping him from checking his phone for hours as he watched her at work. She was a natural with people. She had this easy way of talking, smiling, making people relax. Even old Fred Barrow was swept off his feet and the look on his face when she gave him a hug was a picture. He'd probably not been hugged since Jeannie died a few years ago and he moved into Heart of Honeybridge. Etienne did what he could to put a smile on his face, but he'd not been rewarded with a toothy grin like that one ever. He'd watched the swing of Isabella's hips in her dress that swished around the knees and gave a rather tempting view of her cleavage as she bent to pick up dishes in the kitchen or placed them in front of the diner. She looked good enough to eat herself. It was a shame she was opening her own restaurant, otherwise he would have offered her a job on the spot. He had a feeling she would be good for custom.

But then again, thinking about it, that probably wouldn't be a good idea. Because he had every intention of sleeping with her at some point. Maybe not immediately. But sometime for sure. Better not to be working together. No awkwardness afterwards.

He remembered the feel of her foot in his hand. The softness of her skin. The way her foot pushed back against him, like a cat butting you with its head, nudging for more attention. One day, Isabella. One day. He checked his watch. But not today. Today he had an appointment with the bank. He locked the restaurant door and strode towards the high street.

'Ah, Mr MarTIN,' Mr Andrews, the bank manager, welcomed him, using the English pronunciation of his surname ending in Tin, rather than as his French parents had said it, ending in Tan. He shrugged it off, used to it. 'Nice to see you. Would you like a cup of tea?'

Etienne shook the hand he offered, and sat, keen to get on with business.

'I'm fine, thanks, Mr Andrews. Thanks for fitting me in at such short notice.'

Mr Andrews indicated the computer screen on his desk. 'It looks like the restaurant is making a decent return at the moment, Mr Martin, so how can I help you today?'

'I wondered how much money I'd be able to access immediately?' Etienne said.

'Well, this is unexpected.' The bank manager clasped his hands in front of him. 'Are you planning a refurbishment?'

'No,' Etienne said.

'A holiday?' the man persisted.

'No,' Etienne repeated.

'An extension?'

'No. I just want to know how much money I have managed to save since I opened The Bistro, and when I can get my hands on it.'

Mr Andrews pressed his mouth together, obviously much happier at the thought of taking money into the bank than giving it out.

'Believe me, Mr Martin, it's much safer to leave the money where it is, earning a steady rate of interest, unless you have a specific need for it?'

'I do have a specific need for it,' Etienne said and clasped his own hands in front of him. The two men stared at each other.

'Well, let's see then . . .' Mr Andrews said reluctantly and swivelled his screen again to run through columns and figures. He cleared his throat.

'Total savings of almost forty thousand pounds.'

Etienne nodded as his stomach fell. Ten thousand pounds short of what he needed.

'A very good amount,' the bank manager said, wistfully.

But not enough, Etienne thought.

'Can I access it today?' Etienne asked.

'Normally there is a ten-thousand-pound limit to how much you can transfer on any one day, Mr Martin . . .'

'So, can you authorise raising that limit so that I can transfer forty thousand on one day then, please?' Etienne leaned forward in his chair. Red tape and bank bureaucracy were not going to stop him being able to get that money out when he needed it. The two men stared at each other again. Mr Andrews blinked first.

'Of course,' the bank manager said. 'We'll just have to work through the documentation.' He took a long sip of his tea and pulled up a new form on his computer. He tapped away, humming to himself before hitting the final key with a flourish.

'Done, Mr Martin. You can now transfer the whole amount whenever you feel the need.' He sipped his tea.

Etienne nodded slowly.

'What about if I wanted it in cash? Could I get that out today?'

The bank manager snorted tea all over the desk in a fine spray as he tried unsuccessfully to swallow his mouthful.

'Today won't be possible for that amount, Mr Martin.' He dabbed his mouth with a handkerchief. 'It will take a few days for us to organise that sum of cash.'

He pursed his lips.

'How much notice would I need to give you if I wanted it in cash?'

'Two working days.'

'No wriggle room on that?' Etienne asked hopefully.

'Unfortunately not, Mr Martin.'

'But, just to be clear, if I ring you on Monday morning, I can have the cash on Wednesday?'

The bank manager nodded and Etienne exhaled. It was the best he was going to get.

'Thank you, Mr Andrews. That's good to know.'

As he stood, a thought struck him. 'What about a loan for another ten thousand pounds?' he asked, keeping his tone businesslike.

Mr Andrews straightened in his chair and widened his eyes silently, before opening a drawer and extricating a form.

'Just fill this in and pop it back to me as soon as possible and we can assess the situation.'

Etienne extended his hand across the table, shaking the bank manager firmly, and optimistically, by the hand.

The bank manager's personal assistant, whose name badge said she was called Melissa, came in to show him out. She flashed lustful eyes at Etienne from under her eyelashes and led the way, wafting Chanel No.5 perfume. But Etienne didn't even notice, he was too busy wracking his brains as to where he could find another ten thousand pounds if this loan didn't come through.

Chapter Nineteen

Isabella

The restaurant was starting to look like a restaurant. The walls were plastered, the floorboards laid. It needed decorating and styling, but it was coming along. Isabella left Tutto Mio with a smile, feeling the need to stretch her body after a morning poring over forms and paperwork. She ignored the flash of disappointment as she glanced at the empty doorway of The Bistro and headed towards The Lit Lounge.

Wren gave her a wave from behind the counter when the doorbell jangled and Rosie glanced across from her position at a bookshelf where she was talking to a family, her expression downcast as she pulled one of the children in for a hug. Some customers seemed to be happy browsing, taking their time to choose their next read. Others had already chosen and purchased their books and were now curled in the armchairs, with or without a cat on their laps. The Keyboard Corner had a smattering of people on their laptops. Barney sprawled over one whole desk space to himself.

'Espresso?' Wren asked, already reaching for a tiny cup to fill.

The coffee was hot and strong and they chatted over their drinks. Wren was excited about a play she was taking Rosie to see that evening. Isabella was equally excited about some opening publicity she was planning for Tutto Mio.

Rosie suddenly appeared with the family beside her. They shuffled anxiously and the woman wiped her red eyes, holding one of the children tight to her front, as though frightened to let her go. An older girl, about sixteen, looked at her trainers where the toe dug into the carpet.

'Isabella might be able to help!' Rosie said with forced hope in her voice.

The man was sandy blond and it was only then she noticed his firefighter uniform T-shirt. He had shoulders that looked like he could lift a car off a child if needed.

'Isabella, this is my friend Walker,' Rosie said, 'and this is the Malone family.'

Aha, Walker. Etienne's friend. Well, they say like attracts like, and they were both equally gorgeous. Isabella lifted a hand in hello but was conscious of the grave expressions on their faces.

'There was a house fire at the Malones' last night,' said Walker in a soft Scottish accent. 'Luckily, we got everyone out, including the dog.' He threw an encouraging smile at the youngest child. 'But Millie's bedroom was badly damaged, being directly next to the kitchen where the fire started.' He nodded towards the older girl, who still hung her head.

'Oh, my goodness, how awful,' Isabella said, wondering immediately how Rosie thought she could help.

'They're staying with friends for the moment, until the house is made safe and the insurers have visited,' Walker continued. 'But I'm trying to make sure they have everything they need for the immediate time ahead. We don't know how long it will be before they can move back in.' Isabella nodded respectfully, wondering if the fire service usually went this far above and beyond.

'And Millie is finding year eleven tough already with GCSEs next year,' the mum said, wringing her hands together and throwing an anguished look at her older daughter. 'That's stressful enough for her, without the house burning down on top.' Rosie passed her a tissue as fresh tears threatened to fall.

'All of Millie's revision books were in her bedroom. All her work from the last few years. She has nothing to revise from.'

'Walker has already contacted the school and they are pulling together spares for all the textbooks,' Rosie said with a sweet smile towards him, 'and we're trying to add to it from the bookshop – for free of course,' she said, patting Mrs Malone's arm, who immediately needed another tissue.

'Thank you so much. I can't afford to replace everything, I'm in debt up to my eyeballs as it is. Pay day loans aren't what they're cracked up to be. All my own fault.' She shook herself. 'Anyway, it's Millie's language we're most worried about,' Mrs Malone snuffled. 'She wants to study languages at college and then hopefully university, but her teachers have already said she needs to put in the effort to get a good grade . . .'

'So, we wondered whether you might know of any good foreign language podcasts or YouTube channels?' Rosie raised her eyebrows so high that they peeked over the top of her glasses. Mrs Malone wrung her tissue as Millie continued to stare at her feet. Isabella wondered if the girl might still be in shock.

'What language are you doing?' Isabella asked Millie quietly. When she didn't immediately answer, her mum put a soft hand on her shoulder.

'Italian,' Mrs Malone answered for her daughter.

'That's why we thought of you . . .' Rosie chipped in.

Isabella cocked her head, considering.

'*Posso aiutare*,' she said then, directly to Millie.

Nobody else spoke, not knowing what she'd said.

'Millie, *posso aiutare*,' she repeated. *I can help.*

Inch by inch, Millie lifted her head. Her face was white as paper, her eyes as wide as pools. She'd had a real scare, that was for sure. She bit her lower lip as she stared back at Isabella.

'I need to pass,' she said.

'I can help,' Isabella clarified. 'We don't need a tape, it's better to practise in person. I'm Italian. You're keen. You'll be fluent before you know it.'

'We just thought you could recommend an audio,' the mum stammered, but Millie was looking at Isabella hopefully and Isabella flapped her hands to dismiss the suggestion.

What with the imminent restaurant opening she already had her work cut out for her, but she couldn't just stand by if she could help. She thought for a moment.

'Do you do art at school as well?' she asked abruptly.

Millie looked blind-sided by the change of direction, but nodded.

'Great, then you're good with a paintbrush?'

Millie nodded again, unsure as to where this was going.

'How about an hour after school, every day, you help me with the painting at the restaurant and we'll practise Italian? Deal?'

Millie glanced at her mum, who widened her eyes and gave a quick single nod of her head.

'That would be great,' she said, adding a shy, '*Grazie.*'

Isabella smiled. '*Prego.* You're going to be best in your class.'

Back at Tutto Mio, Isabella added the name Millie to the bottom of her to-do list. She ran a finger down it, checking the items in her head as she went. There was a lot to do before opening night, but she was feeling in control. Happy, even.

Amber had come over the day before and presented her with a list of people she thought they should approach for waiting staff. Most of them were people she knew from school or the rowing club. She'd already run the numbers on how many staff hours they needed and worked out potential shift patterns. She promised to sound out the potentials and then bring the interested ones to interview with Isabella. It removed six points on Isabella's to-do list in one go. She could have kissed her, but instead they clinked their mugs of tea together and celebrated with a Hobnob.

Her phone rang. Gabriella. She lay back on the sofa, preparing for a long catch-up, but Gabi's voice had a strange tone to it, one that didn't bode well.

'What's new?' Gabi asked, but Isabella got the feeling she wasn't listening to her reply.

'Sounds like things are going well,' Gabi said and Isabella heard her sigh at the other end of the line.

'Is something wrong?' she asked. 'You don't sound too happy.'

There was a silence, and she could imagine Gabi biting her lip as she always did when trying to think of the right thing to say.

'Gabi?' She was worried now. Gabi was normally so full of energy, and fearless, that this nervous version of her was terrifying.

'I need to tell you something,' Gabi said quietly, and Isabella realised how hard she was clutching the phone. She forced herself to breathe.

'Are you okay?' she asked. Her mind immediately went to bad places.

She couldn't bear it if Gabi was ill.

'I'm fine,' Gabi reassured quickly. 'Nothing wrong with me.' Isabella shut her eyes in relief. 'But I heard something today that I have to tell you. I didn't want you to find out online.'

Isabella knew then that it would be something about Daniel. And that it would hurt. Sure enough, Gabi took a breath and continued: 'Daniel and Vicky are engaged. It's all over their socials.'

She had expected it would hurt but she wasn't expecting the gut punch pain of it. She opened her mouth but had no words.

'Apparently, he took her out to dinner last night and popped the ring in her drink. Highly original.'

Isabella could picture it. The ring glistening at the bottom of the champagne glass. The waiting staff all watching to see whether they should put another bottle on ice for celebration or quietly prepare the bill so that the couple could leave. She could picture it exactly in fact, as it was precisely the same way Daniel had proposed to her. For all the good it had done.

'I'm so sorry,' Gabi said quietly.

Isabella forced herself to respond.

'Well, I guess he has been divorced almost a whole ten and

a half months. I don't know what kept him!' She dragged out a laugh.

'It *is* pretty quick, isn't it?' Gabi agreed.

'It's fine, Gabi, honestly. We both know I'm better off out of it,' Isabella made herself say. 'But I'm glad you told me.'

Four hours later, Isabella was prowling the flat. How had her good mood and happy day changed so quickly? The news about Daniel had sparked such a jumble of emotions, she wasn't sure whether she was sad, angry, upset or jealous. But what she did know was that she didn't want to be on her own. She needed company. A drink. A chat. Someone to make her feel better. She wanted her mamma, but a quick check of the time told her it was the middle of the night in Thailand, and it wouldn't be fair to ring her now.

She texted Jesse, with a quick note. Got time to chat? And he replied immediately, as always, but with a Sorry! I'm interviewing my potential future husband over a prosecco. When a second later he followed up with Everything okay? she quickly reassured him to let him get back to his date.

Opening her phone, she was about to call Rosie when she remembered the play that Wren had tickets for.

She went to message Amber but remembered she was taking Jayden to see the new Marvel film.

She threw her phone on the sofa and stood up, then sat down, then resumed pacing the room. She felt more alone than she had done since she signed her divorce papers. Without taking a second to consider what she was doing, she picked up her phone, and went to see the only other person she knew in Honeybridge . . . Etienne.

Chapter Twenty

Etienne

Sunday nights were always quiet at The Bistro. By 9 p.m., there was only one table left and soon those customers would be asking for the bill. He'd let Katie go early, promising it wouldn't affect her wages; she'd grabbed her coat and left before he changed his mind. He was studying the staff rota for the next day and wondering how long the lingering diners could make a shared banana split last when the front door opened. He lifted his head to say that the kitchen was now closed, and there was Isabella. Her heels had been replaced by trainers; she looked Sunday evening casual. But her jumper still didn't quite meet the low waistband of her jeans, and that belly button sat perfectly symmetrical in the curve of her stomach.

She paused before shutting the door and threw him an almost apologetic smile as if she wasn't quite sure what she was doing there.

'Hi,' he said.

'Hi,' she replied.

At last, one of the diners on table ten put his hand up and did the age-old sign for the bill.

'Here,' Etienne said to Isabella, pulling out a stool at the bar. 'Have a seat. I'll be right with you.' He watched her climb up onto the stool, cross her long legs and run her hands through her wavy hair as the diners paid and packed up their things.

Closing the door behind them, he turned the sign to closed, then flicked the restaurant lights off, leaving just the cosy glow of the bar.

'Whisky?' he asked and when she nodded, he set about the drinks, adding an oversized cube of ice into each of the heavy glasses. They clinked. He leaned on the bar from the serving side, facing her.

'I hope you don't mind,' Isabella said. 'I needed some company. I was driving myself mad over there.' She sipped and sighed.

'Not at all,' he said.

'And just because I'm here doesn't mean I want a foot rub.' She spoke sternly, looking him directly in the eye.

He laughed, liking her straight talking as he remembered the way she'd put Andy in his place at The Bolthole.

'Your feet are safe with me,' he said, thinking the rest of her might not be. 'Bad day?'

'You don't want to know.'

'Try me.' He put the bottle of whisky between them on the bar and pulled up a stool. 'I'm a good listener. Comes with the territory.'

An hour later, Etienne knew the whole story. Her marriage to a man with floppy hair. His cheating. The divorce. And now the proposal. He asked questions, which she answered. But in the main, he just let her talk. It was a story he wouldn't have expected her to tell. He admired her honesty, but could feel her hurt. It was obviously a raw wound.

'I feel like such a fool. Again,' she finished. 'He's moving on – and I'm not.' She lifted her drink and threw it back. Etienne filled a glass of water and put it next to her on the bar.

'How can you say that?' he asked. 'Look at what you're doing with your restaurant. I can't believe you're doing all that on your own. That's what I call moving on. Setting up a whole new life.'

She pursed her full lips, and he felt a jolt of desire.

'That's because I promised myself I'd have my new life up and running in a year.' She hid a smile as if something was funny. 'I gave myself three hundred and sixty-five days to reinvent my life. Isabella 2.0. I want to prove that I can be single and successful.' He noticed the jut of her chin.

'Prove to yourself – or to him?' he asked. She smiled ruefully.

'Both, probably.' She shrugged. 'I just want to prove I can do it.'

Etienne poured them another measure and she added the ice from the bucket. He sipped slowly and thought about his own ambitions. To never allow a woman to come in between him and his brother. To never let his brother down again. He knew that his mistake to Alex reinforced his loyalty to his Brothers from Another Mother too. He'd do anything for them, and would always be there to help, whether it was making dinosaurs for Fox's son or propping Walker up on the anniversary of his grandmother's death. He put them above any one-night stand. They were his priority until he could prove to Alex he was trustworthy. That he had his back. Now, his chance was almost here. He would pay the money back for Alex and have his brother back in his life.

'But my year is almost up,' Isabella said, swilling the amber liquid in her glass over the ice before taking a long swallow. 'And I've still got a long way to go. So, until then, no distractions.' She leaned closer across the bar and wagged her finger at him. He caught it in his hand, holding it between them.

'Like what?' he asked, their faces mere inches apart.

'Like you,' she said breathily. Her face was flushed and her eyes held his.

Damn. At exactly that moment he'd been thinking he'd like to distract her until she couldn't think straight.

He grinned and saw her eyes spark.

'You never know, it could be good for you. Moving on. You know what they say . . . to get over someone . . .'

'You get under someone else . . .' Her lips were slightly apart and he could feel the warmth of her breath on his face.

Time stopped. He loved these moments. The anticipation. The knowledge that in a moment, he'd feel how soft those lips were. He'd wind a hand in the hair at the back of her head and expose her neck for his mouth to taste.

'Not me,' she said softly, and he wasn't sure if she was trying to clarify it for him or reaffirm it to herself. 'I *promised* myself a year of no sex.'

He growled lightly in the back of his throat. He still held her finger and he tugged it lightly until it touched his lower lip. Her eyes widened. He opened his lips and touched her fingertip with his tongue. When her breath hitched he encircled it, holding it to the first knuckle in the heat of his mouth. She gasped but her eyes didn't leave his.

'I mean it,' she said but her voice trembled. 'No sex.'

He sucked softly and saw the way her nipples hardened, saw the push of them against the cotton of her sweater. Wanted to reach for them and fill his hands with the weight of her breasts.

Smiling, she shook her head slowly at him, her eyes holding his, and he reluctantly released her finger with an almost inaudible pop.

Fuck, he was hard.

'I should definitely go,' she said, slipping off the stool.

'I think the exact opposite,' he said. 'You should definitely stay.' He rounded the bar and stood close enough to make her lift her head to look at him.

'If I have any chance of sticking to my rules, I have to leave this minute.'

'Rules are made to be broken,' he tried again, wanting to crash his mouth onto hers.

'Not this one,' she insisted and managed a smile. 'It's important to me.' She stepped back.

'Do you feel better at least?' he asked, hiding the fact he wanted to lift her back onto the stool, spread her legs with his hips, and hold her so tightly she'd feel the press of him through his jeans, right at her core.

'You've definitely changed my mood,' she said with a flash of her normal cheeky smile as she headed towards the door.

'Glad to be of service,' Etienne said, coming to escort her to the door, ignoring the pulsing in his boxer shorts. Acknowledging the strength of her resolve. Because he knew she wanted him just as much as he wanted her.

'Does your sex ban only mean you can't have sex with someone else?' he asked and saw the flicker of confusion. He clarified, 'I take it you can still satisfy yourself?'

He liked the way she lifted her chin defiantly. 'Of course. How else do you think I'm getting through the year?'

'Then stand still,' he said. 'Trust me.'

To his surprise, she didn't question him, but stopped and waited.

He took her phone from her hand and opened the camera. Leaning forward, he put one hand flat on her exposed stomach, his thumb fractionally tucked into the waistband on her jeans, his fingers spanning up towards those fucking amazing-looking breasts. He heard the intake of her breath on contact. He took a picture of his hand on her body and then handed the phone back. Thinking she wasn't the only one with good self-control. He wanted to rip her clothes off piece by piece and fuck her on the bar.

'Next time you're going to make yourself come, look at that picture,' he said. 'And think about what we could do next.'

He opened the door for her and watched her across the dark square until she closed her own front door.

Chapter Twenty-One

Isabella

Isabella closed the door for the flat behind her and leaned back on it. Her legs felt like she'd run a marathon though she'd only walked across the square. She would have put money on the fact that Etienne watched every step. She could feel his eyes burning into her as she left.

What the *hell* had just happened?

Holding the banister, she pulled herself up the stairs, conscious of the roughness of her breath. Normally she would take them two at a time. Now, her legs shook with each step as she made her way to the bathroom. She turned on the bulbs that lit the mirror.

That man.

He'd started off as exactly what she needed tonight. A pair of ears. A person to talk to. Company. That's all she'd gone over there for, wasn't it? So how had it gone from a friendly chat to a finger suck in an hour? Who was this man who thought he could lick her arm, rub her feet or suck her finger whenever he felt like it? She tore off her sweater and threw it in the wash bin with more force than necessary. She peeled off her jeans and socks and kicked them into the corner.

The *nerve* of him.

Even when she told him about her sex ban, it didn't stop him. He'd looked her straight in the eye and opened his mouth and ... oh *God*. Her stomach tumbled as she remembered the warm wet of his tongue against her finger, the pressure of his lips. And him still half smiling. Like the pleasure was all his. She gripped the enamel of the sink and held on.

He was the cockiest man she'd ever met.

But that thought made her think about his cock and roll her eyes at herself in the bathroom mirror. She had a feeling he had earned his sexual reputation by being pretty good in bed. If he could make her feel like this with all her clothes on, then what would it feel like to be naked with him? Her eyes found her own again in the mirror. They were wild-looking, dark, her cheeks pink. She threw her head back in frustration and growled low in her throat.

God, she was horny.

Opening her bathroom drawer, she selected a vibrator – a big one – with him in mind. The quiet buzz was like the hello of an old friend. She held it lightly to her chest bone and watched herself. The white lacy bra and matching knickers she wore would have offered no resistance if he'd wanted to remove them. She flicked one strap from her shoulder and revealed one of her full breasts, noticing the peak of the nipple tighten as the air in the bathroom touched it. She cupped herself, letting her fingers run trails around the areola. Her eyes were darker now and she reached round to release her bra, letting it fall to the floor. She held the vibrator between them and allowed the hum to throb through her body.

What would he think if he saw her now?

She let her gaze run up and down her body. The strong arms from physical work in the restaurant. The slim waist between heavy breasts and rounded hips. The soft curve of her belly where it disappeared into her underwear. She focused on the exact place he had put his hand earlier. Felt his gentle touch. Wished it was still there. And realised that her vibrator was not going to do the job tonight.

She wanted his hands on her.

She turned the vibrator off and tossed it back into its drawer. Opening her phone, she scrolled to photos and clicked on 'most recent'. There it was. She heard a sound escape her mouth as she looked at the image. His thumb, almost but not quite touching the top of her pants. His fingers spanning towards her breasts. Her own skin felt feverish to the touch when she replaced his hand with hers.

Excruciatingly slowly, as if it was the first time she was being touched by him, she skimmed her hand downwards. She pushed forward involuntarily, wanting more pressure, more contact. Her palm cupped her sex, allowing her fingers to reach beneath her and feel the sodden silk of her underwear.

She looked again at the photo, imagining what Etienne would do next. She could imagine the green glints of his eyes, the curl of hair at the nape of his neck. Drawing her hand back up to her stomach, she parted her legs and felt the cool of the air there. Her fingers eased under her pants, gliding over the soft skin of her until she slid her middle finger between her slick lips. The heat was intense as she pushed one finger, then two, deep inside her, feeling her eyes close at the same time. Her body set its own rhythm, moving forwards and back with each thrust. She imagined his fingers moving out and up to massage her clitoris, and jolted with the pleasure of the first circle, her mouth falling open, her knees feeling weak. She was so close.

The speed of her fingers increased, driving a moan from her mouth, and she felt the internal pressure building until she could hear her own breath, ragged and panting as she imagined his fingers on the swollen bud of her body. She pinched her clitoris once, twice, and then she was clutching the sink, holding on for dear life as she exploded inside.

She opened her eyes in the mirror and saw herself come undone.

Chapter Twenty-Two

Etienne

Etienne's bedroom faced directly across the square to Isabella's flat. He watched the lights go on upstairs and imagined her inside. Turning off his own lights, he stood in the shadows, faced the window and waited, imagining her wandering around, taking off make-up, removing clothes.

She'd surprised him tonight. Firstly, with her honesty about her story. Why she was here. And secondly, by not giving in to him.

It had been the perfect scenario. An empty restaurant, a bed upstairs, a good measure of whisky. And yet she'd still managed to say no to him.

Why she would do it was beyond him. Why deny herself the pleasure?

Her silhouette appeared in the window briefly, tugging the gap in the curtains shut. He hardened at the memory of her stomach under his hand, the way her pulse had fluttered in the skin of her belly beneath his palm.

As Isabella's flat was plunged into darkness, he wanted to plunge his hands into her pants and feel the silkiness of her.

She might have said no to him tonight, but he could see she was fighting herself on it.

He couldn't wait for her to give in.

He loosened his jeans and let his cock spring free. Taking his hot, thick shaft in his hands, he thought about how it would feel to have her hands on him. He closed his eyes and stroked the length of himself, imagining her skin on his own.

Chapter Twenty-Three

Isabella

The following weekend, half of the population of Honeybridge made the most of a sunny day in September and turned out at the fire service fundraiser. The fire station was bedecked with bunting, and the fire engines were parked on the forecourt, teeming with kids. Loudspeakers played music and heralded announcements. There was to be a static bike challenge, a cash prize hoopla, a car wash service and the secondary school jazz band were performing. All proceeds went to help those people in need after they'd been affected by fire, like the Malones that Isabella had met before. Rosie had told her the fundraiser was Walker's brainchild and had become an annual event.

Isabella turned up as the children from the primary school took their places for a street dancing competition. Amber dragged her to the side to watch, pointing out Jayden in the back row. She signed him a good luck message and Jayden signed back, hand to chin, with a thank you. He was rocking a T-shirt tied in a knot in front and had his hair in an Afro Mohican with double tramlines down each side and electric blue hearing aids. He was the coolest ten-year-old boy Isabella had ever seen.

Her impression was reinforced three minutes later, after he'd torn up the makeshift stage, breakdancing at the speed of light. The crowd roared. Amber waved her hands in applause instead of clapping and Isabella copied her, seeing several of the other mums that knew Jayden do the same. He bowed and waved and bowed again, then circled the stage with a collection bucket which was heavy by the time he handed it over to the firefighter standing nearby. He was still grinning as he ran over to his mum. Amber squeezed him tight; he allowed it for a split second before shrugging her off and dashing into the crowd to find his friends.

'God, I love him,' Amber said with a shake of her head. 'I'm grabbing every single minute with him this year because this is his last year at primary and he's going to grow up so fast.'

'He's so good at dancing!' Isabella said, amazed.

'My boy's got rhythm,' Amber said proudly. 'Even if he can't hear the music, he can feel the vibration and count the beat. He loves it.'

Rosie and Wren appeared with Riley swinging happily from their hands between them. When she saw Amber, Riley lunged towards her.

'Is Jayden here?' she cried, tugging on Amber's hand.

'Told you!' said Rosie apologetically.

'Big crush . . .' said Wren with a shrug.

'He's gone to watch the rowing race,' Amber answered and then to the women, 'Shall we all go?'

The fire station backed onto the river and was next door to the rowing club. The banks were lined with picnickers and Amber pulled a blanket from her massive shoulder bag, spreading it on the ground for the women to sit. Riley refused to sit and jigged from leg to leg as she searched the crowd for Jayden. When she spotted him a few feet away with the River Rats, she promised her mums she'd be 'right there' and darted over. Rosie opened her backpack and pulled out a bottle of wine and four plastic glasses.

'I feel somewhat unprepared,' Isabella said, taking the glass on offer with a thanks.

'Don't worry, we came with double,' said Wren, opening her rucksack to show another bottle nestled there.

A firefighter with a microphone announced the Brave Bluetits would be passing in the next few minutes and Isabella shaded her eyes to look at the skies.

'Not up there!' Rosie laughed.

'In there,' Wren said, pointing at the river as the first of the all-woman wild swimming group came into view. Wearing woolly hats and goggles, some in wetsuits, others swimsuits with gloves and booties, a steady procession of more than twenty women swam past, treading water in front of the rowing club to wave and be cheered in return.

The Bluetits adjusted their goggles and swam further upriver to climb out at the jetty. They shook their bodies like dogs drying in the weak sun and then donned dry robes to keep out the chill that would inevitably set in. The first swimmer, who must have been eighty, took the collection bucket and shook it along the bank, grinning and chatting.

'What a woman,' Rosie said.

'Respect,' said Amber.

Millie Malone appeared out of the crowd with a couple of other young girls.

'*Ciao*, Millie,' Isabella called and the girl grabbed her two friends by the elbows and steered them over.

'*Ciao*,' she replied shyly, flashing a look at the other women.

'*Come stai?*' Isabella asked, keen to see if their sessions were paying off and Millie would be more confident in her next reply. They'd been painting side by side for a week now; the main restaurant walls were finished, and they were now onto the more time-consuming woodwork, the gloss. Millie had turned up quiet and shy the first day, listening more than she spoke. But by the end of the week, when Millie was back in her own home, she turned up with brighter eyes, keen to answer any question Isabella threw her way. Always, at the end of the hour, Isabella asked whether she would like a drink of lemonade and Millie would grin and say, '*Sì, grazie.*'

'*Sto bene, grazie.*' Millie grinned now. It was a good answer. *I'm fine, thank you*, instead of just 'good' or 'fine'. Isabella grinned back.

'Next week it's getting harder,' she warned but she knew that Millie would be up for it.

'I don't know if it's okay to ask, because you're being so kind already,' Millie said, biting her lip, 'but this is Ava and Bex and they wondered if they could come along to our Italian sessions?'

'We can paint too?' said the girl on the left, twiddling her nose ring.

'Or help with something else?' the other girl added, from somewhere underneath a sweeping black fringe.

Isabella thought about it for a second.

'Sure,' she said, nodding. 'See you Monday.'

Millie replied with an immediate '*Grazie*,' and the two new recruits shyly added their thanks before heading off up the bank.

'Told you she was cool,' the women heard Millie say and Isabella felt a rush of pleasure. Amber clinked plastic glasses with her.

'As if you haven't got enough on your plate . . .' Rosie mused.

'They'll be a help,' said Isabella, thinking of the toilets that needed painting and the windowsills, and the wine cellar, and, and, and . . . The list went on. 'In fact, while we've been talking Italian, Millie's been a godsend. So with another couple of helping hands, we'll get the painting done in no time.'

The firefighter on the microphone cleared his throat.

'Next, we have the men's rowing race. They started two kilometres upriver at Kettles Bridge. They should be here within the next few minutes.'

'Walker's in this,' said Rosie, kneeling up to get a better view of the river. 'He's in a four with Fox and Etienne.'

Isabella felt her face flush at his name.

'But that's only three,' she said.

'Fourth man is Walker's watch commander, Dean Appleby.'

Isabella stretched back on the blanket, secretly pleased she'd changed out of her decorating gear beforehand. Glad that she'd washed her hair and slicked her lips with a natural-looking gloss. The thought of seeing Etienne set up an ache of excitement low in her belly. She'd avoided The Bistro at all costs this week, not trusting herself to go anywhere near him and his sexy eyes. Although the photo on her phone was practically her screensaver at this point and she thought he might have ruined vibrators for ever for her. She felt like she was getting closer and closer to breaking her rules every time she got near to him. Like a moth to a flame. But surely she was safe at a public picnic to just enjoy the view?

Shouting sounded further upriver and spectators on the bank jumped up and down. Rosie kneeled taller and Isabella sat forward, shading her eyes to look upstream where the trees along the banks were starting to turn orange and red.

Two boats appeared on the water, neck and neck. Other boats followed behind, maybe four or five, in a straggly procession.

'That's them!' Rosie shouted, pointing at the nearside boat. Isabella recognised Walker's sandy quiff and Etienne's brown waves. A third rower had strikingly silver hair and must be the well-named Fox. The watch commander was wearing his helmet. Their strokes were in perfect time, their bodies moving backwards and forwards as one. They called as they pulled, keeping their progress straight and steady; their focus was spellbinding. Isabella realised she was even finding rowing sexy and breathed out slowly. Another six weeks to go.

Their boat pulled forward an inch. The other boat pulled alongside. They edged ahead again, but this time they held the position. Everyone on the bank was standing now, the River Rats running along the front of the bank to keep up with the boats, screaming their encouragement. Jayden had Riley on his back, and she looked overjoyed. With the next stroke Walker's boat gained again, one inch became two and they crossed the finish line with a three-inch lead.

'See,' Amber said quietly to Isabella so that Riley and the

other children nearby couldn't hear, 'every inch counts.' Isabella groaned softly.

The commentator announced Walker's boat as the champions and the four men in the boat collapsed, panting against each other. Dean took his helmet off and waved it at the bank. Isabella couldn't take her eyes off Etienne. He lay back, resting against Walker's chest, eyes shut but smiling, his own chest heaving through his T-shirt.

'Winners' dip!' someone shouted from the bank and soon everyone was joining in.

'Winners' dip! Winners' dip!'

'What's going on?' Isabella asked, but Amber didn't have time to reply as Fox stood up on the boat, causing it to wobble perilously from side to side. He put his hands in the air in a sign of victory and then jumped over the side. Quickly followed by Walker, Etienne and Dean, who managed to both keep hold of the rope and his helmet above water as he jumped in.

They swam to the bank, towing the boat between them as the uniformed fire crew moved into position, collection buckets at the ready. As the four men climbed out on to the riverbank, their T-shirts and shorts clung to their bodies, highlighting the definition of every muscle, the strength of their shoulders, and the crowd erupted into whistles and cheers.

'Come on, boys,' the commentator said over the microphone, 'it *is* for charity!'

Walker went first, peeling his T-shirt over his head, river water running between his pecs. Etienne went second, taking hold of his T-shirt at the bottom hem and lifting slowly until it was all the way off. Fox and the watch commander must have gone third and fourth, but Isabella was stuck staring at Etienne's torso. His chest was smooth enough to eat her dinner from, the only hair a trail from his navel to the top of his shorts which almost had Isabella weak in her own knees. They stood in a line and took a bow. The crowd started throwing their money into the buckets. Isabella thought she might have to go home for a cold shower.

'Worth every penny, every year,' one woman said as she opened her purse and waved a note in the air. Hordes of women surrounded the men, some handing towels, others going so far as to offer to pat the men down. Isabella noticed the biggest crowd of admirers seemed to be around Etienne.

'Your mouth's open,' said Amber as Etienne wrung his T-shirt out on the bank.

'Your nipples are out,' said Wren.

Etienne scanned the crowd. When he saw her standing there on the bank, he shook his head briskly, sending droplets of water from his waves in all directions. He pushed his hand through his hair to hold it back from his face and then grinned at her. Isabella knew she was grinning back. Damn him.

Chapter Twenty-Four

Etienne

It was his kind of day. He always wanted to win and he was not averse to adoration. The rowing race had become a local tradition, and the Brothers from Another Mother had won for the past four years and he wasn't about to let that change. Although today was the closest they'd come to losing their title. They'd better step up their training before next year's race.

He'd seen Isabella on the bank with the other women and had caught the look on her face as her eyes swept up and down his body. That gut-punching look of lust, mouth slightly open, eyes dazed. He remembered the softness of her skin under his hand and wondered briefly if she'd used the photograph yet. She wanted him, he knew that. But she wasn't letting herself have him. It would happen. Soon. He knew it.

The Brothers disengaged themselves to get showered and changed into long-sleeved tops and jeans before heading to the rowing club bar to celebrate.

'Just the one,' said Fox. 'Abbie from next door has been

looking after the boys at the ball pit for an hour. I'll text her and tell her to bring them here afterwards. She'll be exhausted.'

'First one's on me,' Dean the watch commander called over, making a signal to the barman to put it on his tab.

Etienne and Fox both ordered a bottle of beer and Walker had a mineral water. He was still officially at work.

'Should earn lots today,' Etienne said as they made their way out to the patio seating area and found a picnic bench in the sun, which was bright but losing any heat now. The bank was being set up for the next event, the dog agility course.

'We need it,' Walker said. 'Only just had enough to help out the Malones after their fire the other week. And they're exactly the type of people that need the help most. They didn't have much before the fire, let alone afterwards.'

'I can't imagine it,' Fox said. 'She's got a son in Reggie's class. All the parents offered school uniform and things like that.'

'Everyone has been so good. Fiona Malone keeps saying she doesn't deserve it. But people have given all kinds of things. Homemade meals, a new set of saucepans, a new rug from the carpet shop. Even Isabella offered daily Italian revision for Millie to get her in shape for her oral exam.'

Etienne swigged his beer, thinking he'd like to give Isabella an oral exam. He could picture that mouth, that tiny beauty spot, as she wrapped her lips around his cock. He swallowed too quickly and coughed.

'That's nice of her. She must be busy with the opening,' Fox said, just as a waist-high, Reggie-shaped tornado rounded the corner and threw himself at his dad. George, a thigh-high terror, came sprinting after. Abbie staggered behind with a rusty-coloured cocker-something on a lead and sighed with relief at the sight of Fox.

'Everything okay?' he asked, taking in her grass-stained knees, flushed face, hair half escaped from her hairband.

'Fine, all fine,' she said. 'I don't know how you do it!' She laughed. 'The energy they've got.' She thrust the lead into Fox's hand, and tucked a roll of clean poo bags into his top pocket.

'Thanks so much, Abbie,' he said, but she was gone already, making her escape as quickly as she could. She waved over her shoulder and headed for the bar.

'Uncle Etienne!' George shrieked when he saw him and clambered up onto his knee. Etienne pushed him up higher until he was on his shoulders and George bounced around on his neck.

Reggie scampered to the bank and started performing forward rolls. The dog jumped on the picnic bench and scoured the table for leftovers.

Rosie appeared, sliding her arms around Walker's waist.

'Well done, Walker,' she said with a squeeze, which he reciprocated, dropping a casual kiss on her head.

'Hands off my girl,' Wren said, not in the least bit bothered. She stood on tiptoe to kiss Walker's cheek. 'Way to go, bro.'

'What about the rest of us?' Fox asked, nodding at Etienne.

'Not a bad performance, you two,' Rosie said with a shrug.

'Don't think you slowed him down too much,' Wren laughed.

Etienne's eyes found what they were looking for. Isabella, approaching with Amber, jacket tied around her waist now. Arms bare in the autumn sunshine. The two children with them, Jayden and Riley, immediately set off headfirst down the bank after Reggie.

'He looks comfy,' Amber said as they reached the table, nodding at George as he wrapped himself around Etienne's head.

'Me, not so much, though.' Etienne laughed, standing and swinging George down from his perch. He tumbled George in a surprise somersault on the way to the ground, his face lit with delight when he found himself back on two feet.

'Again!' he shouted, jumping on the spot.

'Later, George,' Fox said, trying to get the dog off the table where it was now finishing off someone's burger. 'Go and roll with your brother.'

George switched his attention to the bank and ran there making the sound of a siren.

'Sorry,' said Fox, rolling his eyes. 'His nursery has been learning about the police force. I'll be glad when they move on to something quieter.'

They watched George throwing himself onto his brother's back, squealing.

'Although it probably won't make much difference to the noise levels in our house, to tell the truth.' He smiled sheepishly at Isabella. 'I'm Fox,' he said, sticking out a hand. 'The two feral children are mine. And this is Dingbat, the dog. He's on at four p.m. in the cutest dog arena.' Dingbat looked up at exactly the right moment and cocked his head adorably.

'Isabella.' She shook firmly. 'And they are all gorgeous.'

Everyone shifted around the picnic table. Etienne found himself budged to the end as Rosie and Wren squeezed on next to Walker. Ending up opposite Isabella, he took a long appreciative look at her cleavage as she got herself settled. It was a good view.

Everyone wanted to know about the new restaurant, and he watched her face light up as she discussed the developments.

'So, when will you open?' Walker asked. 'Have you got a date?'

'Bonfire Night weekend!'

'That's quick!' Fox said.

'It's a personal deadline,' said Isabella. 'I want it open within a year of being divorced.'

Etienne again had two thoughts at once. Firstly, he admired her honesty. Secondly, he wondered if that meant Guy Fawkes' weekend was also the end of her self-imposed sex ban.

'Good on you, girl,' Amber said. 'Successful and single.'

They banged plastic glasses together across the wooden tabletop.

'And it's Italian?' Walker asked.

'Traditional, old school, communal eating – but I'm not telling you anything more, what with the competition present . . .' She glanced at Etienne from under black lashes. 'You'll just have to come along.'

Fred Barrow shuffled past on his way to the clubhouse. It was unusual for Etienne to see him anywhere apart from at the restaurant when he came for his weekly dinner. Fred seemed to be leaning heavily on his stick.

'Everything okay, Fred?' Etienne called and the old man turned, taking a moment to find who had spoken. His face creased into a smile.

'All fine, Etienne, thank you.' He edged closer. 'Off to put a bet on the horses.' He tapped the side of his nose and winked.

'Be lucky,' Etienne said.

'And it's nice to see you out with your lovely girlfriend,' Fred said next, his eyes alighting on Isabella. 'Isabella,' he said, taking her hand in his and dropping a kiss to it.

She laughed.

'No, we're not—' Etienne said hurriedly, but the old man wasn't listening.

'Thank you for the maps you delivered,' he said to Isabella. 'I have had a wonderful time retracing our routes. Truly wonderful.'

'You're welcome, Mr Barrow. Keep them, please.'

'Fred, please,' he said before planting another kiss on her hand and shuffling off.

'What's all that about?' Etienne asked her.

'When I met him at your restaurant he told me that he travelled through Italy in the sixties. It was where he proposed to his wife. I had some old maps of the area he mentioned so I dropped them in to him.' She shrugged. 'Glad he liked them.'

Etienne raised his beer bottle to her, acknowledging her effort. It was only a small thing, but it would mean a lot to Fred. She held his gaze and it immediately turned into something more fiery, before she dropped her eyes to concentrate on her drink.

'So have you come up with anything for the rocket yet, Fox?' Walker asked and Fox put his head in his hands.

'The next school project,' he clarified to the women. 'We've had mountains, castles, dinosaurs and now rockets.'

'When he says "we", he means "we",' Walker said, indicating Etienne and himself.

'True. You're lifesavers, both of you,' Fox agreed. 'Next one is on food so hopefully that will be easier – a batch of flapjacks or something, which even I can manage. Anyway, from my quick look on Google, yoghurt pots seem to be the way to go for rockets.'

Conversation turned to the advantages of plastic models over ones made from clay. Etienne stretched his legs under the table, other things on his mind. He met Isabella's feet on the floor beneath the table. She flicked a questioning glance at him. He grinned.

'Have you thought about using papier-mâché?' Wren asked up the other end of the table. Discussion followed on the messiness of the wet paper, and the fact that George would probably glue his own eyelids together.

Etienne pushed gently against Isabella's shoe, moving his own foot forwards until it nestled directly in between hers.

She glanced at him again, and this time he imagined her parted knees under the table.

Rosie flashed her phone screen across the table to Fox.

'YouTube has videos on how to make them out of toilet rolls . . .'

Etienne ran his foot alongside hers, increasing the gap between her feet. Her eyes widened and she took a long swallow of wine. A spot of colour had appeared on each of her cheeks. He'd bet she was a blusher after sex. His dick came to life in his shorts.

'Make sure you take a photo,' he said to the group, but keeping his eyes on her. 'It's always good to take a photo for reference.' He wondered if Isabella had used the one he took for her.

He moved his other foot so he now had both between hers.

He hoped she was throbbing as he was. This time when she met his eye, she held the contact. She squeezed lightly on the outside edges of his ankles and he pushed back, holding her open. Her eyes flashed wider but she didn't look away. He could imagine her looking at him like that when he drove inside her.

Suddenly, a joyful screech ripped through the air and everyone jumped.

'Found you!' shouted a petite woman with a black pixie cut. 'At last, Isabella!'

Isabella took a second to react, eyes locked in lust as they were with Etienne's, but when she turned and recognised the woman, her jaw dropped in delight and she scrambled up, all thoughts of foot sex with him obviously forgotten.

'Surprise!' The woman launched herself at Isabella, and the two women collided in arms and kisses.

'What are you doing here?' Isabella choked.

'I've got a day off so here I am.' They hugged again. 'Wanted to make sure you were okay,' the newcomer said, more seriously.

'Everyone,' said Isabella, turning to the table, 'this is my cousin, Gabriella. Gabi for short.'

Standing next to Isabella, Gabi was almost a head smaller, but equally beautiful in a pixie like way.

'And that's one thing I am,' she said to a collective laugh.

Etienne closed the empty space between his two feet, swigged his beer and swallowed disappointment along with it. He'd just been starting to enjoy that. Never mind. Next time.

Chapter Twenty-Five

Isabella

Back at the flat, the two women sat at either end of the sofa, their toes touching in the middle, cupping a large coffee each and both wearing huge grins at being reunited.

There had been periods in their lives when they'd seen each other every day, when they were young and Gabi moved in to live with Isabella's parents for a while when her own parents divorced, and most recently when she moved in to get Isabella through the tsunami of her breakup. But there'd also been times when they didn't see each other for months on end. Gabi's job took her to far-off places and film sets all around the world. One of the best stuntwomen in the business, she had appeared in a dozen box office hits, not that you'd recognise her. Standing in for the leading ladies, the stunts Gabi performed were normally at such high speed that you'd miss her on screen if you blinked. She earned mega money and had to go where the work was. But it didn't matter how long they were apart, they were connected. They were family.

'So, tell me what you think of everyone . . .' Isabella was keen to know if Gabi liked the new crowd as much as she did.

'Rosie and Wren are the cutest. Real-life couple goals right there,' Gabi started first.

'And Amber seems so determined to do things on her own and be a good role model for Jayden. She's a lot like you in that way.' Gabi inclined her head at her cousin. 'She'll be great to have at the restaurant.' She paused, considering.

'I didn't get to talk to Walker. But he *looked* good!' She grinned. Walker had been called back to work almost as soon as Gabi arrived, so she'd only had a hello and a goodbye.

'Oh, Walker's great. He was the one who introduced me to Millie, the girl needing help with Italian?' Isabella clarified and Gabi nodded, piecing the puzzle together.

'And the silver Fox is the hot daddy,' Gabi said. 'Shame I'm not the mummy type.'

'Still not feeling the maternal urge?' Isabella asked. It had been a topic of conversation for years between the two cousins. Isabella had always known that she would want to try to have a family one day, although that seemed further away than ever. Whereas Gabriella had always said she thought she might not have a maternal streak.

'Nope,' said Gabi, scrunching up her nose. 'Plus, I don't think I could throw myself off a burning building if I were six months pregnant.'

'There is that,' Isabella agreed. And then, as casually as she could, 'What did you think of Etienne?' She shut her mouth firmly after the question, conscious even to say his name, knowing she'd called it out loud several times in the last week in her bathroom, her bedroom and even on the sofa where they now sat. Damn that photo.

'The guy opposite you?' Gabi asked.

'Hmmm,' Isabella said, playing for time.

'Looks dangerous to me,' Gabi said. 'Too gorgeous for his own good.' Isabella slumped, not sure what to say, but then decided on the truth.

'It was a good job you turned up when you did, otherwise I might have started humping his leg under the table.'

In the space of a minute, Gabi had swapped their coffees for glasses of wine and sat herself back down.

'Right, tell me everything.'

Half an hour later, it was all out.

'What do the girls say?' Gabi asked. 'They obviously know him.'

'That's just it,' said Isabella, 'everyone knows him. You could say he has a bit of a reputation.'

'A player?'

'Sounds like it. A series of one-nighters. No relationships. There's even a local phrase – *have you been Etienne'd?*'

Gabi eyed her sternly. 'Do you like him?'

'No, it's not even that.' Isabella rolled her eyes. 'It's that my body goes into some kind of sexual frenzy whenever he's around. I can't think straight.'

'So have a fantastic one-night stand and get it out of your system!' Gabi said, as if it was the simplest thing in the world. Isabella felt a stomach tug of lust in response, but something still held her back.

Gabi had never been left so publicly that she couldn't show her face in the local shops. Gabi had never had to build herself up again from not wanting to get out of bed in the morning. And Gabi had never felt the need to prove herself successfully single. She'd worked her way up the stuntwoman ladder since she left college – all on her own, without any help from anyone.

'But what about my promise to myself?' she said.

'Break it.'

Isabella couldn't believe it could be that easy. She could go across the road and ride Etienne round every room of his restaurant. And that would be the end of it.

But she knew it didn't work like that. If she had sex, that was breaking half of the promise. What if it jinxed the other half? What if she couldn't make the restaurant a success?

No. She'd made herself a promise. Given herself the luxury of time to be single, with no sex, and make a success of things. That was what she'd been telling herself for months.

'No. I think I should stay away. Stick my year out,' she said grimly. 'It's only a few more weeks . . . and it wouldn't be worth breaking my promise on something that's just a bit of fun.'

'Probably a good plan,' Gabi said. 'Especially because you've just heard the news about Daniel's engagement. You don't want it to be a knee-jerk reaction.'

'I think it would make my knees weak, not jerk,' Isabella said. Gabi snorted and topped up their glasses.

Isabella wondered briefly if she should delete the photo on her phone. But then decided sometimes life was all about small pleasures and she saved it to her favourites instead.

Mia Famiglia WhatsApp group

Isabella: Look who came to surprise me! (uploads picture of Gabi raising a glass in cheers)

Mamma: Gabi! Looking beautiful!

Papà: My favourite niece.

Mamma: You're not supposed to say that!

Papà: Don't worry, I say it to all my nieces.

Isabella: I love you, Papà. You're adorable.

Girl Gang WhatsApp group

Amber: Gabi's so cool!

Wren: Rosie and I were just saying the same!

Isabella: She loved you guys too!

Rosie: Do you think she'd like to Bolthole next time we go?

Isabella: Definitely!

Chapter Twenty-Six

Etienne

Brothers from Another Mother WhatsApp group

Fox: The good news – the investors fucking love the game!

Walker: Well done, bud.

Etienne: You going to be rich now then?

Fox: The bad news – they want a couple of extensions designed over the coming months before they buy.

Etienne: So, I guess Walker and I are making rockets this weekend?

Fox: Lifesavers.

Fox: Talking about projects, Etienne – they're planning a project on cooking at school. I gave your name to the class teacher . . . She wants you to go in and cook something French.

Etienne: You owe me, mate.

Fox: I know.

Etienne felt a rush of love for Fox. He worked bloody hard, putting in long hours after his boys were in bed. He deserved success. Maybe his game would take off and be a worldwide phenomenon, the next *Fortnite* or *Roblox*, and Fox would never have to work again. You never knew what was around the corner. He touched a wooden windowsill nearby, an old superstition since losing his parents, trying to hold luck close to him.

Things were going well on two fronts, and he wanted to keep it that way. Firstly, bookings for the restaurant were full for weeks and he could add to the £40,000 for Alex with every good day's work. And secondly, the hot Italian Isabella was caving in. He just knew it.

He threw a look out the window, as he often did, to see if he could catch a glimpse of her painting the frontage or planting window boxes, hair in a messy bun or tucked under a baseball cap. She was hot even when she was decorating. But not today. In fact, he hadn't seen her for a few days, maybe close to a week. Hmmm.

The phone rang in his hand and he half expected it to be Fox again, laughingly apologising for volunteering him to go into a class of children and teach them how to cook. Him, the most child-free man in town. What was he going to do with a bunch of six-year-olds? When he glanced at the screen and saw Alex's name, he sank down on the nearest seat to answer.

'Hello?' he said hesitantly.

'Et?' Alex said, sounding equally anxious, but Etienne held the phone tighter at the sound of his brother's voice. It had been so long.

'Al,' he said back and his face broke into a grin. 'How are you doing?'

'I'm okay,' he answered and Etienne could hear the smile in his voice too.

'Where are you?' Etienne could hear other sounds down the phone, people talking, something clanking in the distance.

'The train station.'

Etienne's stomach dropped. Was he leaving again? Before he even came home? What was going on?

'Where? Where are you going?'

'Don't worry, I'm moving around until I get this sorted. Now that I've made contact with the Dougalls, I don't feel safe staying in one place.'

'But you've told them you want to clear your debt?' Etienne said. 'How did you do it?'

'Contacted the pub landlord where they run the poker games from. Told him to pass on my message. He said they'd be in touch.' They both considered that in silence for a moment. It sounded ominous.

'How long ago was that?'

'A few days. But nothing yet.'

'You worried?' Etienne asked quietly.

'Been worried for years, Et. But now it feels worse. Like I'm so close to getting out of it, you know?' Alex's voice shook. Although they were twins, Etienne suddenly felt older than him. Responsible for making everything better. Alex paused while a train announcement sounded far away, mentioning Newcastle and other places.

'I want to come home. To start a real life. I've made a lot of wrong decisions over the past few years, all because I couldn't trust myself.'

Etienne watched out of the restaurant window as he tried to imagine where his brother was. Somewhere in the north

by the sound of it. Faraway cities flashed through his mind –
Middlesbrough, Leeds . . . He could be anywhere.

'What's the plan then, with the Dougalls?' he asked.

When Alex replied, it was in a whisper. As though he didn't
want people to hear.

'When they contact me, I won't give them any clues as to
where I am. I need to do this on my terms. It's safer. That's why
I want to stay on the move until it's done.'

Etienne imagined his brother existing in cheap bed and
breakfasts and living out of a suitcase. He closed his eyes.

'Hopefully I can just transfer the funds, or arrange a drop-off
point for the money and hand it over. And that will be it. A
clean slate.'

It sounded a bit too easy to Etienne. Were they being terribly
naive?

'Why don't you come here now? And wait for them to contact
you? I've got a spare room. You can hide out upstairs.'

'Etienne . . .'

'You wouldn't even have to come downstairs if you don't want
to. Just think, you could place your order and it would be like
having a fantastic French bistro delivery service, three times a day.'

'No.'

'But I could look after you here, Al,' Etienne said, realising
how urgent he sounded. How much he wanted to do the right
thing this time.

'I don't want to put you in danger.'

They listened to each other breathing down the phone. As
they had done in their cots, and in their twin beds in their
shared room before they fell asleep. It was oddly comforting.

'Are the Dougalls that bad?' Etienne asked.

'You don't want to know,' Alex said.

'Like what?' Etienne said, unable to leave it alone, morbidly curious.

'Like people getting branded for cheating in a game. On the face. With a hot screwdriver. Which they make the cheat heat up themselves on the fire. They carve the letter D on their cheek.'

Etienne flinched. Images of cattle branding flooding his mind. The branding iron, the red glow of the hot iron, the sizzle as it touched flesh. The smell, he could imagine the smell.

'And someone didn't pay their debt quickly enough, so they got their thugs to pay his wife a visit and beat her until he got home with the money.'

Etienne exhaled slowly. He hadn't realised that all those terrible stories he'd heard were actually true.

'So, now you see why I'm staying on the move. And why I don't want anyone linking us together.'

'I get it.'

'It would be safer all round to keep it between us until it's over.'

'It's okay, Al. I understand.'

They were silent again, as if taking in the severity of the situation.

'It would be good to think I might be home in time for Mum and Dad's anniversary.'

Etienne took a deep breath. He was aware of the turn of the calendar as it got closer to October. He felt the date looming over him. The day his parents died in a car crash five years ago. It had been a day like any other for him, for them. A bright and breezy autumn day which blew leaves from the trees. He'd been working as assistant manager in a hotel in Ealing. He'd been on the late shift and started at midday, by chance calling his parents as he hurried along a side street in West London to work. His mum had been happy to hear from him, but then she always was. She put him on speaker to tell him about a character in the new book she was writing, an old lady who owned a fish and chip shop who had never been to the sea. 'So, guess where we're going now?' his dad called in the background and his mum laughed. 'The seaside!' she said. 'For ice cream and paddling. Research purposes of course!' And that was last time he spoke to them. A lorry travelling at seventy miles per hour on the M27 burst its tyre, lost control and smashed their blue Volkswagen Golf into the central reservation of the motorway. Emergency services said that his parents would have died instantly. The one happy thought, that Etienne clung to, was that they were on their way home from the coast. They had eaten their ice creams and done their paddling.

'That would be good,' he answered Alex softly, thinking of how he normally marked the anniversary. A closed restaurant. A good bottle of French wine. Alone.

'So, I'll let you know when they make contact. And then I can arrange next steps. I'll have to get the money from you . . .'

'I'm almost there with it.' Etienne felt his jaw pop as he clenched his teeth together.

'And I'll pay you back, Et. Every penny.'

'I know,' Etienne agreed with him, not intending to take a penny. Because as Alex paid off his debts, so Etienne would have a clean slate too.

Chapter Twenty-Seven

Isabella

Girl Gang WhatsApp group

Rosie: Late-night opening at ours tonight if you want to come and listen to Story Stars?

Isabella: What's Story Stars?

Wren: We eat snacks while the kids listen to someone read them a bedtime story.

Rosie: FYI. Grapes count as snacks too.

Isabella: You mean, you drink wine while someone reads a book out loud?

Wren: Yup. It's a winner with all the parents.

Rosie: Come over. Unless you've got something else to do.

Wren: Or someone else to do.

Isabella: I'll be there. But after 6 p.m. I'm meeting the team Amber has put together.

Wren: Is Gabi still here? Bring her along.

Isabella: No, she got called back to work at the weekend. Throwing herself off a tall building or something similar.

Wren: And how are your nipples?

Isabella: In solitary confinement.

Rosie: 🌀

The waiting staff filed into the restaurant, taking in the new floorboards laid from reclaimed wood, the whitewashed walls, the stripped-back wooden windowsills. Amber led the way. Isabella overheard snatches of whispers, how different it looked, how much nicer, and glanced round at her handiwork as if seeing it for the first time. The main dining area was almost complete. It was the kitchen, bathrooms and backstage areas that were still majorly under construction. Plus, there was still the damp problem in the wine cellar.

The group collected in the middle of the room and Isabella hung back in the doorway of the kitchen, watching them. They all looked to Amber for directions already, which would be helpful when she was organising their rotas and training. It was a mixed bunch. Men and women, ages ranging from what looked like eighteen to retirement. Amber spotted her and beckoned her over.

'Everyone, this is Isabella.'

Everyone turned to look at her.

'Hi,' she said, before opening her arms wide. 'Welcome to Tutto Mio.'

Amber stepped out of the huddle to stand beside her.

'Isabella, before I introduce you to your team, can you tell them a bit about what you want Tutto Mio to be?' Isabella felt a surge of excitement at the words 'your team'. It was a real 'pinch me' moment. A team of people to help bring her dream to life. They were looking at her expectantly, and she clasped her hands together under her chin.

'I want Tutto Mio to feel like being at home with your family,' she began and saw the raise of an eyebrow from one woman. She smiled and carried on, sure of the image she had in her head.

'I don't want tables pushed through in an hour and a half if they're not finished. Your mother wouldn't shoo you away from the dinner table, would she? She'd want you to linger, to talk. To have another glass of wine, or a coffee, or the dessert you didn't think you wanted earlier. That's what I want for our diners. I want them to have time to be together.

'We're going to have the best homecooked Italian family food there is. You can be sure of that. And I want everyone who comes in here to leave with a full tummy, a happy heart and a smile on their face.'

Nobody cringed at the sentiment of it. There were in fact nods and smiles in response. There was an energy in the air; she could feel the buzz already.

'So, let me introduce you to everyone,' Amber said. 'It might seem like we have a large team, but you'll understand why in a while. I'll be managing the daytime shift, and Sinead will manage the evening shift.' Sinead, a woman who looked to be in her fifties, waved cheerfully at Isabella.

'Hello, so,' she said in a lilting Irish accent. 'Pleased to meet you, Isabella. This is an opportunity, to be sure.'

'Nice to meet you too,' smiled Isabella. 'Tell me about yourself?'

Sinead smoothed her dress over her thighs.

'Well, I've five boys.' She glanced at the woman next to her, bringing her into the conversation. 'Great hulking lads they are now. And the last one, Aaron, recently moved out – he's gone to London to join his brother Tony. The others are in Dublin, Dubai and Derry can you believe?' The woman next to her smiled sympathetically. 'And Barry, that's my husband,' she clarified to the man in a suit on the other side of her, 'well, he works evening shifts so I'm on my own.' She turned back to Isabella as if that answered everything.

'And where have you worked before?' Isabella asked, wondering if she'd not been clear with her question.

'I worked in the school kitchen for a while.' Sinead nodded, as if that clinched the deal. Her smile was so wide, you couldn't help but like her. But was she waiting staff material?

Isabella flicked a look at Amber, who nodded encouragingly and said, 'The other staff will have regular shifts, a mixture of daytimes and evenings working with either myself or Sinead. We'll sort the rotas out around their needs.'

Did Amber mean she'd sort the rota out around the restaurant's needs? That would surely make more sense.

'So, let me introduce the rest of the team. Paul, would you like to start?'

Next to Sinead, Paul lifted his hand. Wiry, white-haired and impeccably dressed in a suit, he must have been early sixties. His moustache was finely tuned into a curl on either side of his mouth. He tugged his waistcoat straight and cleared his throat.

'I'm Paul Metcalfe, and I've lived in Honeybridge my whole life,' he said in a rich tone, deeper than you'd expect from his slight frame. 'I've got a deep love of wine, Italian wine being the finest in the world.'

'I agree!' Isabella said, adding it to her mental to-do list. Sort the wines. Maybe he could help with that.

'And where have you worked before?' Isabella asked.

'I've not worked since my wife was wheelchair-bound with multiple sclerosis twenty-five years ago,' he said, shaking his head. 'But the house is too quiet now that's she's passed away and I'm a fast learner.' Sinead leaned over and clutched his arm, making a clucking sound, while someone else put a hand on his shoulder.

Isabella nodded, taken aback by this but unsure of the direction this was going. Amber just nodded again, as if she knew something that Isabella didn't. Isabella held her tongue and waited for the next person to introduce themselves.

The youngest girl stepped forward. Probably eighteen.

'I'm Harry, short for Harriet,' she said, daring a peep from under her fringe. 'I'm in my second year at college. I've done my Duke of Edinburgh award. You have to do volunteering, physical challenge and learn a skill.' She glanced more confidently at Amber and Isabella caught the encouraging nod from her friend. Harry took a deep breath and continued: 'For my volunteering, I helped at the Heart of Honeybridge nursing home. I went in at mealtimes.'

'Ah, great,' Isabella said, smiling in relief. Someone with waiting experience. 'Were you serving the meals?'

Harry bit her lip. 'No, I wasn't allowed in the kitchen to collect the trays, some kind of training rules. But I sat with the older people while they ate and talked to them. They were lovely.' Isabella started to wonder what on earth was going on.

Next it was Meryl, a single woman in her twenties. She

stepped forward confidently and shook hands. Please, Isabella silently prayed, please have some kind of serving experience.

'I was abandoned as a baby,' she said. She said it matter-of-factly, but Sinead's eyes filled up immediately. 'I was in the care system until I was adopted at the age of five.'

Isabella's eyes widened.

'My adopted mum and dad already had six children. Three older, three younger, and I slotted right in the middle.'

Isabella was starting to think she was in some kind of alternate universe.

Meryl carried on, chin up, eyes bright. 'I've never waitressed but I know I'll be good at it.'

The three remaining members of 'the team' looked at each other, waiting to see who'd go next. Isabella wondered what sort of 'team' this was going to be. She glanced at Amber again. Had she made a big mistake?

Next Naomi, who had set up a community network to check on your neighbours as a school project and it was still going five years later.

After her, Denzil, with a highly autistic son who had started at the local residential college and left him and his wife with an empty nest.

Lastly, a woman with sun-streaked hair and a smattering of freckles.

'I'm Angie from Australia,' she said with a broad grin. 'I miss the sun!' Everyone laughed. Isabella winced.

Not a single day of serving work between them. Nobody had ever taken an order or placed it with a kitchen. Nobody knew how to carry plates balanced up their arms or clear a table in one go. It was clear nobody knew how to tot up a bill, suggest a wine, or use a payment card machine.

Eight faces beamed at her. Amber nodded expectantly. Isabella blew out slowly.

'Can I see you for a moment?' she said, indicating the door with a nod of her head.

'Be right back,' Amber said happily to the team.

Isabella pulled the door shut behind them and they both stood in the empty shell of her kitchen.

'What do you think?' Amber asked, looking pleased with herself.

Isabella considered her words. She didn't want to lose a friend.

'They all seem like lovely people,' she started.

'Right.' Amber nodded.

'All with interesting backgrounds.'

'I know,' Amber agreed.

'And you've obviously gone to great lengths to find them,' Isabella said at the same time as wondering where on earth Amber had found such a random group of people.

'They're the best.'

'But they're not waiting staff.' Isabella exhaled.

Amber's wide eyes got wider. She blinked, once, twice. The silence grew between them, and Isabella imagined she could also hear the group in the restaurant holding its collective breath.

Amber laughed. In fact, she put her head back and roared. Then, clapping a hand to her mouth to hold it in, she reached her other hand out to Isabella, waving it up and down.

'You're right,' she said. 'You're right.' She let her own laughter die down and then wiped her eye. 'They are not waiting staff.'

Isabella was now confused, conscious of the people in the next room that she was going to have to disappoint.

'Not yet,' Amber said. 'They are not waiting staff – *yet*.'

'I don't understand,' Isabella confessed. Amber took Isabella by the shoulder.

'You hired me to run the waiting staff, right?' She only paused long enough to see Isabella nod. 'Well, we have four weeks until opening and I am the best waitress I know and I promise you I will make the greatest waiting team you have ever seen from this group of people.'

Amber's sea blue eyes held Isabella's.

'I promise you,' she repeated.

Isabella pressed her mouth together, unsure of what to say. She so wanted to believe Amber.

'Because these people bring more than waiting experience with them,' Amber said. 'These are the people that will bring your dream to life. This is *your* team.'

Isabella rolled her eyes without meaning to.

'I mean it,' Amber said. 'I chose every single person for a reason.'

'I think we need professional staff . . .' Isabella said, as quietly as she could, not wanting the team next door to hear. It was Amber's turn to roll her eyes, but she was smiling.

'Come with me,' she said, opening the door and pulling Isabella back into the restaurant. The 'team' braced themselves, looking hopeful but hesitant.

'Next question for you all,' Amber said and all eyes turned to her. 'I'd like you to tell Isabella your best memory, or feeling, or experience.'

Isabella stopped herself from groaning out loud. This was a restaurant, or would be, not a therapy group. Sinead stepped forward.

'All my family around the table. On the odd occasion we all get together now. And it's a bit of a squeeze what with the size of them!' She put her arms around herself. 'Feeding them food they like. Making sure they've all got what they want. Seeing them all happy.' Several people made a noise of approval; Angie nodded.

Paul twiddled his moustache. 'Looking after Jane. Trying to think ahead for all the things she might need and making sure they were nearby. The smile on her face when she realised I'd thought about her.' He flushed and Sinead clucked, patting his arm.

'Ah, bless you,' she whispered.

Harry flicked her fringe out of her face to answer this time. She had the darkest brown eyes. 'Sitting with the clients at Heart of Honeybridge and spending time with them. They loved to tell me stories, and I liked to listen.'

Meryl stepped forward before Harry even stepped back. 'For me, it was those family meals around the table when I was first adopted. Coming from care, it was my first experience of family. It was amazing.'

Angie from Australia put her arm around her. 'Me too, babes. That's my favourite memory and I miss my crazy old Australian family now. Barbies and bevvies. I feel on my ownsome some-times over here and I don't want anyone else to be lonely.'

Denzil cleared his throat. 'I don't have a large family, just the one son. But I miss looking after him. I've always been a carer, I guess.'

'It takes a special kind of person,' Meryl said.

Naomi was last, the girl who'd set up the neighbourhood check-in system. 'I like being part of a community,' she said with a shrug. 'It makes me happy to be part of something.'

'Hear, hear,' said Paul suddenly and everyone laughed. When it subsided, their words echoed around Isabella's head, creating a fuzzy feeling of love and family and food. Kindness and caring.

Amber nudged her.

'You want people to linger and talk,' she said and then nodded towards the team who shuffled closer together, a united front.

'You want people to feel looked after as if they were at home,' she continued, as the team threw arms around each other's shoulders or linked arms in solidarity.

'You want our diners to feel as if they were part of a family, a community,' she added, and the team stood taller, chests out, chins up.

Isabella looked at their faces, one by one. She felt the prick of tears behind her eyes and saw it reciprocated in Amber's. She wondered if she was hormonal or mad. She cleared her throat.

'I want everyone who comes in here to leave with a full tummy, a happy heart and a smile on their face,' she said, repeating her earlier speech. The team waited in pin-drop silence.

'You're all perfect,' she said with a nod and a squeeze of Amber's hand. 'I can't wait to see you bring this dream to life.'

As they all hugged each other and slapped each other on the back, she felt one step closer to being successful and single.

Mia Famiglia WhatsApp group

Isabella: I have a fully recruited restaurant team!

Mamma: My baby's a boss!

Papà: Follow that dream!

Isabella: Where has your dream taken you two today?

Mamma: We swam in a waterfall!

Isabella: How cool.

Papà: Not cool actually. Cold. In fact, freezing!

Chapter Twenty-Eight

Etienne

Brothers from Another Mother WhatsApp group

Fox: 2 p.m. at our house. George's birthday party. Don't be late.

Walker: I'll be there.

Etienne: Me too.

Fox: Bring ear protectors. It's going to be a noisy day.

Walker: Oops. Not just a noisy day, I'm afraid. Noisy year ahead . . .

Fox: Eh?

Walker: Are you going to tell him, Etienne, or shall I?

Fox: Tell me what?

Etienne: We bought him a drum kit. 😊

Fox: 😣

Etienne: Just kidding. 😊

Fox: 👍

Fox was not wrong about the noise. Ten three- and four-year-olds and their parents, plus some brothers and sisters and *their* friends, packed into Fox's four-bedroomed family home almost had Etienne's ears bleeding within ten minutes. The fact that the children were existing on sugar and adrenaline also raised the decibel levels.

He made his way through the house to the kitchen diner which opened onto the back garden. On his way, he passed Fox's study where the door had been taped closed with police incident tape and a notice had been stuck firmly in place: *STAY OUT OR DIE*. Obviously, the game design was at a crucial stage then and couldn't be put at risk by cake-high partygoers.

As he picked up a beer from the table marked *Adults only*, the birthday boy barrelled into his thighs and hugged him tight. Etienne scooped him up to shoulder height so that he could see him properly.

'Happy birthday, George,' he said to the freckled face, who grinned widely before wiggling like a bag of cats to be returned to the floor, where he took off through the sea of legs towards the garden.

Etienne followed, saying hello to those he knew, and nodding to those he didn't. A couple of the mums watched him with heavy eyes as he walked past; smiling politely, he moved on.

Fox's kitchen was the most family place he knew. It reminded him of his own home growing up: pictures on the fridge, birthday cards on the windowsill, photographs on a corkboard on the wall. A shelf full of cookery books – which Fox used daily to make sure he was getting nutrition into the boys – a calendar full of play dates in red, work deadlines in black. A wooden table with spaghetti Bolognese stains deeply ingrained. All that was missing was their mum. Many a night he and Walker had sat with Fox around that table in the early days, offering beer and friendship while Fox kept one ear on the baby monitor and one eye on the clock for the next feed. Today a *Happy 4th Birthday!* banner hung across the ceiling, while red and blue balloons were tied in bunches in the corners of the room. It was amazing how much things had changed. Etienne was here to celebrate that today, just as much as he was here to chuck his godson around.

That had been a surprise too. When Fox finally came out of his shock at having two children and no wife, George had been almost six months old: a chubby baby who always wore more of his food than he swallowed. Fox asked if Etienne would be his godfather, saying with a smile, 'Walker got Reggie, it's only fair.' But then, in all seriousness, 'Honestly, mate, you've been a lifesaver. I'd love it if you said yes.' He'd been choked up, tears filling his eyes.

Etienne glanced at the corkboard as he went past. Fox had a passion for photo booths. Earlier photos had Fox holding fat-cheeked George wearing bibs and rompers, with Reggie hanging on the side. The boys changed across the corkboard, George growing teeth, Reggie losing teeth, both getting curly hair. Fox looked exactly the same in every picture – same smile, same silver hair, just a different checked shirt. Right at the bottom of the corkboard there was one of Fox and Meg. In that one, his hair was darker with a silver fleck at the temples. He smiled widely at the camera, as Meg pressed a kiss to his cheek.

'You're late!' Fox shouted from the garden. 'But I see you found the beer.' He beckoned Etienne over to the circle he was in where everyone still wore coats and rosy cheeks.

'And I've already seen the birthday boy,' Etienne said, lifting his bottle to cheers with Walker as he joined the group, grinning at Rosie and Wren who had brought Riley, who was in the same nursery as George.

The garden had been set up with a bouncy castle, and children were flying in all directions. Etienne spotted Reggie as he ricocheted from one side to the other.

'Here you go, Wren, Rosie.' He knew, by the husky tone, that it was Isabella. She squeezed in alongside him, handing over glasses of lemonade to her friends while juggling a wine herself.

'Not drinking?' Fox asked. 'Is there something we should know?'

'Only that we are responsible parents at a birthday party for a four-year-old,' Rosie said haughtily, sipping her lemonade.

'And we do have a nice bottle chilling in the fridge at home for after we leave Riley here for her sleepover. So don't worry about us.'

'That's a relief,' Etienne said and then turned to Isabella. 'How are you?' he asked.

She paused momentarily before dropping her eyes and asking, 'Fox, where's your bathroom?' And when he told her, she gave her glass to Walker, muttered an 'excuse me' and disappeared off into the house. Had she blanked him?

His suspicions were aroused again when, a few minutes later, she rejoined the group and slotted in on the other side of the circle, next to Rosie and Wren. He watched her, but she seemed to always be deep in conversation, never once looking his way. Although this didn't give him the chance to catch her eye, it did give him the opportunity to admire her. Wavy hair hanging loose. Bright red trainers and ankle-length jeans. Her coat open to reveal her shirt tied at the front, offering a glimpse of her midriff. He thrust his free hand into his pocket, thinking about the way her skin had felt under his fingers. Still, she didn't look at him.

'Time for pass the parcel,' Fox announced loudly, and a dozen children appeared from nowhere, assembling to sit cross-legged in a circle. They knew the rules. The music started, but it wasn't a tinny nursery rhyme. Thanks to Fox, who always played music as he worked, Reggie and George knew their stuff. This game of pass the parcel was soundtracked by Usher. Fox handed a wrapped-up parcel to George, and he sniffed it and shook it and squeezed it before passing it on. Wren and Rosie edged nearer to help Riley if she needed it and Etienne saw his moment.

'Hi,' he said, closing the gap to Isabella. She looked even better up close. Her blue eyes flicked to look at him, then away, and her mouth parted slightly as if to speak before closing again.

'How's everything going?' he asked. Suddenly, she pulled her phone from her pocket and, glancing at the screen, said hurriedly, 'Sorry, I've got to get this,' before turning away and rushing inside. What the hell?

The birthday cake came out and Fox lit the candles, and a million children leaned in to breathe their germs over the icing. Fox was in his element.

'Blow out every candle and then make a wish,' he said to George, who blew the longest exhale possible then screwed his eyes tight shut. Etienne smiled at his godson's faith in wishes coming true.

'Always make sure the candle is properly blown out, though,

kids.' Walker's fire safety advice went unobserved by the crowd as they all surged forward for a slice of heaven.

Etienne saw Isabella out the corner of his eye, and she seemed to spot him at the same time and moved away to talk to some of the parents. She kept her eyes downcast, studiously *not* looking in his direction.

Once was nothing. Twice was a coincidence. Three times was obvious. She was avoiding him. Interesting. He sauntered over to join her. She was talking to a couple, the woman holding a sticky toddler on her hip.

'So, how are you finding Honeybridge?' the man was asking. 'Settling in?'

'I'm loving it,' she said with a smile that faltered as Etienne approached. 'Everyone's so friendly.'

'Did you move here with your husband?' the woman asked, dabbing at her child's grubby hands with a wipe.

'No, just me,' Isabella replied, and Etienne watched her back straighten at the question. He also saw the woman edge closer to her husband, laying claim on him.

'You'll want to join lots of clubs then, to meet local people,' the woman said. 'The rowing club has lots of single men,' she said, making it abundantly clear her husband was taken. Etienne couldn't help but smile.

'Oh, I'm not looking for a man at the moment,' said Isabella and she chose this exact moment to look directly at Etienne. 'I'm concentrating on the restaurant. It's easier without distractions. I might join some clubs, though. Good suggestion.'

'What sort of things do you like? There's archery? Running? Watercolour painting at the Maltings?' the man suggested.

'Or maybe photography?' Etienne chipped in and couldn't help but notice the flush that spread up her neck. Ha. Got her. So, she'd definitely looked at the photo.

'Thanks,' she said to the couple. 'I'll do some research.' And with that, she turned and practically ran in the opposite direction, back towards the house.

'She was nice,' the husband said as they headed towards the bouncy castle.

'Very pretty,' the wife said, sniffing.

'Was she? I didn't notice,' the husband replied, lying through his teeth for the sake of his marriage. Etienne snorted and had to turn it into a cough.

An hour later, most children had been taken home. All of them had a slice of cake, a party bag, a balloon, and a sugar high.

After the last acquaintances had left, Fox finally opened a beer and slumped in a deckchair beside Etienne and Walker. Wren, Rosie and Isabella sat on a bench seat. Riley, Reggie and George returned to the bouncy castle.

'That went well,' Fox said, watching the children slam into the inflatable walls like mini cannonballs. 'George has had a great day.'

'Four already. Can you believe it?' Rosie said, watching Riley and George jump together, holding hands.

'He's a lovely boy,' Isabella said.

'And that's all down to you, Fox,' Wren said. 'You should be proud.'

There was a short silence while everyone thought about the fact that he had raised the boys on his own. Meg's sudden death had been such a shock.

'Did George ask about Meg this year?' Walker asked.

Fox took a swig of his beer before shaking his head. 'Nope.' Etienne put a hand on his shoulder.

'But I told him she would love to have celebrated his birthday with him and that she's blowing kisses from heaven.'

'That's lovely,' Rosie said, rising from the blanket to give him a hug. Wren wiped a tear from the corner of her eye.

'The good thing is that the boys don't remember her to miss her.' Fox laughed softly. 'It's just me that does that.'

George torpedoed across the lawn and sprang into Etienne's lap, narrowly missing kneeing him right in the nuts.

'Let's play hide-and-seek!' he yelled far too loud and far too close to Etienne's ear. Riley and Reggie stopped mid-bounce and turned like meerkats, awaiting the next words. Maybe it was on the back of what Fox had just said, but at that moment in time Etienne would have done anything in his power to make George happy.

'Go on then!' he said, tickling George's ribs and making him squirm. 'Everyone playing?' He saw Wren pull Rosie to her feet and then extend a hand to Isabella. Walker's eyes were already scouting the garden for hiding places.

'I'll seek first,' said Fox, making the most of an extra minute in his deckchair.

'Count to fifty!' George shouted and took off, arms pumping like pistons, towards the house.

'The office is out of bounds!' Fox shouted back, before closing his eyes and counting out loud, 'One, two, three . . .'

'No peeking, Dad,' Reggie warned before legging it round the corner.

Walker was already halfway up a tree, Rosie and Wren ran off holding hands and Isabella disappeared into the house. Etienne mentally scanned Fox's house, thinking of best spots. Deciding that behind the sofa was a good option, he padded through to the living room only to find Reggie already lying there.

'Taken!' the boy said, looking surprisingly fierce, pointing at the door for Etienne to leave.

'Okay, okay.' Etienne raised his hands and backed away, laughing.

'. . . thirty-five, thirty-six, thirty-seven . . .' Fox shouted from his deckchair.

Heading through the lounge, Etienne saw Riley's purple trainers poking out from under the coat stand and heard Wren and Rosie giggling in another room and hushing each other. Glancing out the window, he saw Walker pull his legs up into the canopy of the tree and disappear from view. He was running out of time.

'. . . forty-five, forty-six, forty-seven . . .'

He jogged past the cupboard under the stairs – too obvious by far – and through the hall to the big wardrobe where he knew they kept coats and skateboards. He only had a few seconds left as he pulled open the door. Isabella, standing inside surrounded by raincoats and woolly hats, blinked at the sudden light. Eyes wide, she wagged her finger at him fiercely. 'No!' she exclaimed.

'Coming, ready or not!' Fox shouted and Etienne stepped inside and pulled the door shut behind him.

'What are you doing?' Isabella hissed.

'Shhhh,' he replied and slid in beside her in the dark.

'Go and find your own hiding place,' she whispered, and he felt her breath on his face.

'Shhh,' he urged again, as they heard footsteps approach the hall and then pass by, taking the stairs above their heads two at a time.

He could hear her breathing as they listened, and her body was pressed against his in the cramped space. She smelled of lemons, but he wasn't sure if it was her shampoo or just *her*. She shifted, as though trying to put some distance between them but it was impossible. He grinned in the darkness as they followed Fox's searching from room to room, punctuated with the odd floorboard creak and stifled laughter.

'Found you!' Fox suddenly shouted somewhere upstairs, as George's giggles rang out. A second later the two of them passed the cupboard door again, talking about who they might find next. Isabella wriggled and the floor creaked. Etienne put his hand on her thigh to still her so that they wouldn't be detected. He heard her sharp intake of breath at his touch but she didn't remove his hand. As they listened to the seekers disappearing on their mission, he started to move his hand slowly, fingers spread wide, pushing it down her thigh to her knee and back towards the side of her hip, feeling the shape of her leg under the denim. She was strong and slender. He pictured her thighs wrapped around his waist.

'Found you!' Fox and George shouted together from a room nearby and Rosie and Wren's laughter rang out, followed by exclamations and chatter and noises of furniture being moved.

Etienne had played this game hundreds of times with the boys, but the act of hiding had never felt so delicious than standing here, in the dark, with his hand on Isabella's leg. It was exciting in lots of ways that were nothing to do with children's games.

'So, why have you been avoiding me?' he asked, his voice low, as his hand once again brushed down to her knee and squeezed.

'I think it's probably for the best,' Isabella replied quietly.

'Because of your sex ban?' He drew delicate circles on her thigh with his thumb.

'Because of my *promise*,' she breathed into his ear.

'Have you at least looked at the photograph?' he teased and she growled, low in the back of her throat, a sound so sexual that he immediately wanted her to repeat it.

'I'm taking that as a yes,' he whispered, moving his hand millimetre by millimetre to her buttock. The seeking troop made a discovery outside in the garden, and there was a round of applause, no doubt for Walker up the tree. His lack of vision seemed to heighten Etienne's other senses and he swallowed, smelling Isabella's scent, feeling the tremor in her thigh.

'Surely we don't have to avoid each other, though?' he said. 'Do we, Isabella?'

'It's not that I want to exactly . . .' Isabella's voice trailed off and he heard her lick her lips.

His whole hand spread across her bum and squeezed.

'What *do* you want then?' he asked, thinking he knew exactly what he wanted. Her. Now. In this cupboard if needs be.

He heard the hitch in her breath.

'This,' she said, turning towards him, and then her mouth was on his in the black. Momentarily stunned, it took him a split second to respond to her full, parted lips. Her hand on his chest, gripping the front of his polo shirt, pulling him closer, deeper in. But then they crashed together, his hand winding into her hair, her curls tumbling over his arm. His other hand on her tightened and she made a sound into her kiss, a moan. The feel of her body drove him on. Her tongue searching his, he pressed her to him and she met him with every move.

The door opened without warning. As the light streamed in they turned as one, still entwined. Etienne blinked, disorientated. Isabella pressed the back of her hand to her swollen mouth.

The seekers stood as a surprised group in the hallway. Fox and Walker raised their eyebrows and nudged each other like kids. Rosie and Wren put hands over each other's mouths to stop the other laughing out loud. Reggie, George and Riley stood straight-faced in the doorway.

'Wrong game, Uncle Et,' said George, obviously disappointed with his godfather. 'It's not kiss chase!'

Chapter Twenty-Nine

Isabella

Girl Gang WhatsApp group

Wren: Code red.

Rosie: Come now. Drinks at The Wayside.

Amber: Can't. Gotta collect Jayden from street dance in an hour.

Rosie: You won't want to miss this.

Amber: What happened?

Isabella: I kissed Etienne. 🙈

Amber: 😲 Be there in ten.

The women were already huddled around a round table in the back bar of The Wayside, all cradling large glasses of dry white wine, when Amber skidded in wearing denim dungarees over a cropped top, hair in two plaits, looking like some sort of sexy children's entertainer. Wren pointed to the seat beside her and the waiting glass of Coke Zero with a straw. Amber sat.

'You did WHAT?' she said to Isabella, getting straight to the point.

Isabella lifted her face from her hands. 'I kissed him. Etienne.' As if she needed to clarify.

'Where?' Amber asked, as if that was important.

'On his mouth,' Isabella said, confused.

'No, girl, I mean, where *were* you?' Amber said.

'Oh. In a cupboard.' Now Amber looked confused. Rosie snorted.

'Back up here,' Amber said, propping her chin on her fists and sipping from her straw. 'Tell me from the beginning.'

Isabella took a glug of wine and exhaled.

'We were all at George's birthday and ended up playing hide-and-seek. I hid in the cupboard under the stairs and then Etienne got in too.'

'Cheeky . . .' Amber said.

'I told him to get out. I mean, it was dark in there, and crowded, and he was pressed right up against me. After I'd done my best to avoid him all day. In fact, I'd done my best to avoid him since he sucked my finger . . .'

'What?!' Rosie choked on an olive.

'You never said!' Wren accused, banging Rosie's back.

'And especially since he took this . . .'

She opened her phone on the table, and they all peered at the photo of his hand on her skin.

Amber fanned herself and rolled her eyes.

'That's seriously hot, Isabella,' she said.

'Why did he take that?' Rosie asked, turning the screen to get a better look.

Isabella shifted in her seat.

'In case I needed any visual stimulation to get me through my year of no sex.'

They all took a moment to look at the picture again.

'That'd certainly help,' Amber said and they all nodded. Isabella didn't add that it had in fact been 'helping' every night since he'd taken it. She flicked the phone off.

'Anyway, so I've been avoiding him because it seems every time I get near him, I can't control myself. I mean, I've never let someone lick my arm, rub my foot, suck my finger before. And then all of a sudden, I'm in a cupboard in the dark with him and he was so close and . . .' She crossed her legs under the table at the memory of his hands.

'Oh my God, this was at a child's party?!' Amber said.

'This is definitely not PG behaviour!' Wren laughed, leaning back and putting her arm around Rosie. 'To think we were hiding behind the curtains upstairs waiting to be found by a four-year-old while this was going on.'

'And then I kissed him,' Isabella said, shrugging, as a flush pinked her cheeks. She took another long sip of wine.

'And then we found them!' Rosie said, leaning back into Wren, symbolising end of story.

'Omigod?' Amber looked at Isabella for clarification and she nodded.

'Yup. There we were for all to see. Me with my tongue down his throat.' Isabella's head sank into her hands again and she groaned. Amber threw her head back and laughed so loudly one of the waiters jumped as he walked past.

'But the question is,' Amber said, getting control of herself again, 'was it any good?'

Isabella raised her head, and looked into the eyes of each of the three women in turn. They all leaned in.

'It wasn't good,' Isabella whispered. 'It was amazing.'

'Yes!' Amber said and gave her a high five across the table. 'So, what now?'

'You going to sample the Etienne platter?' Wren said.

'She's going to drink of the Etienne juice . . .' Amber said.

'You're going to get Etienne'd,' Rosie proclaimed with finality.

Isabella swung her head from side to side, definitively.

'Nope, I am most definitely NOT breaking my promise.'

'But you've said it yourself, you can't trust yourself around him,' Wren said.

'And he's everywhere here, you can't avoid him,' Rosie added. 'I mean, we're all in the same friendship group.'

'What do your nipples think about that?' Amber asked.

'Believe me, I've taken my nipples into consideration,' Isabella said with a smile. 'And I'm also taking my own personal journey into consideration. And I've got an idea of how to combine both. We'll just have to see if Etienne is up for it.'

She checked her surroundings again and beckoned the women in until their heads were almost touching over the table. When she'd finished whispering, Amber slumped back in her chair.

'If you can pull that off, then you're a stronger woman than me.'

Later that night, Isabella watched as the last diners left The Bistro, and Etienne waved his staff goodbye before flipping the sign to closed and dimming the lights. It took her exactly one minute and ten seconds to lock her flat, hurry across the windy square and tap lightly on the front door. Etienne appeared from the kitchen, squinting to see outside, and she caught the glint of his smile in the shadows when he spotted her waiting.

Chapter Thirty

Etienne

Brothers from Another Mother WhatsApp group

Fox: Thanks for coming today, guys. George and Riley finally asleep in the den in the lounge. Reggie in bed. I'm shattered.

Walker: Glad George had a good day.

Fox: I think he had almost as much fun as you, Etienne.

Etienne: I doubt that somehow. 😳

Fox: She was in quite a hurry to get out of the cupboard, though.

Walker: And leave. 😊

Etienne: Don't you worry. She'll be back.

Fox: Not sure. Maybe you've met your match. 😳

Walker: Just got a callout to help the on-shift crew. Another house fire. Update you tomorrow.

Fox: Be careful.

Walker: Yes, Dad.

Fox: Fuck off.

Etienne heard the tapping on the door and saw Isabella's face through the glass and his first thought was, Yes, she's back, like he'd predicted. He grinned as he ambled over to let her in. She wafted fresh air and lemon scent behind her as she passed him, heading straight to the bar.

'Drink?' he asked, already taking down two glasses and putting the whisky between them. She used her fingers to drop in the ice and suddenly he was having a déjà vu of the last time they met like this. He pulled a stool beside her, closing the distance between them.

'Hi,' she said. 'Sorry it's late.'

He swallowed a slug of whisky, feeling the burn, thinking about the way her mouth tasted this afternoon. The unexpected fierceness of it.

'Nice to see you again. I was hoping you wouldn't keep avoiding me.'

She held his eyes at the words, and they were a startling blue, even in the subdued lighting.

'I'm realising it's quite hard to do that,' she said. 'Honeybridge is a small town.'

He grinned and moved his stool even closer. She put her elbow on the bar and rested her chin on her hand, watching him. He swore he could see the point of a nipple through her top. Tonight was going to be a good night.

'It was fun today, wasn't it?' he prompted, mirroring her pose, resting his chin on his hand, their faces just too far apart to make a move.

'It *was* fun,' she said and the tip of her tongue wet her bottom lip. Fuck, she was sexy.

'But I'm not going to sleep with you,' she said, with a tilt of her head.

'Who said anything about sleeping?' he replied, with a lift of his glass. She laughed before reaching out a hand and poking his elbow on the bar.

'Let's be honest, Etienne,' she said. 'I find you extremely attractive.'

His eyes widened. She was so honest, always saying exactly what she felt.

'And I think you're hot as hell,' he replied. She nodded seriously.

'And I can't seem to control myself when you're around – even at a children's birthday party . . .' she continued.

'So, maybe you should go with the flow.' He shrugged, moving his legs to put them under her stool, next to her feet, closing the gap.

'But I have made a promise to myself, and I take promises seriously.' She sipped her whisky, grimacing slightly as she swallowed. 'Especially after everything that has happened to me.'

'You're denying yourself pleasure,' he said quietly. She held his gaze again and he wondered if this was it, the moment when she would finally give in. When she would press herself against him. He felt his breath catch in readiness.

'I know, I realise that now,' she nodded. 'But I've only got a few weeks to go – and I want to be true to myself and complete my mission. A year being single to be successful with *no sex*.'

He exhaled slowly.

'I already feel so much better than I did straight after the divorce,' she continued. 'The restaurant is coming along. The staff's been hired. Training has started. I'm beginning to think of Honeybridge as home. I have friends, a local, a coffee shop that knows my order. It's a big thing to me. In fact, it's massive. When I think about how low I was, how sad, how lonely. I'm making such great progress.' She paused for breath.

'But the thing is, I'm facing temptation every time I'm in a room with you. And I'm fighting a losing battle.'

He grinned, feeling more on track again.

'So, I'm wondering if we can give in to some of that temptation without breaking my promise.' She circled the rim of the glass with her finger and licked it, looking at him from under her lashes. 'Spend some different sort of time together.'

'I'm not a relationship type of guy,' he said immediately.

'I'm not looking for that either.'

He rubbed the skin between his eyebrows, confused.

'So, what do you want?' he asked.

She took a deep breath.

'Perhaps we can enjoy each other without having actual sex?'

He felt his mouth drop open slightly.

'Define "actual sex",' he said quietly.

'Penetrative sex,' she said. 'Your cock inside me.'

The words set off a chain reaction of images in his brain, him on top of her on the floor, the bed, the bar and seeing the widening of her eyes as she finally took all of him.

He took a swallow of his drink and she did the same, maintaining eye contact above their glasses.

'So, to be clear, touching each other with our hands would be okay?' he asked.

'Uh-huh.' She nodded.

'And mouths?'

She pressed her lips together and nodded again.

'Yep.'

'And tongues?'

She rolled her eyes and grinned. 'Definitely, yes.'

'To give each other pleasure,' he asked and watched the flush of her neck. 'But no penetrative sex,' he confirmed.

'Exactly.'

'Is your promise that important to you?'

'Yes,' she said with a light laugh at herself. 'It is. But I guess I've realised I have needs too.' He was so full of need right now that he was hard for her for the second time that day.

He chuckled and let his eyes linger on her face, sweep down to her top, flick over her chest. She was delicious. And if she was on the menu, he was hungry. If it wasn't time for the main course yet, then fine. He could still snack. He imagined peeling her shirt back from her shoulders and then cupping those breasts. He visualised pulling her jeans down her long legs and seeing what was between them. She put her finger under his chin and brought his gaze back up to her face.

'What do you think, Etienne? Can I trust you?'

'To what?'

'To *not* have sex.' Her face was serious, and he felt the depth of the question.

'Of course.' He would never take it further than anyone wanted it to go.

'Then shall we have some fun?'

'When do we start?' he said eagerly, and she laughed, putting her finger against his lips. She swallowed the last of her whisky and slipped from the stool.

'Soon.'

Girl Gang WhatsApp group

Isabella: He went for it.

Amber: I bet he did. But can you stick to it?

Isabella: Yup. 👍

Wren: So, when will you start?

Rosie: Or have you already?

Isabella: Not yet. Need to book a wax!

Chapter Thirty-One

Isabella

Staff training was in full swing. Amber, now free from the rowing club, had turned all her attention to Tutto Mio and their first waiting masterclass. Returning after a visit to a supplier, Isabella found Amber demonstrating how to carry three plates at a time as she strolled up and down the dining floor. It looked easy when she did it, but Isabella was glad to see they were practising with plastic plates when Sinead, Paul and Harry had their first go. Sinead sped up the closer she got to the table, until she was almost at a run. Paul inched along focusing on his hands as if he was doing an egg and spoon race. Harry sang to herself with every step she took. More plates hit the ground than made the table. And the ones that made the table only did so by sheer luck.

'Don't worry, you'll get it,' said Amber, picking up the plates and stacking them again. 'Look, let's do it together again.' Everyone gathered around. Paul pulled out a notebook and licked a pencil.

'You lay the first plate on your middle three fingers, like this.' Amber demonstrated. 'Then you hold it in place with your thumb and pinky.' Paul wrote it down.

'Now, you lay the second plate on the same hand,' Amber said, laying it flat on the underside of her wrist and balancing it on the fleshy bit of her thumb. Paul sighed and scribbled. Denzil nodded.

'Then you carry the third in your other hand.' Amber expertly lifted the final plate and repeated her saunter across the dining floor, where she carefully unloaded onto the table.

'Fair dinkum,' said Australian Angie in awe.

'Who's next?' Amber asked and the team all looked at each other hopefully until Sinead stepped forward again, followed cautiously by Naomi and Harry. They loaded up the plates as Amber had directed and made their way to the table at the other end. Sinead only ran the last few steps and managed to get all three plates down, although in a real-life scenario one of the diners would be wearing their dinner. Naomi managed two of the three and Harry got all three down but still sounded like a backing singer on her way across the floor.

'Better!' Amber cried and beckoned the four awaiting their turn. Paul tucked his pencil behind his ear and picked up his plates, looking calm and comfortable. Meryl, Angie and Denzil followed his lead and soon they were all at the other end, slapping each other on the back, all plates down safely.

'Whoop, whoop, looking good!' Amber called and then she noticed Isabella in the doorway, watching.

'What do you think then, Boss?' she asked and everyone turned to her. 'Not bad for a first session?'

'Fantastic.'

'Not all of us, though,' Naomi said, sighing. 'I dropped one of mine.' The group moved in around her and Sinead put her arm around the younger girl. The team dynamic was strong.

'There's loads of time to practise,' said Paul.

'You've only had one go,' said Denzil.

'You'll get it next time,' said Amber.

Naomi looked downcast.

'It's not only this, though, is it? Serving the food is only one part of it. I've got to learn so many other things as well. Types of drinks, how to make cocktails, working the card machine!' She was working herself up now, hands flapping by her side.

'We'll take them one step at a time, Naomi,' Amber said. 'Try not to worry.'

'And that's before we even get to the menu,' Naomi whispered. 'How am I going to cope with the menu? Recommending different things, remembering what's on the specials? Bringing the right sauces for the various meats?' Isabella could see the rising panic and thought it was time to step in.

'That's where I can help, Naomi,' Isabella said. 'Because yes, you'll have to learn drinks and how to work the card machine and serve tables, but I guarantee you the menu at Tutto Mio will be the easiest part of your job.'

Isabella motioned for everyone to pull up a chair and a circle was swiftly formed. She checked the builders had the door shut to the kitchen and began.

'This is highly confidential. Nobody else is to know what we will be serving at Tutto Mio until we launch. I don't want any other local restaurants to find out.'

She was met with nods from a wide-eyed team.

'I've told you before that the food here will be Italian. But not "vaguely" Italian. The food cooked here will be to an old family recipe of mine that has been passed down the generations. It has never been outside my family.'

Paul pulled out his pencil and pad and then thought better of it. He winked at Isabella and tapped the side of his nose.

'The menu will be extremely easy to remember because there will only be one thing on it.' Australian Angie raised her eyebrows. Isabella again checked behind her.

'Meatballs,' she said, smiling as Harry grinned and licked her lips.

'Just meatballs?' Amber sat back in her chair.

'With a couple of variations . . .' Isabella continued. Sinead made a quiet 'oh' sound.

'So, we're a meatball restaurant?' Naomi asked blankly.

'I've never been to a meatball restaurant,' Paul said.

'I've never even heard of a meatball restaurant,' Angie agreed.

'We are not just any old meatball restaurant!' Isabella laughed. 'We will be the best, most authentic meatball restaurant this side of London.'

The team glanced at each other. Isabella tried again.

'Let me ask you all – do you like meatballs?' Everyone nodded.

'Would you like them with spaghetti or rice?' Everyone answered; it was a hung jury.

'What about in a sub for lunch?'

'Oh yes,' said Meryl, literally licking her lips.

'Or meat-free meatballs if you're vegetarian?'

'I'm in!' said Naomi.

'What about mini meatballs for the children?'

'Ah, cute,' said Australian Angie.

'And maxi ones for the super hungry?'

'That's me sorted,' said Denzil.

'Washed down with the best Italian wines?' Isabella said with a nod to Paul, who saluted her in return.

'And followed by some of the best Italian desserts, biscuits and ice creams, which I'm still perfecting . . . ?'

Everyone looked enthused. Isabella grinned. It was the first time she'd told anyone since Gabi and Jesse and the reaction was good. In fact, it was better than good.

'So, all I have to know about is meatballs?' Naomi laughed.

'Yep.'

'Meaty, meat-free, maxi or mini?'

'You're an expert already,' Isabella said and Naomi took a bow. Isabella checked her watch and stood. It was almost time for her next important announcement.

'So – confidential, please. Until we launch.' Everyone nodded gravely.

'That brings us on to the elephant in the room,' said Amber before breathing out slowly. 'Who will be cooking these meatballs? Where's the chef?'

The twenty-four-million-dollar question. Isabella had wondered about this since the day she had the idea for the restaurant. The recipes were precious to her. They needed treating with the care and respect they deserved. She wanted someone who would continue the family ways and keep them secret. What she didn't want was a chef who felt the need to put their own stamp on something. To add a pinch of turmeric because it was the latest 'wonder spice'. She'd toyed with the idea of being the chef herself, but knew she wouldn't have the time – or skill – to do the job properly. What she needed was an expert.

A car tooted outside in the drop-off zone of the square and Isabella hurried to the window. She clapped her hands in delight as she watched a taxi drive away.

'Right on time,' she said and pulled the door open wide.

A tiny lady, no taller than five feet, stood on the pavement wearing a bright red woollen cape. Her long white hair was in a plait that wrapped around her head like a crown. Her face was weathered and wrinkled but her bright blue eyes shone with a surprising twinkle, even if she was easily over seventy years old. Isabella heaved her suitcase over the threshold before bending to envelop her in the biggest hug. The older woman squeezed her fiercely in return and Isabella was reminded of what a good yoga class can do. When she looked back at the team, she knew her eyes were gleaming with tears.

'Team, meet Chef,' she said, 'maker of the best meatballs in history. Keeper of the family's secret recipes since the nineteen fifties.' Isabella wrapped her arm around the woman's shoulders and pulled her in tight. 'Tutto Mio's secret weapon. Otherwise known as my grandmother.'

The woman undid her cape with a flourish and plucked a white cotton apron from the bag at her feet. She tied it around her waist and pulled herself up to her full four feet eleven inches. She rubbed her hands together in happy anticipation, armfuls of bracelets clinking.

'Call me Nonna,' she said.

Nonna knew everyone in the team by name by the time Isabella led her up to the flat. She announced that Amber was a beautiful and strong woman when she heard she was bringing up Jayden alone. She particularly liked Denzil's handwashing and admired Harry's manners. She'd impressed them in return by asking them if they knew of a local Pilates club she could join, and Australian Angie declared that she was bonza when she'd enquired where the nearest escape room was.

Sinead promised to introduce her to the macrame gang and Harry's face lit up when she said she'd never been geocaching, but it was 'on her list'.

After the team left, Isabella showed her the newly refurbed restaurant. When Isabella opened the doors to the kitchen and Nonna saw the new stainless-steel worktops and the shiny white tiles on the wall, she turned around and hugged herself.

'Now, here's a kitchen to make meatballs,' Nonna said.

'You don't think this is going to be too much for you, do you?' Isabella asked for the hundredth time. She'd been begging Nonna to come and stay with her for months, ever since Mamma and Papà left for their extended travels. She hated the thought of Nonna living alone and wanted her where she could look out for her more. The only way she'd been able to finally get her to say yes was with the suggestion that Nonna did the cooking for the restaurant. Nonna jumped at the opportunity so quickly it made Isabella question whose idea it was in the first place, but she was delighted that her grandmother would be close by – and she was the best possible chef for Tutto Mio.

'I've told you, *mia cara*, that cooking and family are the two best things in my life. So, no, this will not be too much for me.'

'But if it does start to be—'

'Then I will train someone else,' Nonna said with a shrug and then a nod. 'I like the look of that Sinead already.'

'I don't want to wear you out.'

'I'd like to see you try.'

Isabella laughed.

As Nonna unpacked her things in the spare bedroom, she hummed away to herself. It was an old Italian folk song that reminded Isabella of being tiny and going to stay with Nonno and Nonna in the school holidays. The patchwork quilt, the smell of lemons. The sounds of her grandparents cooking and talking in the next room when she went to bed. She'd spend a few weeks there every summer, playing under pine trees, swimming in the lake, meeting up with Gabriella and playing with her other cousins. As she closed her eyes to listen, a text came in and brought her reminiscing bang up to date.

Etienne: Wanna play tonight?

Isabella felt a rush of pure lust. But she couldn't leave Nonna on the first night. It wouldn't be fair.

Isabella: Sorry, can't. My nonna's here.

It was tempting but she hadn't seen her nonna for almost a year and they had a lot to catch up on.

Etienne: Shame . . . Without upsetting your grandmother, I was imagining what I might do to you first . . .

Isabella chuckled at the same time that her thighs tightened. Nonna started to hum a new tune in her room.

Isabella: Where did you decide to start?

She grinned to herself, hoping this message chain was having the same effect on him as it was her. Heightening the anticipation. She watched the screen. He was typing.

Etienne: Undoing your shirt buttons, one at a time . . .

Isabella automatically put her fingers to the button between her breasts. Her breathing was deepening.

Isabella: And then?

She flicked a glance at the door to Nonna's bedroom, at the opposite end of the flat to hers.

Etienne: Tugging your bra out of the way . . .

Isabella's nipples stood to attention, knowing they were being talked about.

Isabella: What would you do next?
Etienne: I'd roll my hands around your boobs . . .
Isabella: Omigod, you've got to stop. My grandma's in the next room!
Etienne: We can be quiet . . .

Isabella laughed out loud and clapped a hand over her mouth. She sagged on the sofa, a hot ache in her lower belly. There was no more putting this off.

Isabella: Tomorrow?

Even as she wrote it, that felt a long way off. At least twenty-four hours too far away if Isabella was totally honest with herself.

Etienne: It's my birthday. Everyone's going to The Bolthole. Come along.

Isabella's fingers were a blur in her hurry to reply.

Isabella: I'll be there – oh, so will my friends! Gabi and Jesse are coming to visit. Might make things a bit difficult to be alone . . .

Etienne: We'll find a way. Remember the cupboard under the stairs at Fox's?

Isabella: Yes?

Etienne: Keep that in mind.

Chapter Thirty-Two

Etienne

The sounds from the market outside woke him. Stalls being assembled, produce being wheeled in. Shouts and cries as people greeted each other even if it wasn't even 7 a.m. His phone beeped.

Brothers from Another Mother WhatsApp group

Walker: Happy birthday, bro. Just coming off shift.

Etienne: Thanks, bro.

Fox: Just starting my shift here. Happy big 4-0.

Etienne: Ha ha. 39, arsehole.

Fox: See you at The Bolthole. Abbie is coming over for the boys.

Walker: I'm sleeping till then. It's been a week. Two house fires in two days.

Etienne: Love you guys.

Walker: Back at you.

Fox: Same.

Etienne put his hands behind his head and stared at the

ceiling. His birthday was always a weird day. The absence of his parents rolled over him like a steamroller, and for most of the last five years, he'd got through it without knowing where Alex was either. Fox and Walker had been the people that got him through those days. Not that he'd told them about Alex's existence until recently; he'd been too ashamed of his part in his brother's absence. But they knew about his parents. And they'd stepped in on their behalf. They'd had sober birthdays, drunken celebrations and everything in between.

But this year, he already had a better birthday ahead. Because Alex was coming home, and Etienne was going to put things right. He rolled over in bed and lifted his phone again, typing quickly.

Etienne: Happy birthday, Al, you old git.

Alex always made the most of the fact that he was the older twin. At every birthday party when they were young, he'd told people that he was born first. As if that made him more important. Until Etienne learned the rhyme, 'First the worst, second the best, third the one with the hairy chest,' and then, funnily enough, Alex stopped mentioning it. His phone beeped.

Alex: Happy birthday, Et. Hope we can spend the next one together.

Etienne grinned.

Etienne: Any news?
Alex: Nothing.
Etienne: Let me know when you hear.

There were a handful of cards on the doormat of the restaurant from Katie and some of the other waiting team, old Fred Barrow and others. Mile End Mickey gave him a cheery wave from the kitchen as he shouted through, 'Happy Birthday, my old mucker.' Etienne was setting about getting the restaurant ready for the day when his phone beeped again.

Isabella: Happy birthday.

Etienne: Thanks.

Isabella: Can't wait to give you your present.

He grinned. Today was most definitely going to be a good day.

Chapter Thirty-Three

Isabella

If Gabi and Jesse hadn't arrived that day and distracted her, Isabella might have self-combusted with sexual excitement. Knowing she was finally going to give in to the urge and put her hands on Etienne made her tingle in all the right places.

Jesse's first visit to Honeybridge demanded a tour of the town and Gabi was happy to tag along, showing off her newly acquired stunt skills as they went. Walking on her hands along the riverbank, and doing parkour jumps across the bollards marking the square.

'Believe me, you never know when they'll come in handy in my line of work . . .'

Nonna pinched the cheeks of her other granddaughter until they were pink and treated Jesse like an adopted grandson, complimenting the precision of his beard and his expensive-smelling cologne.

'I spray it on my sheets before I put them in the tumble dryer!' He cupped Nonna's hand to her ear theatrically, to share one of his trade secrets for being the best-scented man Isabella had ever encountered. That is, until Etienne. That woody fragrance that followed him around was intoxicating.

When she got dressed that night, she put on a silky top with buttons, remembering Etienne's text messages. She slipped into a mini skirt which sat low on her hip and high on her thigh, teaming it with strappy high heels. Gabi's eyes widened when she saw her.

'You look hot!' she said. 'Am I underdressed?'

She most certainly wasn't – with hot pants and knee-high boots, her pixie cut pointed to her cheekbones, she looked perfect, elfin.

'Special effort for someone tonight?' Gabi went on. 'Etienne by any chance? The one whose leg you were nearly humping last time I came?'

'Pre-drinks for the gossip!' Jesse announced, joining them with a bottle.

A glass of prosecco later, Isabella had told them of the no-sex deal. Jesse pretended to tip his hat to her.

'If there's ever a woman who knows her own mind, it's you, Isabella . . .' He winked at Gabi. 'And you of course, darling.'

Gabi agreed, with an admiring tilt of her head.

'Good on you, girl,' she said. 'Keeping your promise and eating your cake!'

'Can't wait to check him out!' Jesse rubbed his hands together and Isabella made them swear to be discreet, or at least not to make a show of her when they met.

By the time she got to The Bolthole, Isabella was like a fuse waiting to be lit. Rosie whistled as she shimmied out of her coat.

'He doesn't stand a chance,' she said, shaking her head.

Wren arched an eyebrow in agreement. 'I almost feel sorry for him,' she said.

Gabi kissed them both and Jesse enveloped them in a hello hug they weren't expecting but seemed to love when they got close enough to smell him.

The bar was two-deep, but Amber had a friend working and they were soon settled in a booth with their drinks. Isabella tried not to be obvious as she scanned the dance floor.

'He's not here yet,' Rosie said. 'Walker said they're coming at nine.'

Isabella resisted the urge to check her watch and leaned into Amber's conversation, who was telling the others about Nonna's arrival.

'So, she's living with you? How sweet!' Rosie clapped her hands.

'For the time being,' Isabella said. 'I managed to persuade her at last. But she doesn't want to live with me for ever. She's a very independent woman. Ideally, she'd like somewhere of her own so that she can bring a boyfriend home if she wants to.'

Amber spluttered on her drink.

'Boyfriend?'

Isabella laughed. 'My nonno has been dead a long time. I guess she still has needs!'

'Must be nice for you to have some family around, with your parents being away.'

'It's so lovely to see her. And the restaurant is all about family, so it feels right that she's here at the start. How long she stays is up to her. I think a lot of it will depend on how long my parents travel, and how long she wants to cook for. We agreed that when she'd had enough, she'll train someone else on the family recipes.'

'Has she settled in? She didn't mind you coming out tonight?' Rosie asked.

'You obviously haven't met her yet!' Gabi laughed. 'She's out herself. Went to join the local chess club.'

'I guess that answers my question then. Good on Grandma.'

'Tell us about you, Jesse?'

Jesse wiggled in excitement in his seat at being the centre of attention.

'What do you want to know?'

'Everything!' Rosie said. 'Like, why you smell so good for a start!'

Gabi and Isabella rolled their eyes at each other as Jesse beckoned the girls closer with his finger to stage-whisper about the aftershave tumble dryer trick.

'And talking of laundry, did you hear how I met Isabella?' He then proceeded to tell them in excruciating detail how he met her in the first week of university when she was so drunk she peed in the laundry basket for their dorm.

'Lifelong friends ever since!'

They all clinked glasses, Isabella distracted by the door opening as Fox, Walker and, finally, Etienne entered the club and headed for the bar.

All nine of them were now squeezed into the booth. Isabella was trapped at the back, hemmed in by Gabi on one side and Amber on the other. She felt something tap her foot and locked eyes with Etienne, who was half smiling at her across the table. Her stomach lurched.

Birthday drinks were ordered, toasts were made.

'Is there a band on tonight?' Isabella asked, thinking of Throwback Thursday, and that it might give her a chance to get up close and personal with Etienne on the dance floor.

Wren looked up, surprised. Rosie snorted.

'Didn't you tell her?' Wren asked. Amber bit her lip to stop herself laughing.

'It's a thing we do – for birthdays,' she explained.

'Whoever's birthday it is,' Amber said, and everyone pointed at Etienne, 'has to do karaoke first. Then there's a DJ later.'

Etienne nodded, almost sheepishly.

'It's been running at The Bolthole for ages. That's why Etienne's name is up there.' Amber pointed to a chalkboard above the bar, where it had two names printed in capital letters. SYLVIA and then ETIENNE.

'Looks like there are two birthday parties today.'

'That's why the guys got here at nine, because that's normally when the karaoke starts.'

As if on cue, the bar manager jumped the bar and leaped onto the stage. His long hipster beard was impeccably groomed; he must have spent a fortune on beard oil to make it gleam in the spotlights.

'Welcome to The Bolthole!' he said, doing a quick spin on the spot, arms wide, dozens of leather bracelets tied around each wrist. The crowd cheered.

'First to the stage tonight for Birthday Karaoke is the lovely Sylvia!'

A booth on the other side of the stage erupted into cheers and whistles as a petite blonde girl stood up and waved before downing the drink in front of her. A spotlight followed her onto the stage, where she smoothed her hair off her face and straightened her shoulders.

'Have you had a good birthday, Sylvia?' the bar manager asked. She nodded and hiccupped at the same time. 'And what are you going to be singing tonight for us, Sylvia?'

Sylvia took the microphone he offered her and said, '"It's Not Unusual"!'

'Over to you, Sylvia!' The bar manager spun on the spot again and then jumped off the stage. The music started and Sylvia was straight into it, sidestepping in time.

The entire club joined in immediately and Sylvia's smile widened. By the end of the song, she was absolutely belting it out. Once Sylvia had taken a bow to the crowd's deafening applause, the bar manager bounded back up to the stage.

'Is it you now?' Isabella said across the table to Etienne. He grinned.

'Not quite yet,' he said.

'So as is customary, the birthday girl's table will now have their go!' Three girls in Sylvia's booth jumped up and down before running to the stage.

'Sorry, we didn't tell you the whole story!' Amber said with a nudge.

'You mean, I have to do it?' Isabella swallowed, every sexy feeling draining away and being replaced by horror.

'Etienne's doing his with the boys,' Wren said.

'So, we four girls can go up together!' Rosie looked delighted about this while Isabella's face fell.

'Wait, what about Jesse and Gabi?'

'I'm happy to watch!' Gabi laughed. 'This is going to be brilliant,' she said, throwing a knowing look at Isabella.

'We'll get the crowd going down here!' Jesse said. 'Leave that to us.'

'Sorted,' said Amber.

'But I can't sing!' Isabella said, grasping Amber's arm.

'It'll be fine!' Amber said as the music started again and the three girls on stage started 'Mamma Mia', complete with poses and synchronised dance routine. Isabella took a long gulp of her drink and filled it again before the girls finished, running off the stage back to their booth.

Fox, Etienne and Walker all stood.

'Wish us luck!' Fox said as they headed to the sound man.

'Next up is the ageless heartthrob of Honeybridge . . . Etienne!' Isabella noticed a surge of women moving towards the front. The manager pumped Etienne's hand and asked, 'Good birthday so far, Etienne?'

Etienne peered into the spotlight in the direction of Isabella's booth. 'It's been a great day, thanks,' he said with a wolfish smile. 'But I think somehow the best is yet to come.'

Isabella crossed her bare legs under the table, pressing her thighs together.

'And what are you singing tonight?' the beard asked.

Etienne shaded his eyes again, still looking directly at the booth.

'The Rolling Stones,' he said. '"Satisfaction".'

'I can help with that!' someone shouted from the dark edges of the dance floor, to much hilarity.

Wren put her two fingers in her mouth and wolf whistled. Women stamped their feet on the floor. Isabella made a noise deep in her throat as she looked at him in the spotlight, shirt undone at the top, sleeves pushed up, belted jeans fitting like a glove.

'Holy Mary, Mother of God,' Jesse mouthed across the table to her, crossing himself at the same time.

That famous guitar introduction sounded, and Fox and Walker positioned themselves slightly behind Etienne, one to either side, a triangle of gorgeousness.

Etienne pouted and shook his waves out at the familiar beat, apparently channelling his inner Mick Jagger.

He turned to the audience and started belting out the opening to 'Satisfaction'.

He stalked one way across the stage, then the other as he sang, in a perfect imitation of the original. Fox and Walker played air guitar behind him, swaying in perfect rhythm. Either they'd been practising, or they'd done this before. Gabi cheered, Amber whooped and Wren whistled. Isabella and Jesse were both struck dumb.

Was there anything Etienne couldn't do?

The dance floor was in chaos. People were whirling around in circles, jumping on the spot, shouting along. Isabella leaped up to join Amber at the front of the booth and found herself doing some kind of flying angel. Jesse and Gabi were stamping their feet so hard the glasses on their table rattled.

As the last chord sounded, the crowd roared. Etienne wiped

a hand across his brow and grinned. Walker saluted and Fox pretended to stagger off stage clutching his heart.

Isabella threw a panicked glance at the girls as she realised what it meant. Their turn.

'Help me,' she mouthed to Gabi but Amber had grabbed her by the wrist before she could escape. Wren and Rosie jumped down from their bench and Isabella was swept along to the stage. Halfway there, they met the men on their way back.

'You smashed it!' Rosie said to Walker.

'Tough act to follow,' Wren agreed.

'Especially with a karaoke virgin in our midst,' Amber said, indicating Isabella.

'And I can't sing,' Isabella exclaimed wildly, wondering why nobody was listening to her.

'You'll be fine,' they all chorused as she stumbled into the spotlights. A microphone was thrust into her hand and the bar manager ran off the stage. Just as she was considering running after him, the song title appeared on the screen in front of her and the immediately recognisable electro strains of the intro sounded. Well, at least she knew the words to Human League's 'Don't You Want Me'.

Amber jumped to the centre of the stage in time to start and Isabella sighed in relief. Of course Amber would take the lead, she was sassy and confident and obviously loved karaoke. Isbella joined in with what Wren and Rosie were doing at the back, swaying and clicking their fingers until the chorus, when they all leaned in to join in with the refrain over a shared microphone. This wasn't too bad.

As Wren and Rosie sang, Isabella made sure to keep her

mouth as far away as possible from the microphone. The crowd bellowed along and suddenly it was feeling better. Almost like fun. She could be part of the backing singers – no problem. She grinned and struck a pose on the next line, feeling more confident with every second.

Rosie and Wren grabbed a mic each and faced each other, taking the next couple of lines on their own. Isabella was happy to leave them to it, and did a little dance in the background. She was having a blast.

Until the next verse was about to start and Amber turned and shoved the mike into her hand. 'Your turn,' she shouted and stepped back, leaving Isabella out front on her own. In a spotlight. Facing a crowd.

Isabella shook her head frantically, but the other women waved their hands at her to get on with it. They didn't understand and it was too late to tell them now. There was a reason Isabella didn't do karaoke. An extremely good one. She couldn't sing. *At all.* She was, as the music teacher at school had factually stated, tone deaf.

Amber pushed her forward again, and it was too late to do anything but go for it.

'Sorry about this!' she shouted into the microphone to the audience, then she grinned and began to sing.

The look of shock on people's faces rippled down the front row. She shrugged and carried on, nothing else for it. She couldn't let the girls down. She sang the next line and it came out a bit louder, which made someone at the nearest booth put their hands over their ears. People were looking at each other in disbelief. A handful laughed out loud. The others looked horrified. She'd seen it before at school and it had hurt then, but tonight, it just seemed funny.

'Yay, Isabella!' Gabi shouted from the audience.

'You go, girl!' Amber said behind her and she heard Wren's two-finger whistle.

She felt a giggle building inside her as she heard the girls all cheering her on. All of a sudden, it didn't matter. She was having fun. And probably her last glass of wine had kicked in.

She sidestepped back and forth, then did a wiggle, which got a laugh. The more she threw herself into it, the more the audience joined in and by the time she'd finished her verse she was enjoying herself so much that the audience couldn't help but go along with her.

They finished the track and the audience cheered and pumped the air with their fists. The girls collapsed into each other in a hot hug.

'Girl, you could have warned us!' Amber said, which set Rosie off cackling.

They made their way back to the booth. Fox and Walker were already there, lifting their beers in a salute.

'Some performance, ladies!' Walker said, which led to a thump on the arm by Rosie.

'Truly never heard anything like it,' Fox said with a wink.

'Believe me, once you've heard that voice, you never forget it,' laughed Jesse.

Isabella was waiting for everyone to move in and sit down as a hand snaked around her from behind. Although she glanced backwards over her shoulder, she knew by the way her body responded that it was Etienne.

'I still want you,' he said into her ear, chin resting on her shoulder. The words turned her innards to butter, hot and melting. 'Even if you do sound like a cat dying when you sing.' He pulled her back against his body. Her legs suddenly felt weaker than they had on stage.

'Come with me,' he said, picking up her jacket from the back of the booth.

'Where are we going?' she asked, turning to face him.

'To put your coat in the cloakroom,' he said, with a half-smile which made her want to bite him.

'But the night's nearly over?' she said in confusion.

'Not yet it's not.' He took her by the hand and led her through the crowd.

The cloakroom was full of coats and empty of attendants. Etienne confidently opened the door and tugged her inside, closing the door behind them, leaving them half lit.

'What is it with you and cupboards?' Isabella whispered.

'The excitement,' he murmured back.

'What if someone comes in?' she said.

'They won't. Not until closing.'

She didn't even care how he knew that. She didn't care about anything apart from him, right in front of her.

He turned to look at her. A long look that swept her entire body. She saw the twitch of his mouth as he appreciated her long, smooth legs. Every nerve in her body was straining. She had never felt such anticipation in her life.

They both moved at the same time, crushing together, his mouth on hers, hard and demanding. She pushed back against him with just as much wanting. He backed her up against the wall of coats, and she pulled him in closer, her arms round his neck, never losing contact with his mouth. His tongue flicked in to meet her own and her stomach hollowed.

They turned together, Isabella pressing Etienne against the wall now. She pushed the length of her body against his as his hands skimmed her back and grasped her butt. She moaned as he turned her around, dropped his mouth to her throat and her head fell back against the wall. He trailed the length of her neck, biting and licking and making her gasp. His knee worked its way between hers, and she felt the rush of air against her already wet pants.

His hand joined his mouth at her neck, moving down until he reached the first button of her top. It gave no resistance, and he moved his mouth to follow. She was glad of the wall behind her, holding her up, as the second button popped and then he was laying bare her bra. She could hear the hoarseness of his breathing as he pulled back to study her shape. He ran his fingertips along the edge of the lacy cup where it met her skin and her nipples tightened into buds. She put her hands into his hair, urging him on as he pushed the flimsy fabric out of the way and filled his hands with her breasts. His head dipped and he caught her nipple between his lips and she moaned out loud as he nipped with his teeth. She cradled his head, holding him against her. God, she wanted this.

He moved quickly and turned her again, this time swivelling her on the spot, so that she faced the cloakroom wall, her bare chest rubbing against the soft leather of someone's jacket and him tight behind her body. She could feel his hardness pressed against her. His hands and mouth seemed to be everywhere at once. She pushed against his erection and he growled into her hair.

His hand moved down, stroking over her stomach and skimming the front of her mini skirt until it skated across the smooth skin of her thigh. Her eyes closed as he tugged up the hem. She gasped as he ran the heel of his hand over her mound and between her legs, once, twice, three times. Easing his fingers under the elastic, she finally felt him where she wanted him, rubbing the hot, throbbing core of her. Her head fell back against his shoulder and a noise vibrated from deep inside her.

'Is it good?' he asked into her neck, and she moaned a response.

'No, you have to tell me,' he said, circling her clit with his thumb. She could hear her own ragged breathing. 'Is it good?'

'Yes,' she whispered and her voice was hoarse. 'It's good. It's so good.' She gritted her teeth together as the feeling built inside.

He thrust against her, holding her in position against his hand, as his thumb increased speed and her legs started to tremble. His other hand still cupped her breast as he used his thumb and forefinger to roll her nipple. Her legs shook and she put one hand to the wall to hold on, reaching a coat hook for support as she approached the summit.

He flicked with both thumbs, nipple and clit at the same time, and she went over the brink. Eyes shut, the only thing holding her up was him as her knees buckled and she fell into the biggest orgasm of her life as he murmured, '*Yes, yes, yes,*' into her hair.

It took her a minute to come back to herself. She panted and slumped against him until she found the strength to force herself upright. She pushed her hair away from her damp cheeks and turned to face him. He didn't move away and she could feel the heat from his groin against her hip.

His green eyes glinted and he half smiled at her, letting his tongue run over his bottom lip.

'I think we got that wrong,' she rasped.

He raised an eyebrow. 'You think? How?'

'Normally if it's your birthday, *you* get a present . . .'

'I did.' He laughed, nodding down at her boobs, still exposed over her bra.

'I was thinking more of . . .' Isabella reached a hand down between their bodies and saw his mouth part as she traced the huge outline of his cock, like rock in his jeans. She ran her fingers along the length of him and watched as his breath caught. She moved her hand to his zip. She could not wait to get her hands on him.

The door opened, flooding light into the room. Isabella shrieked and Etienne stepped in front of her while she stuffed herself back into her top and did the buttons up.

The cloakroom attendant raised an eyebrow but sighed like she'd seen it all before.

'Sorry about that!' Isabella stammered, shuffling past Etienne to the door.

'We were just looking for something . . .' Etienne said as he followed her.

'Yeah,' said the woman knowingly. 'Satisfaction.'

Back at the booth, things had progressed in terms of drunkenness.

Walker and Rosie were doing some kind of waltz together on the dance floor while Wren was teaching Jesse basic pole. His open shirt buttons were exposing a fair amount of fake-tanned chest as he spun around. Amber was breakdancing, moves it looked like Jayden might have taught her, and Gabi was walking on her hands along the bar to cheers from a line of spectators.

Fox broke off from proudly showing pictures of his boys to a mum from school. 'You're back!' he slurred. 'Where've you been?'

'Just showing Isabella around,' Etienne said, sliding into the booth beside her and lifting a beer from the bucket. He tipped his head back and drank, swallowing until half the bottle had disappeared. She scoured the table for something to quench her own thirst, but the water jug was empty and the wine bottle was turned upside down in the ice. He handed the beer over and she nodded her thanks as she sank the rest of the bottle.

'Happy birthday,' she said, wiping her mouth on the back of her hand. 'I still owe you a present.'

He nodded.

'Looking forward to it,' he said and then, putting his hands on her shoulder, he led her to the floor to dance on legs that were still shaking.

Chapter Thirty-Four

Etienne

The banging in his head eventually beat his need for sleep and he stumbled to the bathroom cabinet for painkillers, glugging water straight from the tap. What a night. Free-flowing drinks, old and new friends. Karaoke, and Isabella's body. He splashed water on his face and patted it dry, thinking of the way her head fell back on his shoulder as she came. This 'not having sex' pact was fun after all. Back in his bedroom, he flicked to his messages before he started his day.

Fox: Thank fuck you only have a birthday once a year.

Walker: Someone on the way to work just told me I'm a good waltzer?

Mile End Mickey: You've double locked the door, you plonker. We can't get in.

He staggered down the stairs in his boxers and opened the restaurant door to a grey, foggy square. Mickey sauntered in with a chuckle.

'That's a fine state to start your year in,' he said as he held the door open for Katie and then headed to the kitchen. She in turn looked Etienne up and down, before sighing.

'I'll set up. You go and sort yourself out.'

He tried to nod but it hurt too much. Halfway up the stairs, she called after him, 'Oh, I don't think I told you before, but my cousin works in the cloakroom at The Bolthole.'

He ignored her and carried on up to the flat, her laughter echoing behind him. 'She says it's amazing the things people leave in there!'

An hour later he was showered, shaved, and back to life. His phone pinged as he was about to go downstairs for first serving.

Alex: Can you talk?

Etienne immediately went to call him. Alex answered before he heard it ring.

'You okay?' Etienne said quickly, only relaxing when Alex replied, 'I'm fine.'

'Heard anything?'

'I got a message from the pub landlord. The Dougalls were happy to hear from me.'

'That's good, isn't it?' Etienne said.

'Apparently they said that there were lessons to be learned.'

Etienne sank back onto the sofa.

'You need to be careful, Al,' he urged.

'I know. But what if they want to make an example of me? I'm the one that got away – for years . . .' Etienne could picture Alex's face. The furrow of worry between his eyebrows. The clenched set of his jaw.

'Don't think about that,' Etienne said. 'Focus on doing the next right thing.'

'Which is?' Alex sounded panicked.

'You find out how they want the money.' Etienne spoke calmly, keeping his own fear tucked away. He was still £10K short. 'Then I get it to you.'

'What if they find me first?' Alex's voice was just above a whisper.

Etienne stood up again, made his voice strong, authoritative.

'Nobody knows where you are,' he said. 'It will be fine.'

Silence.

'Al, trust me. Keep your nerve. How will they contact you?'

'The landlord gave them my number. That was two days ago apparently. Nothing yet.'

'They're playing with you, Al. Trying to make you sweat.'

Alex gave a shaky laugh. 'It's working,' he said.

'Let me know when you hear from them,' Etienne said. 'Day or night, I'll be here.' He closed his eyes as he said the words, conscious of the irony. If he'd been there day and night for him in the past, Alex wouldn't be in this predicament now.

'I will, bro,' Alex said. 'Thanks.'

As Etienne was about to hang up, Alex spoke again.

'You have got the money for me, though, Et?'

Etienne rubbed his face roughly.

'Nearly there, mate. Nearly there.'

Chapter Thirty-Five

Isabella

Girl Gang WhatsApp group

Rosie: Anyone fancy Story Stars tonight?

Wren: Fox is reading so the yummy mummies will be here.

Amber: Can't. Am training the squad on card machines.

Isabella: Can't. Am doing my food hygiene certificate online with Nonna.

Rosie: Jesse gone?

Isabella: Jesse flew to Paris for a meeting.

Rosie: Gabi gone too?

Isabella: Gabi went to America to free dive through a cave for a celebrity advert where the celebrity can't actually swim.

Rosie: Shame. Etienne and Walker might pop in too . . . Sure you can't make it?

Wren: We all know what too much work and no play makes . . .

Isabella: Yes. A successful restaurant. 😊

Amber: Well said, sister.

Isabella put the phone down with a sigh and a twinge of regret that she couldn't join them. She hadn't seen anything of Etienne since he saw a lot of her in the cloakroom. And that was fine, because she'd been more focused and more driven and had slept better than she had in weeks, maybe months, since their mind-blowing non-sex.

He was the first person to touch her since Daniel. She had never thought of her married sex life as boring. They'd had a regular sex life, maybe twice or three times a week. Of course, she knew now that while she might have been having sex twice or three times a week, he was having it a lot more. But she'd been content. The sex was good. Maybe a bit routine, but good. But now, having been touched and turned and tweaked by Etienne, she thought maybe it had been a bit . . . pedestrian. Run-of-the-mill. A bit, dare she say . . . missionary. Daniel had never, and would never, think about pressing her to the wall in a cloakroom. He would wait until they got home and had locked the door and gone upstairs to bed. 'More comfortable,' she could hear him saying.

She'd not texted Etienne since that night, almost a week ago. She wanted to ration herself. Only give in when her sexual appetite really needed satisfying. That way, the rest of the time she could focus on what mattered. The restaurant.

It had been a productive week. She'd applied for her premises licence and personal licence so that she could sell alcohol. She'd scheduled a date for the Environmental Health Department inspection. She'd registered her food business and smiled at the sight of it in black and white. *Tutto Mio Restaurant. Proprietor Ms Isabella Tucci.*

But the paperwork that went with it seemed never-ending and Isabella had to steel herself to stay focused and plough through endless sections on hygiene, allergens and food storage. Before she reached the end, Nonna nudged her hard in the ribs and she realised she was asleep.

When they'd started the course after lunch, she could hear Amber whooping downstairs every now and then, when another member of the team managed a successful transaction on the card machine. She wished she had something as exciting to do up in the flat now that might keep her awake. She knew *one* thing that would keep her awake, but she was trying not to think about him.

She refocused her eyes and her efforts; half an hour later she punched the air as she closed her laptop.

'Done!' she said.

'Wondered what was taking you so long,' said Nonna and Isabella realised she'd already finished and was now playing online poker.

Isabella stood and stretched, feeling like she used to at uni after pulling an all-nighter. She wanted to go and let off steam.

'Want to go out for dinner, Nonna? Check out the competition?' she asked. Nonna patted her arm as she too closed her laptop.

'Sorry. I'm booked in to tai chi at eight.' She struck a pose, looking at something in the middle distance while lifting one leg in front of her. Isabella wondered where she got the energy.

She checked her watch and remembered Wren's earlier invitation but it was approaching seven; Story Stars would be over.

They'd be closing up and taking Riley home to bed. And Amber would be home with Jayden.

She drummed her fingers on the bar and considered her options. She could go downstairs and find a windowsill that still needed painting. She could luxuriate in a hot bath with a face pack and a hair mask. She could ring Gabi and Jesse and have a long gossipy catch-up. Or she could do what she truly wanted to do, and text Etienne to see if he wanted 'part two'.

Maybe it was the fact she'd been sitting still all day that she felt the need to go and do something wild. Maybe it was because it had been a week without feeling his skin on hers and that was long enough. It wasn't technically sex after all. It was fun. And she deserved it after all the work she'd done that week.

Nonna came back downstairs wearing purple sparkly leggings and a sweatband round her head. She dashed a slick of fuchsia lipstick on as she picked up her house keys and then threw a wave over her shoulder. Isabella listened to the front door close and then lifted her phone.

Isabella: Hi.

No immediate response. She moved to look out the front window across the square, squinting to see if she could see him inside The Bistro. But it was too far away. She could see the lights on, glowing through the windows. Maybe he was busy. And then:

Etienne: Hi. ☺

She grinned to herself and then took the bull by the horns. She'd never put herself out there like this before, but she figured, if you don't ask, you don't get.

Isabella: You free tonight? Thought I could give you your delayed birthday present.

Her stomach lurched at the thought of putting her hands on him. Of finding out what he had in those snug-fitting jeans. She wanted to see him, suck him, taste him. She pressed her thighs together while she waited for the reply.

Etienne: Nice thought but I don't think I need your birthday present tonight.

Isabella slumped in shock. What kind of message was that? He didn't *need* it? Did that mean he'd had his 'needs' fulfilled elsewhere? Of course he must have done. He was the town player after all. She was about to throw the phone onto the sofa when another came through.

Etienne: What I really need is some help!

That stopped her in her tracks. She shrugged, looking around her empty flat, having nothing else to do tonight.

Isabella: What's happening?
Etienne: Can you come to Fox's?
Isabella: Be there in ten.

Etienne opened the door holding George against his chest. The tiny boy's pale face was tear-stained and he refused to look at Isabella. Reggie ran around in the background wearing a pair of pants on his head and chasing Dingbat.

'Welcome to the madhouse.' Etienne's normally perfect waves were stuck up with what looked like peanut butter. 'Come on through.'

The kitchen looked like something had exploded. Water pooled on the floor, the table was covered with half-eaten food and reading books, the sink overflowed with dirty dishes. And a funny smell, almost medicinal, hung in the air.

Dingbat streaked past, something in his mouth. Reggie raced after him, now circling a lasso over his head.

'He has a lot of energy for this time of night?' Isabella said.

'I think I gave him too much sugar . . .' Etienne said, pulling her out of the way of the rope with his free hand as it whistled past her ear.

'Tea?' Etienne asked, patting the back of George's head as he sniffled into his shirt.

'I'll do it,' said Isabella, taking off her coat and rolling up her shirtsleeves. Etienne slumped onto one of the kitchen chairs and adjusted George's position on his lap. George still refused to look at anyone and stuck his head in Etienne's armpit.

Tea made, Isabella took the chair opposite and Etienne took a thirsty slurp.

'Thanks. Don't think I've had a drink all day. Last thing was a coffee before Fox left.'

'Where's he gone?'

'He's gone to see the games investors he's working for. They're in London for a games convention and wanted to see the latest on the extension he's designing.'

'Bit last minute, isn't it?'

Etienne scrunched his nose. 'Abbie from next door was booked to look after the boys but she's gone down with a bug. So, I got a call this morning to see if I could step in.' He rubbed

George's back rhythmically, automatically, and the boy's bottom lip wobbled.

'It was all going fine until George started throwing up everywhere – I think he has the same bug as Abbie.' He tried to look into George's face, but the boy snuggled deeper and turned his head away. 'Not feeling very well, are you, mate?' George closed his eyes and sneaked his thumb into his mouth.

Reggie tore through the kitchen, now wearing a tutu, and this time he had the dog on reins.

'What time is Fox back?' Isabella asked.

'He's not. They've asked him to stay for the dinner later, to meet some of the other investors. I said I'd stay over. I didn't tell him about George or he'd have worried and he needs to be focused on his meeting. It's a big deal.'

He looked around the debris of the kitchen and exhaled apprehensively. George lifted his head for the first time and yawned loudly.

'I could do with some help getting them into bed,' Etienne said with a hopeful look at Isabella. 'I did try Walker but he's on shift. I think this little guy will feel better with a good sleep,' he said with a downward nod at George. 'And then I can set about clearing up.'

Isabella nodded.

'I have no experience of children at all, but hey,' she said optimistically, 'how hard can this be?'

An hour later – after George had thrown up again twice (once down Etienne's shirt), Reggie had demanded four bedtime stories, the dog had eaten the leftover dinner from the plates on the table and Etienne had trodden barefoot on some Lego which resulted in some language that was definitely not child-friendly – they had two boys in bed. George sucked steadfastly on his thumb and his eyelids drooped. Reggie screwed his eyes shut and counted sheep out loud.

They reconvened at the kitchen table, Etienne now wearing one of Fox's checked shirts and limping. Isabella was dazed.

'Are we allowed alcohol now?' Isabella asked. Etienne stumbled to the fridge and held up a beer. She nodded. They clinked bottles together and slumped back in their seats. Etienne glanced around the kitchen.

'I'll sort this out in a minute,' he said, closing his eyes.

'How does he do that every day?' she said.

'And on his own too,' Etienne agreed. 'He's a superman.'

'What happened to his wife?' Isabella asked. 'It never seemed right to ask.'

Etienne opened one eye and pointed at a photo on the edge of the corkboard that Isabella hadn't noticed before. She stood to examine it, the profile shot of lips pressed to Fox's cheek. The happy crinkle of her eyes as she kissed.

'That's Meg,' he said. 'She drove to the local shop for milk one Saturday morning about two weeks after George was born and suffered a brain aneurysm. She drove off the road and hit a tree.'

'How awful.' Isabella slumped back into her kitchen chair, her eyes blurring as she tried to focus on the corkboard. All the happy pictures of Fox and his sons. Everything that Meg was missing out on.

'Walker's crew were called out. It was him that cut her free of the car but she didn't make it into the ambulance. Walker told Fox he was as gentle with her as she died as he had been the first time he held her babies.'

Isabella closed her eyes as that hit home. 'That explains why they are so close.'

'I met Fox about a week after she'd died. He was a real mess. Not surprisingly.'

'And you've not left him since,' Isabella said.

'Never.'

'Do you think he'll ever move on?' Isabella turned to face him.

'Maybe one day,' Etienne said. 'In his own time.'

Isabella's heart hurt for Fox. Bringing up the boys alone.

'He's lucky to have you,' she said, a break in her voice.

'I'm the lucky one.' Etienne swore, his eyes fierce.

The moment lengthened. Her stomach somersaulted as she held the look, thinking about her earlier message. He wet his full lower lip and she wondered if he was thinking the same thing. Even with food in his hair and bags under his eyes, he was still the sexiest man she'd ever met. The house around them was silent. Etienne's eyebrow raised. Was this it? Part two?

'Uncle Et . . .' George stood in the doorway, with dinosaur pyjamas, bare feet and the whitest face she'd ever seen. 'I don't feel so good.'

Etienne stood and was halfway across the kitchen when George projectile vomited. Etienne expertly sidestepped its trajectory and swung the boy into his arms. George's chin wobbled as he started to cry, and Etienne cradled him against his chest.

'Back soon,' Etienne said to Isabella before carrying George back up the stairs to clean him up and sort him out. She could hear him talking gently to the boy, and then the sound of the bath running. She couldn't just sit there, so she found some bleach under the sink and got busy with the mop.

An hour later, the kitchen was sparkling. The front room was tidy and all Lego was back in the box. Dingbat had been fed and was spread out on the hearth, farting. Even the plants had been watered. Still Etienne hadn't reappeared. She watched half an hour of television, and even then, he didn't come back down.

'Etienne!' she stage-whispered from the bottom of the stairs. Nothing. She crept up to the landing and saw the night lights were still on in George's room. Maybe he hadn't got off to sleep yet. She poked her head around the door.

Etienne and George were both in bed. George wore a clean pair of pyjamas and had a touch more colour in his cheeks. Etienne lay beside him wearing yet another of Fox's shirts, snoring lightly, a children's book on his chest. Isabella tiptoed over and switched off the bedside light. Let them sleep. She'd leave them to it and head home.

She pulled the bedroom door to and was on the top step to head down when the other bedroom door opened and Reggie appeared, white like a ghost with shadows under his eyes.

'Isabella,' he groaned, holding his tummy. 'When's Daddy home? I feel a bit sick.'

She moved as fast as she could to get him to the bathroom. It wasn't fast enough.

Chapter Thirty-Six

Etienne

Etienne woke with George poking his fingers up his nose. He snorted, or sneezed, and George dissolved into a fit of giggles. He was practically sitting on Etienne's head.

'What are you doing in my bed, Uncle Et?' George said as Etienne pulled himself up to lean on the headboard, pushing a hand through his hair. It snagged on something sticky which smelled of peanuts.

'I must have fallen asleep,' Etienne said, stretching.

'And why are you wearing Daddy's shirt?' George ran his fingers over the fabric.

'Because you – YOU . . .' Etienne said, grabbing the boy and tickling him hard, 'got sick all over me!'

George squealed and wriggled out of his grasp. He slid off the bed saying, 'Oops, sorry about that!' As he widened his eyes apologetically, George looked so much like Fox that Etienne had to laugh.

He ran a hand over his face, scratching his stubble, then

checked his watch, wondering how much sleep he'd had. It had been a mad, crazy day yesterday. Thank God for Isabella who had been brilliant. He couldn't remember exactly what time it was when Isabella went home . . . Wait. He sat bolt upright. *Had* she gone home?

The last thing he could in fact remember was lying on the bed with George in fresh pyjamas after his bath, to read him a quick bedtime story. He'd thought it would only be a minute and he could slip off and leave him to it, go back downstairs and clear up. And then, he might have helped himself to a slice of Isabella if she was still on the menu. He remembered the look between them. The promise. But he must have fallen asleep. He threw the Power Rangers duvet off and sprang out of bed, taking the stairs two at a time. George sat on his bottom and bumped down behind him.

Dingbat nearly wagged his tail off to see him in the kitchen and stood pointedly in front of his doggie bowl. Etienne threw him a handful of dog biscuits and then turned in wonder on the spot. It was unrecognisable from the ruins of yesterday. The kitchen was gleaming. The washing-up was dry on the rack. The table was scrubbed. The floor was immaculate. No signs of playtime or mealtime or worse. He definitely needed to message Isabella and thank her. He hadn't expected this.

'Can I have my tablet time now, please?' George asked, pointing at the iPad, and Etienne nodded, relieved to see the boy looking so much better.

'Go get comfy then and I'll bring us some breakfast,' Etienne said, lifting the front of the bread bin to explore the contents. George plodded off, already navigating to his cartoons on the screen.

As Etienne had delivered his mini-master a plate of hot bagels and jam, he noticed the Lego boxes cleared away and the reading books stacked back on the shelf. He reached for his phone; he should message Isabella. She'd done so much. He cringed at the thought of being asleep while she cleared up. She must be livid. He heard a creak overhead from Reggie's room and pocketed his phone again. It would have to wait. He needed to think of the right words. He'd do it once he was home.

Taking the stairs two at a time again, he headed along the landing to Reggie's room. Pushing open the door, he stopped dead in his tracks. Reggie was sitting up in bed, both fists rubbing the sleep out of his eyes, hair flat on one side. And Isabella was sleeping on a bunch of cushions on the floor, wearing yet another of Fox's checked shirts.

Reggie blinked his eyes open, frowned at Etienne and pointed at Isabella.

'Why is she on my floor?' he asked loudly, and Isabella pulled herself upright groggily, immediately looking towards his bed.

'Feeling better, Reggie?' she asked and he nodded happily. 'That's good.'

She crossed her legs and stretched before spotting Etienne and attempting a laugh. Her hair was wild, her mouth was sleep-swollen, and her bare legs peeked out under Fox's shirt. Etienne exhaled slowly. The things he wanted to do to her.

'Breakfast?' he asked instead. Reggie tumbled out of bed and ran whooping down the stairs.

An hour later, Reggie was dressed and fed. George was dressed apart from his joggers, which he had put on the dog. All three of them were playing happily in the front room. Isabella sat at the breakfast table with her legs tucked under herself, nibbling toast.

'Quite a night, eh?' Etienne said as a starter.

'When I heard that everyone wanted to spend the night with you, I don't think this was quite what they were imagining.'

He spread his arms to take in the kitchen. 'I do want to thank you, though. The clean-up was amazing. But staying with Reggie when he was sick was above and beyond.'

'Didn't seem fair to leave, you'd have two of them on your hands,' she said, pushing her plate away. 'Think it's put me off my food, though.' He nodded. He knew the feeling. He'd only managed coffee himself.

'So, we'll have to replan the giving of the birthday present,' he said and she lifted her head in surprise.

'You can't be talking about that with me looking like this, sitting here covered in vomit and just out of bed.' She laughed self-consciously.

'Oh, believe me, I can.' He saw the colour hit her cheeks and his dick hardened. Today might not be the day, but he couldn't wait much longer.

A key in the lock and the front door opened. Fox staggered in, hair more tousled than ever. One of his shirt buttons was done up wrong and he looked decidedly hungover.

'Daddy!' The boys hit his legs like mini tornadoes, nearly taking him out.

'Go gently with me, boys, I'm a broken man,' he whispered, which only seemed to work in reverse as they climbed up his legs. He gave in, kneeling to hug them both in the hall before dragging himself through to the kitchen. The boys followed. In the doorway, Fox looked first at Etienne and then eyed Isabella, both wearing his shirts.

'What is this? Fancy dress? Let me guess, you've both come as me?'

Isabella tugged her shirt down a bit lower. Etienne pushed his sleeves up.

'I was sick on Uncle Et!' George said proudly.

'And I was sick on Isabella!' Reggie said, pushing out his pigeon chest. 'Twice!'

Fox whipped his head from one boy to the other.

'Uncle Et slept in my bed,' George said. 'He snored LOUD!' He started snoring impressions to demonstrate.

'Isabella didn't snore,' Reggie said, considering. 'Maybe it was because she was on my bedroom floor.'

Fox turned wide eyes to Etienne for clarification. Etienne and Isabella both nodded.

'Oh God. You should have called me!'

'Never,' Etienne said. 'I called in reinforcements.' He nodded at Isabella, who saluted Fox with her coffee cup. 'How was the meeting?' Etienne continued. Dingbat barked in the garden and the boys ran out to play.

Fox collapsed into a chair and rubbed his face.

'The meeting was good,' he said. 'In fact, *brilliant*. The investors like the extension and they think it's going to be big. Let's hope they're right.' 'Big' in Fox's gaming world meant big money. Big advances for new games and big payouts on sales. It could change his life. And that of the boys.

'So, what did you have to stay on for?'

'Dinner and schmoozing,' Fox answered, averting his eyes. 'Nice food, lots of drinks. Probably too many.'

'Did that go okay too?' Isabella asked, pushing him a cup of coffee.

Fox considered for a moment. He cleared his throat. 'It went *surprisingly well*.' He stirred sugar into his coffee, not making eye contact. 'Unexpectedly so.'

With a quick glance out the kitchen window at the boys racing in the garden, he tapped his teaspoon on the side of his mug three times, as though to make an announcement. Etienne raised an eyebrow, Isabella leaned in.

'I had a one-night stand,' Fox whispered across the table. Etienne choked on his coffee, and Fox reached over to slap him on the back. 'I know, mate. I'm as shocked as you are about it.'

He looked it too. His face was hungover and tired and happy and . . . worried?

'Well, we all knew the day would come.'

'Makes me feel strange, though, you know? Like the end of an era.' He glanced at the photograph on the corkboard of Meg.

'Meg would want you to live your life, Fox,' Etienne said quietly. Fox shrugged but didn't look convinced.

'Will you bump into the woman again then? Was she part of the investment team?'

'No.' He laughed. 'She was a demonstrator. They bring in gamers to show the investors how they work. She was playing my game.' He raised an eyebrow. 'Pretty good she was at it, too.' Fox sipped his coffee and added a fourth sugar.

Etienne laughed. He'd never considered game playing skills

as high on his list of traits he found attractive. Fox obviously rated it highly.

'What was she like?' Isabella asked, elbows on the table, hands under her chin. Etienne laughed again – a typical girl question. It was a one-night stand, what more did Isabella need to know? But Fox answered.

'Funny. Curvy. Long red hair. And a tongue piercing.'

Isabella smiled, as though enjoying the attention to detail. 'So, you liked her then?'

Fox paused, as though coming to a realisation.

'Yeah. She made me laugh.'

Isabella straightened up now, excited.

'So will you see her again?' she asked. 'Have you got her number?'

Fox scratched his head, screwed up his face and then shook his head.

'Truth be told, I panicked this morning when I woke up. I left her sleeping in my hotel room, and caught the early train back to Honeybridge.'

'But it was fun while it lasted,' Etienne encouraged, and Fox agreed.

'It was the best "fun" I've had in years.' He made quote marks around his words, laughing at himself.

Isabella squirmed in her seat and Etienne glanced at her. Surely she couldn't be offended by sex talk? Not with the package she'd put on the table for him? She seemed to know exactly what she wanted, and how to get it.

Her chair screeched on the floor as she stood up. Etienne saw that she was deathly pale. Her stomach made a noise that was audible on his side of the table. Fox looked horrified as she groaned and immediately slapped her hand over her mouth. She sprinted to the downstairs toilet and was the first person in the house in the last twenty-four hours to make it in time.

That night:

Etienne: Are you feeling any better?

Isabella: I feel like death.

Etienne: I feel guilty.

Isabella: So you should.

Etienne: If it makes you feel better, I'm throwing up too.

Isabella: Strangely, that does give me some comfort.

Etienne: Feel better soon.

Isabella: You too.

Chapter Thirty-Seven

Isabella

Etienne: Are you free to meet tonight? I'd like to buy you a drink to say thank you for your help with the boys.

Isabella: I'd love to . . . but I can't. Cocktail and mocktail team training tonight at Tutto Mio.

Etienne: Shame, I was looking forward to thanking you. Personally.

Isabella: You could come and join us. The girl gang will be here. Bring the boys.

Etienne: Sounds crowded.

Isabella: Stay late.

Etienne: Sounds better.

Isabella: I want to see how good you are at saying thank you.

Isabella dressed to impress. Her hair tumbled down her back and she left the third button undone on her silky blouse, tucked into her jeans. She exuded almost as much nervous energy as the team did, buzzing around behind the new wooden bar setting out bottles and glasses. Amber pulled a collection of stools and chairs together around a temporary card table in the middle of the restaurant floor. Naomi followed her and placed a hand-written drinks menu in front of each place. Isabella waited for Amber to give her the nod and then opened the restaurant door to the others for the first time.

Wren and Rosie were first. Rosie wore milkmaid plaits and Wren's red hair was in her usual sleek topknot. They scanned the room, admiring the new paintwork and vintage wooden floorboards. Walker acknowledged the new sprinkler system and fire alarm with an approving nod, Fox came in talking to the babysitter on the phone and Etienne strolled in last looking completely edible. Although they'd been sexting, she hadn't seen him since the babysitting night and now her desire hit her full force. He looked fresh from the shower, his hair still damp where it curled at his neck, and his black jeans emphasised long, muscular thighs. Definitely time for another serving, surely?

Isabella shook her hair back and felt her lower stomach tighten as she watched him survey her restaurant. Tutto Mio was so different to The Bistro, more whitewashed and stripped-back aesthetic than soft lighting and cosy corners. Although she wouldn't mind getting him into one of those cosy corners right now.

Rosie grasped her arm and brought her back into the moment.

'You've done so much in here! I wouldn't recognise it.'

'Yes, it looks so much better,' Fox said, laughing, a take met with a general murmur of assent.

'Grab yourself a seat,' Amber said, 'and let me talk you through the drinks menu.' Isabella aimed for the seat next to

Etienne but was surprised when he scooted into the gap between Fox and Walker.

Amber ran through the list of cocktails and mocktails, encouraging everyone to order something different to give the team as much practice as possible.

'So, what's first then?'

Fox ordered a Black Russian and Etienne asked for an Old-Fashioned. Walker asked for a gin and tonic and everyone did a fancy 'oooooh'.

Rosie and Wren turned to the mocktails, choosing an Orange Sunrise and a Berry Burst.

Isabella ordered a Kir Royale. Gazing across the table at Etienne, what she wanted was sex on the beach. Or bar. Or floor. And nothing to do with the drink. Etienne was unaware of her gaze now, though, as he listened to Walker next to him, rubbing the short stubble of his facial hair in concentration.

'We've not had a run like it ever before,' Walker said. 'I wonder if the next shift will have a quieter time.'

'What's happened?' Rosie asked him, leaning in.

'We've had a few house fires recently – more than normal,' Walker said. 'Over the past four days we've had two, and last shift we had another one. It's a lot for this area. If we were in a busy city, I could understand it.'

The first round of drinks arrived, the team placing them gently in front of the right person and stepping back to watch the first reactions.

'To Tutto Mio,' Isabella said, lifting her Kir Royale and admiring the blackberry sitting on the side of the glass. Nice touch.

'Tutto Mio,' everyone repeated before sipping. The team held its collective breath until various appreciative noises and nods ensued. Isabella glanced Etienne's way, but he was studiously appreciating his drink.

'So how many house fires would you normally deal with each week?' Rosie asked, turning back to Walker.

'Sometimes none at all.' Walker shrugged. 'Normally we are busy with road traffic accidents, or cats in trees. But we seem to be having a spate of them. The weird thing is that the neighbouring county is experiencing the same thing.'

'That's quite a coincidence,' Etienne said.

'Is it arson? Or accident?' Wren asked, sipping her Orange Sunrise through a straw.

'That's what we're trying to ascertain. We're sending in the investigative team.'

'That's worrying.' Fox frowned. 'I need to check my smoke alarms.'

'I did it last week when you were in the garden with George. Replaced the batteries in the downstairs one,' Walker said and Fox fist bumped him across the table.

'Lifesaver.'

The Kir Royale was the first alcohol Isabella had drunk since the beer at Fox's on babysitting duty. She'd hardly eaten for the last two days and was only now starting to feel back to normal. She sipped and let the alcohol ease out her tensions. Although it only seemed to add to the sexual tension she felt, rather than relieve it. She flicked her eyes at him but he was seemingly deep in study of the menu.

'Next orders,' Amber called and choices were made. Rosie and Wren again ordered from the mocktail side of the menu.

'You two got an early start?' Fox asked.

'Not particularly.' Wren shrugged.

'Simply being helpful and trying the menu,' Rosie chipped in.

The next round came and this time, the team member announced the name of their drink before they set it down. Another nice touch. Amber was doing a great job in training them. The only problem was Australian Angie's pronunciation of the word Caipirinha sounded more like 'cup of piranha' but apart from that, all went well. Conversation was flowing now, two cocktails in. Isabella reached for the water jug as Etienne did the same and her hand brushed his, the tiniest touch, and their eyes met across the table. She drew her hand back as though she'd been burned and felt the touch all the way inside her as Etienne told everyone how and why Isabella and he each had one of Fox's shirts in their laundry bins at home.

'Thank God I was on shift,' Walker said and everyone laughed.

Fox admitted his one-night stand to the group, and blushed when Rosie moved around the table to give him a hug.

'Oh Fox,' she said softly, 'I bet that's brought up a whole heap of emotions.' He nodded and moved around so she could take the seat next to him, still holding his hand. Etienne slid, at last, into the seat next to Isabella. She let her elbow press against his on the table, wanting the contact, needing it. He jerked away. She threw a confused glance in his direction but he was intent on the one-night stand conversation.

'Was she nice, though?' Wren asked.

Fox thought for a second. 'She was great,' he said.

'Start thinking about your next orders!' Amber instructed, poking the page.

'I'll get some snacks to soak up the alcohol,' Isabella said, pushing herself to standing and staring at Etienne directly.

'I'll help you,' said Etienne, which drew a quick side-eye from Rosie and a raised eyebrow from Wren, but luckily nothing was said as he followed her to the kitchen.

He let the door swing shut behind him. She pulled open the new shiny fridge and began rummaging, transferring bowls to the worktop and moving jars and sauces.

'You could always be my snack?' he said quietly, and she laughed in relief, catching the glint in his eyes.

'Not yet,' she said. 'But I can be dessert.' Nodding her head towards their friends in the restaurant, she continued, 'Thought you were avoiding me out there.'

'Only because I don't trust myself to keep my hands off you.'

She looked at him under her eyelashes, feeling exactly the same.

'Patience is a virtue, Etienne,' she said teasingly and passed him a bowl. 'Can you sort the olives?'

'Hmmmm.' He laughed and gave in, washing his hands before he began decanting different types of olives and arranging breadsticks. She grabbed the other snacks she'd prepared earlier. Strawberries, plump and red, with a smooth chocolate sauce for dipping. Homemade ice cream in individual portions, gleaming white with purple marbling. She turned to find him watching her.

'Ready?' she asked.

'Always,' he said.

'Only fair to give you a taste,' Isabella said. 'A little something to keep you going.'

His eyes glinted with interest.

She swiped one of the strawberries from the top of the display and dipped it in the smooth sauce. She twirled it in her fingers and then lifted it to his mouth, first letting just the tip enter so he could taste the chocolate. Then, pushing the whole fruit into his mouth for him to bite into. He closed his eyes to swallow his mouthful and made a noise in his throat which was so sexual she missed a breath.

'Come on,' she said, suddenly aware of the hum of conversation next door. 'The rest is for later.'

The third round was ordered and Rosie and Wren again chose from the non-alcoholic page.

'I can try a mocktail next time if you fancy a drink?' said Fox. 'I've got to be up early anyway.'

Rosie glanced sideways at Wren, who grinned and bit her lip.

'What's going on?' Isabella asked.

The two women looked at each other, hesitant smiles lighting their faces. Isabella saw Wren reach for Rosie's hand under the table.

'We thought we might try for another baby,' Rosie blurted with an excited wiggle.

Amber whooped from the bar, obviously listening in.

'That's so exciting!' Isabella said, clasping her hands together. Trying to ignore the fact that Etienne's thumb was brushing against her thigh under the table.

'Riley will be four soon and will be in school come next September. So, we could devote time to the baby,' Wren said.

'So, we talked to Toby about it and he was keen . . .'

'So, why are you both drinking mocktails then?' Fox asked.

'We thought we'd do it differently this time. With Riley, it was Wren's egg and my womb,' Rosie said.

'This time, we're going to try Rosie's egg and my womb.' Wren and Rosie only had eyes for each other. Wren bit her lip hopefully. Rosie crossed her fingers. Everyone clinked glasses.

During the last round everyone had a mocktail, apart from Walker who was starting his four days off and was making the most of it. Everyone else had to be up early or had babysitters to get back to. As everyone sipped, Etienne started to stroke Isabella's thigh under the table, and she fought to keep her face composed. By eleven, the team took a bow to a round of applause and left, congratulating each other with high fives and hugs. There'd been no breakages and no mistakes. Amber seemed to sag with relief.

Fox invited Walker back to his house to play the latest stage of his game and Rosie and Wren offered Amber a lift home, which she gratefully accepted, looking beat on her feet. Etienne nodded towards the chaos on the bar, the crushed fruit, the empty bottles and dirty glasses.

'I'll help you clear up,' he said to Isabella.

Isabella bit her lip as she locked the door and turned off the main lights. Her stomach was hollow with anticipation. It was just her and Etienne.

Etienne had already rolled his sleeves up and was stacking glasses in the dishwasher as fast as was humanly possible. She moved behind the bar next to him and began to clear the top. Standing so close, she could smell his scent.

'I think your restaurant is going to be good competition,'

he said, shutting the door and programming the front to start the cycle.

'Do you think you can handle it?' she said, wishing the only thing he would handle was her.

'I like a competition,' he said, turning to face her. There was only a foot between them and she caught her breath. His eyes darkened. Her nipples throbbed.

'It's just a game,' he murmured, letting his eyes skim over her body. 'And you know I like to play.' His eyes glinted, and the air felt charged between them.

Suddenly he was on her, his mouth devouring hers. His tongue pushed into her mouth, his hands on her arse to pull her closer, to hold her tight against him. She could feel the heat of his erection pressing against her stomach through his jeans and knew he was as turned on as she was.

Etienne pulled away and they faced each other, chests heaving. She blinked, unsure as to why he'd stopped. He raised an eyebrow and lifted an ice cube from the bucket beside him. It glinted in the half-light. As he held it between his thumb and forefinger, a drip ran down his hand. Slowly, ever so slowly, he reached out and touched it to her mouth, letting it pull the lower lip as he moved it over her chin and down the side of her neck. She shivered. The ice left a trail of goosebumps behind on her exposed skin, but it felt as though he were touching her with fire.

He undid the buttons on her blouse with the other hand and the ice cube followed, sliding between Isabella's breasts and then over the lace of her bra, tormenting her. Her breath hitched and she pressed towards him, drawing a lazy smile to his face – but he wasn't in a hurry. Propping her back against the bar, he ran the ice around her waist and then into her navel and she gasped. Etienne undid her belt, her jeans, and she spread her arms out on the bar beside her as he pushed his hand, ice first, into her knickers. She moaned and his mouth claimed hers again, his tongue and fingers working to the same rhythm, as he rubbed what was left of the ice cube against the hottest part of her body. It was exquisite. And then she was coming and coming and coming, Etienne holding her up with his body as she fell apart.

As soon as Isabella opened her eyes again, she took control, running her hands under Etienne's shirt, feeling the broad muscles in his back and then up and over his chest. His hands massaged her breasts, but she was not to be distracted this time. She tugged at his belt, undid his jeans and finally put her hands on him. She ran her hands along his length, feeling him leap under her fingers. She selected a cube of ice and dropped to her knees behind the bar. His hands found her head, fingers twining into her hair.

Inch by inch she uncovered him. His head glistening already, shaft throbbing. She could hardly circle him with her fingers and her mouth watered in anticipation as she parted her lips to take him in. Looking up, she saw Etienne's eyes closed, his mouth open, a look of fierce concentration on his face. She slipped the ice cube into her own mouth and felt the delicious chill of it. She took him in again, deep, hearing his gasp at the sensation. She moaned onto his cock and watched him throw his head back. She held on to his muscular thighs and ran her fingers up and down, all the while maintaining her rhythm, feeling the power she had over him. Etienne's hands slowly tightened in her hair and he began to move too, increasing the pace, pushing himself deeper, and she closed her eyes, matching him move for move until he growled and came, and she tasted him deep in her throat.

There was a knock at the door. They froze. Isabella, still on her knees, pushed her boobs back in and zipped up her jeans. Etienne tucked himself away behind the privacy of the bar. There was another knock, this time on the window.

'Can you see anyone?' Isabella asked from the floor.

Etienne nodded.

'A woman wearing a pink bandana. She's waving at me.' He lifted an arm and waved back tentatively.

'Omigod! Nonna!' Isabella exclaimed, scrambling to her feet to see her grandmother outside, hands pressed up against the glass. She ran across to open the door.

'*Ciao, bella*,' Nonna said, giving Isabella's cheek a pinch. 'I must have left my keys upstairs.' She turned her attention to Etienne. 'Are you the new barman?'

Etienne laughed. 'No, although I am pretty good behind the bar.' Never a truer word. Isabella felt the heat on her neck as she introduced him as the owner of The Bistro.

'Nice to meet you, Etienne,' Nonna said. 'Now I need to go up. I have a meeting tomorrow with a meat supplier. Then I'm joining the gym.'

She headed towards the stairs that led to the flat. When she was behind Etienne and he couldn't see her, she widened her eyes at Isabella and did a silent chef's kiss.

Chapter Thirty-Eight

Etienne

The smile was still on Etienne's face a few mornings later as he made his way to Honeybridge Primary School for his promised cookery lesson. He'd been grinning like a Cheshire cat since that night at Tutto Mio and was already looking forward to his next no-sex session with Isabella. It was more fun than he'd ever imagined. Not exactly a one-night stand, but definitely not a relationship. Maybe friends with benefits? Whatever it was, he was enjoying it. Not even a wet and windy morning could take the edge off. He threw a scarf around his neck, picked up his bags of ingredients and set off.

However, his good mood was ruined when his phone rang en route to the school and his bank manager told him politely that his application for a loan had been declined. His shoulders slumped with the weight of it. So, he still had to find almost ten thousand pounds. And quickly. He sighed and then checked himself. Time to put on a happy face again for Reggie's class.

The receptionist tucked an imaginary hair behind her ear and wet her lips before speaking.

'How can I help?' she said, hopefully.

'I'm Etienne Martin,' he said to the woman, who obviously knew who he was already. 'I'm here to teach Year Two some cooking.' He lifted the two carrier bags he was carrying to show her his ingredients. He was excited to see Reggie's face in class.

'Oh,' the woman said, looking flustered, and checking the registration book in front of her. 'That's strange . . .' She ran her finger down the sheet and stopped on an entry. 'It seems someone else is also here to do the same thing.' She nodded her head to the waiting area where Etienne turned to see Isabella, surrounded also by shopping bags and scrolling on her phone, her cheeks blown pink from the wind. She sensed the attention and lifted her head, raising a hand to her lips when she spotted him. He remembered the feel of them wrapped around his dick. He smiled. She blushed. The receptionist buzzed up to the classroom and a moment later the Year Two teacher, Mr Brady, appeared, apologising for his mistake.

'Seems I've invited you both in for the same date,' he flapped. 'You were meant to be a week apart.'

He twiddled his tie, thinking.

'We could reschedule one of you if you like? I'm so sorry for the confusion.'

Etienne looked at Isabella questioningly. She looked torn.

'I won't be able to come back next week – we're so close to opening and there is so much to do.'

The teacher turned hopefully to Etienne.

'I *could* come back, but I've done all the prep . . .' He opened one of the large Tupperware boxes he was carrying and showed them a fresh batch of bread dough. 'You wanted me to cook something from France and so I thought French bread would be perfect.'

'And I've got a lot of fresh ingredients too,' said Isabella, indicating her bags, 'for pizza toppings. You wanted something from Italy.' The three of them looked at each other, unsure of how to proceed.

Etienne looked from the teacher to Isabella, who was the sexiest school cooking teacher he'd ever seen. She had her hair in one of those messy buns that made it look like she'd just got out of bed. That's how she'd look when they could finally get into bed together. It was that image that put the next thought in his mind.

'How about we do it together?' Etienne asked Isabella. 'We make French stick pizzas.'

'Your bread, my toppings?' she asked with the beginning of a smile. He could tell she wanted to laugh. He was fascinated by her mouth. The last time he'd seen her . . . He shook himself. Get it together, man.

'It's a cultural mash-up,' he said.

'It's a food fiasco,' she countered.

'It's a testament to French–Italian relations,' the teacher said, leading the way down the corridor. 'Brace yourselves,' he warned as he threw open the door to thirty excited children.

Mr Brady led them to the front of the class and for the first time Etienne felt a slight hint of nerves as thirty curious children stared back at him.

'So, children, let's give a Honeybridge Primary welcome to

Mr Martin and Ms Tucci, who are going to teach you something about France and Italy.'

The children all clapped politely, and Etienne relaxed a bit. How hard could this be? He scanned the crowd for Reggie and saw him moving his chair to be in front of Isabella. Obviously, her nursing skills the week before had formed a bond for them. He caught himself momentarily imagining Isabella in a nurse's outfit.

'Before we start, and while Chef Etienne gets himself organised,' Isabella said, pulling a stack of white paper out of her bags, 'I need all my chefs to wash their hands and put on their hats.' She demonstrated how to make a hat, literally taping the white paper into a tube wide enough to put on her head. He liked the way her tongue poked from the corner of her mouth as she concentrated. 'And put your names on the front, so that we know who you are.' Thirty kids got busy, and five minutes later everyone was in place at their table.

Etienne gave each pair of children a lump of dough and explained that he'd made it in advance so that it could prove.

'Prove what?' someone shouted.

'That it's bread?' someone else asked.

'Now you need to shape it into a French bread stick.'

Sticky fingers got to work forming baguettes. Etienne worked his way around the tables, and smiled to see Isabella kneel to assist the only girl who didn't have a partner.

'Now, while they cook we're going to learn some French,' Etienne said, closing the oven door. He saw Isabella look up. He hadn't imagined doing this in front of her when he'd had this bright idea. He took a deep breath, then began.

'*Bonjour!*' he cried in a sing-song voice, as he marched towards the class, and they all sang it back to him. Then he turned his back and pretended to walk away. '*Au revoir!*' he sang, waving over his shoulder. '*Au revoir!*' they chorused back.

He did it again, and one by one, the children jumped to their feet to join in. Isabella stood too, holding hands with the girl, and Etienne saw Reggie claim her other hand. Poor kid, he obviously had it bad. By the time the bread had risen and Etienne cut the French sticks in half lengthways so that each child had a pizza base, the whole room was marching up and down, including Mr Brady.

'Now, for the main event – Italian pizza!' Isabella took her turn at the front of the class. 'You can all choose your toppings.' She showed the children the range she had available: tomato, cheese, ham, olives, pepperoni. 'Think about making it tasty and good-looking at the same time.'

Etienne did a double take. Had she winked at him? In a classroom? Reminding him that she had in fact tasted him? He shook himself. Surely not?

Ten minutes later, the pizzas were put back in the oven.

Isabella shushed the class and they all sprang to attention. How come they all sat up like that for her?

'Now, what do you know about Italy?' she asked and a dozen hands shot up. She pointed to a girl on a nearby table.

'You like ice cream!' she said. Isabella nodded.

'We do,' she said. 'We call it *gelato*.'

'You have a tower that fell over,' said a boy with his finger up his nose.

'The Leaning Tower of Pisa,' she said with a laugh. 'It's not fallen over yet!' Half the class stood up to lean over, balancing on one leg.

'You like pizza.'

'We *invented* pizza,' she corrected.

The timer went off and the pizzas came out and Etienne pitied the parents that would be eating those germ-covered creations that night. But the children were hyped, proud of their creations, pointing out their toppings to each other. As Mr Brady stood up to thank them for coming, Etienne exhaled slowly, feeling like he'd just finished a ten-mile run. Isabella on the other hand looked like she'd just opened a present at Christmas.

By the time they'd packed up their bags, the class was putting on coats to go out to break. Etienne spotted Reggie as he ran out the door.

'*Au revoir*, Reggie,' he called.

'*Ciao*, Uncle Et,' Reggie replied with a backward wave.

Isabella snorted.

'Traitor,' Etienne growled.

Chapter Thirty-Nine

Isabella

Isabella knew she was going to the community meeting under false pretences. Yes, of course she wanted to support the fire service safety briefing, but what she wanted more was to set eyes on Etienne. And hands, if at all possible.

The community centre was standing room only when she arrived. A quick scan had her heart sinking: Etienne wasn't there. But she spotted Wren and Rosie and wove her way through the crowd to stand with them, saying hello and waving to a surprising number of people on the way. Honeybridge was really starting to feel like home.

The fire crew were on a stage decked out with a pumpkin display, Walker standing to one side. As the church bells outside chimed seven, the hall doors were closed and Walker picked up the microphone.

'Good evening, Honeybridge, and thank you, everyone, for coming to this community meeting.'

The crowd settled. Isabella undid her coat and noticed Etienne slide in through the door and close it quietly behind him again. His hair was windswept and his cheeks flushed from rushing. All in all, very distracting. She shook herself mentally and focused on Walker, who started to speak.

'Working with neighbouring authorities and the police force, we are investigating a spate of fires locally in both domestic and business premises that we wanted to bring to your attention.'

The word 'business' grabbed her attention. Walker had mentioned the house fires the other night, but not said anything about businesses being affected. Her mind flicked to Tutto Mio and she imagined how devastating it would be to lose it. It didn't bear thinking about.

'Our investigations have shown the fires have been started deliberately, so we are working to assist the police with anything that might help them to catch the arsonists.'

A murmur rippled through the hall. Rosie threaded her fingers through Wren's. Isabella looked over at Etienne but he was on his phone.

'We'd like to ask for your help. Please be on the lookout for any strange or suspicious behaviour and report it immediately. Fire spreads quickly. We can lose a building or business in minutes, so the quicker we get there, the better the chances.'

More anxious whispers and worried looks. Isabella nervously fiddled with a lock of her hair.

'And finally, if any of you would like to schedule a premises check, we would be happy to come out and advise on your fire prevention and safety. We can recommend alarms, monitors and sprinkler services that could make all the difference. Any questions?'

A few hands shot up. Walker pointed at one. 'Yes?'

'Are the cases linked? Or are they random?'

'I'm afraid we don't know the answer to that yet. The police are following up.' He pointed to the next hand. 'Yes?'

'How do we get an appointment for you to come and advise?'

'Speak to one of the crew here.' Walker indicated the team. 'They'll take your details and we'll be in touch.'

'Do you have any fire alarms to give away?'

'We have a moderate fund to help people to buy smoke alarms, if necessary,' the commander said with a nod. 'Of course, we need to make sure they go to those people that need it.'

The community nodded as one.

'Thank you, everyone.' Replacing the microphone on its stand, Walker and the fire crew started to move down the stairs from the stage.

Wren bit her lip and Rosie pulled her in for a hug.

'Walker checked our system last week, you know,' she said.

'I know. It's just all the books. The Lit Lounge would go up in seconds.' Isabella could hear the tension in her voice. Rosie tried a reassuring smile.

'We've got no reason to think we'd be targeted.'

'But if someone likes making fires and they realise what a quick fire our shop would make ...' Wren wrung her hands together. 'What about the cats?'

'Try not to worry,' Rosie said, taking hold of one of those hands she was wringing, and leading her towards the door. 'We've got to try to stay calm.' The three of them threw a wave towards Walker, who was surrounded by a queue of people, and left the hall.

Old Fred Barrow appeared beside them at the exit, and saluted them with a rolled-up newspaper opened on the racing pages.

'Were you lucky today, Fred?' Isabella asked, nodding at his newspaper. He'd circled his hopefuls in red pen. There seemed to be a lot of them. He sucked his false teeth in an expression of disappointment, but then shrugged.

'But tomorrow is another day,' he said, tucking the paper back under his arm.

'I have more maps for you too,' Isabella called as he turned in the direction of Heart of Honeybridge. 'My grandmother brought them with her from Italy for you.'

His face lit up. 'I shall look forward to seeing them, and meeting your grandmother.'

The crowd spilled out into the car park and huddles of people stood chatting, or headed off up the high street. Isabella spotted Etienne ahead, still focused on his phone.

He looked up at that exact moment and she waved, thinking he'd seen her, but he frowned and went back to his screen.

'Hmm,' she said to her friends, feeling strangely let down. 'He can't have seen me.' Rosie threw a strange look at Wren. Isabella stopped walking and put her hand on Rosie's arm. 'What?' she asked. Rosie considered for a second.

'Is everything going okay with your no-sex plan with Etienne?' Rosie asked.

Isabella grinned. 'More than okay as a matter of fact,' she said. 'I can officially confirm that Etienne Martin is incredible at not having sex.' She'd expected them to smile or laugh but instead they swapped another worried look.

'It's just . . . you know it's not more than that, don't you?' Rosie said nervously.

Isabella flinched as they both stared at her, but tried to laugh it off.

'Of course I do,' she said. Of course she did, right?

'Because Etienne doesn't do relationships,' Wren said.

'We love him and all, but he's not the boyfriend type,' Rosie added.

'In all the time we've known him, he's never committed.'

'I truly don't think he has it in him.'

The words were coming thick and fast, tumbling over each other. Isabella held up her hands to stop them speaking, then said, 'That's not an issue, because I don't want him as a boyfriend.'

Her two friends peered into her face, trying to decide if she meant it. 'I don't!' she repeated and laughed. 'All I want from Etienne Martin are orgasms.' They continued to scrutinise her, and Isabella hardly dared move.

'Thank goodness for that,' Rosie eventually said with an exaggerated sigh.

'We were starting to get a bit worried for you. We don't want you to get hurt.'

'We thought we'd seen some feelings—'

'Or a look in your eye—'

'That meant you might be falling for him.'

'Thank *God* you're not.' Wren threw her arm around Isabella's shoulder, and they carried on walking. 'I mean, look at him now, on his phone. Probably on Tinder as we speak.'

Isabella linked her arm with Rosie and let them pull her

along between them, trying to ignore the fact that her mood had soured.

Later that night, she curled up in the window seat she'd created in the bedroom window of her flat. Surrounded by cushions, and lit by scented candles, she would sip her chamomile tea in her cosy place and run through her plans and meetings the next day, mentally packing her bag or planning an outfit. It had become her routine. A ritual.

But as she glanced across the square to The Bistro she finally accepted that it was more than that. It was her last chance of the day to catch sight of Etienne as he closed up. Some nights, she didn't see him at all, only Katie or Mile End Mickey as they left. Other nights, her patience would be rewarded and he might come outside to get some air or look at the stars before heading back inside. And then she'd head off to bed with her phone and that photograph.

She hated to admit it, but Rosie and Wren were right. It wasn't only his sexual prowess she liked. It was him. The full Etienne package.

Now, over the square, she saw the lights go out, without a glimpse of the man himself. Tonight was not her lucky night. She sighed at what she knew deep down. She really liked him.

The feelings had crept up on her. He'd made her laugh at karaoke. She'd seen his softer side with the kids. He'd listened when she told him about Daniel. She was impressed by how much he cared for his friends. He seemed like much, much more than just a player. He'd been a surprise.

But it was a silly crush. And it wasn't going anywhere. She knew that. It wasn't like it was real feelings or anything, was it?

She got up to put her cup in the sink before turning to the calendar, marking the day off with a red cross through it. Ten days until opening. Ten days until her sex ban was over.

Ten days until potentially the end of her no-sex deal with Etienne. And then what? A one-night stand and it would all be over?

She shook herself. Forcing herself to focus on the positives. Ten days to go to smash her goal, to be single and successful.

Suddenly it didn't seem to have the same rousing ring to it.

Chapter Forty

Etienne

After he'd turned out the restaurant lights, Etienne could see Isabella's outline in the window opposite. She often sat there late at night. He thought about waving at her but didn't want her to think he was spying. He snorted at himself. Waving at her across the square, what was that about?

He padded upstairs to the flat, his mind dragging him back to current worries. Ever since the community meeting that evening, he'd been waiting for Alex to get back to him. But however many times he checked his phone, there was nothing. Not since the voicemail that Alex had left earlier saying he had been told to expect a call from the Dougalls. Etienne could hear the fear in his voice.

His phone ringing in his hand made him jump. Alex's name lit up on screen. At last.

'You okay?' he asked even as he accepted the call.

There was a slight pause, a hesitation, before Alex said, 'Yes.'

'You sure?'

Again, the pause. 'I'm sure. But I don't think this is going to be as straightforward as I thought.' Etienne rubbed his hand over his stubble, waiting.

'They want to meet face to face when I hand over the money. And it has to be me.'

'I'll come with you.'

'You can't. It has to be only me.'

A million thoughts rammed Etienne's brain at once. Would they simply take the money and go? He couldn't see it happening. The Dougalls just picking up a suitcase of money and walking away. It wasn't their style. He imagined dark alleyways. Dead end streets. Car headlights in the dark of the woods. Every gangster film stereotype rushed through his mind. Would they beat his brother? A chill ran right through him. Did they want to brand him? Kill him? The silence was so thick, Etienne knew there was something else coming.

'I fucked up, though, Et.'

Alex swallowed anxiously, sounding a million miles away. Etienne could imagine him rubbing his hand through his blond hair like he had done as a kid. When he'd missed a goal, or got caught scratching his name into a desk with a penknife. He waited.

'They were pushing me to deliver it tomorrow at first. They kept saying the price would go up if I didn't. And I panicked and said I couldn't because I had to get it first.' He sighed. 'I had to get it from my brother.'

Etienne froze.

'So, they know I exist then.'

'I'm sorry, bro. I wanted to keep you out of it,' Alex said gruffly. 'It slipped out.'

Etienne's innards contracted but his voice came out strong.

'It doesn't matter. They don't know who I am or where I am. I'm not worried by that. I'm more worried by you meeting them alone.'

The silence the other end said everything that Alex was thinking.

'Did you set a day and location then?'

'Ten days. Place and time to be determined.'

'We'll work it out. This will soon be over.'

'Wish it was sooner,' said Alex. 'It would be good to spend the anniversary together.'

Etienne felt the weight settle on his chest.

'Me too, Al. Me too.'

Chapter Forty-One

Isabella

Isabella looked ahead at her empty calendar that she'd intentionally cleared to focus wholeheartedly on Tutto Mio until opening. Then she turned away with a sigh. That meant no chance of running into Etienne and although that was probably a good thing, her nipples didn't think so.

She glanced at her ridiculously long to-do list; the closer they got to launch day, she only seemed to add items, rather than tick them off.

She'd started her social media posts, steadily building likes and followers and promoting the opening event on TikTok. The most important thing was that people give the restaurant a try. Because hopefully if they tried it once, they'd be back again in the future.

She'd already visited each of her suppliers and now had to put in final orders for meat, vegetables, pastas and condiments. Plus, she needed to get her membership at the local cash and carry for alcohol and stock the bar.

The vintage tables and chairs she had ordered would be arriving in the next few days and she couldn't wait to dress them with candles and flowers.

Menus were at the printer's. Aprons and napkins and tea towels hadn't yet arrived, and she needed to chase the delivery.

The list went on. And on. And on.

Well, at least she had lots to do to keep her mind off a certain French man who was good with his hands.

Nonna was cooking rum biscuits by the tray load. She was always in a good mood after making a batch, probably because she sampled the rum every time.

'Right on time,' Nonna said and pushed the still-hot tray to Isabella.

'Not for me,' said Isabella, shaking her head.

'But they're so good,' said Nonna, reaching for one herself. She took a bite and closed her eyes. '*Bellissima!* Why would you deny yourself pleasure like that?' She set about transferring the biscuits to a cooling tray, helping herself to another sip of rum as she went.

Isabella watched her grandmother thoughtfully as she worked. Perhaps she was right. Why would she want to deny herself pleasure? And she wasn't thinking about biscuits. Even if she had caught a case of the feels for Etienne, that didn't change the deal they currently had on the table. They could enjoy no-sex fun until her sex ban was up. Then, if they had sex and it was of his usual one-night variety, it would be the last time she got to enjoy the pleasure that was Etienne Martin. So, shouldn't she enjoy it as much as she could before then?

She marched back out of the kitchen and up to the window.

The Bistro was closed; it was too early for the lunchtime serving. But it was not too early for the type of snack she had in mind.

Her to-do list could wait. She glanced at herself in the mirror, her shining eyes and full lips smiling back at her. She pulled her hair from its messy bun and let the waves fall down her back.

'See you later, Nonna,' she called back to the kitchen, pulling on her coat and throwing a scarf around her neck. 'Errands to run.' And she meant run too, as she speed walked across the square, one thing and one thing only on her mind.

It wasn't until she got to the door of The Bistro that she saw the taped-up handwritten note there that stopped her in her tracks.

Closed today. Personal circumstances.

She bit her lip. That put a spoke in her plan. Now what? She put her hands to the glass and peered in. There were no lights on but the tables were already dressed for the next sitting. She scanned the room. The restaurant was empty, apart from one person in the corner. Head in hands, with a bottle of red wine in front of them. Etienne.

The feeling inside her flipped to concern. The slump of his shoulders. The wine at this time of the day. He literally looked like a study in sadness. She didn't think about what she was going to do, she just did it. She knocked on the door, loudly.

He lifted his head towards her. She watched indecision cross his face before he stood up and came to open the door, holding the wine bottle by its neck.

'We're closed,' he said flatly.

'I can see that,' she said, indicating the sign. 'I wanted to check' – she paused and nodded at him – 'are you okay?'

'I'm fine, thanks,' he said, starting to close the door again. She leaned on it, propping it open.

'You don't look it,' she said, eyeing the wine bottle in his hands.

'It's for a toast,' he said, defensively. But the bottle was more than half empty already.

'Has something happened?' Isabella asked. 'The sign says personal circumstances . . .' She knew she was being pushy now, but somehow suspected he needed to be pushed.

Etienne blinked at her, then took a swig from the bottle. Suddenly he looked exhausted. He pushed a hand through his hair.

'My parents died,' he said.

Isabella dived inside the door and grasped his arms with both hands. His eyes widened.

'I am so sorry,' she gasped. 'What? When?'

He stepped away, freeing himself from her.

'Five years ago today actually.' Etienne sighed and pressed his mouth together, as though stopping himself from saying anything else.

'God, that must be so hard,' Isabella said, trying to imagine a life where her parents didn't FaceTime her all times of the day and night and get her to show them how she was getting on with the restaurant. The other day, Mamma had even demanded she show her the new sinks they'd had fitted in the ladies' toilets. Even though her parents weren't nearby, they were still a major support, a daily part of her life. Her chest hurt to think about it. She reached out for Etienne's arm again. 'I'm so sorry.'

He sighed and rubbed his hand through his hair.

'Have you not slept?' she asked, as he sank down again at the nearest table. His shirt was crumpled and his stubble longer than usual.

'I've got a lot on my mind.'

'Do you want to talk about it?' She hovered nearby, unsure as to how to help.

'I can't,' he muttered and she heard the worry in it.

'You listened to me, when I was upset about Daniel. I could listen to you,' she said, pulling out a chair and facing him, but he shook his head, not looking at her. She bit her lip. Etienne obviously didn't want to tell her what was bothering him, but it didn't feel right to leave him on his own like this.

'So, you're going to stay in here drinking all day?' she asked and he lifted a surprised face towards her.

'Probably, yes. It's what I do every year to remember them,' he drawled sarcastically.

'Why don't you go to their graves? Are they in France?' she asked and he flinched.

'No, they're in London. In Kensington Cemetery.'

'Why don't you go there then?' she asked simply.

He let his head roll back on his shoulders and closed his eyes before answering.

'I went the first year after they died,' he said. 'I used to go there with someone else. But now *they're* not here, I can't face going on my own.' His breath shuddered and he took another swig of red wine. Isabella couldn't help but wonder who that person was. Someone in his past that he had relied on. Someone he had trusted. It gave her a sharp, stupid stab of jealousy. She purposefully pushed it away and did what she thought was right.

She checked her phone for timings and directions. As she did, she saw the list of things she was supposed to do today and decided they'd have to wait. Some things were more important. They could be there in an hour and a half if she drove, which would give Etienne time to sober up. They could buy flowers on the way.

'Come on,' she said, pulling him to his feet. 'I'll take you.'

The entrance to the cemetery was through an imposing grey stone archway. Leaves fell from the avenue of trees as they walked through. Row upon row of headstones and memorials surrounded them as Etienne led the way to the left-hand side of the grounds. He'd changed his shirt before they left and drunk a large coffee in the car. He hadn't talked, looking silently out the window. The landscape changed as they left the countryside and neared London, brown fields turning to suburbs and then city. Isabella stopped once on a high street and Etienne chose a large bouquet of bright yellow sunflowers. The last of the season according to the florist.

'There were fields of these in France where Mum grew up,' he'd said as she pulled away again.

Now, he hesitated. An old man looking cold in an ageing black leather jacket and with slicked-back white hair shuffled past, glancing in their direction on his way to a visit of his own.

'My parents are there,' Etienne said, nodding at a gravestone across the way.

Isabella sat on the bench, knowing she'd come as far as she should. She pulled her scarf tightly around her neck and ducked her chin into its warmth.

'I'll wait here for you,' she said and he nodded, seeming to pluck up some courage as he turned and approached the grave.

Etienne was far enough away that she couldn't hear what he was saying as he spoke to them. But she could see the care with which he laid out the flowers as he talked. He traced the stone with his fingertip and pulled tiny bits of moss from the monument. Doing what he could to make things nice for them, even after their death.

She texted a message to Mamma and Papà. Suddenly wanting to have that contact with them, having seen the grief of someone who had lost it.

Isabella: Ciao, Mamma and Papà. I just wanted to say I love you.

A few seconds later a reply came in.

We love you too.

Her heart swelled with love, and she slipped her phone back in her pocket in time to see Etienne put his lips to the headstone on one side and then the other, in the French way of kissing both cheeks. Her heart hurt as she blinked a tear away, only to spot a robin sitting on the grave next to him. She'd heard the sentimental stories about how a robin's visit is meant to signify a loved one reaching out from the other side.

'Etienne,' she called, pointing out the bird when he raised his head. The bird cocked its head. Etienne did the same. The bird tweeted. Etienne smiled. Something moved inside Isabella, seeing him so vulnerable. She saw the old man was watching too as the bird flew away.

'Thank you,' Etienne said, returning to the bench. 'I don't think even I knew how much I needed that.'

His eyes were brighter, his shoulders back.

'Sometimes you just need to let other people help you,' she said.

'Maybe,' he said, not looking convinced.

'You'd do anything for your friends,' she said. 'They'd do anything for you. You don't have to do everything on your own.'

'You're a fine one to talk,' he said, with the first real smile of the day. 'Ms Successful and Single.' They turned to leave. 'Anyway, thank you,' he said and pulled her in for a hug. She felt her stomach turn over as he held her against his chest for a second, warm and briefly protected from the wind. The old man in the leather jacket was still watching them from his graveside. Maybe he was wishing he had someone with him.

'You're a real friend,' Etienne said as he let her go and she had to remind herself that he was right. The wind whipped around her face again and her heart sank, but she managed to hide her disappointment in a smile.

Mia Famiglia WhatsApp group

Mamma: We've been offered an off-road camping trip with a native guide!

Papà: And we'll get to trek with elephants and follow the jungle trail.

Mamma: It's the only time to go because of the weather.

Papà: But it's the week of your launch . . .

Isabella: Follow your dreams! That's what you always tell me to do!

Mamma: But we feel like we're letting you down.

Isabella: Not at all. There will always be a table for you at Tutto Mio.

Papà: Thank you, my darling.

Chapter Forty-Two

Etienne

Several hours later, they arrived back in Honeybridge and Etienne watched Isabella head back across the square. Even now, today of all days, he couldn't help but admire her bum. The thought made him grin involuntarily. Again. In fact, Isabella had been responsible for all of his smiles today. Not that there had been many of them, but they'd chatted on the way back, and some of the heaviness had disappeared as she told him about other epic car journeys.

Like when she and Gabi had decided to do a camping holiday through France. Neither of them ever having put up a tent or speaking a word of French. And how she made Gabi put her feet out the window as they drove because they smelled so bad.

'It was a long time ago,' she'd reassured him. 'She never smells now.' It had made him smile. The easy way she chatted about Gabriella, and the obvious love she had for her. It reminded him of how close he and Alex used to be.

The thought of Alex brought back the gnawing in his stomach.

The worry. The money – or lack of it. And he had to admit he didn't like it one bit that the Dougalls now knew of his existence either. They were the kind of people it was much better if they never knew you were alive. And you certainly didn't want to cross paths with them. But he couldn't let Alex face them alone. He was going to find a way to go too. Although there was something he needed to do first. He watched as Isabella closed the door to her flat behind her and imagined her running up the stairs, hips swaying. Then he pulled his phone out of his pocket.

Fox was rocking a three-day stubble with his checked shirt and looked like he needed a good night's sleep. Walker had just come off shift and was looking like he wanted a beer. Etienne was somewhere in the middle, wanting both.

'Tough day today, mate,' Walker said, knocking Etienne's shoulder with his own as he came into Fox's kitchen. It wasn't a question, simply an acknowledgement. The friends knew it was the anniversary of his parents' death. Fox looked questioningly at him from his position at the fridge, which was now covered in hand-drawn paintings of pumpkins.

Etienne nodded. 'The usual,' he said, as he accepted the beer Fox held out to him, but then he caught himself. It hadn't been the same as other years. He hadn't sat on his own and disappeared into a well of grief, or not for long at least. And he hadn't drunk too much of his own wine cellar this year. He realised he'd done something more positive with his day. He'd celebrated his parents rather than grieved them.

'Boys in bed?' Walker asked.

Fox nodded. 'Both asleep as soon as their heads hit the pillow.

Reggie's been to River Rats and George tried ballet dancing at the community centre, so they're both exhausted.'

Etienne grinned. 'Is my godson going to be the next Billy Elliot?'

Fox laughed. 'He can't decide between ballet and Meccano club. They both take place on Wednesdays so he's trying them both.'

'Is that why you look so tired?'

Fox rubbed his hands around his bristly face.

'No, it's this game extension. It's killing me. But if I can pull it off, it will be worth it.'

Etienne waited until they all sat with a beer in front of them. Their faces were as familiar to him as his own. Or Alex's. Walker and Fox had become his family and he had sworn time and time again to never let them down or put a woman between them. To not let history repeat itself. But he rarely asked them for anything in return. He never gave them the chance to support him. It was enough for him to feel like he had their backs. Until now.

Isabella had hit home when she said that he didn't have to do everything on his own. That he had friends that would support him. Looking round the table today, he was suddenly sure that he could tell them anything and they would still be there for him. They wouldn't judge him for what he'd done, or not done, when Alex needed him. He needed to confide in somebody, he couldn't keep everything bottled up any more.

'I want to talk to you,' he said and had their immediate attention with this serious tone of voice. 'About my brother. I told you we weren't close any more. That's not strictly true.'

He didn't leave anything unsaid. He told them of how Alex

had been a gambler for years, starting small with the local arcade slot machines, working his way up to the bookie's on the corner. But it was their parents' deaths that sent him off the rails, when he started online betting and back-room poker games, placing higher stakes each time, burning through his inheritance and more. Selling his car, losing his house deposit, until he owed so much he had to run for his life, literally.

Etienne didn't gloss over the part he'd played. How he'd lent him money in the past to help him out and Alex had always gambled it away. So when the call came in that night, he turned his phone over and ignored it so that he could carry on making out with Kira. How he hadn't been there when he was most needed and it had haunted him ever since.

Etienne talked about wondering where Alex was for the past four years, blaming himself that his brother was living somewhere in fear. Even worse, wondering if the Dougalls had caught up with him and he would never come home again. He told them how the phone call a few weeks earlier had come out of the blue and now he could think of nothing other than having his brother home. His friends had finished their beers by the time he stopped talking. He took a long swig from his own bottle in the ensuing silence as Fox got up to replenish them.

'So, you're going to give him the money, to pay off the Dougalls?' Fox said, passing him a new bottle. Etienne nodded and exhaled slowly.

'I have to.'

Fox and Walker exchanged glances which Etienne couldn't read.

'What?'

They looked at each other again, before Fox said, 'You're going to give fifty thousand pounds to a gambler?' Both of them studied his face, waiting for a reply.

'Yes.' Etienne shrugged.

'How do you know he won't gamble it away rather than pay the debt off?'

Etienne recalled Alex's voice on the phone, his promises that he didn't gamble any more and the shake in his voice when he talked about wanting to come back.

'I'm certain,' he said. 'He won't do that. Not this time.'

Fox and Etienne exchanged glances.

'Will he pay you back?' Walker said. 'That's a hell of a lot of money. That's the extension you were talking about at The Bistro to open up the back garden.'

'He will, over time,' Etienne said, acknowledging that all these questions came from a good place. Their desire to look out for him, like Isabella had said. 'I told you, I owe him.'

'This seems above and beyond to me,' said Walker, sitting back in his chair.

'It's not your debt to pay,' said Fox.

'It might not be my debt, but he *is* my brother and I let him down before. Because of that, I haven't seen him for over four years. I can't let him down again.' Fox and Walker sipped their beers without passing comment. 'I just need to find a way of raising the last chunk of money. I applied to the bank but they turned me down. I'll find another way.'

'So where is this money being handed over?'

Etienne told them what he knew, which wasn't a lot, but added in the bit he was sure of.

'I'm going to go with him.'

Fox sat forward. 'They said he had to be alone.'

'I'll be nearby, in case Alex needs me. But I'm going to be there, somewhere.'

'Don't you want to tell the police?' Walker asked, his uniformed training springing into action.

'No. I can't risk it,' Etienne said. The thought of police cars or sirens would surely spook the Dougalls. And Alex needed this deal done if he was to come home.

'But you're risking yourself instead,' Fox said.

Etienne swigged his beer and swallowed.

'I just wanted to tell you what was happening. So that someone knew.'

Silence hung over the table as that sank in. Etienne watched the tiny glance between his two friends. A silent communication.

'We'll lend you the money between us,' said Fox. 'I've still got some of Meg's life insurance handy.'

'And I've got savings,' Walker said.

'No way,' said Etienne, shaking his head.

'Yes way,' said Walker.

'And if you're going, I'm coming too,' said Walker, sitting forward.

'Me too,' said Fox. 'You don't have to do this on your own. But we keep it between ourselves. These guys sound dangerous. Nobody else needs to be involved.'

'I can't let you do that,' Etienne said.

'You're doing it for your brother,' Fox said. 'We're doing it for ours.'

Fox lifted his phone from the table with the Brothers from Another WhatsApp group, and scrolled back, showing the other men page after page of comments, chat and day-to-day arrangements between them. It went back years and suddenly meant much more than any old group chat.

The three men leaned in and clinked their bottles.

Brothers from Another Mother WhatsApp group, later that night

Fox: Et, just wondering, why did you decide to tell us today? About Alex?

Etienne: It was something Isabella said when she took me to the graveyard to see my parents.

Walker: She did what?? That's nice.

Fox: What did she say?

Etienne: She said I didn't have to do everything alone. That I had friends I could rely on.

Fox: Smart woman, that Isabella.

Walker: Talking of Isabella, Rosie tells me you're in some kind of sex pact.

Etienne: That makes it sound weird. We're having non-sex as she's on a sex ban for a year until she's become successful as a single woman.

Walker: And you thought I made it sound weird?

Fox: So, it's a sexual thing then?

Etienne: Yup.

Walker: Casual?

Etienne: Yup.

Fox: Shame. She's lovely. So good of her to help you with the boys that time when they were sick.

Walker: Hard agree. After the fire at the Malones', she offered to help Millie with her Italian without a second thought.

Etienne: Got to go, boys. Commitment warning bells are ringing.

Fox: Some things never change.

Walker: 😊

Chapter Forty-Three

Isabella

Nonna already seemed to know almost as many people as Isabella did in Honeybridge. As they walked the high street and admired the pumpkin displays, Nonna waved her mittened hands and called out and promised people biscuits.

'How many clubs have you joined, Nonna?' Isabella asked, thinking she seemed to be out almost every night.

'Five,' Nonna said. 'Tai chi, chess, book club, the Women's Institute and DJ skills. Wait there.' Isabella paused on the pavement as Nonna disappeared into the baker's. She herself might not have joined any clubs – unless you could call The Bolthole and The Lit Lounge clubs – but she felt completely at home now in Honeybridge. Her old life with Daniel felt a million miles away. In fact, she realised, she hadn't thought about him in weeks. Probably not since she heard the news that he was engaged. God help that woman. But it wasn't just her life with Daniel that seemed a world away. Her old nine-to-five job in a marketing agency felt like another life too. She'd got used to being her own boss, setting her own schedule, being the master of her own career. She loved creating the vision for the restaurant and the way in which Amber and the team were bringing it to life. And now, having Nonna here was the icing on the cake. Or the rum in the biscuit.

Nonna reappeared, clutching a paper bag, which she opened to show Isabella the contents: white biscuits sprinkled with sugar.

'Checking out the competition like you,' Nonna whispered. She plucked one mitten from her hand and selected a cookie with her fingers, holding it between their faces. 'Overpriced, I think, for the size of them.' She bit into it and chewed thoughtfully. 'Good flavour, though, I'll give him that.' She finished the biscuit and brushed the crumbs from her lips, waving at the baker happily through the window.

The siren made them both jump. The fire engine rounded the corner towards them, the noise deafening as it passed. Isabella spotted Walker in the front passenger seat but didn't wave. It didn't feel appropriate. Nonna crossed herself, whispering, as they watched it turn towards the park. Isabella bit her lip, the thought of another arson attack making her anxious.

'I think Sinead would make a good chef,' Nonna said as she plunged her hand back into her glove and they started walking again. 'My initial suspicions were right.'

'We haven't even opened yet,' Isabella protested. 'Don't tell me you're thinking of leaving already? And Mamma and Papà are still travelling, so there's nothing to rush home to.'

'Not at all,' Nonna said. 'I'm succession planning. It's crucial to your business.'

Isabella grinned.

'Have you talked to her about it?' she asked.

'Not yet, but I've sounded her out. She's not fazed by batch cooking, she did it for her boys. And she follows recipes all the time, saying she doesn't like to deviate from what's proven to work well. So, I know our family recipe would remain true.'

'We could always make that part of the contract,' Isabella said.

'Better if we don't need to. That she sticks to it because she believes in it.'

Nonna was right. Isabella nodded.

Another siren sounded. A police car this time, lights flashing, whizzed past. A second later a second fire truck followed in its wake. Whatever was happening was serious.

A crowd gathered on the pavement, watching as an ambulance tore past and another police car. A shopkeeper came out and scanned the high street. Isabella recognised him from the community meeting.

'Not another one,' he said, and people muttered their assent.

'What's happening?' Nonna asked, grasping the forearm of the person next to her. A young mum, with a child in a buggy.

'By the looks of it,' she said, pointing towards the park where a roof could be seen with black smoke pluming from it, 'Heart of Honeybridge is on fire.'

Nonna crossed herself again. 'Is that the retirement village?' she whispered and Isabella nodded.

'Brigitta from chess club lives there. She's the stylish one I told you about.'

'So does Fred Barrow,' said Isabella, thinking of the last time she visited him. He had invited her into his flat and made her a cup of coffee. They had sat for an hour looking through the maps together, while he reminisced. He was such a lovely man. 'Let's go. Maybe there's something we can do to help.'

Nonna didn't need persuading. Handing the bag of biscuits to the child in the buggy, she linked arms with Isabella and urged her on.

A crowd had already gathered at the park, held back by a hastily erected police cordon. Some people were talking on phones, others huddled with friends and family, watching. Sure enough, Heart of Honeybridge was burning. Isabella and Nonna picked their way through, until they were at the police ribbon where they could feel the heat of the blaze even through the October chill.

The fire service already had three trucks and crew in operation. Three huge arcs of water streamed from the engines as hoses were aimed at the source of the fire. Isabella gasped when she saw the accommodation that seemed worst affected was Fred Barrow's unit. His apartment at the end of the row was ablaze, flames licking through the roof. And the fire was spreading quickly, moving in all directions into the other retirement homes. The smoke billowing across the park was bitter and stung the back of her throat. She held her sleeve over her mouth, frantically looking for Fred as the fire crew helped people out into a waiting area, where the ambulance service was on standby. Nonna coughed, peering into the crowd.

Etienne appeared beside her, out of breath.

'I just heard,' he said. 'Have you seen Fred yet?'

She shook her head wordlessly and he shaded his eyes with his hands, squinting towards the blaze.

'His flat looks bad,' he said.

'I'm sure they would have got him out,' Isabella said as confidently as she could, but she gasped as the roof suddenly gave in, flames roaring through. The crowd cowered in the fierceness of the heat that blasted out.

'Move back, please.' The police force pushed the cordon to clear more space. Etienne resisted, straining to see from his higher vantage point. Isabella tugged at his elbow and he gave in and fell back.

The fire crew were bringing out some of the residents in their wheelchairs, and some of the older, bedbound residents were still wearing their nightclothes.

'Can you imagine how scared they must have been?' Nonna said. 'Lying there waiting to be rescued.' And then she clapped her hands together in relief. 'That's Brigitta there,' she said, 'safe and well.' She pointed to a lady with what appeared to be a Burberry scarf tied around her face to protect her breathing. 'I'll go and see her,' she said, disappearing into the wall of people. A loud crack made Isabella duck against Etienne's shoulder and cover her ears.

'Why isn't he out already?' Etienne said. 'If it started with his house?'

'You don't think he's still in there, do you?' Isabella asked, running through the interior of his house in her head. It was compact, a one-bedroomed unit with a front door out to the park and a back door to the communal gardens at the rear of the complex. 'Maybe he went out the back rather than the front? When it started?' she said.

At that moment, she saw Walker. Even though he was kitted

up with breathing apparatus, she'd still recognise the sandy hair and width of his shoulders. He seemed to have the same idea, as he and a crewmate were forging a path between the two buildings to get to the gardens behind.

'Move back.' The policeman pushed the crowd away again. People were constantly arriving, worried family and friends. This was the biggest fire the community had ever seen.

'You don't think this is arson, do you?' Isabella said. 'Nobody would do anything so terrible, would they?'

Etienne's jaw was set hard.

'God, I hope not,' he muttered.

Both wings of the building were now on fire. The sound was incredible. The roar of flames, the cracking and creaking of the building. Isabella found tears springing to her eyes and brushed them away. The elderly people being helped out were now being given oxygen and medical assistance. They looked terrified, somehow their fear making them childlike, even in their old age. And still no sign of Fred.

One of the ambulances set up a triage station on the grass.

The smoke was thicker now, rolling out of every open window in the building.

'There!' Etienne shouted, pointing between the buildings. Walker was supporting Fred through the smoke, followed by his crew member and another resident.

Etienne pushed forward through the crowd, but not before grabbing Isabella by the hand and dragging her with him, until they reached the ambulance bank.

'Walker!' Etienne called and waved with his free hand. 'Is he okay?'

Walker was grim-faced as he nodded.

'Can you look after him?' he said. 'I have to get back.'

Etienne lifted the rope cordon for Isabella and they slipped through, his hand strong and warm in hers.

'There you are!' she said to Fred, who blinked at her through sore, red eyes, clutching a book under his arm and some papers.

'Gave us quite a scare there, Fred,' Etienne said, letting go of Isabella and pulling the old man into a ferocious hug. Isabella felt the air against her hand where his skin had been.

'I was in the back garden when it started, showing my maps to someone,' Fred croaked when Etienne released him. 'I couldn't get through.' His face was smoke stained, the creases and wrinkles showing white against the soot.

Etienne hugged him again and Isabella was shocked to see the tears in his eyes.

'People are saying it started in my house?' he asked and his face seemed to collapse as tears ran down the wrinkles in his cheeks. 'I can't think straight, Etienne. But I'm sure I didn't have the oven on. I'm sure.' He looked like he was bearing the weight of the world on his shoulders.

A paramedic approached and took him gently by the arm, leading him away to the front of the queue.

'I think we should check you out, Mr Barrow,' he said as they went. 'You can wait over there,' he added to Etienne and Isabella, pointing to an area filled with friends and family. Nonna was already there with her friend Brigitta. They headed over.

'How did you get to know Fred so well?' Isabella asked, remembering meeting him in The Bistro on the first night she went there.

'I met him and his wife, Jeannie, when I first moved here. They dined in The Bistro one night and we got talking. I think they realised how lonely I was. It was just after my parents died . . .' He broke off and shook his head. 'It was a bad time for me. Anyway, they invited me to their house for a Sunday meal. And they invited me every weekend after that until Jeannie died. They were such a loving couple. They made me feel less lonely, like I still had a family.'

Isabella blinked. Having seen him at the graveside earlier in the week, she knew how much he missed being a part of something. She saw Fred was now in a seat, the ambulance man shining a light into his eyes.

'He must miss her dreadfully,' she said. Etienne nodded.

'So, when she died, we switched it around. He now comes to the restaurant every week for a free dinner on me. I always try to sit with him for dessert.'

'That's a lovely idea,' Isabella said. 'Gets him out of the house and saves him money.' They watched as the paramedic put a stethoscope to his chest and listened.

'He doesn't have a lot.' Etienne shrugged. 'And he likes a bet on the horses every now and then.'

Fred was being helped out of the chair and steered in their direction.

'I'm all fine,' he said. 'My ticker's making good time.' He pointed to his heart.

Etienne helped him under the rope and Fred got his first look back at what had been Heart of Honeybridge. The fire now seemed to be out. The streams of water still arced through the air, but it was mainly smoke now. The flames had died. The place was swarming with emergency services, uniforms of all colours setting about their duties. Walker appeared, removing his helmet and rubbing his hand through his hair.

'Any idea what started it?' Etienne asked as soon as he was close enough.

'We'll find out,' Walker said. 'It could have been a tragedy. As it is, the only casualties we have are minor.'

Etienne slapped him hard on the shoulder, acknowledging what the services had achieved.

'But this place is going to be out of use for a few days at least. Some of the units will need cleaning for smoke damage, but others are ruined and will be uninhabitable for a long time.'

'I'm guessing Fred's will be one of those?' Etienne asked. Walker nodded. Fred's chin trembled.

'Right, we'd better go and get you settled in at home then,' Etienne said. 'You're staying with me until it's sorted.'

Fred started shaking his head, but Etienne gave him a look and he changed his mind. Shoulders sagging, he mouthed a thank you.

'I said the same to Brigitta,' Nonna said as they arrived. 'She can stay with us, can't she, Isabella?' The woman with the Burberry scarf also seemed to have reapplied some Dior lipstick. 'It will only be for a couple of days – her apartment hasn't been damaged.'

'Of course,' Isabella said, thinking the woman looked more stylish having just escaped a fire than she herself did on a night out. 'Nice to meet you, Brigitta.'

'That will be the next job,' said Walker. 'Finding all these other people somewhere to stay. Not everyone has friends or family here. And the local authority won't be able to place them all immediately. It might be a few nights sleeping on the floor at the community centre for some of them.'

Isabella's mouth fell open. The community centre was a fantastic public facility, new and well kept. But it was hard-floored and impersonal. And cold at this time of year. It didn't have a warm bed or a comfy pillow for someone to sleep away the shock of what they'd been through. There were no armchairs or footstools to rest while they were so tired. There wasn't even a television to watch to distract them from what they'd been through.

'They need to be in a home environment,' Isabella said and Walker nodded and shrugged at the same time.

'I agree,' he said sadly and put his helmet back on to return to work.

Isabella grabbed his forearm.

'Walker, I've got an idea. Can I talk to your watch commander about something? I can help. I know I can.'

'Sure,' he said. 'We could do with all the help we can get. Come on through.'

'See you at home,' Isabella said over her shoulder to Nonna and Brigitta. 'And Nonna . . .' she called as she trotted after Walker, 'can you put my laptop on charge? I'm going to need it.'

Chapter Forty-Four

Etienne

The first Etienne knew of Isabella's plan was when it popped up on his socials later that day. He'd come home with Fred and got him set up in the spare bedroom. Then he'd gone out and bought him a toothbrush, pyjamas and some essentials he might need to be comfortable, a change of clothes and a newspaper; he always had one of those tucked under his arm. When Fred was showered, changed and dozing in the armchair nearest the TV, Etienne finally picked up his phone and checked his messages.

Nothing from Alex. Nothing from Isabella.

He jolted. Wait a minute. Nothing from Isabella? Why should there be anything from Isabella? Why was he looking for her name on his phone?

Probably because they'd both been together that morning. Maybe he expected an update on how she was getting on with her new housemate. He tapped the phone against his palm. Should he message her to ask? She'd probably be busy. He mindlessly flicked to his social feed instead.

All across his feed were tags of the Spare Room Sleepover, a bright, bold campaign which grabbed attention right off the screen. It was a rallying call, with Isabella directly asking local people to show their big hearts by opening their homes to a special guest for a while. It showed smiling head shots of some of the residents of Heart of Honeybridge and footage of the fire that morning.

It was everywhere, and from what he could see it was working. The comments, growing by the minute, were all from people signing up to the scheme, offering to lend their spare rooms. The local news site had picked up the campaign too; everyone was getting behind it. He couldn't believe Isabella had turned it around so quickly.

Fred Barrow woke in his chair and ambled over, looking at the campaign over Etienne's shoulder.

'She's some woman,' he said, nodding, before going back to watch the racing on the television.

Etienne felt something move inside him, a bit like indigestion. He swallowed and rubbed his chest.

He looked back at his feed and saw the increase in the number of comments. She'd created something amazing, in such a short time. He was blown away. Surely she had enough to do without setting up and organising a community campaign as well? Now he had to message her. It was only neighbourly.

Etienne: The campaign looks amazing!

Nothing. She was probably busy working.

He went to make a coffee, purposefully leaving his phone

on the table as he did so, but there was still nothing when he arrived back.

He glanced across at Tutto Mio. The front door was open, as deliveries of tables and chairs were being unloaded from a van and carried inside. Aha. That explained it. Maybe she needed a hand? It would be quite physical work, moving all of that. She'd do the same for him, he knew, if he needed some help at The Bistro. Not allowing himself to hesitate, he headed across the square. He was just going to help.

Faced with two delivery drivers who wore their trousers too low, Etienne realised she wasn't there and they definitely did not need his help. A glance at his phone told him his message was unread.

Maybe he'd head down to the retirement home and see how things were going. He might run into Walker down there. And it would be good to congratulate Isabella in person. This feeling of wanting to see her must come from the need to say well done. That was all.

Chapter Forty-Five

Isabella

The Salvation Army had arrived at the park as soon as they heard about the fire. By the time Isabella had created her social media campaign, they had erected a huge tent to give the burned-out residents some protection from the weather and from prying eyes. By the time she'd posted it, the marquee was set up with deckchairs and trestle tables and the residents were drinking tea. Someone had even found a solar radio.

Isabella had used all her marketing knowledge to get the campaign out there as quickly as possible. She rang the local council and outlined her idea, and they'd been positively thrilled with the help. Walker had confirmed she could use some money from the hardship fund for the adverts on Facebook and she'd filmed the TikTok content herself and posted it live. She'd not had time to eat and she was bursting for the toilet, but watching the likes reaching their first hundred, first thousand, first *ten thousand*, was the most amazing feeling in the world. Well, *almost* the most amazing feeling in the world – but she wasn't thinking about that, or him, today. She wandered over from her workstation in the back of a fire service van to peek into the tent and see how everyone was doing.

The first thing she saw was Nonna and Brigitta, back again and handing out trays of rum biscuits to tired residents. Brigitta might have also been testing the rum with Nonna as her Burberry scarf was now tied on the wonk.

A lady with a white bob cried out loud and stood from her deckchair to turn the radio up. Hearing the introduction to a certain song, she turned to a man with a handlebar moustache and led him to the middle of the tent. He clasped her hand and put his other around her waist and they pulled in tight to dance. The grass beneath their feet was uneven and she was wearing her slippers, but they didn't miss a step. As the song ended, he turned her for a final spin before taking their seats, and everyone clapped. Isabella felt her eyes burn hot with tears, but blinked them away.

Just outside the tent, she spotted Walker with his team, discussing next steps and comparing notes on the investigation so far.

She blinked again, her eyes almost overflowing. People were lovely. It was amazing to see how everyone was keeping their spirits up in such an awful situation. Honeybridge was a good place and it had done her good to move there. The people here would do anything for anybody.

Rosie, Wren and Amber had welcomed her in with no other purpose than to make friends. They were fantastic, hardworking women with the most amazing hearts. They'd opened hers again.

She also no longer hated or distrusted men as she had when she'd first arrived. Because she'd met three who showed her every day that they were good men. Walker, the everyday hero. Fox, the wonder dad. And Etienne . . . Etienne.

She felt the usual surge inside as she thought of him. There was no point in trying to deny it. She had fallen for him. She knew it was ill fated but there it was.

And there he was. Walking towards her, with the biggest smile on his face. And just like that, her heart swelled to fill her chest to bursting.

Chapter Forty-Six

Etienne

There she was, her hair up in a messy bun, laptop under her arm. Etienne waved and realised he was smiling. Not just smiling. *Beaming*.

'Look what you did!' he said, pointing his thumb over his shoulder at the growing crowd of people there to offer a spare room. The queue was long and wound around the bandstand, where the local school orchestra were setting up to play to entertain the crowd. He watched Isabella's eyes widen as she saw more people filing in from the high street, clutching coffees and hot chocolates to join the end of the line. He checked his phone and held the screen towards her in amazement.

'Nearly one hundred thousand likes!'

She grabbed his phone and her mouth fell open.

'You did that!' Etienne said, shaking the phone at her. 'You did that!' he said again, and swung his arm back to take in everyone waiting to play their part for the community. A ripple of emotion seemed to cross her face, and then a laugh bubbled out of her, starting hesitantly and building until she threw her head back, causing her bun to fall out, her hair to tumble down her back.

Without thinking, he put his arms around her and pulled her into a hug. Her body felt small, soft but strong at the same time. Isabella froze for an instant and then melted against him. Her hair smelled like lemons. Her arms wound around his neck and squeezed back. She fitted perfectly.

'This is the woman you want, right here,' someone said and Isabella pulled away. Etienne felt the gap where she'd been all the way down his body.

One of the firefighters was leading a woman with headphones around her neck in their direction, followed by a cameraman.

'This is Isabella Tucci. She's the one who started the community campaign.'

'Michelle Carter,' the woman in headphones said, introducing herself as she shook Isabella's hand. 'Regional television news.' The cameraman caught up, shielding his eyes to choose a good aspect.

'Love what you've done here,' Michelle said. 'We'd like to record a piece for the evening news.'

Isabella flushed and touched her hair. As if she had anything to worry about. She'd look beautiful getting out of bed in the morning. Probably especially getting out of bed in the morning. Wait, why was he thinking about that now?

'If we film from here,' the cameraman said, indicating an angle, 'we can get the queue behind you and then pan round to show what's happening inside the tent.'

'Perfect,' Michelle agreed. 'Then we'll do some pieces to

camera from the people with spare rooms, and those who need to stay with them.'

Isabella clutched Etienne's forearm and he saw the panic cross her face.

'You'll be fine,' he said quietly.

She moved a few steps away from the media team who were busy setting up, pulling him with her.

'We had to do practice interviews at university as part of my business marketing degree, and I . . .'

Her hand on his arm was shaking. Etienne had a weird urge to hug her again.

'What happened?'

'I froze when they asked me a question. Not once, but twice. They pointed the microphone at me and I opened my mouth and nothing came out. I was like a goldfish looking for air.' She closed her eyes at the memory.

'What was the interview about?'

'What difference does that make?' She frowned. 'It was just awful.'

He waited and after a second, she huffed and answered.

'It was a scenario, a made-up thing, where we had to defend our business that had been accused of flouting employment laws.'

He took her hand and was surprised at how perfectly it fit into his own, her small delicate one enfolded in his.

'This is different,' Etienne said. 'Totally different. You're going to tell them how happy you are to be able to help your community. How much you love it here. How great it is to see the residents of Heart of Honeybridge going to family homes until things are sorted out.'

She didn't say anything. She was still looking at his hand.

'Plus, you are amazing. You can do anything you set your mind to. You've proven that already with Tutto Mio.' Still nothing. It was as though she were hypnotised.

'Isabella?'

She lifted her face and it had a new kind of nervousness on it. Hope. If the camera caught that look, she was going to be the best interview they ever got.

'Would you do it with me?' she whispered, squeezing his hand between them. 'You *were* the first one to take Fred in.'

Etienne pulled a face and she laughed.

'You'll be fine,' she repeated back at him. 'You don't even have to say anything if you don't want to. Just stand with me.' She squeezed his hand again and he found himself looking at it this time. 'Please.'

'Okay,' he said and she beamed.

'Then later, maybe I could buy you a drink?' she said unexpectedly. She opened her mouth to say something else, but then closed it again. She gave no excuses, or reasons. She left the invitation out there, hanging between them.

Her eyes were looking directly into his and he realised he was still holding her hand. His thumb ran over her knuckles.

He thought about his evening ahead and realised there was nothing he would rather do than spend it with her.

'I'm buying the second round,' he said, and her mouth curved into a smile and Etienne had a realisation like a punch in the face. He had feelings. Ones that he couldn't control. Ones that fluttered in his stomach like a romance novel. Ones that made him want to see her, even without any non-sex. Ones that made him want to, right now, not let go of her hand.

'We're ready for you,' Michelle Carter called and Isabella waved in acknowledgement. They walked over together, hands joined.

Isabella quickly updated Michelle on Etienne's part in the process and she was happy to 'add more colour' to the story. The cameraman positioned them where he wanted them and still Etienne was holding her hand.

Chapter Forty-Seven

Isabella

Isabella's heart was flapping like a trapped butterfly in her chest. But it had nothing to do with the cameraman pointing his lens at her, or Michelle preparing to ask the first question. It was all due to the fact that Etienne was holding her hand. Every now and then his thumb smoothed over her skin or he tightened his grip, but he hadn't let go.

She'd seen something in his face, she knew it. That had been a true-life, real romance moment that they had shared. More than just a pep talk, or him trying to give her confidence. And he was *still* holding her hand. Surely, if they were just friends, he would have dropped it as soon as she agreed to do the interview?

And they were going for a drink. Okay, maybe just a friendly drink. A drink to celebrate the day. A drink to relax after the interview. They'd been for drinks before, in a group, and obviously for karaoke, but this time she had asked him simply because she didn't want him to leave. She wanted to spend the evening with him and he had said yes. And he was still holding her hand.

Michelle Carter moved into position and counted them in. Etienne moved fractionally closer, and she could feel the touch of his elbow on her arm.

'This is Isabella Tucci,' said Michelle in her 'on air' voice, 'the person behind the campaign for Spare Room Sleepover, created to come to the rescue of the elderly residents of Heart of Honeybridge, which suffered a serious fire earlier this morning. How did you come up with the idea, Isabella?'

She thrust the fluffy microphone towards Isabella. Etienne squeezed her hand encouragingly and she felt the smile stretching her cheeks as she answered. This time, she didn't freeze and she wasn't shy. She was happier in that moment than she could remember being for months – maybe ever.

'It just came to me,' she said. 'I'm lucky enough to live with my own grandmother and thought that a lot of other people would love to do the same – have an honorary grandparent come to stay, even if it's just for a few days.'

'The council tells us that fifty-nine residents have already been matched for home stays,' Michelle said. 'How do you feel about that?'

'It's fantastic news,' said Isabella. 'Because every resident we match will have a home environment to recover in, and they can be part of a family, which is so important.'

'And this is Etienne Martin,' Michelle said, turning towards him. 'The first person to take in one of the residents. How did that happen, Mr Martin?'

'It was an easy decision,' said Etienne. 'I would class Fred

Barrow as a friend of mine, so it seemed natural to ask him to come home with me until all this is sorted.'

Isabella watched him speak and bet that every woman watching this section on the news would be salivating on their sofas. And, out of shot of camera, he was still holding her hand.

'Is this normal for Honeybridge?' Michelle asked, indicating the queue of people waiting to sign up to the scheme. 'This level of community spirit?'

All the sides of the community that Isabella had experienced in the last three months rushed through her head. From karaoke at The Bolthole to Story Stars with Rosie and Wren, the Italian lessons to the fundraiser and the market on the square.

'Definitely,' she said, glancing at Etienne, who nodded in agreement. 'We wouldn't live anywhere else, would we?'

'Have you lived here long then?' Michelle asked and Isabella recognised an opportunity when it was presented to her. After all, she did have a marketing degree.

'Not that long, just long enough to set up a new restaurant. It's called Tutto Mio. It's all family recipes – Italian meatballs – and we open this weekend.' She turned away from Michelle and looked straight down the lens of the camera. 'Everyone's welcome!'

'And cut,' said Michelle, taking her headphones off and checking with the cameraman to make sure he was happy. He finished reviewing the footage and then gave her a thumbs up.

'That was perfect, thanks,' Michelle said, carefully winding her microphone wire up. 'It will probably go out tonight unless something else happens nationally to push it out. But if not tonight, then tomorrow night.'

'Sorry about the promotion at the end.' Isabella laughed, not sorry at all. 'I couldn't help myself.'

'No worries,' said Michelle. 'Those kinds of things normally get edited out, but I'll see what I can do.' She winked.

'Isabella, can I get some shots of you walking by the queue? And then a few in the tent?' the cameraman asked.

She let her fingers squeeze Etienne's one more time, saying, 'See you after for that drink.'

He nodded and squeezed back. 'Told you you'd be brilliant. You're amazing.'

The burst of emotion almost brought tears to her eyes. She reluctantly let go of his hand and followed the cameraman, fighting the urge with every step to skip and laugh out loud like a five-year-old. Giving in to looking over her shoulder as they got to the queue, she saw Etienne lifting the phone to his ear and turning away to talk.

Chapter Forty-Eight

Etienne

Etienne was watching Isabella walk away – admiring her bum as usual – when his phone rang. Alex's name on his screen grabbed his attention.

'You okay?' he asked reflexively as he pressed green.

'I'm okay,' Alex replied and Etienne wondered when they would be free of those first questions. When they might be able to relax and simply say hello.

'Got any news?'

'I have a location,' Alex said. 'It's an old farm building in Shentford. I've had a look on Google Maps. It's quite remote.'

Dread flooded through Etienne.

'I'm coming too,' said Etienne. 'And so are Fox and Walker. We'll wait somewhere nearby—'

'You can't,' Alex cut in.

'They won't know we're there. It's so that we can get to you if needs be . . .'

'No. I just need you to help with the money. Nothing else. Especially now.'

'What do you mean?'

Alex fell silent, and Etienne watched the cameraman trailing Isabella along the queue. People were smiling and waving to be on the television; Isabella was laughing.

'What do you mean, Al?' he repeated.

'They know who you are, Et,' he said quietly, and Etienne covered his other ear to hear better. 'Not only that I have a brother. They know who you are.'

'What? How?'

'Old Man Dougall saw you, at Mum and Dad's grave. He thought you were me, that I'd dyed my hair in some kind of disguise, an attempt to change my looks.'

Etienne realised how hard he was clutching the phone and tried to relax his grip. It was true, he and Alex looked similar although they were not identical. There were differences you would see and know if you saw them together. The colour of their hair was the most obvious. Alex had blue eyes, Etienne green. Their jaws were different, the shape of their nose. Alex looked somehow softer than Etienne. But their build and height were the same – or had been last time he'd seen him. They were easily confused if seen separately, and from a distance.

'He couldn't believe his eyes apparently. Thought I'd walked straight into his day. Then he heard you being called Etienne by whoever you were with. And after you'd gone, he checked the grave. It says beloved parents of Alex and Etienne Martin. So, he figured it out and told the brothers. They know your name, Et.'

Images of the graveyard flicked through his mind. Isabella

calling him to point out the robin. The old man who walked past.

'I can't believe he was there at the same time as you. Apparently, all he does these days is watch television and visit his wife in the cemetery. Of all the chances . . .'

Etienne's brain was going in a million different directions at once. They knew his name. Etienne Martin was quite an unusual name. Memorable. So, they could easily find him if they wanted to. He shook himself, tried to think calmly.

Why would the Dougalls want anything to do with him? It was Alex they had the problem with. If the debt was paid – which it would be in a matter of days – they had no reason to need to pay Etienne a visit. It was only if Alex didn't pay the money back for any reason that they might come looking. He swallowed. Fox's face resurfaced in his mind, the concerned look on his face as he asked, 'So you're going to give fifty thousand pounds to a gambler?' He squashed the thought as quickly as it appeared. He trusted Alex, one hundred per cent.

'It doesn't make any difference, though, does it? We stick to the plan. I still transfer the money to you. You pay them off. You come home.'

'They told me I'm not calling the shots. And to remember that.' Alex's voice had a tremor in it again. 'Then they told me they knew about you. It felt like a direct threat.'

Etienne's skin crawled.

'Who were you with, Et? At the graveyard?'

'Isabella. A . . . friend.' He stumbled over the word; it didn't sit right. He wasn't sure what to call her, but it wouldn't be a friend. He watched her as she walked back across the park towards him. When she saw him looking, her face lit up. 'Why do you ask?'

'Because they commented on it. After they said about knowing you. They said, "His wife's a looker."'

Etienne felt his breath stop. Isabella was pulled into the crowd by the bandstand to watch Jayden breakdance.

'I don't like it, Et,' Alex said.

'Me neither,' said Etienne, watching Isabella applaud Jayden spinning on his head, and it felt like the understatement of the century. The thought of someone threatening Isabella was like a blow to the stomach. It changed everything. 'Call me if you hear anything else.'

As he hung up, his jaw hurt as he realised how hard he'd been clenching his teeth. He watched Isabella laughing and clapping along and knew he couldn't put her at risk. Him being in danger was one thing, but he would not bring her into it. And the only way he could do that was to make sure she was nowhere near him, ever. All he wanted to do was spend time with her, but he had to stay away – to protect her. To make sure she was safe.

Isabella fist bumped Jayden and waved to the others. He heard them calling '*Ciao*' after her as she turned away, her eyes immediately seeking Etienne out, searching for him. When she spotted him, she lifted a hand, her mouth already curving upwards. But she must have seen something on his face, something in his expression that made her falter. She slowed in her step, suddenly uncertain, as she stood before him.

'Ready for that drink then?' she said, but even the tone of her voice was different, hopeful but hesitant.

He made his face hard, hating himself as he did it.

'I can't,' he said and his voice was flat, harsher than he'd intended. She blinked.

'Oh,' Isabella said, momentarily searching for words, the confusion clear on her face. 'Has something come up? I saw you on the phone.'

'Yes, something came up,' Etienne said, wanting to take her by the hand again, and pull her closer, to shield her from what he was about to say. Instead, he looked her in the eye and said it anyway. 'A better offer.'

She flinched. A flush started on her neck, blooming there as quickly as if he'd slapped her. Her eyes widened and then she blinked, and he thought for one awful moment she might cry.

'Come on, Isabella, this was only ever about the sex. Or non-sex, actually,' he said, the words dripping with sarcasm as if the whole idea was ridiculous. 'It's never going to be more than that.'

She turned her face away. By the way her throat was moving, he knew she was trying to swallow down a sob. But she held her ground; he wanted to hold her tight and tell her he was sorry. Instead, he thought of the Dougalls, letting his mind dwell on the words *His wife's a looker*. He steeled himself and knew he was doing the right thing. Even if it didn't feel like it. She had to stay away.

'You've made that crystal clear now, thanks,' she said and he had to admire her voice. It didn't crack or break. She looked him straight in the face as that flush crept up her throat and flooded her cheeks. 'My mistake. See you around, Etienne.' She even tried a smile and he felt something physically break inside himself.

As she huddled into her coat and walked away, it was all he could do to stop from running after her.

Chapter Forty-Nine

Isabella

Isabella didn't know how she managed to get home without breaking down. She stumbled tear-blind through the park, and then almost ran home to the safety of her own front door, which she closed behind her with a relief so strong she thought she would fall to the ground.

Nonna believed her when she said she was sick; Isabella let her think maybe it was food poisoning. Amber told her that if she had food poisoning, she should stay out of the restaurant and look after herself. Which gave her the perfect excuse to shut her bedroom door and block the world out. Lying down on her bed, she didn't know how she would ever get up again.

How could she have got it so wrong?

She and Etienne *had* had a moment, she knew it. She'd bet her entire restaurant on the fact that something had passed between them. She *knew* he felt it too.

The thing was, she'd let herself go with it. She'd believed it to the extent that it seemed like the beginning of something.

She'd been so ready to think his feelings might match hers. That he might be falling for her the way she was for him. Because that's what it was for her. She knew that now. Full-blown, life-changing, heartbreaking love. She was in love with Etienne Martin. And for a blissful, exciting few minutes, she had fooled herself into believing he felt the same. Stupid, stupid, stupid.

She should have known that her feelings were never matched.

With Daniel, she had loved him and believed he loved her. She had been loyal, and trusted he was the same. Wrong, wrong, wrong.

She should have listened to the girls.

Because Etienne doesn't do relationships . . . he's not the boyfriend type . . .

I truly don't think he has it in him . . .

Well, he'd proved them all right this afternoon. He'd stayed true to his reputation, and she was the fool for thinking he could have been anything different. She slammed her fists into the pillow as she collapsed onto the bed, finally letting herself cry.

She wanted to hate him. She wanted to feel like she did after Daniel betrayed her, filled with blazing fury and white-hot rage. She wanted to hate all men because none of them could be trusted to be honest and faithful. Because feeling angry and righteous would be better than this. But instead, as her sobs subsided, she just felt hollow and sad.

She dragged herself up from the bed to sit at her dressing table. The mirror reflected the shadows of her cheeks, the empty expression in her eyes. She squeezed make-up remover onto a cotton pad and gently wiped it around her face, removing any traces of the day. It was one she would rather forget.

Isabella had a restaurant to open in three days. It was so nearly here, the day she had envisaged since signing her name on the divorce papers, the last time she ever signed as Isabella Simmons. The day she opened Tutto Mio, she thought, would mark a high point in her life as a successful, single woman.

And yet, here she was, devastated. She'd let herself fall for a man – again. A man who couldn't love her the way she wanted him to – again. And she hated herself for it. Because, if Etienne turned up now, knocking at her flat door, she'd want to answer. If he pulled her into his arms, she'd want to fall against him. And if he kissed her, she'd want nothing more than to kiss him back. For the rest of her life.

She plaited her hair into one single rope down the back of her head. She rubbed lip balm onto her lips, then pulled on her pyjamas. Yes, it might only be six o'clock in the evening but for her, the day was over. She refused to look at The Bistro as she pulled the blinds closed, in case she caught a glimpse of the man she so desperately wanted to see. It wouldn't help.

The only thing she could do now was to focus on what she'd come here for. To finalise all the last points for the opening and make sure the launch of Tutto Mio was the biggest success it could be.

Her phone pinged and her heart stopped. She reached for it with trembling hands.

It wasn't him. She closed her eyes tight against the sting. Instead, a message from Michelle Carter.

The Prime Minister's announcement has pushed our news piece out of tonight's programme. Will be tomorrow instead. Thanks again. And well done.

Isabella sighed. She didn't care if it was today or tomorrow any more, she wouldn't be watching. Hopefully they would keep the segment in about her promoting Tutto Mio because that would be great free advertising. But she would never watch it because whilst everyone saw her smiling face, the crowds and the community, she wouldn't be able to forget that out of shot, Etienne was holding her hand.

Getting into bed, she put her phone on silent on the bedside table. She didn't have the words to talk to anyone and she certainly didn't want her mamma to FaceTime her because she would see through her fake smile in a second and be worried. Isabella sent her a quick message, letting her know about the 'food poisoning' and the fact that she was going to sleep, knowing that would prevent her from calling until tomorrow.

She drank a few mouthfuls of water, as she always did. She plumped her pillows as usual before lying down. She arranged herself in her side sleeping position as if this was just another normal day. She flicked out the light. But this wasn't a normal day. This was the day she got her heart broken.

Shutting her eyes, she let the tears come again. They seeped out from under her closed lids and ran down her cheeks to the pillow. Tonight was the only night she would let herself feel it. Tomorrow she would get up, move on and focus on her restaurant. And forget the hell about Etienne Martin.

Chapter Fifty

Etienne

The next day, Etienne tried to distract himself with coffees at the park with Fox and Walker. He watched Reggie and George kick dried leaves at each other and tear around the almost-bare trees.

'Not working today then, Walker?' he asked.

'Going in later,' Walker said, stretching. 'Extra shift because of the arsonist. Everyone is on high alert and we've got all the normal firework worries to cope with too.' He circled his arms; he'd done five days in a row. He looked tired. Etienne yawned too.

'You working hard as well?' Fox asked him. 'Or hot date?'

'Neither,' Etienne said. 'I just didn't sleep well.' When he said he didn't sleep well, he wasn't sure if he'd slept at all. Any time he closed his eyes, he had kept seeing the way Isabella had straightened her spine to look him in the eye. The way that flush of colour crept up her neck, giving her real feelings away. Her embarrassment, her hurt, because of him.

At one point in the night, he'd found himself wandering the

apartment, barefoot so as not to disturb Fred snoring in the spare bedroom. The square was quiet and empty, the glow from the street lights throwing golden circles on the paving. Across the way, Tutto Mio was in darkness. His chest was heavy as he thought about Isabella sleeping inside.

'Worrying about your brother?' Fox asked and Etienne nodded.

'Things got more serious.' He told them about the Dougalls now knowing who he was and thinking that Isabella was his wife. Fox rubbed his forehead on hearing Isabella's name. Walker whistled low.

'Does she know anything about this?'

'No,' said Etienne. 'I told you, it's only us.'

'But they have no reason to come for you if Alex pays up as planned.'

'Exactly. And we have less than a week to go.' Etienne paused. 'And even if they did pay me a visit, there's no way Isabella would be within a mile of me.'

'No?' Walker said. 'I thought you were getting on so well yesterday at the community event. You almost looked like a couple . . .'

'Let's just say, I'm not her favourite person any more,' he said, ignoring the stab in his insides. 'So, she'll be safe and sound away from me no matter what happens.'

'What does that mean?' Walker probed. 'Do you want to be her favourite person?'

'Were things going somewhere?' Fox asked.

'Forget it,' Etienne said. 'It's not happening.' He pressed his lips together so tightly he felt the strain in his jaw.

'We're always around, Et,' Fox said. 'If you need us.' He

clapped a hand on Etienne's shoulder and then stood to check on the boys, happy when he saw them on the swings, Reggie pushing George in a rare moment of sibling teamwork.

Walker stretched again, checked his watch.

'Gotta go,' he said, rising to his feet. 'Staff meeting this afternoon. Police are coming in to brief us.'

'What's the score with Heart of Honeybridge?' Fox asked. 'How long will it be out of action for?'

'One wing will be a week; the other wing will be more like a month. Looks like you'll have Fred Barrow with you for a while, Et, as his room was worst hit.'

Etienne nodded. The thought of Fred being in the apartment in the evenings was oddly comforting, especially seeing as he had absolutely no inclination to bring any women home for the foreseeable future.

'The Spare Room Sleepover was a massive success,' Walker said. 'There were only ten people that had to be housed in emergency council accommodation and that was only because they have extra medical needs. Isabella did an amazing job.'

She had done an amazing job, it was true. Because *she* was amazing.

Walker picked up his rucksack.

'Seems like Fred's room was where the fire started. Lucky he was out in the back garden.'

Etienne frowned.

'Why would anyone want to burn down a home for old folks? I don't get it.'

'And especially Fred Barrow? Why would anyone want to hurt him?'

Walker hitched his rucksack onto his back.

'The police have been trying to find a link between all recent events. The house fire that started at the Malones'. A new hire company business that got torched overnight. A man in Shalford that came home from work to a burning house. An office in town that had a burning package put through the letter box. There's so many and they all seem so different.'

'And no CCTV footage that might help?' Etienne asked. Walker shook his head.

'Whoever is doing it certainly knows what they are doing.'

'What are the boys playing at now?' Fox said, standing to watch as they ran across the park and threw themselves at—

'*Ciao, Bella,*' Reggie cried with delight as he wrapped himself around Isabella's legs. She bent to ruffle his hair and then tickle George under the armpit. Something leaped inside Etienne at the sight of her.

Both boys hanging off her, she scanned the nearby benches, obviously looking for Fox. Etienne saw her expression change as she spotted him there beside Fox. Something rippled across her face which was immediately replaced by a stoic resignation that they would have to talk.

'Hi,' she said, a boy swinging on each arm.

'Hi,' Etienne said, his heart plummeting.

'Great job yesterday,' Walker said to Isabella as he left, tucking a pound coin into the boys' hands for lollies on the way home.

'You smashed it,' said Fox and she made sure she was focusing all her attention on Fox as he talked, so that she hardly glanced at Etienne. She looked pale, he thought, as though maybe she hadn't slept well either.

'Are you all ready for opening night?' Fox asked and she talked for a while about Tutto Mio, last-minute arrangements, more marketing. How she was hopeful because they had steady bookings for several weeks ahead now. She was saying all the right words but her tone lacked her normal enthusiasm.

'We'll all be there to celebrate,' Fox said, trying to disentangle the boys from around her legs. 'These two love meatballs.'

'Great.' She squatted in front of the two boys. 'I'll save you both a mega portion!'

Straightening up, she finally looked directly at Etienne. Her blue eyes met his.

'I'm sure *you'll* be far too busy to come, with so many better options,' she said and it wasn't a question. 'Anyway,' she kissed Fox on the cheek. 'See you there.' She left to a chorus of *ciaos* from the boys and lots of blown kisses.

'Wow, you weren't wrong,' said Fox. 'She really hates you.'

Chapter Fifty-One

Isabella

When Isabella arrived, The Lit Lounge was temporarily quiet: the calligraphy club had already been and gone, the lunchtime knit and natter group not yet arrived. Rosie and Wren were behind the counter, Wren sipping a coffee, Rosie reading a book, taking a well-earned ten-minute break. Barney lay on the counter, belly up, purring. As Isabella walked in, Amber caught the door behind her and linked her arm.

Wren put two cups under the coffee machine and by the time they pulled up stools at the central reading bar, an espresso was in front of Isabella and a cappuccino was in front of Amber.

'Don't go holding back on the good stuff, sister,' Amber said as Wren shook the powdered chocolate on top. 'This is what I live for.'

Isabella saw Amber was wearing the Tutto Mio blue shirt and knew she would have come from the restaurant for a break. She'd been working so hard.

'How's the food poisoning?' Amber asked. 'Feeling better?'

Wren and Rosie looked over. Isabella opened her mouth to smile, or say that she felt fine, but nothing came out. Just a sudden and overwhelming fear she was going to cry.

'Are you still feeling ill?' Wren asked.

'You do look pale,' Rosie added, putting the back of her hand to Isabella's forehead.

Isabella slumped and put her head in her hands.

'Something tells me this isn't food poisoning.' Rosie pulled her stool closer and put her hand to Isabella's head, stroking her hair. Isabella wanted nothing more than to close her eyes and go to sleep. To forget everything.

'I got Etienne'd,' she said, sitting back up, 'without even getting properly Etienne'd.'

She saw the sympathy on her friends' faces, the way they reached out to her, the arms around her shoulders.

'You haven't had sex?' Rosie asked and Isabella shook her head. The sex, or lack of it, wasn't even the thing that she was missing.

'You fell for him?' Wren asked.

Isabella nodded, tears spilling from her eyes. She brushed them away, frustrated. She'd promised herself she wouldn't cry after last night. But seeing him this morning in the park had been a step too far. She hadn't been expecting it, and the sight of him knocked the air out of her lungs like a slap on the back. She'd hardly dared look at him, scared to see the coldness on his face again as she had yesterday. But when she had finally looked at him this morning, he looked . . . sad, resigned. And that made it worse, and more confusing, and now she was crying. Again.

Nobody said *I told you so*. Nobody said she had been warned. Everybody just piled on to hug her and hold on.

Finally, she wiped her eyes, blew her nose and slurped her espresso down in one gulp.

'Honestly, that man,' Wren said.

'Lucky we're not attracted to them,' agreed Rosie.

Isabella laughed and it hiccupped over all the tears she'd cried.

'I honestly thought there was something there,' Isabella said. 'How wrong could I be?'

'It's his loss, honey,' said Amber. 'You remember that.'

Isabella forced a smile and wished it felt like that.

'On to happier things,' Wren encouraged. 'The launch.'

'And Gabi coming,' Rosie added.

'And meatballs to make . . .'

Isabella checked her watch and blew her nose again. The women were right. It was time to get her show on the road. Hopefully she wouldn't be seeing Etienne Martin again in a very long time.

Mia Famiglia WhatsApp group

Mamma: Everything okay, darling?

Isabella: All fine, Mamma. Just busy.

Mamma: Just thought you'd been a bit quiet.

Isabella: One of those weeks. Don't worry.

Mamma: You're not too disappointed we won't make opening day?

Isabella: No, Mamma. It's not that.

Mamma: Okay. Only checking. You know we love you.

Isabella: I love you too, Mamma.

Chapter Fifty-Two

Etienne

Etienne's phone rang and he wished it could be Isabella, even knowing how impossible that was. But instead it was Walker and his voice was slightly out of breath. He was walking and talking at the same time.

'Etienne. I've come out of the police briefing to tell you they've found a link between all the victims of the arson attacks,' he said, the sound of his boots echoing on the pavement. Etienne moved away from where Fred was watching the evening news on an overly loud television and made his way over to the window.

'Go on,' he said.

'Everyone who has been targeted has got into money troubles. They've borrowed money that they couldn't pay back. Susie Malone took out pay day loans after her husband left them high and dry. The hire company took out loans to buy the hire equipment in the first place and when the business didn't take off they couldn't pay it back. The man in Shalford borrowed money for a new car. Another family owed money for a holiday. Fred Barrow, we think, ran up some debts through betting . . .'

'On the horses . . .' Etienne finished, glancing across at Fred, who'd had the racing on the television all afternoon and his feet, in his new slippers, on the footstool in front of his armchair.

'Exactly,' Walker said. 'So, all of these people owed money and all of these people got burned for not paying it back quick enough. And I think your problem just got much, much worse.' Etienne heard him take a deep breath the other end of the line.

'They all owed money to the Dougalls.'

Etienne felt his blood slow in his veins. Life paused for a single second as the impact of it struck home.

'How much did they owe? Do you know?'

'All of them less than fifty thousand pounds. So, all of them less than Alex.'

Etienne pushed a hand through his hair.

'How late were they with their payments?' he asked.

'Between a week and a couple of months,' Walker said, not needing to say the rest. Etienne rubbed his stubble on his jaw.

'I think you need to be on the lookout,' Walker said quietly. 'Call me if you need me.'

'Thanks.'

Etienne hung up. He looked out the window at the street-lit square, trying to assemble his thoughts into some kind of order. The Dougalls were punishing people who owed them money and didn't pay it back fast enough. The Dougalls were the ones responsible for burning families and businesses and old people out of their homes. The Dougalls were the ones pulling the strings for Alex. But he wasn't weeks late or months late in making good on his debt. He was four years late. What kind of interest were they going to add to that?

A taxi pulled up opposite on the square and Gabriella climbed out of the back seat, dragging a large bag with her. Isabella ran out of the front door of Tutto Mio and scooped her into a long hug in the dusk. Etienne could almost feel the intensity of it, and wished it were him she was holding so tight. Nonna appeared in the doorway, wiping her hands on her apron as she waited for the opportunity to hug her other granddaughter.

At least he'd done the right thing by Isabella. She was safe even if he wasn't. He'd made sure of that.

'Ooh, look, you're on the telly!' Fred pointed at the television and Etienne turned away from Isabella outside to see her face on the screen instead. Her grin was so wide it stretched her cheeks. Her hair tumbled around her face as she gestured and laughed. He remembered the warmth of her fingers in his, the gentle pressure of her thumb against his skin. He turned away, unable to watch it any more.

'I'm going to meet Walker and Fox for a drink,' he called to Fred, who gave him a double thumbs up from the armchair.

Chapter Fifty-Three

Isabella

An hour or so later, after a catch-up in the flat with Gabi and Nonna, Isabella offered Gabi a preview of the restaurant. She felt a rush of pride as she watched Gabi turn in a slow circle in the middle of the floor, taking everything in.

'I cannot believe how good this looks!' Gabriella clapped her hands to her face. Moving slowly to take everything in, she trailed a finger over the vintage wooden tabletops. 'It's transformed,' she said. 'It's gorgeous.'

It was true. The hard work had paid off and the restaurant was dressed and ready to go. Glass jars and vases of differing heights and sizes were on each table, ready for the flowers to be added on opening day. The aged glass mirrors on every freshly painted wall bounced light around beautifully, and the whole effect was calm and warm and welcoming. She couldn't wait for the first customers to see it in a few days' time.

'I'll get us all some coffee,' said Nonna. 'And some biscuits.'

Which Isabella knew by now meant she'd come back in with the rum.

'Is Brigitta here too?' Isabella asked. 'Shall I call her?'

'No, she's at art class this evening,' Nonna said as she disappeared into the kitchen.

'Honestly, Issy, this is amazing.' Gabriella caught her in another hug. When they separated, she studied her face. 'So why are you not looking ecstatic? You okay?'

Isabella couldn't help but sigh. There was no hiding anything from Gabi. But she put a finger to her lips and whispered, 'Tell you later,' as Nonna banged cupboards in the kitchen.

'Daniel?' Gabi whispered, frowning, and it took Isabella a second to remember who Daniel was. She laughed, confusing Gabi even more.

'No,' she said. 'In fact, I'd forgotten Daniel existed.'

Gabi's interest was piqued now and she opened her mouth to get the gossip when the front door banged open and a large man in a black leather jacket stepped inside. His hair was thinning on top and swept back with oil. Another man stood behind him in the entrance. Slightly younger looking but with the same thinning widow's peak.

'Is it a delivery?' Isabella called, looking past them to see the van. He didn't reply, but took another step inside, looking about him, surveying the place. The second man followed.

'Sorry, we're not open yet . . .' Isabella said, confused.

'So I heard,' the man said, lifting one of the glass vases from the table in his pawlike hand. His knuckles were thick, and he wore a gold signet ring on one finger. He turned the glass in his fingers, inspecting it carefully.

'Here we are,' announced Nonna, coming through the swing doors to the restaurant, carrying a tray laden with coffees, biscuits and a bottle of rum. She stopped in her tracks when she saw the extra guests and looked from Isabella to Gabi and back again.

'Now there's a good idea,' the man said, reaching for the rum. He let the vase drop from his grasp, and it smashed on the wooden floorboards. Nonna flinched as he grabbed the bottle by the neck and slammed it onto the nearest table. He pulled out a chair and lowered himself into it, focusing his heavy-lidded eyes on Isabella.

'Shut the door,' he said over his shoulder and the second man pushed the front door closed behind him. Then locked it.

Chapter Fifty-Four

Etienne

The boys were not in bed before Walker and Etienne arrived and now Fox was letting them officially 'wear themselves out' before trying again. To say Reggie and George were pleased with the reprieve was an understatement. They immediately set up position at the back window, noses pressed to the glass, to spot any early fireworks.

Fox wiped a hand across his face. 'You never know, they might one day decide they *want* to go to bed,' he said, lifting his bottle of beer. The three of them took their usual seats at Fox's kitchen table.

'Only if they're older and there is someone they fancy in it,' Walker said, deadpan. The boys were now having an earnest, whispered conversation. It looked like trouble. Reggie skidded across the kitchen and landed at Etienne's chair.

'Is Isabella your girlfriend?' he demanded, poking him with a surprisingly pointy finger.

Etienne's beer went down the wrong way and he swallowed painfully.

'No,' he sighed. 'We're just friends.' He noticed Walker and Fox glance at each other.

In fact, they weren't even that any more. He'd be surprised if she ever spoke to him again after the way he treated her. Maybe he could try to explain it after Alex came home. When it was safe. But until then, he had to live with it. And without her.

'Good,' Reggie said with a satisfied nod. ''Cos I'm going to marry her.'

Etienne spat his beer out. Walker clapped him on the back.

'Don't you think she might be a bit old for you?' Fox said, smiling.

'She won't be when I've grown up to her age.' Reggie shrugged in perfect child logic before turning on the spot and legging it to the front room. George ran after him.

'He's been like this since you guys went into his school that day,' Fox said, shaking his head. 'Smitten.'

'Is that true?' Walker asked him, studying his face.

'What?'

'The "just good friends" story?' Both of them were watching him now.

Etienne rubbed his hands through his hair.

'I don't think we're even that any more,' Etienne muttered. Fox put another beer on the table in front of him, seeing as he'd snorted half of his across the kitchen. He took a long sip but it didn't make him feel any better.

'We were friends,' he started, 'at the beginning. Then we

were having non-sex and that was amazing.' He closed his eyes for a moment. 'Better than most of the actual sex I've ever had.'

He sighed. Walker and Fox waited.

'And then we ended up spending more time together. The karaoke, the cocktails, the school visit. And she's fun, you know?' His friends both nodded in agreement as if they'd known this all along and Etienne was catching up.

'And then I realised I was looking out for her. Making opportunities to see her. I kept looking at her window to catch a glimpse.' He threw an almost embarrassed look at Walker, who took a long swig of his beer but said nothing.

'And she's kind. Like, she'd help anyone, wouldn't she?' Again, he looked at them for confirmation he didn't need. They nodded. 'Even when she was so busy with Tutto Mio, she took time out to take me to the grave. She organised the Spare Room Sleepover.'

He rubbed his stubble.

'And then I thought I had indigestion, but it only ever happened when she was around. And I realised it wasn't anything to do with a dodgy meal. It was proper feelings, right here.' He put his hand on his chest.

'And then I held her hand.' He dropped his face into his hands for a full ten seconds before raising it to face them and saying, 'And never wanted to let go.'

Fox raised an eyebrow. Walker sat forward in his chair.

'But I had to make her stay away from me, in case the Dougalls were going to target me. So, I told her I had a better offer. I really hurt her. And I can't think of anything else apart from how much I want to be with her.'

There followed a silence so complete they realised the boys

were no longer playing noisily in the front room. Instead, they were standing side by side in the doorway, listening to every word: Reggie wide-eyed, George sucking his thumb.

'I love her, don't I?' Etienne said slowly, feeling the awe and relief in saying the words out loud for the first time.

Walker and Fox looked at each other and clinked beer bottles.

'That's what we think,' Fox said.

'You knew?' Etienne asked in disbelief.

'Have done for ages,' Walker agreed, high fiving Fox across the table.

'No!' said Reggie, kicking the table leg with a tiny foot. 'Not fair.'

'Oh my God,' said Etienne. 'I'm in love with Isabella Tucci.'

Reggie harrumphed and grabbed an unsuspecting George in a headlock, marching him through and out of the kitchen. 'We're going to bed,' he said as they stomped up the stairs.

'Two miracles in one day,' Fox muttered as he followed them swiftly to make sure the job got done.

Walker grinned at him and clinked his bottle against Etienne's, who sat back in his chair, winded by his own feelings.

Isabella had worked her way so far under his skin that she'd embedded herself right in his heart. He finally acknowledged all his trips past Tutto Mio were to bump into her. He realised that he'd accepted her 'no-sex' deal in the first place only because he wanted to spend more time with her. Every time she smiled at him, his heart lifted. And every time he held her, he never wanted to let go.

His phone rang. Alex's name on the screen dragged him back to the present with a jolt. He showed Walker the screen as he answered it, putting it on loudspeaker.

This time Alex didn't wait for Etienne to speak before starting himself.

'Et, you're in danger! It's all gone wrong!'

Etienne stood up with his fists on the table, leaving the phone between them. 'What's happened?'

'The Dougalls suddenly rang, saying they wanted the money transferred now.'

'I thought we still had six days to get it together . . .' Etienne said. 'But I can do that—'

Alex cut in.

'I knew you'd say that so I told them I didn't have it, but I would get it from you and could transfer it straight away.'

Etienne made a noise of agreement.

'And then they got really mad and said they'd already waited too long. Four years too long.'

Walker's eyes widened as he focused on the phone screen.

'And they said they'd come and get it themselves.'

Walker and Etienne's eyes locked. This was bad. They both knew it.

'Have they found out where I am?' Etienne asked, trying to keep his voice level, thinking about old Fred Barrow at home watching the television in his slippers.

'Old Man Dougall saw you on the evening news. They know the name of your restaurant.'

Fox appeared in the doorway having put the boys to bed, glancing between the two, sensing the tense atmosphere.

Etienne put his hands to his head and wracked his brain, forcing himself to recall the interview. Had they asked him about The Bistro?

'Did you see it?' he mouthed at Walker and Fox but they both shook their heads.

He thought back. Isabella explaining how she organised the scheme. The interviewer asking whether they liked living in Honeybridge. And Isabella's happy promotion of the restaurant, Tutto Mio.

The Dougalls thought they were a couple. And they now thought they owned a restaurant together.

'They're going to Tutto Mio,' Etienne gasped down the phone. 'Isabella . . .' he said aloud, helplessly, and Walker stood too now, all three men moving instinctively together.

'Did they say anything else?' Etienne asked, needing to get off the phone, to move. He had only one thought in his head and that was to get there before the Dougalls did. To keep Isabella safe, to hold her tight.

Alex's voice shuddered as it came through the phone speaker.

'They said if you play with fire, you're going to get burned.'

Etienne's brain was laser sharp, focused only on working out the steps to take to keep Isabella safe. He glanced at his friends. Fox and Walker already had their phones out and were accessing their online bank accounts.

'Transferred to you,' Fox said.

'Done.' Walker pressed the button.

Etienne heard the double ping on his phone, notifying him of a deposit to his account. He checked the balance. £50,000. All there.

'I'm transferring the money now, Al. Pay it to the Dougalls and let them know that it's done.' He hung up the phone and immediately accessed his bank app. The transfer took seconds his end but he knew it might take longer to show up in Alex's account. He pulled on his jacket and headed to the front door.

'They're dangerous, Etienne,' Walker said, following behind, still on his phone. 'I'll notify the police and I can scramble my fire crew on the substantial threat of fire.' Etienne pulled on his coat, and zipped it purposefully.

Fox held the door for them, stopping Etienne as he went through with a firm grip on the shoulder.

'If this was a game I was designing, I'd say the element of surprise would be your winning strategy.'

Etienne locked eyes with him and nodded his understanding, before sprinting in the direction of Tutto Mio.

Chapter Fifty-Five

Isabella

Isabella moved closer to Nonna, who stood frozen in the doorway, still holding the tray. Gabi looked urgently at her and Isabella could only look back and make a minute shake of her head. She cleared her throat.

'Sorry,' Isabella said again. 'I think there's been some confusion. I'm going to have to ask you to leave.'

The first man laughed, a spray of his spit misting the air.

'You don't give us orders,' he said, sticking a toothpick in the corner of his mouth.

Nonna laid the tray down on the nearest table and Isabella moved in front of her.

'The Dougalls give the orders.'

The other man, who had a chest the size of a beer keg, checked his phone.

'They haven't received the money yet,' Barrel Chest said in a wide south London accent.

'That's okay,' Toothpick replied. 'We've got all the time in the world.'

This didn't make any sense. Isabella looked from one to the other before trying again.

'Look, I don't know any Dougalls,' she said. 'And I don't owe anyone any money.'

'Your husband does, though, love,' Toothpick said.

'I don't have a husband,' she said, trying her best to keep her voice calm and even, but even she could hear the shake in it. 'There must be some kind of misunderstanding. I'll have to ask you to leave. Otherwise, I'll have to call the police to sort it out.'

Toothpick lunged. For a big man, he was surprisingly fast. He slapped her phone out of her hand with such violence that it smashed on the floor. Nonna gasped. Isabella grasped her sore hand against her chest and shot a glance out the window towards the square, but it was dark and deserted.

'Obviously your husband hasn't told you his family secrets,' Toothpick said. 'But he and his brother owe a *lot* of money to the Dougalls. And we're here to make sure he pays up.'

Barrel kicked the wooden chair beside him at the wall. It splintered into pieces and Gabi ducked reflexively.

'Please don't,' Isabella heard herself say, and then wished she'd kept quiet as it seemed to enrage him more. He turned over the entire table, kicking and stamping on the wooden chairs until they were nothing more than a pile of broken limbs.

In the silence afterwards, she heard his breathing, ragged with the exertion.

'Anything yet?' Toothpick asked.

Barrel checked his phone again and gave a mocking thumbs down.

'Well,' Toothpick said, 'I guess we should start claiming interest.'

They looked round the restaurant as if surveying a playground and deciding what fun to have first.

Toothpick walked casually to the largest mirror that hung behind the bar. Gripping it by the top in his two paws, he heaved it from the wall with a roar. It crashed to the dining floor. The aged glass shattered, shards spinning across the floorboards, the frame cracking in two.

Nonna shrieked, Gabi ran to her and Isabella clapped both hands to her face. But the men didn't stop. Menus were ripped up and thrown in the air like confetti. Glasses were dropped one by one on the floor. Isabella's chest was pounding, anger raging as she watched them destroy her hard work, but fear held her in place. If they could do this to property, they could hurt them too. She glanced at Nonna and saw the pallor of her face. She had to get them out of there.

The men regrouped, panting with their efforts, and Barrel checked his phone again. He shook his head and Toothpick turned to another table.

'Wait, wait!' Isabella rushed forward, no idea what she was doing, but unable to stand still and watch the destruction of her dream.

'You stay right there,' Toothpick said, stopping her in her tracks with a hard shove on the shoulder and snapping a photo of her on his phone. 'That might make them pay a bit quicker,' he said. 'You're our insurance.' With a humourless smile, he flicked his old toothpick to the floor before taking a new one from a pack in his jacket pocket. She realised they weren't toothpicks – they were red-headed matches.

He nodded at Barrel and they lunged again, kicking stools, smashing shot glasses, breaking mirrors. The noise was incredible. Toothpick pulled the bar shelves from the wall and glasses fell like a waterfall to the floor. Gabi bent Nonna into her chest, protecting her in the corner. Isabella stood still, alone and exposed in the middle of the dining room. Her eyes flashed around the room, looking for a weapon or a way out, or something – anything – that might help.

What she spotted was Etienne's eyes as he peeked through the gap in the kitchen door. Her breath hitched in hope and he put a single finger to his lips. She blinked, too scared to nod. Terrified to draw attention to him. Afraid that someone was going to get seriously hurt.

Barrel paused, out of breath. He had single-handedly destroyed the majority of tables.

Toothpick had focused mainly on accessories. The floor was littered with glasses and pictures that his boot had stamped through. The entire restaurant was like a bomb site. Isabella swallowed a sob and flicked her eyes to Etienne again.

Barrel checked his phone and grinned, showing a gold tooth front right.

'They've got their money,' he said with a certain amount of satisfaction. 'Lucky for you.'

Barrel hoicked his jeans up by the belt loops, and stretched, surveying the damage.

'A job well done,' he agreed. 'Now we can claim the rest of the interest.'

He opened the canvas holdall he'd slung to the floor and pulled out some ripped-up rags and a can of petrol. Unscrewing the lid, he took a long hard sniff, eyes closed. Isabella could smell it from where she was. Her eyes watered.

'Please,' she gasped. 'You said it yourself: they have the money.'

'Your husband and his brother can't fuck about with the Dougalls, you know,' Barrel said.

'I keep telling you I haven't got a husband.'

'Your boyfriend then,' Toothpick said. 'Etienne Martin.'

Isabella resisted looking at Etienne as she heard his name. It took every ounce of self-control she had to keep her eyes on the two men.

'Him and his brother can't keep the Dougalls waiting without expecting to pay the penalty . . .'

Barrel lifted the petrol in front of him and, tauntingly slowly, tilted the bottle until the amber liquid began to pour, splashing on the floorboards. He then jerked his arm and sent an arc of it over the nearest piles of broken wood. Isabella surged forward but Toothpick forced her away again, pushing her back towards the other women. She saw the fury simmering in Gabi's face, the way she bore her weight on the balls of her feet, her stance ready to spring. Isabella realised that if she made a move, Gabi would be right there with her.

'Wait a minute,' Toothpick said to Barrel, before moving closer to Isabella. She saw something different on his face as he let his eyes linger on her body.

'Old Man Dougall said she was a looker.' He swapped his match from one side of his mouth to the other. 'He wasn't wrong.' Barrel grinned again, flashing that gold tooth, before screwing the lid back onto the can of petrol.

'They've got their money,' he said thoughtfully. 'And they'll get their interest paid in ashes.' He nodded at the petrol pooling on the floor before slowly removing his box of matches from his jacket pocket. He shook them, in silent consideration, before tossing the pack to Barrel, who caught them one-handed.

'I'm thinking I might take me a bonus,' Toothpick said, his tongue turning the toothpick over and over as he stared at Isabella. 'And that's you.'

Chapter Fifty-Six

Etienne

The air was heavy with the smell of petrol and the echo of those words. They changed everything. Etienne had held back, thinking the police or fire crew would be there by now, but the street outside was quiet and the restaurant already trashed. When the money was confirmed, he'd thought for one moment that would be enough. But now, the look on that man's face, the way he licked his lips as he leered at her. Etienne would not let them touch Isabella. Never while he had breath in his body would that man lay a single finger on her. He groped about him frantically for a weapon, something he could use to strike. His hand closed on the shiny metal handle of the fire extinguisher.

He watched her through the crack of the door, barely ajar, his heart in his mouth. She straightened her back, steeling herself.

'No,' she said.

Toothpick raised his eyebrows at her and smiled. His teeth were as pointed and yellow as a rat's as he pulled a revolver from his inside pocket and aimed it directly at her chest.

'Nobody says no to me,' he said.

Barrel laughed and his whole belly shook, as if he were watching one of the funniest films he'd ever seen.

'Maybe I'll take myself a bonus afterwards too,' he said, turning his sweaty face to wink at Gabi.

Isabella shot a glance at Etienne, and he silently lifted one finger in front of his face and turned it in a tiny circle. She blinked. God, he hoped she understood. Turn him around. Get his back to the kitchen door. He tightened his grip on the extinguisher and readied himself.

She sidestepped left and the thug mirrored her, moving one step closer to Etienne.

'It won't take long,' he said. 'Don't worry, I can be sweet . . .' He flicked his tongue in and out like a snake, balancing the match on it before tossing it back in his mouth.

Isabella took another step to the left.

Toothpick waved the gun at her and smiled, as though they were dancing. As if this was all part of the fun. Like he had all the time in the world. It was like watching a cat play with a mouse, knowing there was only one way the story was going to end.

Isabella took another step and the man followed, closing the distance between them. He was so close now and could grab her at any time. Isabella moved quicker again, darting to the left, and the man turned and lunged for her, his back to the kitchen. Etienne seized his chance and barged through the door so hard it flew back on its hinges, slamming against the wall. He hit the back of the man's head with the fire extinguisher with such force that they both staggered forward and fell in a jumble of arms and legs. As they hit the floor, the gun went off.

Chapter Fifty-Seven

Isabella

The noise of the gun reverberated in Isabella's head and echoed around the decimated room. The smell of gunfire mingled with petrol and rum where the bottle lay spilled and dripping amongst the debris.

Isabella wasn't hurt, but someone was moaning. She ran to Nonna, who was crouching on the floor, hands over her head. Gabi was standing over her like a lioness. They were both unscathed.

God, no, not Etienne. Her heart thumped. Was it Etienne? He lay flat out on top of Toothpick, and one them was bleeding. Blood bloomed across the floorboards from beneath them.

'Etienne,' she gasped and threw herself onto the floor beside him.

Etienne lifted his head, bleeding from something he'd hit on the floor. He crawled backwards off the man's body and pushed himself to his feet. Isabella ran her hands over his chest, looking for blood but there was nothing. He wasn't shot. He dragged her to him, away from the man writhing in agony on the floor, and she felt his arm around her like a life raft.

Toothpick moaned again, clutching his leg where blood was pumping through his jeans. He spotted the gun, forgotten on the floor, and made a last-ditch grab at it, but Isabella beat him to it by kicking it towards the corner. It skimmed away across the floor.

'Do it now,' hissed Toothpick at Barrel, 'and then get me out of here.' Barrel struck a match, and it hissed into life. He held it momentarily in the air to let it take hold. The flame spluttered into life.

It all seemed to happen in slow motion. The horror of it playing out around her like a film. Isabella heard her own shout and saw Etienne already diving for the fire extinguisher. The flame flickered taller, and Barrel tossed the match casually towards the petrol. It arced through the air, and Isabella's shout rose to a scream of pure anger. This couldn't be the way her dream ended.

Gabi took her moment. Crouching low before leaping upwards to grasp hold of one of the exposed timber beams across the restaurant ceiling, she used all her acrobatic training and strength to swing her legs backwards before flinging herself forwards, kicking the match perfectly with her pointed toe before it hit the ground. The impact of her foot kicked the flame clean out. Nonna flew in behind her and tipped the coffee pot on the dead match, just to be sure. Etienne put the icing on the cake by letting the fire extinguisher rip at the same spot.

Barrel had heaved Toothpick to his feet and they were lurching together to leave, leaving a trail of blood as they went. Sirens wailed as the emergency services closed in on the restaurant and by the time the two men had opened the door, the entire square was lit by the swirl of blue lights. Isabella saw the police outside rushing in to apprehend them. Walker was there too with his crew, parked in the middle of the square and aiming the fire hose at the restaurant frontage. How they all knew to be there, she couldn't even guess.

Etienne went out to talk to them, leaving her standing alone for a second before Nonna and Gabi rushed to envelop her in family arms.

They watched, still holding each other as Walker stood his team down. It took two policemen to handcuff Barrel and fit him into a police car, and Toothpick was handcuffed too before being loaded onto a stretcher and wheeled into a waiting ambulance.

They saw Etienne pause in the centre of the square, alone. He pulled his phone from his pocket and held it to his ear, looking upwards, jaw taut. Then, whatever he heard on the other end made him squeeze his eyes tight shut, his head sagging backwards on his shoulders in relief. Blood ran through his hairline and dripped down his forehead, but he seemed not to notice it as he pocketed his phone again, then walked decisively towards Tutto Mio. A single firework shot into the sky behind him, exploding into a million white stars.

The other women drifted away from her as Etienne stepped in the doorway. But she didn't notice. She only registered the noise of his feet as he crunched through glass towards her.

He stopped before her, within touching distance. His eyes were searching her face and they looked hopeful, apologetic, fierce, terrified. She could feel the tears trembling on her own lashes. Neither of them spoke, but when he put his arms around her and pulled her to his chest, she weaved her arms about his neck, holding on.

'I'm sorry,' he whispered, pulling her tightly so that she fit against every part of him. 'I'm so sorry, Bella.'

Chapter Fifty-Eight

Etienne

It was almost midnight and Etienne had only let Isabella out of his arms while he took his turn to give the police his statement.

His interview had taken the longest as he shared the entire story of Alex's debt and the link to the Dougalls. The two police officers shared a look.

'This might be just what we need to nail them,' one said, but the other looked unconvinced. Etienne knew he was debating the fact that the Dougalls were nowhere near the attack itself.

'Even if it's not, it's enough to bring them in for questioning.'

While Etienne would love to see them thrown in jail, so long as they left Alex and Isabella alone from now on, it was enough. And with the two-word message Alex had told him he received on transfer of the money; it seemed it was over. Debt Paid. Thank God.

The ambulance crew had dressed Etienne's head wound and Isabella had held his hand throughout. Gabi had used Isabella's phone and texted the Girl Gang WhatsApp and Wren, Rosie and

Amber had dropped everything, turning up to sweep broken glass and make tea. Walker had organised a skip for the following day to clear out the piles of broken furniture. Nonna had passed around several glasses of rum and then taken herself off to bed.

Since finalising his statement, he had kept hold of Isabella's hand. It felt like the most natural and obvious thing in the world and he wasn't letting go.

Once everyone had gone, and Gabi had also gone to bed to watch an action film for research, Etienne sat with Isabella on the sofa and told her everything. Starting five years ago – no, before that, he corrected himself – when Alex started his gambling. How it got worse when their parents died. How Etienne had let him down by not giving him the money, by putting a woman first. He'd dropped his head at that point, not through embarrassment but through the realisation that what he felt those years ago was nothing, *nothing*, compared to what he felt for Isabella.

'So that's the whole fear of commitment thing,' she said gently, finally understanding.

He told her about Alex's phone call. How he would do anything to right his wrong and get what was left of his family back together.

'You could have told me,' she said. 'I would have helped.' It was such an Isabella thing to say that it stopped him in his tracks, wondering how he could have got it all so wrong.

He wound his fingers through hers. 'Everything I did, I did to keep you safe,' he said, squeezing her hand gently to make his point. 'I've never felt like this for anyone before and I promise I will never hurt you again.'

He passed her a cushion to get comfy and told her the whole story, explained about Walker's concern that the Dougalls were behind the fires. The sudden fear when Alex told him the Dougalls knew who he was. The overriding worry he was going to drag her into danger.

When he stopped talking, she was curled in the corner of the sofa so that she could face him, still holding his hand. In the silence he could hear the clock in the square chime midnight.

'I feel the same, you know,' Isabella said quietly. 'About you.'

Their eyes met and held, and there was something burning so strongly there that it hurt his chest.

'Since the first time I saw you, I haven't been able to get you out of my mind. I was drawn back, time and time again,' she said. 'I just want to be with you.'

He smoothed her hair away from her face. 'That's good, because I'm not letting you go again. Not ever.'

He couldn't stay away any longer. He pulled her into his arms and kissed her, gently, conscious of her bruises. Her lips met his and his heart swelled with the tenderness of the kiss.

He pulled away to look into her face, only then noticing the shadows under her eyes, the paleness of her skin. Isabella smiled but it turned into a yawn, and he wanted to wrap her up in a blanket and watch her sleep. She stretched her arms above her head, letting go of his hand, and it felt strange and empty without her. She pushed herself to standing and he felt his shoulders sag. It was obviously time to go. She stretched again, before looking back at him.

'Do you need to go home?' she asked, tilting her head to one side.

He exhaled slowly.

'No,' he said. 'I *need* to stay here.'

'I was hoping you'd say that.'

She extended her hand to him again and he stood with her, pulled her into him, and she sighed, long and slow.

'I'll need to get up early in the morning to sort everything out,' she said into his shoulder. 'Cancel the bookings and the opening arrangements, change the social media adverts . . . fill the skip.' She sighed again and he felt her disappointment inside his own body. Everything she'd worked so hard for, smashed to smithereens. The focus of her whole year, her adult life even, snatched away just as it was within taking distance.

'Don't cancel anything,' he said. 'Leave it all to me.'

She pulled away to see his face. Her skin was pale with shock and fatigue.

'I can't do that . . .' she said, shaking her head and wrinkling her nose. 'It's my business.'

He moved his hands to the top of her arms, shaking her ever so gently so that she listened.

'I know you want to do everything on your own,' he said. 'I know you're an independent, successful woman. But let me help. You helped me. You help everyone. I won't let you down.' It was suddenly vitally important to prove it to her. To show her he was a man of his word.

She lifted an eyebrow, considering.

'You'll open on Saturday as planned,' he insisted and a tiny light of hope rekindled in her eyes.

'But that's the day after tomorrow.' She lifted her hands to the sky in despair. 'And there's nothing left of the restaurant.'

'Trust me,' Etienne said, pulling her back against him. 'I have an idea.'

Mia Famiglia WhatsApp group

Mamma: Everything ready for the launch?

Isabella: Hmm. Not quite. We're having a few last-minute setbacks.

Papà: I'm sure you'll work it out. You always do.

Isabella: Let's hope so!

Mamma: I'm so sorry we can't be there.

Papà: But we'll be thinking of you.

Mamma: And we're proud of you, darling.

Papà: So proud.

Chapter Fifty-Nine

Isabella

She couldn't stop looking at Etienne there in her flat, touching him as he sat on her sofa, his hands entwined with hers. She'd watched him help Nonna on with her coat before she went out, help Gabi lift the heavy bar cabinets, find brooms and mops for Amber, Wren and Rosie. Since hearing his story and his reasons for pushing her away, she understood the man behind the reputation. She saw Etienne as the loyal, fiercely family-loving man he was. As well as being a total sex god. And now he was going to stay the night. Or what was left of it.

'And don't worry,' he said, with a half-laugh. 'I know what day it is.' They'd both glanced at the calendar hanging there on the kitchen wall. The one with all the red Xs on it marking off the year. The day after tomorrow was supposed to be opening day – the last day of her year's promise to herself. 'I'm just here to hold you.'

She considered that for a split mini second. The thought of Etienne spooning her all night, folded around her like a blanket, made her go gooey inside. But her nipples didn't seem to understand they'd recently been in a near-death situation and were screaming for attention.

'Maybe we could relax the rules for the night . . .' she said, unconsciously pulling her lower lip with her teeth. His eyes glinted as he looked back at her from the calendar. He put his hand under her chin and lifted her face to his.

He was so close she could feel his breath on her face as he whispered, 'We only have a couple of nights left until you'll have kept your promise to yourself.'

'So, no sex then?' she said, almost sulkily, and he laughed.

'No sex,' he agreed. 'I'm not going to be the one that breaks your promise. I'm going to be the one that helps you keep it.'

She could feel herself straining towards him, aching to be touched. He ran a finger down her forehead, down her nose and to her mouth. She parted her lips and took it inside, sucking on it greedily.

'But anything else goes, right?'

He used her spare toothbrush and they cleaned their teeth, watching each other in the bathroom mirror. The strangeness of the situation bringing that half-smile to his face, his mouth irresistible even when it was frothing with foam. Damn.

'Can I shower?' he asked and she nodded at his reflection, suddenly having lost the ability to speak. Reaching into the cubicle, he turned the water to full pelt. As she tied her hair up to wash her face, Etienne began to undress behind her. He undid the buttons of his shirt, peeling it off to reveal his muscular and smooth chest. The line of hair starting from his belly button and heading down. His shoulder had a bruise forming on it already, from where he hit the floor, showing blue-green under the skin. She smoothed her cleanser over her face on autopilot, her eyes glued to him. He pulled at his belt and then released the buttons of his jeans. Shucking them down over his hips, they fell to the floor and he stepped out of them, standing only now in his fitted boxers. She put the hot cloth to her cheeks and began to massage off the cleanser in careful circles, thinking about what was under those shorts.

He raised one eyebrow at her in the mirror and then turned. She let her eyes feast on the contours of his back, the round of his buttocks, the long, strong legs. Using both thumbs, he pulled down the shorts. She realised she'd stopped attempting any kind of face washing and let the hot cloth fall in the sink. He looked at her over his shoulder and flashed her a smile, before stepping into the shower, back still turned. She was gripping the sink with both hands.

She'd never seen him naked. He'd never seen her naked. Not completely. She wanted to see him all, feel all of him.

She pulled her top over her head in one movement. Her own shoulder smarted where Toothpick had shoved her, but she didn't give it a second thought. She pushed down her jeans and left them there on the floor. Unclipping her bra, she let it fall and she kicked her thong to join his pile of clothes.

His back was still to her as he ran his hands through his hair under the jet, sending the water cascading down his body. Opening the shower door, she stepped inside, pressing herself against his back and hearing his gasp above the sound of the beating water as she wrapped her arms around him from behind.

'Bella,' he said quietly, and she smiled to herself, her forehead to his shoulder, her breasts to his ribs. He was the only person in the world to call her that and she loved the sound of it. She explored his chest with her fingers, feeling his nipples bud like hers under her fingertips. She trailed her fingers lower, skating over the taut abs which quivered slightly at her touch, brushing the tiny trail of hair from his navel and down. He turned in her grasp before she could reach his cock, his body soap slippery against her, and pulled her further into the torrent of water so that it ran in rivulets from her breasts, and down between her legs. She widened her stance, letting the water run where she wanted his fingers, his breath, his cock.

'I want you,' she said, voice husky. She put her hands to his head, gently avoiding the cut, and held his face to hers. The first touch of his lips was soft and tender. It grew and deepened until he was holding her so tightly and kissing her so completely that it felt never-ending. God, she loved him. His hands roamed, hers searched, they learned each other's backs and shoulders as they tightened their grips on each other. Turning each other this way and that underneath the water, pressing her back at one point onto shockingly cold tiles, the heat of his erection searing her stomach.

Slowly, without her realising what he was doing at first, he loosened his grip and pulled away, putting a few inches between their bodies. He turned the lever and the water stopped. Her breath shuddered with anticipation.

'I want you, Etienne,' she said again. 'I want all of you.'

He led her by the hand out of the shower and she saw his eyes flick over her body, the clench of his jaw.

'I want you too,' he said, voice rough. 'But not tonight, Bella.'

She growled low in her throat and he laughed. Pulling one of her fluffy white bath towels from the rail, he wrapped her in it and began to rub her shoulders, her arms, her breasts. She felt her body strain for him, but he calmly smiled that half-smile and continued to dry her.

'You only have a few days left,' he said. 'We can wait. And I'm not going to make it harder for you.'

She growled again in frustration.

'Although it's hard for me too,' he said, tucking the towel around her. 'Very hard indeed.' He took her hand and wrapped it around his cock, holding it there against the throb and heat for a second. She gasped. He removed her hand and she groaned.

'Tonight, I'm going to make this easy for you . . .' Etienne continued, leading her from the bathroom to her bedroom and sitting her on the end of her bed. She wanted to pull him onto her, to wrap her legs around his body. But he sank to his knees in front of her instead.

'I'm going to make this easy for you to enjoy.'

Etienne tugged at the towel and it fell away. He knelt before her and his tongue flicked his bottom lip as he swept his eyes over her breasts, her belly and down. Running his hands lightly over her, he pushed her backwards on the bed so that she lay flat on her back with her knees off the end. She reached her hands above her head, holding on to the bed sheets.

'I'm going to make it easy for you to come . . .'

Etienne put his hands on her knees. Her stomach flipped over.

'And then you're going to rest . . .'

His hands gently eased her knees apart until she knew he was staring right at her most secret part.

'And then you're going to sleep.'

She wasn't listening any more. Her breathing was ragged already and his fingers were only skimming her inner thighs, heading inwards to where she wanted them so badly. Holding her legs wide now, he parted her lips and she realised how wet she was. His fingers stroked the slickness, dipped inside her and then again, one finger, then two. And she arched her back on the bed at the penetration, wanting more.

Then, nothing.

He withdrew.

Isabella's whole body throbbed with longing. With the need to be touched, kissed, filled. She writhed on her sheets, creasing the cotton between her fists.

Etienne held her in place, one hand on each thigh, stilling her. She glanced at him there, his face between her legs, the hint of a smile playing on his mouth. She dropped her head back to the pillow and knew he was making her wait.

He rubbed the stubble of his beard on her left inner thigh and she groaned at the proximity of him. He pressed his lips to her mound, his beard scratching her softness and leaving it tingling. And then the tip of his tongue flicked out, so soft, so gentle as to be almost not there. But the next pushed firmly against her clit and she gasped at the current that charged through her. Her back arched like a bow, breasts pushing to the sky. Isabella closed her eyes to feel everything, to lose herself to this feeling. This moment. Again, and again, flicking, licking, gently at first, as though exploring, tasting, testing reactions.

Then longer strokes, covering all of her, his moans vibrating against her core. She filled her hands with her own full breasts, and put her fingers to her nipples, pulling them to peaks. His hand came between her legs, two fingers inside her plunging, again and again and again as he pressed his whole mouth over her clit and sucked it inside his mouth, holding it between his teeth for a second before tugging with his lips. His other hand reached over her belly to her breasts and he put his hand over hers and suddenly she was reaching and reaching for something that crashed over her in such waves that behind her closed eyes she saw sparks and then stars and fell a thousand miles into a warm black nothing.

Chapter Sixty

Etienne

Etienne opened his eyes into a mass of chestnut-brown waves on the pillow. Isabella was still sleeping, the rise and fall of her chest almost, but not quite, soundless – like a cat in the second it begins to purr. His arm was still slung over her waist and she fitted perfectly to his front. Her bottom pushed into his groin was having an immediate effect now that he was awake, or maybe her closeness had woken him.

He breathed her in – the lemony shampoo, the cream of her skin – before exhaling slowly, fully. The light was already shining through the gaps in the wooden blinds and it was time to go. However nice this was – and it was probably the nicest way in which he'd ever woken up – he had to get out of bed. He had a lot to do if his plan was going to work.

He shifted in the bed and she awoke, turning towards him, winding her arm around him even before she had opened her eyes. She was sleep-smudged and beautiful, bare-faced, and he could have stayed there all day, looking at her, touching her . . .

But there was no time for distractions. The thought made him laugh. He was turning into Isabella.

Last night, after she'd come, Etienne had rolled her into bed and switched out the light. He'd held her and stroked her head as she'd drifted immediately into a deep sleep, exhausted by the shock of the day.

He lay there for a long time, not daring to move in case he woke her up. But also, to watch her as he still tasted her on his mouth. The twitch of her nose when a stray hair fell on it. Her slightly parted lips. The way her eyelids moved occasionally with dreams underneath. His heart swelled with love.

Finally, she woke. As her eyes adjusted to the light and she spotted him there, she smiled.

'I have to go,' Etienne said, pressing a kiss to her mouth, and she made a noise of protest and pulled him in tight. He laughed and kissed her again, before scooting out of the bed.

'You sort the skip out. I'll sort the rest,' he said, pulling his boxers on and noticing her admiring the view. His jeans came next. 'I'm going home to check Fred is okay and have a shower and then I'll get to work.'

'Are you sure I shouldn't postpone the opening? Cancel the bookings?' She sat up and stretched her arms above her head, letting the sheet fall from her breasts. He stopped with one sock midway on, and blinked, trying to keep his focus. Stuffing his foot into his trainer, he knew the only way to get out of here without ravishing that body was to leave fast. He grabbed his shirt from the bathroom, blew her a kiss and ran out the door.

Once he was showered – which was quite a feat with an

erection like a flagpole thinking about the shower he'd had with Isabella the night before – and was at the kitchen table, he began making his list of contacts. It would take everyone he knew to make the plan come to life but he was determined to make it work. Isabella was depending on him and he wouldn't let her down.

He rang Rosie and Wren first. They immediately promised to pass the word on to all the clubs that met in The Lit Lounge. Walker promised to email everyone who had taken in a Spare Room Sleepover guest, and also contact the Malones so that Millie could pass on to her friends on Snapchat. Fox put the word out on Reggie's class WhatsApp group. That was already more than one hundred people who knew Isabella that he was sure would want to help. After everything she'd done for Honeybridge, it was time for Honeybridge to repay the gesture.

Once he'd called everyone, he wrote up the list.

Wooden chairs x 60
Tables x 12 (wood if possible)
Mirrors – as many as possible – different sizes and shapes welcome
Glasses x hundreds

Luckily the crockery and cutlery just needed putting through the dishwasher and nothing had been touched in the kitchen.

It was the dining room that he needed to focus on. And the marketing. But he had an idea for that too.

'You okay, Boss?' Mile End Mickey asked, pulling on his apron. 'I heard you were the hero of the day yesterday at Tutto Mio.'

'Not so hard to believe, is it?' Etienne said and added *pictures/ art* to his list of things to do.

'Finally realised you fancied her then?' Mile End Mickey waved a rolling pin his way. 'Thank fuck for that.'

Chapter Sixty-One

Isabella

By four o'clock in the afternoon, Isabella was starting to panic. The restaurant was still an empty space, although it was clean and free of debris and glass, and she was meant to open the next day. There was a brown bloodstain soaked into one section of the old floorboards which hadn't scrubbed out, but it didn't look out of place as the floorboards were reclaimed and bore bruises and memories from their previous lives anyway. It was now another piece of history – and one she felt curiously proud of. No matter what people threw at her, she was going to get through it.

She messaged Etienne again. This time a single question mark. She couldn't see how this was going to work. The closer it got to the end of the day, the less she could imagine opening tomorrow lunchtime with a fully functioning restaurant. All day, he'd replied saying not to worry, to focus on the kitchen and the team.

Nonna had cooked endlessly, tray after tray of meatballs,

preparing for the grand opening. Whenever Isabella expressed any kind of concern about whether it would happen, she'd shrugged and patted her arm, and said that Etienne was sorting it.

But by four o'clock, her anxiety was kicking in. Her message to him whizzed off into hyperspace and she awaited his reply. But it came in person. He rushed through the front door, rosy from the cold and with an excited smile.

'Come outside,' he said. 'We're ready for you.'

She frowned, confused. Who was he with and what was he doing and how was this going to get a restaurant open tomorrow? What was with all the mystery? She stepped into the coat that Etienne held out for her and let him wrap a scarf around her neck. He kissed her quickly on the nose, then gestured for her to lead the way out to the square.

The cheering took her by surprise. The TV camera in her face was also a bit of a shock. But the long line of people waiting outside the restaurant was the most astonishing thing she'd ever seen. The queue went all round the four sides of the square. People of all ages, some she recognised, others she didn't, all bundled up in coats and hats, holding various items in their hands or in bags.

She recognised the cameraman. It was the same guy from the Spare Room Sleepover, and there beside him was the reporter, Michelle Carter. The camera was firmly focused on Isabella, capturing the confusion and the wonder on her face.

Etienne wrapped her in his arms and even though she'd only missed him since this morning, it had already been too long.

'What's going on?' she whispered into his shoulder.

'You'll see,' he said, pressing a kiss to her mouth.

Michelle Carter cleared her throat and puffed her hair with one hand.

'Ready?' she said to Isabella, who had absolutely no idea what she should be ready for. Michelle, without waiting, beamed down the camera as she started.

'Here we are back in Honeybridge, the riverside town which doesn't often get media attention. But twice in the last week, it has shown itself to be *the* place to live if you love community and friendship.'

Michelle spread her arm wide, and the cameraman panned from her to Isabella and Etienne and then slowly along the waiting line of residents, following them on all sides. As they saw the camera pointed their way they did a crazy-looking Mexican wave, with various household items in their hands.

'A few days ago we reported on the Spare Room Sleepover. A genius campaign created by Isabella Tucci, here with her boyfriend, Etienne Martin.' Michelle moved to stand next to them. Etienne's arm remained around her shoulders, holding her in place. The camera refocused on them and Isabella was glad she'd taken her apron off already.

'Her campaign brought the entire community together to make sure the residents affected by a fire in the elderly residential home had somewhere safe and comfortable to stay. She organised it all even though she's only lived here for a few months, putting people first and helping where she could.'

Isabella could feel a flush creeping up her neck.

'So, when Isabella's family and her new restaurant were the

victims of a brutal attack which destroyed all her hard work, the community were more than happy to step up for her too.'

Michelle gestured with her arm again, showing the sheer numbers of people gathered in the square.

'Right, let's get this restaurant sorted out!' she called to the waiting line.

The cameraman stepped aside and Michelle waved the first people forward. It was like a receiving line at a wedding, Isabella and Etienne standing by the door of Tutto Mio as the line slowly edged towards them. First in line were the waiting team, all wearing their blue shirts and jeans under their jackets. They proceeded past her into the restaurant, talking about 'taking positions'.

Wren and Rosie came next, carrying a whitewashed wooden table between them which would seat four. Isabella recognised it from The Lit Lounge.

'From us to you,' Wren said, pausing to give her a squeeze as they carried it inside. The camera caught it all, including the brimming tears as Isabella finally realised what Etienne had organised. He winked at her and followed Wren inside to direct where everything went.

The next table was a six-seater, old and pine, carried by a family with a bespectacled six-year-old girl who said '*Ciao*' with a shy smile.

The next were Amber's next-door neighbours, who she had never met, but who told her they had heard so much about her. She blinked, taken aback by people's kindness.

After another fifteen tables of various sizes were brought

in by people she recognised, and others she didn't, the chairs started. She put her hands to her head in astonishment.

Wooden chairs, white-painted chairs, wicker chairs and a couple of benches came through. A gorgeous dark-haired man introduced himself as Toby, Riley's dad, and presented her with a high chair and a hug, saying, 'Every restaurant needs one.'

Everyone headed one by one into the restaurant with their offerings and reappeared a few moments later, waving at the camera, smiling, happy.

Next came glasses. She recognised a few of the older people from the Heart of Honeybridge. Brigitta turned up with a set of sherry glasses, beautiful and stylish, as Isabella would expect.

'We managed to get into some of the units to claim some items,' Brigitta said, tapping her nose, and Isabella gave her a tearful smile as she went in the front door.

The next couple were grinning at her. The man looked vaguely familiar, but she couldn't place the woman as she lifted a beautiful antique-looking set of champagne coupes in an aged box.

'They're beautiful!' Isabella exclaimed. 'Sorry, have we met before?'

'Not me, but you might recognise my *boyfriend* . . .' the woman said. The man leaned forward conspiratorially and suddenly Isabella recognised him. Andy, the drunken lothario from The Bolthole.

'You recommended an app to him on how to talk to women? Well, it worked. He asked me out. And we wanted to say thank you.'

Isabella was quite overwhelmed, and even more so when

Jesse was next in the queue. His beard was trimmed so perfectly that it looked to be drawn on and he pulled her into a hug that smelled reassuringly expensive.

'Gabi rang me!' he said. 'And you know how much I love you – so I brought you my Emma Bridgewater mug collection for your coffees.'

She gasped, knowing how much he loved his pottery, but he flapped a hand at her, and whispered, 'And the visit's been more than worth it already, as I met that gorgeous man over there.' He smiled, waving as Toby emerged again from the restaurant, now empty-handed. Toby mouthed 'call me' as he held his thumb to his ear and his pinky to his mouth. Jesse danced on the spot and Isabella laughed.

'Can't stay today, my darling, but I will be back!' he said, and then, throwing a last look over at Toby's departing rear, 'That's for certain!'

Millie Malone and some of her art class friends came next, carrying between them a ten-foot canvas which had *Tutto Mio* painted across it in beautiful cursive script. In every corner there were vines which trailed around the frame.

'*Grazie mille,*' Millie said, grinning. 'Guess what?'

'What?' Isabella's head was so scrambled she couldn't even attempt a guess.

'I've been predicted an A* for my Italian.' Millie was bursting with excitement to tell her. The words ran over themselves in her grin.

'*Auguri!*' Isabella said and Millie extended her hand for a shy fist bump.

The rest of her art class followed with terracotta plant pots for each table and the windowsills, painted and decorated with shells and glass and stones, each and every one different.

Last came mirrors and art and accessories. People of all ages brought all kinds of art. Metal wall hangings, photographs and paintings. The calligraphy group at The Lit Lounge turned up with hand-scripted menus and drinks cards. The garden centre brought a tray of plants for the tables and windowsills.

The last person in the queue, the very last, was Fred Barrow. The cameraman zoomed in. Michelle Carter got ready to wrap up.

'This is for you,' Fred said, handing over a rectangular parcel wrapped in brown paper and tied with string.

It was a framed map. But not just any old framed map. It was one of Nonna's that she'd lent him, that had been saved from the fire because he'd been showing it to someone else outside at the time the fire began at Heart of Honeybridge. It showed the region where Nonna grew up all those years ago, the mountain that protected the village in which she lived. The river she played in as a child. It was perfect to have on the wall of Tutto Mio. Tears streamed down Isabella's face as she threw her arms around Fred.

'So, community spirit is alive and well in Honeybridge,' Michelle Carter said to the camera, stepping back into shot. 'And because of that, Tutto Mio will open for business tomorrow as planned. Is there anything you'd like to say, Isabella?'

The fluffy microphone was pointing her way. She wiped her eyes and felt the ache in her cheek from smiling.

'A huge thank you to Honeybridge for welcoming me in. It truly is the most wonderful place to live. And I can't wait to open the doors to Tutto Mio tomorrow.' She flashed a glance at Michelle, who rolled her eyes and gave a quick single nod. Isabella looked straight down the camera and beamed.

'Everyone's welcome!'

Chapter Sixty-Two

Etienne

Etienne could hear Isabella outside thanking Michelle and the cameraman and knew she'd be in at any moment.

'Positions!' he hissed. The team dashed to their tables and held their breath as the door opened.

She stopped in her tracks, putting her hands to her mouth. Etienne watched her face as she took it in.

The mismatched collection of tables and chairs from homes around the community. The Tutto Mio mural taking pride of place. Flowers or pot plants on every table with an assortment of candlesticks, all lit and flickering softly. Mirrors on every wall, reflecting light into every corner. Brightly coloured cushions on the benches, knitted and crocheted blankets hanging on the backs of a few chairs. All the glasses were lined up on the shelves, awaiting all the future toasts and celebrations of engagements, birthdays or anniversaries. Or a nice family meal out, just because.

And the team standing by their waiting stations, brimming with pride.

Isabella turned in a slow circle in the centre of the dining room, absorbing every detail, running her hand over a chair back. Finally, she lifted her hands as if weighing the air and then let them fall to her sides.

'It's perfect,' she said on a sob. 'Absolutely perfect. Thank you.'

Amber got there first, wrapping her up with a, 'Yes, girl!' which made Isabella laugh through her tears. Angie from Australia was next, putting her arms around both of them, followed by Naomi and Paul and the rest of the team in the biggest, most affectionate team huddle Etienne had ever seen. 'We're ready!' they all agreed. 'We open tomorrow!'

Breaking the circle apart to excited chatter, Isabella extricated herself and finally, finally came towards Etienne. His breath caught as she put her arms around his neck and pressed herself to him.

'Thank you,' she said, in a low, urgent voice.

'You don't have to do everything on your own,' he said, repeating her own words back to her. 'You have me now.'

She grinned and glanced around at the fully kitted out restaurant.

'And Honeybridge,' she said. 'And it feels so good.'

Chapter Sixty-Three

Isabella

Isabella awoke thinking that Etienne was curved behind her. She stretched and turned to him before she was even fully conscious, before she realised the other side of the bed was empty. In that moment, when she thought he was there, she was happier than she had been in . . . for ever.

She flopped onto her back and stared at the ceiling. She loved him, she knew that. It wasn't just infatuation, or desire. She hadn't said the words to him yet, but she would. She was madly, passionately, wholeheartedly, wonderfully in love with him, and although he hadn't said the words to her yet either, she recognised the same look in his eyes and hoped, believed, he felt the same.

Last night, after Nonna and Gabi had gone to bed, they'd talked late into the night, sharing stories and pasts on the sofa, always wrapped around each other. There was something different again between them, a recognition and a depth. It got late; the clock in the square rang ten, then eleven, but she didn't want to give in to the time. She didn't want the night to end. She yawned and tried to cover it with her hand, but he laughed and smoothed her hair away from her face.

She was aching inside, however tired she was, with the want to pull him to her, run her fingers over his chest, mount him on the sofa and ride him, ride him, ride him. But it was also the last day of her year. The very last day of a promise she had made to herself. She opened her mouth to say something, to explain why she had to stay away from him that night, but he put a finger on her lips.

'I'm going to The Bistro now,' Etienne had said. 'You need to sleep. You've got a big day tomorrow.' He sucked the air through his teeth. 'And you can't fall at the last hurdle. You have to pass the finish line in one piece' – he chuckled – 'even if it's killing me.'

She'd kissed the finger against her lips and smiled. He got it.

'It's killing me too, if that makes you feel any better?' she'd said, letting her eyes skim his chest again, fall to his lap. She was wet just thinking about being with him. Was he hard too? She'd wanted to extend a hand, rest it on his lap, tease him; she'd groaned and clenched her fist instead.

Etienne got up, pulling her to stand with him. Holding her face between his hands, he'd lowered his lips to hers. The kiss was slow and soft. She'd twined her hands into the curling hair at the back of his head and let herself fall into him, not wanting it to stop.

'Good luck tomorrow,' he'd said at the door. 'Text me when you're ready for me to come over.' As he went out, over his shoulder, he'd called, 'Night, Bella,' and she'd locked the door and gone upstairs to find her phone and her trusty photograph of his hand on her skin.

Now it was opening day and Bonfire Night. The day she'd been dreaming about for a year. Which was even better today than it was before the Dougalls, because Tutto Mio had become something else, something bigger. Not just the result of her efforts, her work, but the evidence that she'd made an impact in this new place. That the community here welcomed her and that she had a brand-new home. Her mismatched, beautifully eclectic dining room was proof of that. Luckily, she had showered and dressed before the phone rang for the first time in the restaurant for a customer to make a booking.

By ten o'clock in the morning, she had to put Gabi on phone answering duty. Everyone who had seen the segment on the evening news wanted to book in, to show their support. Gabi sat with the laptop at a table in the corner, trying to navigate the calendar and book callers in, even as the online bookings flooded through. Sometimes a slot would disappear while she was talking to someone on the telephone, and they'd have to try the next day. By lunchtime and before they'd even opened for the first time ever, they were fully booked for the month ahead.

Isabella checked her watch and called the team together. They huddled in a circle, each putting a hand in the centre, grinning at each other nervously. She made sure to make eye contact with each and every one, starting and finishing with Amber.

'*You* are by far the best waiting team there has ever been,' Isabella said. 'Now, let's go spread some sunshine to every single person that walks in that door.'

The clock chimed twelve and it was officially lunchtime. Amber high fived Isabella.

'You got this, sister.'

Isabella snapped a quick photo of the restaurant on her phone and sent it to her family WhatsApp group with the message *And we're open!* before taking her position at the front desk, butterflies the size of sparrows in her stomach. Amber opened the door and Tutto Mio was up and running. Isabella greeted every diner as they entered, her cheeks soon aching with so much smiling, but she couldn't stop.

The guests exclaimed at the restaurant; they'd all heard the story. Some pointed out their own possessions in the room, an old chair or a donated cushion, and they did so with pride, feeling like a part of something. By half past twelve, every table was full. The buzz of people eating and talking and laughing was like music. When Nonna came out of the kitchen for a moment, drying her hands to stand by Isabella, they both looked out in awe.

By the time the first sitting were eating puddings, they were booked for three months ahead. And by the time Australian Angie, Naomi and Paul left and were replaced by the evening team, they were fully booked for six months and Gabi had lost her voice.

Isabella didn't get a moment in the bathroom to freshen up before the evening sitting. She talked to the lunchtime crowd on their way to the firework display and then she heard about how wonderful it had been from the later diners. It was ten o'clock before she reapplied a slick of lipstick, rearranged her waves and spritzed some perfume. Her face in the mirror glowed back at her, even if she'd been on her feet for twelve hours by then. It didn't matter. Today was the best day of her life. All her dreams were coming true.

She resumed her station back at the entrance and checked the iPad bookings in front of her for the next day. She was running a check on the table plan when someone cleared their throat in front of her.

'Sorry I'm late. I have a booking for a table for two,' a voice said. One which she recognised immediately. Her head snapped up. Daniel.

He looked the same: his floppy hair was a bit longer, but his expression was the same from the last time she'd seen him. The day she signed the divorce papers. Slightly sheepish. He probably thought he looked cute. She thought he looked infuriating. Like the popular boy at school who thought he could get away with anything by flashing a smile.

'What are you doing here?' she asked.

'Um, eating?' Daniel said hopefully, trying to make everything a joke. As always. He peered past her into the restaurant. 'Looks amazing, Issy.' Something inside her hardened. How dare he think he had the right to turn up here on her opening day and call her by old nicknames?

'I don't have your booking here,' she said brusquely, scanning the list.

'I booked under Mr Daniels,' he said with that bloody annoying look again which made her want to smack him. Sure enough, there it was. Table for two. Nine thirty.

She selected two menus.

'This way,' she said and didn't look back as she led him to a corner table, the only one empty in the entire room. She pulled his chair out for him and he paused for a moment, unsure as to their changed dynamic, with her in control. He sat.

'Table for two?' she said stiffly, placing the menus on the table. 'Are you waiting for someone?'

'Yes,' he said. The sheepish smile finally dropped and suddenly his face was lit by something else entirely. He raised his eyebrows in a question. 'You.'

Chapter Sixty-Four

Etienne

Etienne had seen the steady stream of diners heading across the square since lunchtime and had felt ridiculously happy for Isabella. His own restaurant was still full, showing there was plenty of opportunity for both of them. He found himself craning his neck for a glimpse of her across the square several times during the day, but she'd be busy, and so was he, with a group booking of a French family reunion who told him The Bistro was a true taste of home. He'd smiled to himself and promised to pass it on to the chef – though he didn't tell them the chef was a larger-than-life cockney who'd never been across the Channel.

By the time the last customer paid, he was aching to see her. Fred Barrow was already in bed and Mile End Mickey had closed the kitchen and gone. She hadn't texted 'come over' yet but he couldn't wait any longer. He did the quickest close down ever and turned off the lights. All he could think of was seeing her, hearing about her first day, and then taking off her clothes, one by one by one. His cock twitched at the thought. She was a drug and he couldn't get enough of her. All of a sudden, he understood Alex, the addiction, the compulsion to do something again and again and again. Because he was well and truly addicted to Isabella. He wanted to be with her every second possible. He tucked his chin into his coat collar and set off.

The square was dark and quiet as Etienne crossed. The fireworks were over. The clock chimed midnight and he couldn't believe it had been less than a day since he'd seen her but he missed her this much. He knew what it meant. He loved her. He'd never known the feeling before, this deep certainty, the warmth, the glow. But he recognised it as though he'd been waiting for it his whole life. He loved her. And he wanted to tell her tonight.

Tutto Mio's main lights were off but there was still enough glow to see in from outside as he got closer. The dining room was empty, the team had gone home. As he neared the front window, he caught sight of a candle burning in the corner and smiled at the thought of Isabella sitting there waiting for him.

She was there. But she wasn't alone. Etienne slowed, trying to work out what he was seeing.

Isabella sat opposite a man at the table, who had his head in his hands. There was a strange kind of intensity between them. Etienne had stumbled into the middle of something, he knew it. Isabella spoke; the man shook his head, without lifting it. Isabella shut her eyes and rubbed the spot between them as though thinking, before standing, putting a hand under the man's arm and pulling him up from his seat.

Etienne saw the man's face then, saw his floppy hair and

knew who it was immediately. His chest sank but he couldn't tear his eyes away as Daniel stumbled forward and wrapped his arms around Isabella.

Unable to help himself, Etienne stepped closer, not wanting to see but needing a clearer view.

Isabella disentangled herself and he felt a leap of hope. But then she secured her arm around Daniel's waist, leading him across the restaurant to the stairs up to the flat. Daniel encircled her shoulders, leaning against her.

Etienne put a hand to his chest and watched as the door closed behind them on their way upstairs, before turning to walk away.

Chapter Sixty-Five

Isabella

Daniel was snoring when Isabella woke up.

She must have passed out, because she couldn't remember falling asleep. But after the excitement of the day and then the emotion of the night, plus a couple of large glasses of wine while they were talking, it was hardly surprising.

But now, hearing him snoring through the wall from his bed on the sofa, she wanted him up and out as soon as possible. He wouldn't have had to stay at all if he'd not sunk a couple of bottles of wine and then told her he was driving home.

Still wearing her shortie pyjamas, she pulled her hair into a sort-of bun and padded through to the living room to wake Daniel up. She had things to do. In fact, she had people to do. A thrill ran through her like a current at the thought. Having to postpone Etienne last night was the last thing she wanted to do, but it would have been impossible to relax with her ex-husband on the sofa. She hoped he'd understand. She'd call him as soon as Daniel had left.

Daniel rubbed his eyes like a small boy and stretched and Isabella felt nothing apart from impatient for him to leave. He scratched at his chin, and she couldn't help but compare his patchy attempts to Etienne's gorgeous stubble.

Eventually, he was ready and she escorted him to the door, to hurry him up more than anything.

The square was quiet and empty, as usual on a Sunday morning. The only sound was from the church bells in the distance. November air nipped her skin and she shivered on the doorstep.

'Thanks again, Issy,' he said. His eyes were bloodshot, and his floppy fringe looked lank. 'It was good to clear the air.'

She exhaled. He was right. It had probably been a part of the process of moving on.

'It was,' she agreed.

'And it was good of you to put me up.'

She nodded again. 'It was,' she agreed.

Daniel laughed and she felt her face relax until she laughed too.

He put his arms out with a hopeful expression on his face and she stepped in for a hug. Let's face it, after this, she would probably never see him again. He was starting a whole new life. And she was doing the same. They hugged for a moment, a strange recognition passing between them that they used to love each other and now they didn't.

Over his shoulder, Isabella saw Etienne standing in the doorway of The Bistro, his face crumpling in disbelief as he watched them. She pulled back from Daniel and put a hand up to Etienne, as if to hold him, as if to tell him to wait, she'd be right there. But his face hardened and he stamped back into the restaurant, slamming the door behind him. Isabella flinched. What had happened? He looked hurt, horrified. It was just a hug, why would he react like that?

'I have to go,' she said to Daniel and began to run, not caring she was barefoot and in pink shortie PJs.

'Take care, Issy,' Daniel called after her but she didn't reply. Her focus was on her future, and he was her past.

Etienne wasn't in the restaurant dining room, or in the manager's office. She called through and heard banging in the kitchen and pushed through the swing door. There he was, cracking eggs into a bowl with more force than was strictly necessary.

'Etienne,' she said. He flashed his eyes towards her and they were dark, hurt.

'Etienne,' she said again, moving close enough to put a hand on his arm, but something held her back. They had to talk. She had to reach him. 'What's wrong?'

He spun towards her, an incredulous look on his face. 'I've just watched you hugging a man goodbye after he *obviously* spent the night and you're asking me what's wrong?' He was searching her face, looking for answers. Isabella frowned in confusion.

'But it wasn't—' she started, trying to keep calm.

'You didn't even try to hide it,' he said and she heard the surprise in his voice.

'Because there's nothing to hide,' she cut in.

'So, you're not denying it?' he asked.

'No,' she said. 'I told you what was happening . . .'

His mystified face stared back at her.

'I sent you a message?'

He continued to look at her blankly.

She pulled her phone from the pocket of her short shorts and opened her messages, frantic fingers now wanting to prove to him it was all above board. She found what she was looking for. A message to Etienne, last night at 12.14 a.m.

So sorry but have to raincheck tonight. Dan has shown up drunk and will be sleeping on the sofa. But I promise to make it up to you tomorrow. Xxxx

She was just about to turn the phone to him to show him when she saw the tiny word next to it on screen. Unsent. She started. *Unsent.* It hadn't gone through. Her mouth fell open. She must have pressed send and then pretty much passed out; she'd been so worn out. Especially after getting a drunk Daniel up the stairs, manhandling him onto the sofa and throwing a blanket over him.

Turning the screen slowly to him, she showed him the message.

'I'm so sorry. It didn't send.' Isabella hardly dared breathe as she imagined him waiting for her to text last night. What would he have been thinking? And then seeing her this morning in these stupid shorts, hugging a man goodbye on the doorstep? Poor Etienne. She couldn't imagine what had been going through his mind.

Etienne took the phone from her and seemed to be having trouble taking the message in. He stared at it for several seconds before raising his face to her.

'He was drunk?' he asked.

'He couldn't drive, so I said he could sleep on the sofa.'

Etienne half smiled and shook his head, as though at himself. His shoulders dropped an inch or two.

'That's such a you thing to do,' he said, closing his eyes for a moment. She could almost feel his relief.

'I might not love him any more, but I don't want him to kill himself drunk driving,' Isabella said with a shrug and he let out a short laugh, before asking, 'Why did he come?'

She shook a long, slow breath and let it go.

'To apologise,' she said simply. 'He wanted to apologise for everything he'd done to me. He wanted to put right past mistakes so that he could move on.'

Etienne breathed out and she could see that it resonated with him. He knew what it was like to feel like you'd let someone down.

'Did you accept?' he said, tilting his head to one side, green eyes reading hers.

'I did. Because I want to move on too.' She swallowed. This was it. The truth. 'I want to move on with you.'

His eyes flashed and she saw the quirk of a smile lifting his lips again.

'And what was that?' Etienne gestured out towards the square. 'This morning?'

'That was goodbye,' she said, holding her hand out towards him, seeing it tremble in the space between them. Her chest hurt with the need to touch him now, to close the gap between them. She heard her jagged gasp as his fingers found hers and they twined together. It was now or never.

'And this is hello.' She tugged his hand and they moved towards each other, wrapping their arms around each other.

She held his head, pushed her fingers through his hair. Held him tight, pressed herself to him. And he pulled her close so that there was no space between them, his body meeting hers at every point, as he inhaled the scent in her hair. Eventually he loosened his grip and she looked up into his face.

'I love you, Etienne,' she said and her voice was certain and sure.

'I love you, Bella,' he replied and she could see the jut of his jaw as he spoke. The honesty behind the words he'd never said to a woman before. She felt the tears seeping out of the corner of her eyes before she could stop them, but she was laughing and smiling and crying all at once as he brushed them away with his thumb.

'What you making?' She nodded to the eggs he'd been cracking.

'Pancakes,' he said with a grin.

She licked her dry lips and felt the ache inside. The anticipation that had built since that day when he licked the batter from her arm, his eyes never leaving hers as his tongue met her skin, was prickling at her.

'Are you hungry?' he asked.

She ran her hands across his chest, spanning the muscles, wanting to feel his skin beneath the shirt.

'Starving,' she said, holding his gaze. His eyes were the darkest green she'd ever seen. They sparked under his heavy lids as he took her hand and led her out of the kitchen.

'Then let's eat,' he said.

Chapter Sixty-Six

Isabella and Etienne

Those pyjamas were the hottest outfit he'd ever seen, but Etienne just wanted them off.

As soon as the bedroom door was closed, they fell on each other, lips crashing together before parting, pushing, pulsing as their tongues danced together. Isabella undid his shirt and ran her hands across his skin, making an unconscious sound of relief as she touched him. He closed his eyes at the sound, knowing that she needed him as much as he needed her.

Etienne peeled the pyjama top over her head in one move, and his hands moved to cup her full breasts, circle her nipples, feel them tighten under his fingers. She dropped her head back and arched her chest towards him and he dipped his mouth to encase her in his lips, pulling lightly, enough to make her moan. Straightening again, Isabella kissed his chest, nipping at it with her teeth, and he gasped, his erection straining in his jeans. Her hand was already there, on him, and she could feel the heat of him through the fabric. He growled in his throat and she moaned back into his mouth.

She flipped open his fly and pushed at his jeans. He'd never felt so hard, so hot. She wrapped her fingers around him, unable to close the loop he was so thick, and she ran her thumb over his end, spreading the moisture already beading there. Dropping to her knees, she tasted him, drawing him into her mouth, and Etienne held her head, controlling the motion, keeping it slow, letting her take him as deep as she could, again and again, until he couldn't risk it any more. He pulled her to her feet, kissing her mouth that tasted of him, letting his hands roam her body, over her breasts and down to those shorts that should be illegal. They skimmed easily over her hips and dropped to the floor. His hands followed, running between her legs and feeling the hot wetness of her. He slipped one, then two fingers into the slick entry to her body, feeling her stumble slightly in his arms as her knees buckled. He brushed her clit with his thumb and she groaned, her head lolling back on her neck, eyes closed. He ran his hands over her, lifting her body. She wrapped her legs around his waist to hold the position and he pushed her back to the wall, straining against her, wanting more.

He carried her across the room as if she weighed nothing and Isabella felt the strength in his chest, his arms, his shoulders. She ran her nails across them, scoring him lightly, leaving red trails. Etienne lowered her to standing beside the bed. His breathing was ragged; her heart was racing as they faced each other.

'Yes?' he asked, his voice gruff.

'Yes,' she said breathlessly. 'Please, yes.'

'Wait,' he said, yanking open the bedside drawer. She heard

the rip of the condom foil and heard her own heartbeat as it pulsed in her veins.

She lay back on the bed, pulling him above her and wrapping her legs again around his waist.

His eyes were half closed, his mouth open. Isabella felt the tension in her legs around him, wanting to draw them closer, force him inside her. But they held the position, chests heaving. They'd waited so long for this. His eyes found hers as the head of his cock opened her up. He was big, he was so big. He stretched her gently as inch by inch, he moved inside her until she was full, completely and utterly full as she never had been before. He paused and she moaned. Their eyes held until he dropped his mouth to kiss her, using the movement to pull back, almost out, before plunging again, smoother this time, not as hesitant, as her body opened for him and he sank to the hilt. Kneeling between her legs now, he loomed above her, holding her knees in his hands, spreading her wider. She felt him shift position, hitting a new deep as he moved, touching parts of her that had never been touched. Her head rolled on the pillow as he moved one hand between her legs and found her core and rubbed in time, so that the sensation took over, the rub, the fullness, the thrust. Nothing else mattered apart from the feeling between their bodies. The electric charge that pulsed.

'Look at me,' he said as she rocked her head back and forth. She opened her eyes in time to see him, his eyes burning.

'Come with me,' he said and she felt his pace change, slamming into her with force and ferocity as he strummed her core and held her eyes and then she was arching her back before falling and falling and falling as she heard him cry out her name.

Chapter Sixty-Seven

Etienne

Etienne collapsed on top of Isabella, his chest heaving, her arms tender now, stroking his back as they recovered. He rolled to one side to lie flat, letting his breathing settle and calm. She rolled onto her side to follow him, head on his shoulder.

'We were pretty good at non-sex,' Isabella said, 'but we're even better at the real thing.'

'I'm going to have to change my karaoke song now,' Etienne said and she laughed, her breath tickling his skin.

'I feel like my pink are cheeks,' she said, putting her hands to her face, and he laughed at her inability to string a sentence together. He had to admit she was flushed, which he hoped was the sign of a good time. He slipped an arm behind her, holding her closer.

'Never had you down as a cuddler,' she said.

'Never been a cuddler – until now.' He laughed. It was true. He'd rarely stayed the night in the past, not wanting the intimacy of it. But with Isabella, he wanted it all. The waking up together, the saying goodnight. Brushing teeth together in front of the bathroom mirror, watching television on the couch. He wanted to share things with her: his days, their nights, her bed. He wanted to share his life with her.

'I love you, Bella,' he said quietly and she lifted her face to look into his eyes as she replied, 'I love you too, Etienne.'

He kissed her softly and she made a tiny sound of contentment in her throat, which he felt in his mouth and made him smile.

The shout made them both jump, slipping as they were back into desire, the kiss building.

'Hey, Boss!' Mile End Mickey shouted from the door in the restaurant that led to the flat. 'There's some geezer down here says he's your brother!'

Chapter Sixty-Eight

Isabella

She could feel the tears in her own eyes as Etienne and his brother hugged for the first time in four years. They didn't bother with the typical male back slaps and thumps, they just hugged long and hard, eyes shut with emotion. Matched in size and shape as they were, they looked like two jigsaw pieces that mirrored perfectly.

Eventually they broke apart and Alex put out his hand to Etienne, his face serious.

'Thank you, brother,' he said, with a slight shake of his head. 'I'll pay you back. I mean it.'

Etienne grasped Alex's hand and shook, slowly.

'Fox and Walker, yes. Me, no. You're worth every penny.'

They hugged again and a tear escaped down Isabella's cheek. She sniffed and brushed it away as Etienne crossed to her, putting his arm around her shoulders.

'Alex, this is Isabella,' he said, and she loved the pride in his voice. 'Isabella, this is Alex.'

They appraised each other. Isabella was fascinated at how two people with such a strong resemblance actually had very different individual features. Etienne had the stronger jaw, the darker hair. Alex was fairer and as he smiled at her, she noticed the blue of his eyes, compared to the glint of Etienne's green.

'Excuse the pyjamas,' she said, self-consciously, still wearing shortie PJs with a hoodie of Etienne's thrown over the top.

'Sorry to bust in on your Sunday morning,' Alex said. 'Lovely to meet you.'

'You'll be seeing lots of her,' Etienne said, pulling her in closer and planting a kiss on the top of her head. 'You'll be seeing her every day, I hope.'

Something fluttered in Isabella's chest. She was still reeling with the events of the last few days. The knowledge that Etienne loved her. The absolutely mind-blowing, earth-shattering sex they'd had. The fact that he wanted her in his life. It was more than she could have hoped for. She wanted to experience things with him for the first time and sing karaoke with him at The Bolthole. She wanted to share things with him, and learn things with him, and cheer from the riverbank when he won next year's rowing race. She wanted a future with Etienne Martin.

'So can I stay?' Alex was saying. 'Until I get myself sorted out?'

Etienne slapped him on the upper arm.

'Of course, Al. Although we're also sharing with an eighty-year-old man for a few weeks, so it might have to be the sofa.'

A movement across the square caught her eye. A glimpse of the back of someone as they slipped into the front door of Tutto Mio. She gasped. She'd never forget that body shape or size. She ducked out of Etienne's arm and ran to the window, straining to see, but the front door of her restaurant slowly closed and blocked her view.

'What is it?' Etienne asked, peering over her shoulder.

'I saw someone, I think – going into Tutto Mio!' she said, already running. 'You'd better come,' she called over her shoulder as she tore across the square for the second time that morning in her shortie pyjamas.

Isabella ignored the calls from behind her, telling her to wait, telling her not to go in. She knew in her bones who it was, but she hadn't expected to see him again nearly so soon.

She flung the front door open and she was right.

Her papà, standing beside a large rucksack, looking tanned and travel weary. Her mamma too, rocking a new blunt bob and an oversized pair of sunglasses, cursing a late flight connection that meant they'd missed the opening of the restaurant. Nonna was beside them, pinching cheeks and kissing them on repeat, and Isabella threw herself in between, to be engulfed in a family hug.

'We were meant to be here yesterday!' Mamma said, holding her away to get a look at her.

'We were only pretending we wouldn't make it – and then we didn't make it!' Papà said.

'You're here now!' Isabella stuttered over the lump in her throat as she pulled them back in for another hug.

Her mamma was laughing and crying at the same time, smiling even as the tears ran down her face and into her mouth. Her father was momentarily speechless, choked with emotion. And she realised how much she'd missed them on their travels. Their never-wavering love and support were always there, but a hug in person was worth more than anything.

The front door slammed again, and Etienne skidded into the dining room, carrying, of all things, an umbrella from his umbrella pot at The Bistro which he waved in the air. Alex crashed in behind him, brandishing another one.

'Where are they?' Etienne said, eyes darting to the corner, the bar.

'Who?' Nonna asked, looking around her too.

Everyone looked at each other in confusion and for a moment it was quiet. Then Mamma giggled and Isabella tipped back her head and laughed. Etienne and Alex slowly dropped their umbrellas and shot each other looks.

'Mamma, Papà, this is Etienne,' Isabella said, putting her hand out for him to join them. 'And his brother Alex.'

Realisation flashed across Etienne's face as he stepped forward and she put an arm around his back, leaning her head momentarily on his shoulder. He extended a hand to her father first and Papà looked at it and then him, reading his face. When he saw what he wanted in Etienne's face, they shook. It seemed a serious connection. A question and answer. A contract.

Etienne turned to her mother.

'Pleased to meet you, Mrs Tucci,' he said, extending his hand again. Mamma ignored the hand and pulled him in to kiss on both cheeks.

Alex filled the gaps left by Etienne and shook and kissed as if he were already part of the family.

'Where were you, out in your pyjamas?' Mamma asked and Isabella laughed when she saw the flush on Etienne's cheeks.

'Long story,' she said. 'It's been a busy morning.'

'Time for coffee and biscuits,' said Nonna. Which

everyone – except Alex – knew meant rum, and soon they were all sitting around a table, chatting in Italian and English and hearing about Mamma's experience swimming with a whale shark in the Maldives and Papà's white-water rafting in Croatia, when Amber opened the front door to set up for lunch.

'Amber!' Isabella called. 'Come and meet my parents!'

Amber approached, grinning already, and they all turned to her. Halfway across the restaurant floor, she stopped, dead in her tracks, and the smile died on her face. Her mouth fell open. Isabella frowned; Amber looked like she'd seen a ghost.

Glancing around the table, she saw the focus of her gaze. Alex. But the expression on his face was one of amazement. Their expressions could not have been more different.

'Amber!' He pushed back his chair.

'You!' Amber said, shaking her head.

Alex stretched a hand towards her and put one hesitant foot forward. Everyone else watched in confusion, not sure which way this was going to go.

Amber moved quickly, closing the space between them, and Isabella saw Alex's eyes widen, a flicker of hope cross his face – before Amber slapped it off in a smack that echoed off the restaurant walls.

Alex put a hand to his cheek as Amber spun on her heel and headed towards the kitchen.

'Amber!' he said again but she put up a hand and carried on walking, her hips swinging exaggeratedly from side to side.

'Never in a fucking month of Sundays, Alex!' She banged open the kitchen door without looking back and let it swing shut behind her.

Alex made a single step towards following her, but Etienne put a hand on his arm.

'Maybe later,' he said quietly, nodding to the family audience. Nonna's mouth was still open. Everyone looked from one to the other, trying to ignore the scarlet handprint on Alex's face as he tucked his chair under the table.

'I'd better go. I'll see you later at home,' Alex said to Etienne and excused himself.

Etienne stood.

'I should probably go too,' he said. 'I need to open up The Bistro. Nice to meet you, everyone.'

Isabella felt a pull inside, not wanting him to go, especially after that drama. His eyes met hers.

'See you later?' he asked quietly and she was flooded with a relief that drove her to her feet to kiss him, softly, gently, repeatedly in front of everyone before he left.

Later that night, after a successful second day in the restaurant, Isabella crossed the dark, deserted square to The Bistro. She'd tried to talk to Amber earlier, but her friend had ruefully told her it was 'a story for a girls' night, over a drink or ten,' and she'd have to wait. Maybe Etienne would know more. He might be able to fill her in. She laughed. In more ways than one.

Etienne had suggested she should stay with him on one of their endless messages during the day. It made sense. Her parents could have her bed for the few nights they were here, before they took off again to see the vivid oranges and yellows of the forests in Japan. With Nonna and Gabi there too, hers was a full house and she could think of no better solution than sleeping with Etienne. Or, hopefully, not sleeping with him.

The door to The Bistro was on the latch and she let herself in, allowing her eyes to adjust to the dark.

The only light came from a single candle at the table in the corner where he sat waiting. Her breath caught in anticipation. A nightcap and then bed, with the man she loved. She wished in that second her parents needed to stay longer.

Etienne's long fingers turned the glass of whisky on the table, the ice cube glinting through the amber liquid in the candlelight. She slipped into the seat beside him and clinked her glass against his.

'I need to talk to you,' he said and the gravity in his voice stopped her glass between table and sip. Her breath halted in her chest; her heart paused. She lowered the glass without drinking.

'I don't want this to be a part-time thing,' he said, and she heard her own exhale at the same time as her blood began to pulse again. Thank God.

'I want you and me to be together for ever,' he said. 'Now that I've found you, I don't want to let you go. I want you to be all mine.'

She reached for him across the table, but he kept his hand in his lap, watching her.

'You're everything I ever wanted but was afraid to look for.' His voice was full of emotion, his eyes holding hers. He was mesmerisingly beautiful. She would never tire of looking at that face.

'I love you, Isabella Tucci, and I want to marry you.'

She blinked, heard her breath hitch.

Now, he raised his hand from under the table and in it he held a black velvet ring box. He placed it on the table between them and carefully lifted the lid. The diamond flashed and she put her hand to her mouth.

'Will you marry me, Bella?'

She swallowed and licked her lips that were suddenly dry as she took it in.

'This was my mother's engagement ring,' Etienne said, tilting the box so that she could see it shine, 'and it would make me the happiest man alive if you would wear it.'

The bells rang midnight in the square and he watched her as her thoughts raced and heart beat so loudly she could hear it. He was waiting.

She reached her hand over the table to the ring box, covering it briefly before shutting it with a quiet click.

He blanched, and she rushed to explain, before he took it the wrong way.

'I love you, Etienne, more than I have ever loved anyone else.' Even as she said the words, she knew they were true. There was no comparison to this craving, this need to be with him. She laced her fingers through his and rubbed the back of his hand with her thumb.

'But sometimes, as we know, it's good to wait for the things you want.'

His eyes were searching hers, looking for an answer, hoping for a future.

'And I want to be with you for ever,' she said, covering his hands with her own. He exhaled slowly, the beginnings of a half-smile lifting his lips.

'So, how about a year of everything but marriage?' she suggested and he raised an eyebrow as he considered the idea.

'Define "everything but marriage",' he said, the glint back in his eye. 'Just so I'm clear.'

'What do you need to know?' she asked.

'Living together?' he asked.

'I'd love to,' she said.

'Committed to each other?'

'Exclusively,' she said.

'Planning a future together?' She knew her smile had turned into a grin.

'Definitely.'

He held her eyes and then nodded.

'Tutto Mio?' he asked, his eyes shy as he said the Italian words.

'All yours,' she confirmed.

'And in a year?' he asked.

She bit her lip, but only to stop the excited laugh that was bubbling there, but it escaped anyway.

'Then I'd love to marry you.'

He laughed and raised his glass.

'One year.'

She lifted her glass to his and they clinked gently together as their eyes met and held.

'One year.'

They drank their toast and came up smiling.

'Only you, Bella, would come up with a plan like that.' He blew out the candle and stood. He pulled her from her chair, lifting her until her legs were wrapped around his waist, and started walking towards the stairs, holding her up. She twined her hands around his neck as he mounted the stairs one by one, carrying her with him to bed. She had the man she loved in her arms and between her legs and things were only going to get better.

'Right, let me show you exactly how good not being married can be,' Etienne said, kicking open his bedroom door.

'Looking forward to it,' she said, twisting her hands in his hair and smiling when he growled.

Acknowledgements

I'd like to thank everyone that has bought this book to life. I wish you all ground-shaking love, and mind-blowing sex, for many years to come.

My amazing agent at Greene and Heaton, Judith Murray, who encouraged me to write some spice.

My brilliant editor at Quercus, Kat Burdon, for loving it enough to publish it.

For my fellow spice girl, Bella North, for the daily encouragements and laughs along the way.

For my women friends who have let me pick their brains and raid their fantasies in the quest for love and satisfaction.

And finally, to my husband. For letting me check that some of the scenes work in practice. I couldn't do it without you.